THE ALPINE YEOMAN

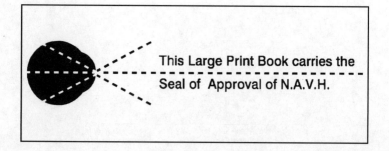

This Large Print Book carries the
Seal of Approval of N.A.V.H.

AN EMMA LORD MYSTERY

The Alpine Yeoman

Mary Daheim

THORNDIKE PRESS
A part of Gale, Cengage Learning

GALE
CENGAGE Learning®

Farmington Hills, Mich • San Francisco • New York • Waterville, Maine
Meriden, Conn • Mason, Ohio • Chicago

GALE
CENGAGE Learning®

LIBRARY OF CONGRESS CATALOGING-IN-PUBLICATION DATA

Daheim, Mary.
  The alpine yeoman : an Emma Lord mystery / by Mary Daheim. — Large print edition.
    pages ; cm. — (Thorndike Press large print mystery)
    ISBN 978-1-4104-6984-7 (hardcover) — ISBN 1-4104-6984-0 (hardcover)
    1. Lord, Emma (Fictitious character)—Fiction. 2. Large type books. I. Title.
PS3554.A264A797 2014b
813'.54—dc23   2014007337

Published in 2014 by arrangement with The Ballantine Publishing Group, a division of Random House LLC, a Penguin Random House Company.

Printed in the United States of America
1 2 3 4 5 6 7 18 17 16 15 14

In gratitude to Pat Burns
for finding the real Alpine. R.I.P.

AUTHOR'S NOTE

The story is set in April 2005.

ONE

My head was pounding.

Delete that. Bad reporting on my part.

It was the pounding *over* my head that was driving me nuts. Silly me, to think I could escape the chaos of my little log cabin by striking out early on a drizzly April morning to *The Alpine Advocate.*

"Paging editor-publisher Emma Lord," intoned my ad manager, Leo Walsh, as he entered my office. "How come you're here before eight?"

The pounding had mercifully stopped long enough so I could hear him. "I forgot that one of the Bourgettes is finally putting a decent roof over our heads here at work. You may recall I canceled doing it last July because I couldn't afford replacing the leaky tin with slate. Not that I'm sorry they . . ." I winced as the pounding resumed. "Oh, hell!" I exclaimed, getting up. "Did you do the bakery run already?"

Leo and I went into the newsroom, where the noise was muffled. "I had advance notice in this week's Upper Crust ad featuring a new kind of Italian slipper. Those things sell fast, so I thought I'd get there when the bakery opened. How's the renovation going at your place?"

"Dick Bourgette and his sons are fine," I said, being my usual perverse self and taking a French doughnut instead of an Italian slipper. "It's the pile drivers or whatever it is that make an awful noise. They have to go down into the rocky face of Tonga Ridge to anchor the addition out back. It feels like an earthquake in the house, and it's really *loud.*"

Leo frowned at the coffee urn, which hadn't quite finished perking. "You sure the ground's thawed out so far below the surface?"

I nodded. "Scott Melville — our architect — assured us it was. We could've started sooner, but the Bourgettes had to repair those homes that were damaged during the March windstorm. When Alpine was founded almost a century ago, there was snow on the ground from September until May. This winter was mild. *Too* mild. We haven't had snow since January and not much rain since then."

The expression on Leo's weathered face was wry. "It's a good thing. I might've headed back to California. I haven't seen my new grandson yet."

My shoulders slumped. "If you took a few days off, you'd come back, wouldn't you?"

"Oh, sure," Leo replied, seeing that the coffee was ready. "I won't be sixty-two until May. I'd like to hang on until sixty-five, but . . ." He shrugged before filling his mug.

"Is Liza willing to take you back after all these years?" I asked.

"I hope she's leaning that way." He smiled wistfully. "It doesn't seem possible, does it?"

I tried to put on a brave front. Leo's defection from his family dated back well over a decade. Between his heavy drinking and the eventual loss of his advertising job, he'd drifted north. I'd hired him ten years ago in desperation. To his credit and my relief, he'd managed to straighten himself out. I'd feel lost without him.

"As I've learned," I said slowly, "all things are possible."

"So," Leo said, picking up an Italian slipper, "how's life with the sheriff? I haven't seen much of him lately."

"That's because he took some time off to help Scott Melville and Dick Bourgette get the remodel project under way," I replied, following Leo to his desk after pouring my coffee. I'd already eaten the French doughnut. "Milo had to supervise some maintenance work on his own house, too. He's back on the job today."

"I don't want to be nosy," Leo said, easing into his chair, "but is Dodge still dividing his time between his daughter and you?"

"Milo isn't staying at his house much now," I replied, but I didn't elaborate as Mitch Laskey entered the newsroom.

"Good morning," my reporter said, looking reasonably cheerful for a Monday morning — and for being Mitch. He often wore an aura of hard-earned gloom. "Vida's outside. She has a flat tire."

Leo laughed. "Is she pumping it up with her own hot air?"

Mitch shook his head. "Watch it. You want the wrath of Runkel to come down on you? As we know, it's awesome to behold."

"She's still not her usual redoubtable self," I remarked. "I suppose she's waiting for Roger to prove himself as the peerless grandson she's always insisted he is despite ample evidence to the contrary."

Mitch frowned. "I missed most of that when I left town to bring Brenda back from Pittsburgh," he said, referring to his wife. In late December she'd suffered a breakdown after their son Troy botched his second escape from the Monroe Correctional Complex. "But I got a dose of the Vida Freeze before I left. She seems in better spirits lately."

"There's still room for improvement," I declared — and wished I'd kept my mouth shut, especially since Vida was making her entrance.

"Well now!" she exclaimed. "This is no way to start the week. Cal Vickers is bringing me another tire, so the Buick doesn't have to be towed to his Chevron station." My House & Home editor paused in the removal of a felt bowler hat plastered with limp paper daffodils. "Goodness, is that noise coming from your office, Emma?"

"It's stalking me," I replied. "I had to endure deafening sounds at home, too."

"I assume," she said archly, "you're not referring to your often overloud husband."

I ignored the comment. It was easier to return to my office and try to ignore the pounding. Vida's disposition had improved only marginally since she'd managed to save her adored great-grandson, Dippy, from the clutches of his mother, the town hooker. But she still blamed Milo, Prosecuting Attorney Rosemary Bourgette, and Judge Diane Proxmire for not putting together a tighter case to prevent Holly Gross from being released on bond after shooting a local drug lord. Never mind that the sheriff should have busted Roger for his own misdeeds. Despite all the problems the spoiled lump of a kid had caused, Vida still doted on him. She refused to appreciate that Milo had gone easy on him, not just because Roger had provided valuable information about the most culpable of the culprits, but for Vida's sake. In fact, she had yet to offer congratulations on February's civil ceremony uniting Milo and me in marriage. But while I was now Mrs. Dodge, I remained Ms. Lord on the newspaper. The sheriff and I agreed that we had to keep the often confrontational nature of our jobs separate from our private lives. I preferred the loud pounding over Vida's sharp tongue.

By eight-thirty, the noise had stopped. John Bourgette, Rosemary's eldest brother, came in to tell me that the cost of the repair would be factored into his father's invoice for the addition to my — *our* — house. That was good news. It wouldn't have to come out of the *Advocate*'s tight budget. It was typical of Milo's attitude that I shouldn't be out of pocket for the remodel. He had wanted to cover the entire cost to ensure

14

that it was *our* home, not just mine. His house in the Icicle Creek Development had been on the market since the third week of March, but real estate wasn't moving fast anywhere, especially in a small town like Alpine. When the property did sell, we'd have to deal with the removal of one entrenched item: his daughter Tanya. She was still recovering from what had been diagnosed as post-traumatic stress disorder after being shot by her fiancé before he killed himself.

Just before nine, Mitch returned from making his early morning tour of the courthouse and the sheriff's headquarters. He was shaking his head when he came into my office to lower his lean and lanky frame into one of my visitor chairs.

"I hope," he said, "that living with Dodge is easier than working for him. The sheriff isn't pleased with the way his staff ran the operation in his absence. He was sparing nobody, his daughter included. Do you think she likes working for her father?"

"It's one way to keep tabs on her," I said. "She can't just sit around his house watching TV all day."

"But Dodge wasn't around much lately," Mitch pointed out.

I couldn't resist a little smile. "It's also a way she can hang out with Deputy Bill

Blatt. And vice versa."

Mitch, who has been in Alpine since coming from Detroit in September, still isn't attuned to small-town ways. He somehow manages to avoid the local grapevine. Back in February, he'd suggested investigating the sheriff's department because he felt Milo had been on the job too long "without some transparency." I'd finally broken the news to him that I was about to become Mrs. Dodge. Incredibly, he'd had no idea we were even dating, let alone that we'd been friends for fifteen years and off-and-on lovers for the past decade.

"No kidding," Mitch murmured. "I thought Bill got married."

"He was engaged," I said, "but they broke up during the holidays."

Mitch nodded absently. "Isn't he somehow related to Vida?"

"Yes," I replied. "Half of Alpine is. She's his aunt. Vida was a Blatt before she married. Is there anything like news coming out of the courthouse or the sheriff's office?"

"A couple of marriage licenses at the courthouse, a divorce filing, and a broken window in the basement," Mitch informed me. "No sign of illegal entry, though. As for the sheriff's log, a cougar sighting, three prowlers, two domestic violence calls, vandalism of the Big Toy at Old Mill Park, one runaway teenager reported . . ."

I held up my hand to interrupt. "That's the second one in a month. The other girl — I forget her name, Samantha Something-or-other — had gone off with her boyfriend. Who's this one?"

"A sixteen-year-old named Erin Johnson. Address is First and Spruce." Mitch's expression was curious. "The trailer park?"

"Probably," I agreed. "Maybe these girls have spring fever. Anything else?"

Mitch nodded. "Four collisions, three on Highway 2 and one on the Burl Creek Road. No fatalities, no serious injuries. Fairly tame on the roads for a weekend. Oh — Ron Bjornson quit as the sheriff's handyman. He got promoted to head of security at the community college."

"Bjornson's a column inch or two of copy," I remarked, thinking that Milo would have to find a replacement. "Keep tabs on the Big Toy thing. It's probably kids."

Mitch got out of the chair. "Hey — thanks for suggesting that Brenda try the Rest-Haven shrink. She likes Dr. Reed."

"Good," I said, smiling. I didn't add that Tanya was also seeing Rosalie Reed, who was treating her for PTSD.

After Mitch went back to his desk, I

turned to my editorial. Off and on for the past two months I'd followed up on Mayor Fuzzy Baugh's plan to reorganize Alpine and Skykomish County. Fuzzy rarely had an idea, let alone a good one, but this time he'd come up with an extraordinary brainstorm. He proposed abolishing his own job, along with the trio of county commissioners, and replacing the positions with a professional manager. This would save money for everybody. I'd tackled the issue slowly, as befit Fuzzy's laid-back native Louisiana roots. Only now was I about to endorse the revolutionary plan. I'd assigned Mitch to a front-page interview with our mayor. While the local citizenry might be opposed to change in any form, they were also tightfisted. Maybe *not* spending their money would trump clinging to the status quo.

It was a tricky editorial to write. I was finishing my opening paragraph when our receptionist, Amanda Hanson, brought me the mail, just before nine-thirty. Her olive complexion looked washed out, though she'd been in good health for the first five months of her pregnancy.

"Are you okay?" I asked.

After setting the mail in my in-basket, Amanda leaned on the desk. "I'm fine. It's

Walt who isn't. He called to say I shouldn't worry if I heard something was going on at the fish hatchery. But I *am* worried. He sounded really weird."

"So it isn't personal with Walt," I said. "It's a work problem, right?"

"I guess." She frowned. "What can go wrong unless the fish died?"

"I'll send Mitch to find out. It sounds like news." I stood up to see if I could spot my reporter, but he wasn't in sight. "Did he go out?" I asked.

"I think he's in the back shop with Kip," Amanda replied, referring to Kip MacDuff, our production manager. "If he comes my way, I'll send him to see you."

I nodded. "Hey, don't get too upset. If Walt can call to tell you something's the matter at the hatchery, then he isn't being held hostage by outraged anglers like Milo who always gripe about the lakes and streams not being planted with enough fish. Maybe I should call my neighbor Viv Marsden. Her husband, Val, might've told her what's going on since he's the hatchery's main man."

"If you learn anything," Amanda said, "let me know." With less than her usual brisk step, she headed back to the front office.

When Mitch reappeared a few minutes

later, I dispatched him to check with the hatchery. A moment later, Vida tromped in to see me.

"There is *no* reason for Maud Dodd to censor my copy," she declared. "Is it my fault that Henrietta Skylstad and Oscar Halvorson prefer dancing with each other instead of their mates at the retirement home? Melvin Skylstad has only one leg and Selma Halvorson is deaf as well as blind."

"Which part is Maud trying to censor?" I asked. "The leg? The blind? The . . . ?"

"The dancing part," Vida broke in. "There's been talk about Henrietta and Oscar for some time. They were sweethearts in high school, you know."

"Ah . . . no, I didn't," I admitted. In fact, I wouldn't recognize the Skylstads or the Halvorsons if they fell through my new roof. But Vida would have every detail of their lives and every other Alpiner's tucked under whichever weird hat she was wearing. "What year did they graduate?" I asked, just to test her remarkable memory.

Vida tapped her cheek. "Oscar was a year ahead of Henrietta. He was in the class of 1928, so she was 1929. Not all that long before I was born. My mother often commented that she thought their breakup was a terrible mistake."

I managed to keep a straight face. "I assume Maud hasn't heard rumors of divorce."

"No. I don't recall anyone separating — certainly not in the nursing home section — despite the Whipps' frequent attempts to kill each other. But Maud feels that mentioning Henrietta and Oscar dancing together at the April Fool's Ball in my 'Scene Around Town' column could fuel ugly gossip. That's absurd, since they were *only* dancing. Maud's role as retirement home news contact has gone to her head."

"It's your column," I pointed out.

"It certainly is," Vida asserted. "However," she added, pivoting on a sensible chunky heel, "I don't want my news source to dry up."

"You be the judge," I said, uncharitably thinking that a lot of the residents at the retirement home had already dried up.

I watched as Vida put on her orange raincoat before leaving to face off with Maud Dodd. She'd been gone less than five minutes when I looked up to see the sheriff loping through the empty newsroom. He paused to pour a mug of coffee and grab a raised sugar doughnut before parking all six foot five of himself in one of my chairs.

"Did your staff quit?" he asked, taking off

his regulation hat and tossing it on the other chair.

"They're working," I said. "They have to earn their meager pay."

He glanced up at the low ceiling. "Got your roof fixed yet?"

"Yes. I was about to buy some earplugs. Did you just wander in to see if I'd survived all the noise, or do you have some news?"

Milo gestured over his shoulder toward the street. "I had to stop at the bank to get a cashier's check for Melville. Except for overseeing the Bourgette crew, his part of the work is done."

"Come on, big guy. I hear you chewed out your crew today. How come you're calling on your wife instead of supervising those rascals?"

"Because she's cuter than my crew?" He ran a hand through his graying sandy hair. "I do have news, my little smart-ass. Jack Blackwell just dropped the charges against Jennifer Hood."

I stared at Milo. "Why? He didn't mind that she tried to kill him?"

The sheriff finished the doughnut before he responded. "She was only trying to scare him for revenge after their long-ago and very brief marriage in California. Frankly, I hoped she might get serious about it and do

22

him in. No such luck."

Milo and Blackwell had a history. As the only mill owner in Alpine and now a county commissioner, Jack considered himself a big mover and shaker. The two men had been at odds since they were both in their twenties. Jack liked to throw his weight around, and even as a deputy, Milo hadn't taken kindly to anyone who tried to bring him to heel. The relationship had been further fractured when Jack ran against Milo for sheriff — unsuccessfully — back when the job was an elected position.

"Since when did Blackwell get so softhearted?" I asked.

"I don't think it's that," Milo replied. "I figure the SOB's embarrassed. Oh, the brake tampering, the attempt to run him down, the shot that only tore his pants — he might've gone with that, but when Jennifer stabbed him in the back after he banged her for old times' sake and then he went to sleep — that was too much. Especially since the moron didn't even know he'd been stabbed and the wound got infected."

I nodded. "That doesn't make Jack look too swift. And even you have to admit he's a shrewd businessman."

"Oh, yeah," Milo conceded, "the asshole is that. Will you write the story or hand it over to Laskey?"

"I'll let him do it. I'd be tempted to turn it into a humor piece. Besides, Mitch gets touchy if he thinks I'm interfering with his beat."

"He's a prickly sort," Milo said, taking a last swig of coffee before standing up and glancing over his shoulder. "Hey — there's still nobody around. You want to close the door and pretend we're in conference?"

"I have an editorial to write, Sheriff," I said primly. "In fact, it's the one where I announce Fuzzy's reorganization plan."

"Sounds like your readers will try to run you and Baugh out of town. Maybe I should assign a deputy to protect you. Too bad I can't afford to do that." He picked up his hat and started out the door.

"Hey!" I called after him. "Wait! What's going on at the fish hatchery? Amanda got a strange call from Walt."

"Oh." Milo turned around and moved to the side of my desk. "I don't know yet. Doe Jamison and Dwight Gould headed out there a few minutes before I went to the bank. Some problem with the hatchery's wetlands." He folded his arms across his chest. "Damnit, now that we're married, why do I still have trouble keeping my hands off of you?"

I looked up at him, craning my neck to make up for the thirteen-inch difference in height. "We promised to not be . . . um . . . *demonstrative* in public now that we're a sedate married couple. It isn't good for our professional images."

His hazel eyes sparked. "That doesn't make sense. Now we've got legal grounds to make fools of ourselves."

I leaned as far away from him as I could without tipping over. "That's my point. Do we really want to look like a pair of idiots?"

His arms fell to his sides. "We've already done that."

"For the first few years we hung out together, you hardly ever touched me. Dare I ask how you exercised such self-restraint?"

"It was tough. I thought if I made a move, I couldn't stop and I'd scare you. We weren't even dating. Oh, hell," he muttered. "See you later, Emma."

I smiled as I watched him stride through the newsroom. I was both happy and content. Yet I still regretted that it had taken me fifteen years to reach that state, when all along Milo Dodge had been right in front of me — and he'd always had my back. *Emma Lord, bat-blind when it came to love.* At least I woke up in time to become Emma Dodge.

■ ■ ■ ■

I'd managed to produce three so-so paragraphs by the time Janie Engelman Borg Engelman showed up in my office looking for Vida.

"I think," I said, "she's at the retirement home. Can I help you?"

"Well . . ." Janie shifted from one foot to the other. "Not sure. I got a wedding picture for her. Of Fred and me. Even if it's the second time."

I was used to Janie's choppy speech. "I think it's fine. Congratulations. I'm glad you and Fred got back together."

"Me and Fred, too. He got out of rehab. Before we married. Again."

"I'm happy for both of you," I said. I didn't add that I was also happy for Milo. The Engelmans' first union had broken up because of Fred's weekend binges. He'd tried to cure himself by checking into the jail Friday nights and staying put until Monday mornings. The sheriff and his staff felt like babysitters. Janie's rebound marriage to Mickey Borg had been rocky from the start. "Say," I went on, "Ron Bjornson quit his handyman's job at headquarters. Would Fred like to take it on when he's not

26

working at Blackwell Timber?"

Janie's gamine face brightened. "He might. We could use the money. Mickey cleaned me out. Of my small savings. And TV."

"I'll mention it to Milo," I said. "I heard Mickey left town."

Janie's brown eyes darted from side to side as if she expected her ex to come through my walls. "Hard to say. About Mickey."

Hard to listen to Janie, I thought. But I smiled. "You can forget Mickey now. Didn't he sell the Icicle Creek Gas 'N Go to a Gustavson?"

Janie nodded. "He kept the money. For himself."

"I suppose he would, if the divorce was final."

"It wasn't." She scowled. "Typical Mickey. Selfish. I asked him to give the TV back. Fred likes to watch baseball. Mickey said no, Fred can listen to the Mariners on the radio. At noon our time. In Chicago. I told him Fred wants to see it. Not just hear it. Mickey didn't care. Fred still wants a TV. Maybe we can. With extra money."

"The main thing," I pointed out, "is you're back with Fred and rid of Mickey. You don't have to worry about him anymore."

Janie smiled faintly. "I hope not. Maybe he's gone by now. For good." She wandered out of my office.

But we hadn't heard the end of Mickey for good — or for bad.

Two

I was deleting all three paragraphs of my feeble editorial when Amanda poked her head in. "Have you heard anything about the hatchery yet? I saw Dodge come in, but I was in the back shop when he left. Walt hasn't called again."

I shook my head. "Milo sent his deputies to check it out. He didn't seem very excited about it."

Amanda looked bemused. "I've never seen the sheriff get excited about anything." She winced. "I mean, he seems . . . ah . . ."

I laughed. "Never mind. On the job, he's usually unflappable. Excitability doesn't become a law enforcement officer. I'll call him when I think he's heard back from Gould and Jamison. He did mention that it had something to do with the wetlands."

Amanda frowned. "The wetlands? What could happen unless they dried up? But it's raining."

"It could be vandalism, I suppose. Mitch told me the Big Toy at Old Mill Park had gotten trashed over the weekend. The schools are on spring break, and that always means trouble."

"You're right. That didn't occur to me." She put a hand on her bulging abdomen. "After so many years of thinking we'd never have our own baby, it still seems like a miracle. It's hard to believe that keeping track of school schedules will be important five years from now."

The idea obviously cheered her. She was smiling as she headed to the front office. Last fall, the Hanson marriage was rocky, with each blaming the other for their childless state. Then, as they considered adoption, Mother Nature stepped in.

Our conversation reminded me to call Viv Marsden to see if she knew what was going on at her husband's hatchery. But Viv wasn't home. I didn't bother to leave her a message. Milo would find out soon enough. Whether or not he'd remember to call me was another matter. Marriage had not changed the sheriff's concept of what was news.

Ten minutes and two more dull editorial starts later, I lectured myself: *This isn't the Queen's Speech. Stop pussyfooting around the issue. No, Skykomish County readers don't like change. Yes, they prefer keeping their money in their pockets. Just say so off the top and go from there.*

"Keep the change. Make the change. This is what Mayor Fuzzy Baugh is asking of SkyCo residents. Change is good when it costs less than the status quo." The writing didn't sparkle, but it might get readers' attention. I gathered steam and kept typing. I was almost done when Vida returned from wherever she'd been for the past hour and a half.

"I managed to reach a rapprochement with Maud," she declared, sitting down in one of my visitor chairs. "I told her that featuring any of those old fools who can stand upright and possibly even move on a dance floor spoke well for the retirement home, especially for the smug and overbearing Lutherans who run it."

I grimaced. "Your exact words?"

"Of course not." Vida removed the bowler and fluffed up her unruly gray curls. "But that was the gist of it. If I could've told her what I really think — which is that the Presbyterians could run a much better facility and in a more thrifty manner. Of course the Lutherans are in the majority, so it can't be helped. At least we finally have a new

31

permanent minister at our church. I do wish he hadn't come from Castle Rock. It'll take him some time to get to know everybody."

What Vida meant was that it would take him some time to get to know *everything* about everybody. According to her, the longtime minster, James Purebeck, had not been reluctant to preach about sins that members of his congregation had recently committed. Naturally, Vida knew enough about her fellow Presbyterians to identify who had committed them. But Pastor Purebeck had disgraced himself six months ago by running off to Mukilteo with Daisy McFee, who, according to Vida, had loose morals and had lived in Alpine for only a short time. In my House & Home editor's eyes, it was hard to tell which was the more serious transgression.

"Pastor McClelland is fairly young, isn't he?" I said.

"Late thirties," Vida replied. "Or course Pastor Purebeck wasn't much older when he came here." She couldn't hide her disgust. "Maturity apparently only aged his exterior, rather than improving his character."

"I believe you wrote that Kenneth McClelland has a wife and two children," I said to allay further criticism of Purebeck.

"Yes. They've moved into the house next to the church where the Purebecks lived. Of course, it's owned by the Presbyterians." She heaved a sigh, her imposing bust straining at the orange-and-blue striped blouse she wore under a black vest. "I noticed Janie Engelman dropped off her latest wedding picture. I wonder where Mickey Borg has gone."

"I don't," I said. "He's a jerk." The words were out of my mouth before I remembered that Mickey had fathered the first two of Holly Gross's three children. Or so Vida had told me when she'd revealed that the third and youngest one belonged to Roger. "By the way," I said hastily, to change the subject, "Father Kelly announced at Mass yesterday that he'll be gone this week to visit family in Houston. We'll have a sub from Monroe. You might want to use that on your page or in 'Scene.' "

"Houston!" Vida shook her head. "Can you imagine living in a huge place like that? So many hurricanes and Enron and heat!"

"Ben's in El Paso," I said. "He's working with the immigrants."

"El Paso." Vida spoke the city's name as if it were a new disease she'd just discovered. "Really, now. I can't imagine it's a very nice place. But I realize that priests must go where they're sent. Has your brother any news of it?"

"He's only been there since the start of Holy Week," I said. "Not yet a full month."

Vida got up from her chair. "He's served in other peculiar areas. I suppose he's used to it." She exited my office in her splay-footed manner.

I decided I'd given Milo enough time to find out what was going on at the hatchery. I dialed his number, but Deputy Sam Heppner answered.

"Dodge isn't here. Call back after lunch." He hung up.

Sam is even more churlish than Dwight Gould when it comes to dealing with women. At least Dwight had finally shown his human side by having a brief encounter with his ex-wife, back in February. I assumed it was brief, though for all I knew, Dwight and Kay Whitman Burns, Rest-Haven's PR person, were whiling away their off-hours in each other's arms. Dwight wasn't inclined to discuss his personal life, even when he didn't have one, so I doubted he'd talk about it now.

It was after eleven-thirty when Mitch returned from his interview with Fuzzy Baugh. "I can't quite figure that guy out," my reporter said, refilling his coffee mug.

"Most of the time he puts on that Louisiana accent and talks drivel, but then he comes up with something kind of shrewd. I think I got a couple of good quotes from him."

"That's more than I've had on some occasions over the years," I admitted. "But the reorganization idea is good. I've wondered if his wife, Irene, came up with it. She always seems savvier than her husband. Still, when Fuzzy and I've discussed it, he makes perfect sense."

"It's a sound proposal," Mitch said. "Why wasn't Alpine incorporated way back when?"

"It was started as a company town by the original mill owner, Carl Clemans, in 1910. Over time, telegraph and railroad employees, along with other related types of workers, moved here. When Mr. Clemans closed the mill in 1929, it appeared the town might wither away. There was no year-round access except by train. But Vida's future father-in-law, Rufus Runkel, and another man, whose name I recall only as Olav the Obese, decided to start a ski operation. The sport was just coming into its own. They saved Alpine from extinction."

Mitch looked grim. "I can understand how a small town could disappear without jobs. The news I hear out of Detroit is damned gloomy with all the problems in the auto industry. Maybe Brenda and I got out just in time. God knows newspapers everywhere are shrinking or going out of business."

"You're preaching to the choir," I said. "The *Oregon Journal* — Portland's afternoon daily — went out of business nine years before I quit *The Oregonian* to move to Alpine. I wonder how long we can hold out, but our relative isolation helps."

Mitch nodded. "It's weird after Detroit. People here don't seem to care much about what happens in the wider world. I suppose it's being surrounded by all the mountains and so far from a big city. I'll work through the lunch hour on Baugh's article. I've still got a couple of features to finish, and I have to cover the county commissioners tonight. I'm glad they switched their meetings from Tuesday to Monday. When they nattered on, as they often do, it made things tight for deadline."

"I agree," I said. "It's just as well they won't see my editorial and the mayor's comments before they meet. Take a look at what I wrote about Fuzzy's plan, to see if it works with your interview. Oh — by the way, Jack Blackwell dropped charges against Jennifer Hood. The news came in after you'd been at the sheriff's headquarters."

Mitch made a face. "She tries to kill the guy four times and he lets her get away with it?"

"Jack's holed up, licking his wounds. Besides, he probably doesn't want Jennifer telling everybody how badly he treats the women in his life. Patti Marsh has taken him back — again."

My reporter shook his head in apparent dismay over the folly of females who stood by their men no matter how many times they'd ended up in the ER. I, too, had wondered about that phenomenon over the years. Doc Dewey had told me recently that he felt such abusers and the abused needed each other. He claimed both had low self-esteem. I still wasn't sure if I bought into his theory, but Young Doc, as he was known, often channeled the wisdom of his late father, Old Doc Dewey.

It was going on noon. I wondered if Milo was free for lunch. Vida had already left, and Leo was out making his rounds. I planned on heading for the Burger Barn, which was catty-corner from the sheriff's office, so I decided to see if he could join me.

The rain had almost stopped by the time I started the block-and-a-half walk to headquarters. I sniffed the fresh mountain air and looked up at Alpine Baldy, where the clouds still lingered below the five-thousand-foot level. The noon whistle blew at Blackwell Timber just as I entered Milo's lair.

The receptionist, Lori Cobb, greeted me with a friendly smile. Deputy Sam Heppner looked as if I'd been ringing a bell to announce that I had plague. I didn't see any sign of Tanya — or her father.

"Did your boss take his daughter to lunch?" I asked Lori.

She shook her head. "Tanya went to the mall. Dodge is still at the hatchery with Dwight and Doe. Mr. Fleetwood was just here, and I think he went out there to see what was going on. It's close to his radio station, but he didn't know anything about it."

I decided to ignore my growling stomach. If my archrival had gone to the hatchery, I'd go there, too. I had no intention of letting Spencer Fleetwood force my husband to help his wife get scooped.

"Thanks, Lori," I said. "Maybe it's worth a trip for me, too. I don't suppose the sheriff or his deputies have let the rest of you know what's going on?"

Sam moved closer to me from behind the

reception area's curving counter. "If they did, it's not for publication," he snarled.

"That's not for you to decide, *Deputy.*" I swiveled around, narrowly missing a cardboard box in front of the counter. Flouncing out the door, I almost collided with a man whose first name I recalled as Gus. I all but ran back down the street to my aging Honda, impervious to the wind that had suddenly picked up and the rumbling of a freight train going through town on the other side of the *Advocate* office. At least I didn't have to cross the tracks to get to the hatchery.

It took me less than ten minutes to drive along Front Street, take a jog onto the Burl Creek Road, go by the modest homes sprinkled along the route, then pass KSKY's cinder-block studio and Skykomish Community College's campus. Entering a dense stand of third-growth forest, I crossed Burl Creek — and finally reached the hatchery, just east of the fork in the Tye and Foss Rivers.

I spotted a SkyCo cruiser, Milo's black Yukon SUV, and Spence's Beamer in the parking lot. I couldn't see any activity around the main building, the wetlands area, or the ponds, which were partially visible behind some steel sheds. I parked my car and headed for the entrance. The small lobby was empty. I hadn't been inside the hatchery in years. I wasn't sure which way to go.

I wandered off to the corridor on the left, where I sighted Derek Norman, who I knew only vaguely from a crisis ten years ago with the parish school board. I hadn't seen much of him since. The Normans weren't Catholics, but they believed in private education.

"Ms. Lord," Derek said, looking older and heavier than I recalled from the last time I'd run into him, "can I help you? It's lunch hour here, so we're a bit shorthanded."

"I'm looking for the sheriff. And Spencer Fleetwood," I added, lest Derek think I was a snoopy wife.

Derek's high forehead — which hadn't been that high a few years ago — furrowed in a frown. "I think they're still in the woods beyond the holding ponds with Val Marsden and the deputies."

I didn't want to admit that I had no idea why any of them would be wandering around in the forest, so I nodded. "I'll see if I can track them down. Is there a back way out?"

Derek pointed over his shoulder. "Straight down the hall you'll see a door that goes to the stairs leading outside."

I thanked him and continued on my way. When I opened the outer door, the wind coming from the south had picked up enough to blow my not-so-tidy brown hair straight back. A few yards ahead of me, small waves ruffled the holding ponds. The tall fir and cedar trees' branches swayed, sending a flock of noisy crows skyward. I'd gotten as far as just beyond the first pond when I saw Milo, Spence, Val, and Walt coming up the trail that led out of the forest. The sheriff had taken off his hat and Mr. Radio was smoothing his usually impeccably groomed hair.

"What now?" Milo called out. "Did the Bourgettes strike gold in our backyard?"

"I'm here on business, Sheriff," I replied in my most formal voice. "Given that the other half of the local media is already on the spot, I sensed news." I shot Spence a dark glance.

Milo and Val had come to where I was standing. Doe Jamison and Dwight Gould moved toward the wetlands, while Spence stopped at the edge of the nearest holding pond. The wind had died down a bit, dampening my hope that he'd be blown away to swim with the fishes.

"No news here," the sheriff asserted. "Why don't you and Fleetwood go eat lunch someplace? The ski lodge, maybe. It's not that far away."

I glanced again at Spence, who lifted his hands in a helpless gesture. I wondered if Milo was talking in some kind of code, but the hazel eyes looked stern.

"Why not?" I retorted. At least Mr. Radio might have a glimmer of what was going on. I motioned to him. "Shall we?"

Spence shrugged. "Fine. I'll meet you there."

We both walked around the building to the parking lot. "You can't know any less than I do," I said when we were out of earshot. "And don't you dare suggest that Dodge plays favorites when it comes to news. You just saw how it still works between us when he's on the job."

"Amazing," Spence remarked in his mellifluous voice. "I fail to understand how he resists your obvious charms."

"Ha! In all the years we've been together — off and on as it's been until now — Milo has kept investigations to himself until he's damned good and ready to go public. You know that."

We'd reached our cars. "Admirable of him," Spence allowed. "I'll meet you in the bar."

I led the way, turning off onto Tonga Road

and crossing the small bridge over Burl Creek. The rest of the short drive was all uphill. Pulling into the parking lot, I noticed that the clouds had been blown away, so that I could see the top of the now moribund ski lifts.

Spence joined me just before I reached the entrance. His expression was quizzical. "You become the sheriff's wife and he sends you off to rendezvous with another man? Is this what's known as an open marriage or some ploy to get rid of us both?"

"The latter," I replied as Spence opened the door. I looked up at his hawklike profile, which reminded me not so much of a buzzard as some other, less ugly bird of prey. "If you think I'm here to seduce you, guess again. You must know more about what's happening at the hatchery than I do. You got there first."

We walked through the lobby, with its high-beamed ceiling, and continued on into the bar. The lodge itself was an architectural homage to the Native American tribes of the region, but the restaurant and bar theme was pure Nordic. Odin and Frigg ruled there, along with other mythical figures out of Europe's northern reaches.

The usual blond waitress — this one's name tag identified her as Belinda — seated us at a corner table and wasted no time taking our drink orders.

"Where," Spence mused after we were alone, "does Henry Bardeen find all these nubile blondes whose names begin with *B*? Or does he rechristen them after they're hired?"

"I've wondered that about the ski lodge manager, too," I admitted.

"Henry's never struck me as a lecher," Spence said, opening a pack of his imported black cigarettes. "Vida told me he was widowed some twenty years ago but never remarried. If he's serious about finding a long-term woman, he might get rid of that all-too-obvious toupee."

"The only woman in his peer group that I ever heard he was interested in is Francine Wells, but not long after that, Francine and her ex, Warren, got back together. Maybe Henry's given up. He must be closer to seventy than sixty." I shook my head, as Spence produced a small portable ashtray and lighted his cigarette. "Are you and the sheriff the only people allowed to smoke in an Alpine eatery?"

"Probably," he conceded. "Rank has its privileges. Or maybe it's sheer gall. Dodge won't arrest himself, so he can't in good conscience arrest me. How is life with our peerless law enforcement leader?"

"It's fine," I said. "How about you and Rosalie Reed?"

Spence put a finger to his lips. "Please. She's still a grieving widow. It's only been two months since her husband's fatal heart attack. We must observe conventional discretion."

I didn't feel like needling Mr. Radio about his longtime liaison with RestHaven's psychiatrist, so I let the subject drop. Our martinis — his of gin, mine of vodka — had arrived. "Okay," I said, "unload about why you showed up at the hatchery and what you found out after you got there."

Spence took a sip of his drink before answering. "Not much. I stopped by your favorite bear's den to make sure I was caught up on the weekend's miscreants. Being fiercely loyal to the print media, you may not know that Bree Kendall does an expanded fifteen-minute Monday wrap-up. Noticing that Dodge's Yukon wasn't parked outside, I asked where the sheriff might be. Lori informed me he'd gone to the hatchery to meet Gould and Jamison. That was two law officers too many for there not to be something newsworthy going on. When I pressed Lori for details, she didn't have any — or maybe the belligerent Sam Heppner had stepped on her foot."

"Gee," I said, "it's good to know that Sam doesn't just pick on women when it comes to a lack of cooperation."

"Heppner strikes me as a man who doesn't like the human race in general." Spence took a drag on his cigarette and another sip from his martini before continuing. "I don't think I was there more than a few minutes ahead of your arrival. Walt Hanson told me Val Marsden and the law officers were somewhere just beyond the holding ponds. I found them about thirty yards into the forest, where the love of your life announced, 'Nothing to see here. Beat it, Fleetwood.' " He gave me an ironic smile. "You can imagine my response. The comment reeked of news. Except there wasn't any."

"And?" I prodded, growing impatient.

"I managed to get an explanation out of the less abrasive Val Marsden. He informed me that a blood trail had been found by the wetlands. Alarmed, he'd called the sheriff's office. Gould and Jamison showed up but couldn't find any sign of a wounded animal, wild, domestic, or human. The blood trail grew fainter and fainter until it petered out by Burl Creek. Still puzzled, they checked back in with their boss, who decided to see for himself. Same result. Sheriff baffled. There's your headline. I dare you to use it."

"Don't kid a kidder," I said. "I'd rather put an item in Vida's 'Scene' about you and Rosalie groping each other in the psych ward."

Spence looked as if the idea appealed to him. "Why not? It's the perfect place to go crazy."

Belinda returned to take our orders, though neither of us had looked at the menu. I asked for the Aegir seafood salad; Spence requested the Scallops a la Olav. With so few restaurants in Alpine, we both knew the offerings by heart.

"Well?" I said after Belinda had gone off again. "It's mildly mysterious. What do you think really happened?"

Spence regarded me with feigned dismay. "You're the one who indulges in solving mysteries. I'll go with the wounded animal theory."

I shrugged. "If the animal was looking for fish, we can rule out a seal or a shark. A bear's most likely. What about paw prints?"

"Not much ground in that area to find prints, especially since it rained today. Obviously, whatever it was that bled was there before anyone came to work this morning. I assume Dodge will try to figure out how long the blood has been on the ground. If there weren't so many trees around there, this morning's drizzle might've washed the trail away by the time the hatchery workers came on the job. Of course, they'll also determine whether the blood belonged to man or beast."

I didn't say anything for a few moments. "It does sound odd. I've never been that far down Burl Creek. What's the terrain like where the blood disappeared?"

"More forest. The creek joins the Skykomish River just after the fork in the Tye and the Foss Rivers. Another fifty yards at most."

Our entrées arrived. Several other patrons had now entered the almost empty bar, apparently needing a hit to get them through the rest of the workday. Among them were Trout and Skunk Nordby, owners of the local GM dealership. They had two men in business suits with them that I didn't recognize, though Spence and I both nodded a greeting.

"Their companions look like bankers," Spence murmured. "Do you think the Nordbys are suffering these days?"

"Doubtful," I said. "Recession or not, this is a GM kind of town. But I do wonder if we'll ever get a permanent president at the Bank of Alpine. Andy Cederberg holds the title, but the buzz is that it's a temporary situation. It hasn't been six months since the last disaster struck the Petersen family and both of the banking heirs announced over KSKY that they weren't interested in following the family tradition."

"Ah, yes, courtesy of 'Vida's Cupboard,' " Spence sighed. "Would that all your House & Home editor's weekly programs were so full of drama as that one was. Not that she still can't command the attention of SkyCo listeners with even the most mundane of topics, including last week's interview with Harvey Adcock about how not to dismember yourself with the latest Weed Eater from his hardware store."

Our conversation turned to other topics so we could avoid being overheard discussing touchier subjects. We adjourned just before one and went our separate ways. Spence and I were rivals in one sense and comrades-in-arms in another. We had seen each other through our own private nightmares, though that didn't mean we were friends. But we had mutual respect as professionals. That meant a lot to both of us in a small town where smaller minds could denounce us for preying on the misfortune of others.

Back at the office, we all engaged in the

usual process of our jobs. Mitch's interview with Fuzzy Baugh meshed nicely with my editorial. Vida had her standard roundup of engagements, births, and a wedding between two people I'd never heard of who were older students at Skykomish Community College. They'd been married in Everett, but Vida gave them five inches of copy because they were making their home in Alpine until they graduated. Leo announced that he thought we'd meet the desirable sixty-forty split between advertising and news copy. Amanda had three and a half columns of classified ads so far. And most importantly, Kip assured me that nothing had gone wrong in the back shop — yet. I had to take his word for it. My expertise when it came to anything involving technology was virtually nonexistent.

It was after four-thirty when the sheriff called. I'd just finished conferring with Vida about which of the retirement home birthday party pictures was the least blurry. They'd been taken by one of the residents who suffered from a form of palsy.

"I've got something for you," the sheriff said, though he didn't sound enthused. "Dwight took off an hour early to make up for overtime he put in this weekend. He wanted to check the Sky where it comes in west of Blackwell's mill. He's getting antsy for trout season." Milo paused, apparently to answer a question from someone about an accident report. I impatiently tapped my fingernails on the desk. "Okay, where was I?"

"Dwight being antsy. So am I. Dish, big guy."

"He found a corpse. Is there anything else you want to know, or can I go help untangle three vehicles and their passengers from a wreck by the Deception Falls Bridge? The sports car involved took out the Milepost 55 sign." He didn't wait for an answer but banged down the phone just as I heard the first of the sirens heading for Highway 2.

THREE

I alerted Mitch immediately. "The sheriff's gone off to deal with a wreck, so you may have to wait until he gets back," I told my reporter. "There's a chance, of course, that one of the deputies might have more information so we can post the bare facts online."

"No ID on the body?" Mitch asked, putting on his raincoat.

"I was lucky to get what I got," I replied. "Be thankful today isn't our deadline."

"What about the wreck? Worth a photo?"

My nose for news seemed dull. "You're right. The stiff's not going anywhere. Try to get a shot of the milepost sign that got knocked over."

Mitch nodded, grabbed his camera, and left just as the last of the sirens faded out of hearing range. Vida, who had been on the phone, motioned for me to come over to her desk.

"Did I hear you say something about a

dead body?" she asked, looking owlish behind her big silver-framed glasses.

"Yes," I said, "near the fork where the Foss and Tye Rivers meet before they go into the Skykomish. It's just this side of Alpine Falls."

Amanda wobbled a bit as she entered the newsroom. "You mean down from the hatchery?"

I paused to mentally reconstruct Burl Creek's path. "Yes, a quarter mile or more away. Have you talked to Walt in the last hour?"

She shook her head. "Not since early afternoon when Val got back from checking out everything with Dodge and the deputies. Everybody at the hatchery figured it was a bear, a cougar, or some other animal."

"That still may be the case," I said. "The sheriff didn't mention that the body was wounded."

"Very negligent of Milo," Vida remarked with a sniff of disapproval. "The least he could do is let you know that much."

I ignored the comment. "It's going on five," I said, heading to my office. "I'll stick around until Mitch gets back. Everybody else might as well go home." I paused at my ad manager's desk. "Where's Leo?"

"At the Grocery Basket," Amanda replied.

"Buzzy O'Toole overordered strawberries and raspberries from California. I guess the younger O'Toole brother has a little trouble with math, so Jake has to put them on special before they spoil. He called Leo a few minutes ago to ask for a change in the weekly ad."

I nodded and kept going. Maybe I'd stop at the Grocery Basket to get some strawberries — if Jake had already marked them down. The store still had chicken breasts on sale. I had no idea if Tanya would be joining us. She was finally able to stay at Milo's house most nights on her own — unless she had a panic attack. Then her father had to abandon me in case his daughter suffered one of her recurring nightmares.

It was almost five-thirty when Mitch returned to the office. "Three out-of-area vehicles, road conditions not that bad, just too much speed for that stretch of highway. One possible fatality, four injured, three treated at the scene, and one downed milepost sign. Even I've been here long enough to respect the hazards of driving Highway 2."

"Same old story," I said as Mitch loaded his photos onto the computer. "People who aren't from around this part of the state don't know that starting outside Monroe on

522, it's called the Highway to Heaven. Oh, you got some good stuff." I gaped as the image of an overturned red sports car appeared on the screen. "Oh, my God! How did that thing land upside down?"

"Ask the driver — if he makes it. He's the possible fatality. Erinel Dobles from Visalia, California. No seat belt. I guess he didn't know it's a law in this state. He almost landed in Deception Creek."

"So what did you learn from the sheriff?"

Mitch looked faintly amused. "I don't get it. You're his wife and he doesn't tell you anything?"

I refrained from rolling my eyes. "As I've explained, nothing changed after Milo and I got married. You know that law enforcement and the media are often at odds. We have to maintain distance in our respective workplaces. He's as tight-lipped about his operation when he's at home as he is at headquarters."

Mitch still looked faintly incredulous. "I have to admit I've never talked a lot about work with Brenda. But so much of what I covered in Detroit was borderline ugly, especially on the police beat. She didn't want to hear it and I tried to leave it back at my desk."

"How is she doing?" I asked, not wanting

to bring up the delicate subject too often since Brenda's late December breakdown.

"Better, I think," Mitch replied, though he frowned. "She's weaving again. That helps. Of course, I try to go home for lunch every day. It just . . . takes time. And Dr. Reed seems helpful."

"Good. She's the first real shrink we've had in SkyCo. It's a wonder half the population isn't lined up outside of RestHaven." I realized we'd gotten off-track. "Did Dodge have any news other than what he told me?"

"Deceased found by the fork in the river was a Hispanic male between twenty and thirty. There was ID, but name's withheld pending notification of survivors. He'd been stabbed in the abdomen. No weapon found. Apparently not a robbery, as he had over thirty dollars in a money clip. Doc Dewey estimated he'd been dead for six to twelve hours. The body's on its way to the Snohomish County ME for a full autopsy."

"Damn. That means we might not have any further information before tomorrow night's deadline. SnoCo's got so many autopsies of their own that SkyCo gets pushed to the end of the line. If only we could get things changed here to free up funds for facilities and services that've been put on hold forever." I smiled wanly. "It'll be interesting to see how the locals respond to your interview with Fuzzy and my editorial."

Mitch ran a hand through his thatch of gray hair. "Let's hope it's not with what you've termed their usual state of negativity — or torpor."

"Yes, let's," I said. "Frankly, hope is all we've got."

I didn't get home until after six. Milo still hadn't arrived, which didn't surprise me. No doubt he had a lot of paperwork, a task he loathed. I'd decided to make stir-fry with the chicken breasts. It was quick and easy. I'd use the strawberries for dessert. Ever since the sheriff had undergone gall bladder surgery, a little over a year ago, I'd tried — not always successfully — to wean him away from some of the less healthful foods he liked. It was hard to avoid grease when dining out in Alpine. Lean cuisine had never gained popularity in the former logging town.

Milo finally showed up a little after six-thirty. He came in through the kitchen door looking grumpy. "I told Gould not to bother checking out the river this soon," he said, taking off his regulation hat. "Then the dumb bastard had to find a stiff late in the day. Why didn't he go there in the morning? The body wasn't going anywhere. It was caught on a snag. Too many of those damned useless alder trees along the river. I can't count how many lures I've lost on those things."

I gazed up at my husband and smiled sweetly. "Hi. Remember me? I'm your wife."

Milo had the grace to look abject. "If you weren't, I couldn't bitch the minute I came in the door. I sure as hell couldn't do that with the ex–Mrs. Dodge." He put his arms around me and kissed me — hard, long, and hungrily. "That better?" he asked, his face still almost touching mine.

"Uh-huh," I said, sounding a bit overcome and then leaning against him. "No Tanya?" I inquired into his chest.

"She's having dinner with Bill and then seeing a movie at The Whistling Marmot. I'm thinking of promoting Bill to . . . something. I sure as hell don't have the money to give him a raise." He let go of me, but not before squeezing my backside.

"Go change," I told him. "I'll make our drinks. You've had a longer day than I have."

"So I have," he said wearily, loping out of the kitchen.

I smiled as I got out his Scotch and my Canadian. I even laughed to myself. Or at myself. For some perverse reason — perversity always having been my middle name — I'd been reluctant to go through the marriage ceremony. My only excuse was that I'd never done it before. There was also the Lord family trait of indecisiveness, shared by my only sibling, Ben. Being a priest, he admitted that the sacrament of Holy Orders meant he had to follow them according to the vow of obedience he'd taken upon his ordination. Otherwise, he conjectured, he'd still be trying to make up his mind about choosing a college major. I understood, though I was glad that somehow my son, Adam, hadn't inherited that particular gene. For years I was afraid he had, jumping from college to college and uncertain about what he wanted to do with his life. Then he'd spent time with Ben in his mission work with the Navajo and Hopi tribes in Tuba City, Arizona. My brother had inspired him, and Adam had discovered that he had a religious vocation. I wasn't very happy about it at the time, mostly for selfish reasons, but my son seemed content serving his parishioners at St. Mary's Igloo in Alaska.

His father, Tom Cavanaugh, had taken Adam's decision in stride. Of course, Tom had only met our son twenty years after his birth. My former lover had impregnated me — and his loony wife — about the same time, when I was still in college. I'd broken off the relationship when Tom said he couldn't leave Sandra Cavanaugh. Father and son had finally met when Adam was in college. A few years later, Sandra died from an overdose of her medications. Tom was free to marry me, and I said yes to his proposal. A bullet erased our future together. He died at my feet. Only in the past few months had I realized that being the second Mrs. Dodge was much better than being the second Mrs. Cavanaugh.

By the time Milo entered the living room, I was already seated on the sofa. He paused on his way to the easy chair and ruffled my hair.

"I figure you're going to keep me from having a stroke someday," he said, ambling over to collect his drink off the side table before he sat down. "All the years I was married to Mulehide," he went on after lighting a cigarette, "I never could say a word about what went on with my job. It was all about her and what had happened to the kids, the house, the bills — everything including the kitchen sink. She wouldn't have cared if I'd found a stack of stiffs piled up in my office."

"So you've told me," I said, laughing. "Don't apologize. You're a news source, big guy. It's what you *don't* tell me that I find annoying. Did Tricia know you *had* an office?"

"The only time she stopped by headquarters was to ask for money," Milo said, stretching out his long legs on the ottoman we'd recently bought. "She controlled our finances, but she knew I had a side account for my fishing and hunting gear. When Mulehide ran short on the home front, she'd ask to dip into that. I usually let her, but it pissed me off." He gestured toward the rear of the house. "Did you take a look at the holes in the ground after you got home?"

I grimaced. "No. I was carrying groceries. I've seen holes in the ground before. We've got gophers and marmots, you know. Are the Bourgettes finished with the pounding?"

"Yeah. Dick Bourgette told me they'd gotten done early this afternoon." Milo paused to sip his Scotch. "If you'd bothered to check outside, you'd have seen that they've taken off some of the logs in back of the house. Those will all get treated when the project is completed. As you may recall, you've neglected the upkeep on them the past few years."

61

"I know. You offered to do it for me, but that was a couple of years ago and I didn't want to impose. I mean, we weren't actually dating."

"Gosh," Milo said in mock dismay, "I'd forgotten all about that."

The reference was to our off-and-on-again sexual relationship, which had resumed after Tom was killed. Our earlier attempt to become a couple had failed when I'd dumped Milo, almost a decade ago.

"We were still involved," I said with a steely glare.

"When it suited you," he responded. "Meanwhile, I had to put up with that asshole from the AP. It's a good thing he took off for France."

My romance with Rolf Fisher had lasted about a year and a half. He was everything I'd thought I wanted in a man — a cultured, charming, attractive widower — but with a gift of gab that drove me nuts. I tried to take Rolf seriously. I even tried to fall in love with him. It didn't work. Maybe the reason was because what I really wanted was the big guy from the small town sitting in the easy chair just a few feet away from me.

I got up from the sofa. "I'll get dinner on. Ten minutes."

"Fine." Milo picked up the *Seattle Times* and all but disappeared behind the sports section.

It took me closer to fifteen minutes, which lured the sheriff out to the kitchen. "Is that chicken?" he asked, peering at the skillet.

"No, it's one of the gophers from the backyard. The Bourgettes bored right through his once-happy home. The little guy committed suicide in despair."

Milo's gaze shifted to the kettle. "Are those noodles? Did you run out of spuds?"

I turned to face my husband. "Damnit, you know I'm trying to change some of your — I mean *our* — eating habits. Maybe you'd like it better if I bought a truckload of those wretched TV dinners you lived on before you moved in here."

"Some of them weren't that bad," Milo said.

I pointed a wooden spoon at him. "You haven't gained back the ten pounds you lost during the Bellevue standoff aftermath with Tanya. Doesn't that make you feel better?"

"Better than what? I didn't feel bad before I lost the weight."

"You're impossible." I turned back to the stove. "Move. I have to drain the noodles."

"I weighed under two hundred when you first met me. It's your fault I gained over twenty-five pounds."

"Huh?" I looked at him over my shoulder. "What do you mean?"

Milo finished his drink and set the glass on the counter. "After Mulehide ran off to Bellevue with Jake the Snake and took the kids with her, I lost my appetite when she decided to become Mrs. Sellers instead of Mrs. Dodge."

"You lost your appetite for five years?"

"That's right." He looked serious. "The divorce dragged on for over two years. You know that. I wasn't used to being on my own. I didn't give a damn what I ate or even *if* I ate."

I'd put the rest of the dinner on the table. As I sat down, I thought back to what Milo had looked like when I'd met him. He had been lanky then, but the change was so gradual I hadn't really noticed.

"You never told me that," I said, touching his hand. "About your weight, I mean. No wonder you look better now than you did back then. But what did I have to do with it?"

"You started feeding me," Milo replied. "Not the first year or so, but we ate lunch together quite a bit, and sometimes we'd go out to dinner. Even after I started dating Honoria Whitman, you kept right on feeding me. I'd gained all the weight back by the time Honoria and I broke up."

I propped up my head with my hand and stared at him. "I guess I never knew what Honoria fed you."

He waved his fork. "A lot of that California health food crap. I liked your cooking better. Hell, let's face it — I liked *you* better, but I kept telling myself I was in love with her because . . ." He heaved a sigh. "I didn't think I stood a chance with you once Cavanaugh showed up on the scene."

"Honest to God, Milo, I still can't believe we finally got it right. No wonder the local grapevine was always buzzing about whether or not we were sleeping together. How do you like the gopher?"

"Tastes like chicken," he said. "How come you aren't asking me a lot of your usual dumb questions about the stiff in the river?"

"Because you won't tell me anything, and I quote, 'this early in the investigation.' "

Milo grinned at me. "You're catching on. You've always been a little slow about that, too."

"It doesn't sound as if it's anybody from around here. Yes, I know we have Hispanics at the college, but you would've told Mitch if the guy's a local."

"He's not. His driver's license says he's

from Wapato. Big Hispanic population over there."

I nodded. "I wonder what he was doing here in the first place. I suppose you're trying to find an abandoned car."

Milo gave me a warning look. "I've told you all you need to know."

"And to think Fleetwood thought I could inveigle information out of you in the bedroom. I told him he was wrong."

Milo's hazel eyes sparked. "You could try it."

I shook my head. "It wouldn't work."

"Would you care?"

"No."

"Want to give it a try after dinner?"

I smiled. "Yes."

Around nine o'clock, I rolled over in bed to poke Milo in the chest. "Hey, is Tanya staying here tonight?" I asked.

"Huh?" He opened his eyes after nodding off for a few minutes. "Damned if I know. Maybe Bill's staying with her."

"Do you think they're sleeping together?"

"I don't ask," he said, wrapping an arm around my waist. "Since they spent our wedding weekend at Lake Chelan after his car broke down, I figure they probably are. That's their business. As long as they aren't rolling around on the floor at headquarters, I don't give a damn. Tanya couldn't find a more solid guy than Bill."

"She hasn't gone for that type in her previous relationships."

"Maybe she learned something." Milo's hand moved to my breasts. "Why don't we just stay here for the rest of the night?"

"I have to make the morning coffee and empty the dishwasher," I said. "Or do you mean we might as well go to sleep so we'll get more rest before the Bourgette gang arrives in the morning?"

Milo rolled over, his chest pressing against me. "You know damned well what I mean, you goofy little twit. Tanya and Bill are at the movies. We're the ones in bed. Let's make good use of the time. I don't count strawberries as real dessert, but this kind was a lot better. Now how about a nightcap?"

I put my arms around his neck and giggled.

FOUR

Making love in the evening was good for us. Getting up in the morning wasn't. We both turned into grumps. We rarely speak to each other before Milo leaves first for work. On this Tuesday morning, the Bourgettes arrived just after the sheriff left. John and Dan were vexingly chipper when they showed up, a little after seven-thirty.

"Say," Dan said, smiling broadly from the carport, "we'll be starting to enlarge your bedroom next week. Are you and the sheriff going to stay here or at his place in the Icicle Creek Development?"

This part of the schedule was news to me. "I don't know," I admitted. "There's not much space in the spare bedroom. We've stored my old bed and some of Milo's things in there."

John had joined his brother. "Why don't you donate the old bed to the women's shelter in the Alpine Hotel? They could use more furniture, according to Father Kelly."

"Good idea," I said. "Milo's dumping a lot of his household items."

"We can collect them," Dan offered. "We like to help Father Den out as much as we can. He's always on overload."

"That's really kind of you," I said. The Bourgettes' good works and good mood were having a salutary effect on me. "Your family does so much for St. Mildred's. I feel like a piker."

John shook his head. "You're the voice of the parish in the paper. You don't ever talk much about religion, but everybody knows you bring a Catholic viewpoint to whatever you write."

"Maybe," I conjectured, "in a mostly Protestant town with a Lutheran majority, it's not always a good thing. Readers aren't fond of spending money on civic projects. Thrift should be their middle names."

Dan shrugged. "That doesn't matter. Well — it does, as far as levies and bond issues are concerned, but it makes the Catholic minority feel better. We all know you're on our side."

"I'm not supposed to take sides," I said. "I mean, except in my editorials. What are you doing today?"

"More log removal," John replied. "We

should finish off the back and the east side of the house today. Tomorrow we'll do the carport side and of course the logs in the front will stay put. We might be able to start framing up the double garage, too."

"Great," I said, sounding a bit wispy. I still couldn't quite get my head around how my little log cabin seemed to be turning into a mini-mansion. "Be careful," I added lamely before going back inside.

I was still musing over the remodel during the five-minute drive to the office. Stopping for the arterial at Fourth and Front, I looked down the street to the sheriff's headquarters. I couldn't see if Milo's black Yukon was parked there or not. Unlike his previous vehicle, the red Grand Cherokee, its replacement wasn't as easy to spot.

Kip, Leo, and Amanda were all in place — that place being the table where the coffee urn was still perking. "Who," I asked, noting that the goodies tray was empty, "has the bakery run?"

"Vida," Amanda replied. "She should be here any minute."

"Okay," I said. "Is everybody set for deadline day?"

Kip frowned. "I have to update a couple of programs, but it shouldn't take long. I hope."

I didn't ask for details. When it came to high tech, I was low Emma.

"The Safeway ad won't be in until this afternoon," Leo said. "They've got some technical problems of their own."

I nodded and looked at Amanda. "You're all set with the classifieds?"

"Yes, unless we get some last-minute ones. Have you heard anything more about that body? Walt and the rest of the people at the fish hatchery are really curious."

"So am I," I said. "If you think the sheriff gave me any late-breaking bulletins, think again."

Mitch made his entrance just as the coffee urn's red light came on. He gazed longingly at the empty tray. For such a skinny guy, he was able to consume large quantities of rich pastry without gaining an ounce. "Did the Upper Crust burn down?" he asked in a plaintive voice.

"Vida's turn," Leo said. "Maybe she's catching up on gossip for her 'Scene Around Town' column."

"Oh." Mitch waited for Amanda and Kip to fill their coffee mugs. "Brenda wasn't feeling very well this morning, so I didn't get breakfast. I suppose the dead guy in the river is our lead or will the mayor's interview still be the big story?"

"Fuzzy wins," I said. "The body isn't one of our own."

Mitch looked faintly dismayed. He still hadn't grasped small-town priorities. "Your call," he murmured, taking Leo's place at the coffee urn.

Vida showed up as I finished filling my own mug. She looked unusually pleased with herself, especially for someone who was wearing a yellow duck on top of her pillbox. The hat was new to me, and my surprise — more like dismay — must have shown.

"Well?" she said, giving me her gimlet eye. "Have you never seen a duck before?"

"Not that duck," I admitted.

"Good thing it's not hunting season, Duchess," Leo said, using the nickname Vida claimed to hate. "You already got shot in the line of duty."

"So did you, Leo," she retorted. "My daughter Amy found this hat at a rummage sale in Sultan. She thought it was quite amusing. I'm wearing it to dinner tonight with her and the rest of the family."

"You have to use it in 'Scene,' " Leo asserted. "Sure, I know we don't usually put staff into the column, but you don't have to name names."

"I most certainly will not use my duck as

72

an item," Vida declared, setting out Danish pastries, cinnamon twists, and cupcakes. "However, I need at least two more items for my column."

"Could we use our new roof?" Kip asked. "I mean, it's not personal, but we'd do it for any other business in town."

"Yes," I said, for once beating Vida to the punch. "It *is* news."

"Very well," she agreed. "Who else has something?"

I, as often is the case, was blank. Leo snapped his fingers. "Scooter Hutchins shaved his goatee."

"Thank goodness!" Vida exclaimed. "He looked absurd. Is he running an ad for his home decor business this week?"

Leo nodded. "Bigger than usual. He's got a sale on flooring."

"Excellent," Vida said, finishing her duties with the pastry tray.

I grabbed a cinnamon twist and headed for my office. All was quiet this morning. In my usual mental fog, I hadn't noticed how our new roof looked when I'd driven down Fourth Street. I'd once again flunked my role as a trained observer. Fifteen minutes later, I observed something I didn't want to see headed for my office.

"Hey, hey, hey," Ed Bronsky called out,

barging through my door and plunking his rotund self in one of my visitor chairs. "Do I have news or what?"

"What do you consider news?" I inquired, noticing that he'd snatched up three cupcakes en route.

Ed licked chocolate frosting off one of the cupcakes before replying. "Remember back in January when you and Dodge were making headlines by almost getting yourselves killed?"

"Yes, I vaguely recall the incident," I said with a straight face.

"Right." My former ad manager paused to flick his tongue over some frosting residue on his upper lip. "You know how my autobiography was made into a Japanese cartoon called *Mr. Pig.* It was never shown over here, but it dawned on me that with all my media experience, why not weave your story into the original, only using Shirley and me as you and Dodge. How's that for an idea?" He wiggled his eyebrows at me.

There are times when I truly don't know how to respond to Ed short of pulling out my hair by the roots and screaming hysterically. This was one of them. All I could say was "Go on," while trying not to slide out of my chair and under the desk.

Ed chuckled, spewing some of the cupcake

crumbs onto my computer. "I can see you're stunned by the idea, but I can't help myself. These things just come to me from nowhere."

Could you please send them back? I thought. In the five years Ed had worked for me, the only idea he'd ever had was to discourage local merchants from advertising. Putting together ads was *work,* a four-letter word Ed found far more offensive than any vulgarity. Having frittered away his sizable inheritance and been forced to sell his ersatz villa to RestHaven, he was still trying to figure out ways to make money from his self-published autobiography, *Mr. Ed.*

". . . a pig with a badge," Ed was saying, though I'd missed what had come before. "But the Smokey the Bear hats Dodge and his deputies wear wouldn't look right. Do you think the sheriff would be offended?"

"In fact," I replied, "Milo has ordered a different kind of hat for himself and the deputies. They should be arriving in another week or two. He's been planning to do that for quite a while."

"Hmm." Ed rubbed two of his three chins. "What are they like?"

"They're similar to Australian hats," I said, for want of a better description. Just

75

being in Ed's presence turned my brain into goo resembling cupcake frosting. "The crown isn't as high. As you know, Milo's kind of tall."

"Right." Ed frowned. "I don't know how Sheriff Pig would look in a hat like that. It's the ears, you see."

My phone rang. "Oh, darn," I said, reaching for the receiver. "Can we talk about this later? I'm expecting an important call."

"That's okay, I can wait."

I tried to control my temper and said hello in what I hoped was an excited tone.

"Is your office on fire?" my brother, Ben, asked in his crackling voice.

"Yes, yes, of course it is!" I replied. "Let me take notes. Or would you rather read me those statements? It doesn't matter how many pages you've got. I don't want to leave out anything."

Even Ed could take that broad of a hint. "Maybe I should come back later," he murmured, still clutching the last cupcake as he heaved himself out of the chair.

"Holy crap," Ben said, "are you being held hostage? Or has Dodge driven you to despair?"

I watched Ed waddle out through the newsroom. "Ed," I replied. "Need I say more?"

"Please don't," my brother begged. "Even Dennis Kelly, who has the patience of a saint, sometimes wishes Bronsky would defect to another religion. What's Ed up to now or dare I ask?"

"Don't," I said. "There are some things that shouldn't be conveyed by telephone. How are things in El Paso?"

"As I told you, it's not what I expected," Ben replied. "It's *huge,* especially when you combine it with Juárez, across the Rio Grande. There's a mountain range on this side and another one in Mexico. The altitude here is higher than Alpine. I thought I'd be hanging out at the border or some damned thing, but mostly I'm helping new immigrants get settled. It's a far cry from the Mississippi delta and the Native American reservations around Tuba City."

"Do you like it?"

"I think so. You know I wanted to be in a city again after spending so much of my priesthood on rural assignments. But the past couple of years filling in for priests in big cities cured me of that. Still, this is a whole different culture in all sorts of ways. And would you believe El Paso is one of the safest big cities in the country? Hell, it may be safer than Alpine."

"You could be right," I admitted. "Dwight

Gould found a body in the Sky late yester-day afternoon."

"Probably easier to do than catch a fish," Ben murmured. "Anybody I know?"

"Not a local," I said. "A Hispanic male from east of the mountains."

"Maybe Catholic. Got a name so I can of-fer up a Mass for him?"

"Dodge isn't releasing any ID until next of kin are notified."

"Okay. I'll do a *folano benecito,* as we call it in Spanish. That's 'blessed stranger' to you. God knows who the guy is, even if I don't. Say — what's up with the annulment process?"

Having been married the first time in a Protestant church, my husband had to go through the process of having his union with Tricia annulled. Then we could have a Catholic ceremony or at least have our mar-riage blessed by a priest. That meant a lot to me, even if Milo didn't give a hoot. He'd been raised as a Congregationalist, but his real religion was fishing. It gave him a sense of peace as well as time for introspection. If, he'd told me, hanging out with fisher-men was good enough for Jesus, it was good enough for him.

"Milo looked through the papers, but he's been busy. The process is . . . daunting.

Don't worry. You know how he is. The sheriff always takes his time, though once he gets onto something, he's thorough."

"I'll take your word for it." Ben paused. "How are you two doing otherwise?"

"Fine, really. Tanya's still hovering, but that's okay. She's dating Bill Blatt."

"Vida's nephew? Oh, my God! Don't tell me that eventually even *you* are going to end up related to Vida in some weird Alpine way?"

"I never thought of that," I said. "She's still mad at Milo — and Rosemary Bourgette and Judge Proxmire."

"Roger, right?" Ben didn't wait for an answer. "They don't teach forgiveness at the Presbyterian church? I expect better of them. And of Vida. Hey — got to go. Jorge Valdez and his six kids just showed up. Peace, Sluggly."

"Same to you, Stench," I said, retaliating with my childhood nickname for him.

I'd no sooner hung up when I saw Mitch come into the newsroom. I went out to meet him. "Anything new at the sheriff's office?" I asked, empty coffee mug in hand.

"If you mean an ID on the body, no, not yet," Mitch replied, shedding his black raincoat. "Otherwise, it's the usual. The sports car driver is still listed in critical condition at the hospital in Monroe. Two other minor accidents in town, the usual traffic violations, one reported prowler up on First Hill, and shoplifters at both Safeway and Grocery Basket. Oh — Dodge is shorthanded. Heppner called in sick."

I was surprised. "Heppner is never sick. He's too ornery. No germ would dare land on his prickly hide."

"He *is* human," Mitch said, beating me to the coffee urn. "Gee, who ate all the cupcakes?"

"Ed Bronsky," I informed him. "You're lucky he left a Danish and a couple of cinnamon twists."

"He seems like a real character," Mitch said, picking up one of the twists. "Was he really such a bad advertising guy?"

"In a word, yes. By the way, what's wrong with Sam?"

Mitch shrugged. "I didn't ask. A virus, probably."

"I suppose even Sam could succumb to one of those."

I filled my mug and returned to my office. Deputy Heppner had never been a warm and fuzzy guy. Over the years, he'd become even more irascible. If he had caught a virus, he'd get over it on his own. That's the way he lived.

It didn't occur to me that it was also the way he could die.

FIVE

Shortly before noon, I called the sheriff. "I'm aware you don't realize this is our deadline day," I began, "but I thought I'd remind you in case you've forgotten to give us the body's name."

"Nope," he replied in an aggravatingly complacent tone. "Do you know how many people named Fernandez live in Wapato?"

"I think you just told me his name," I said.

"You didn't hear that. Besides, you'd never print only a last name and the address on his driver's license is out of date."

"So he may not even live in Wapato?" I asked, tapping my fingernails on the desk.

"Could be. Yakima County's close to forty percent Hispanic. As for his common name, didn't Fleetwood have somebody named Fernandez working for him a few years ago?"

"Right," I said, "but he wasn't from Eastern Washington. Do you have time to eat lunch with me?"

"I don't have time to eat lunch, period," Milo grumbled. "I have to go with Tanya to her appointment with Dr. Reed at twelve-thirty and I'm shorthanded with Heppner out sick. I'll be lucky to be home by six. Tanya's coming for dinner. Bill's pulling night duty."

"Poor you. I'll go away now and leave you alone."

"If I were alone, I'd have some free time." Milo hung up on me. Married or not, there were some habits he couldn't seem to break.

Vida, however, was free for lunch. In fact, she asked if I'd like to join her at the Venison Inn. "One of my Gustavson nieces is working there during the lunch hour. Mandy — you remember her?"

"Yes," I said, not even bothering to try untangling the branches on Vida's enormous family tree. "Wasn't she training to be the daytime bartender before she quit to have a baby?"

"Just briefly," Vida replied, adjusting the duck, which had listed to the pillbox's port side. Maybe he'd spent time at the VI's bar when his owner wasn't looking. "That was a few years ago. Mandy didn't care for the job's rather unsavory aspects. She's filling in for her cousin, Nicole, who's taking college classes. A journalism major, as you may recall. Somehow I inspired her." Vida's attempt to look modest failed.

As usual, Vida chose the booth with the best window view to keep track of the passing parade. "Oh, dear," she said under her breath, "there goes Crazy Eights Neffel on a unicycle. He really shouldn't weave in and out of traffic like that." She gasped; the duck wobbled. "Goodness! He just swerved into the clock tower by the bank!"

I turned around to try to see how our local loony had landed, but a UPS truck blocked my view.

"That's my nephew Ronnie Blatt driving," Vida said. "I wonder if he'll stop to see if Crazy Eights is hurt. It'd serve him right if he is."

Ronnie and the UPS truck moved on. I noticed a couple of people apparently helping Crazy Eights. I suggested it to Vida as a "Scene" item.

She shook her head. "You know I try to avoid sightings of that lunatic. It only eggs him on." She opened the menu and frowned. "The special is a roast beef sandwich with a side of potato salad and a dill pickle. That sounds rather skimpy, don't you think?"

I shrugged. "I'm going for the fish and

chips with the coleslaw."

"Oh." Vida frowned. "Maybe I should have that, too. I suspect it'd be more slimming. You're very fortunate you don't have to count calories," she murmured, putting the menu aside. "Genetics, of course. I'm forced to watch my weight. Oh — here's Mandy."

Vida's niece looked as if she should be watching her weight, too. Mandy hadn't shed most of the pounds she'd gained during pregnancy, despite the baby being almost a year old. But most of the Runkel and Blatt women were big-boned and tall. No matter how much Vida fussed about her diet, I could never tell if she'd gained or lost an ounce.

I drifted while aunt and niece exchanged family chitchat. Finally, Vida inquired about the fish and chips. "There are only *two* pieces of fish?" she asked in dismay.

"They're good-sized portions," Mandy said.

"Hmmm." Vida fretted her upper lip. "Might you be able to add just one more? Smallish, of course."

"Sure, Aunt Vida," Mandy replied. "Anything else?"

"Well . . . I'm not that fond of coleslaw, dear. I noticed there was potato salad with the special. Could you substitute that?"

"I can try," her niece offered.

Vida nodded. "Fine. As for the chips, the last time I had them, there didn't seem to be enough to go around with the fish. I like my fish *and* chips to come out even. They complement each other so nicely, don't you agree?"

"Um . . . sure. I'll make certain that there are some extra fries to go with the extra fish, okay?"

"Of course. And can you bring catsup and mayonnaise along with the tartar sauce? By the way, they put the tartar sauce in such a tiny cup. It's never sufficient for the fish. Is it a bother to bring a bowl?"

"Of course not," Mandy insisted, though I noticed that she looked a bit pained. Maybe her feet hurt. Or her wrist had given out from writing down all of her aunt's requests.

I finally remembered that I knew how to talk and spoke up. "I'll just have the regular fish and chips with a vanilla malt."

"Hot tea for me," her aunt said. "Cream, of course."

Mandy trudged away.

Vida was again looking out onto Front Street. "I see no sign of Crazy Eights or the unicycle. At least he didn't dent the bank's clock tower."

"It *is* cast iron, isn't it?" I said.

"I believe so. It's very old, dating from the bank itself." She leaned forward and lowered her voice. "I hear we may finally be getting a permanent Bank of Alpine president."

"Not Andy Cederberg?"

"That's right. Nobody ever thought Andy would hold down the job permanently. He doesn't have the experience, nor does he possess an executive manner." Vida's gray eyes practically danced. "Do try to guess who would fill the role most admirably."

"I suppose I can eliminate Crazy Eights Neffel. Unless, of course, his executive parking place is the clock tower."

Vida wasn't amused. "If you insist on being obtuse, I shan't tell you until the announcement is official."

Despite all the unpleasant memories from the latest Petersen family bank tragedies of the previous November, I forced myself to recall if Vida had mentioned any names. "I'll eliminate Marv Petersen's grandsons, who declined the honor on your radio show," I said. "Is Marv involved in the decision making or has his brain gone further south than the Arizona retirement community where he and his wife now reside?"

"Marv apparently has some lucid moments," Vida said. "The trustees he put in

87

place upon leaving the bank are the college president, May Hashimoto, and Dr. Bob Starr, Lloyd Campbell, Al Driggers, and Simon Doukas. Quite an upstanding list, you must agree."

I made a face. "Except for Simon Doukas. In case your memory is slipping, he was the first one in town to call me a whore. I haven't spoken to him since."

"That, of course, was of no importance to Marv," Vida said in a reasonable voice. "He wanted one attorney involved, and even if Simon is semi-retired, he comes from an established Alpine family. The other two lawyers, Marisa Foxx and Jonathan Sibley, are relative newcomers."

"Right," I muttered, "they've only been here ten years."

"Now, now," Vida reprimanded me, "you think highly of Bob Starr, who is an excellent dentist. Certainly Al, as the local funeral director, is a longtime fixture, and so is Lloyd, with his appliance store. Admittedly, May Hashimoto hasn't lived in Alpine for very long, but I gather Marv wanted someone from the college. And she's a woman as well as a minority. Surely that means something."

I suspected it meant that whoever was advising Marv felt May's inclusion was necessary to convince a prospective bank president that Alpine was living in the twenty-first century.

"Okay," I said. "The only name I can come up with is from the first set of serious problems at the Bank of Alpine ten years ago. Your old friend Faith Lambrecht had a son who was a higher-up at the Bank of Washington. He came to town when there was talk of a buyout, but nothing happened. In fact, I recall that he went fishing with Milo."

Vida beamed at me as if I'd been able to tell her the earth was round. "Indeed. Bobby Lambrecht longs for his roots."

The prodigal son, I thought. Vida would embrace Bob Lambrecht as if he were her very own. But I had to admit that his acceptance of the job would be a real boon for Skykomish County. I did wonder how Bob liked being called "Bobby." Vida had always called Tom "Tommy," and it made me cringe, but it didn't seem to bother my former lover.

"City life in Seattle has grown so tiresome," Vida was saying, though I think I missed the first part of the family saga. "The four Lambrecht children are off on their own, so it's time for a change. In fact, only the daughter is still in the Seattle area. So wise of Bobby and Miriam to come back to Alpine." She suddenly smiled in her most toothsome fashion. "Here's Mandy with our orders."

Fulfilling her aunt's many special requests had forced Mandy into carrying a tray. She wobbled a bit trying to balance everything and looked relieved to start unloading Vida's meal. "I had to use plates instead of the usual basket for the fish and the chips," she explained. "I'll get your tea. I didn't have room for the pot or the cream."

Vida was looking into the sugar container that was already at our table. "Oh, dear! So much of what's in there is that non-sugar sweetener. It has such an unpleasant taste. Would you mind bringing more of the real sugar, Mandy dear?"

"Yes," Mandy replied. "I mean, no, I don't mind," she amended, putting my basket in front of me. "Be right back."

I returned to our previous topic of conversation. "Did you hear about Bob from his mother, your old chum Faith?"

Dousing salt and pepper on her potato salad, Vida nodded. "I'm urging her to move back here from Spokane. The weather there is so much more extreme. I have a feeling she's never felt at home there since her husband died. She'd be so much better off

90

in Alpine."

I figured Vida would say the same about Queen Elizabeth having to make do at Windsor Castle. *So old, so drafty, so hard to keep up.* "How soon will this news become official?" I inquired, always feeling the need to remind Vida that I was the *Advocate*'s editor and publisher. It was a common enough mistake for many of our readers.

Vida waited to answer until after eating a bite of fish — and a bite of chips. "Maybe at the end of the month. I'm not sure when Bobby is handing in his resignation. Perhaps," she went on with a sly glance, "Milo already knows."

"If so, he hasn't mentioned it."

Vida didn't comment. When she spoke again, it was a change of subject. "I'll be leaving a bit early today. The family dinner, you see."

"That's fine," I said. "You'll have everything in by then?"

"Of course. I finished the last letter for my advice column just before lunch." Vida made a disapproving face. "These silly women who want to apologize for breaking off with an impossible man get my goat. What are they thinking of? He won't change."

"Do you know who this one is?" I asked,

given that most of the time Vida could identify the anonymous advice seeker.

"I must confess I don't. The letter was mailed from Everett. It's quite possible that the writer sent it from there to befuddle me." She pressed her index finger to her cheek. "Now, who do I know who has gone to Everett in the past few days?"

I decided to let the subject drop. It was a wonder Vida didn't keep a log of every SkyCo resident's departure, destination, and return. In fact, she probably did — in her head. My House & Home editor never took notes. If I could see inside her brain, my own head might explode at the sheer volume of data stored there.

We passed the rest of our meal discussing what she thought of Fuzzy Baugh's plan to reorganize the county's government structure. Despite her conviction that it had probably been the mayor's wife, Irene, who had come up with the idea, she grudgingly endorsed it.

"Unfortunately," she said, devouring the last of her potato salad, "the trio of county commissioners grew so old and inept that we've been stalled for the last decade — or two. Granted, Alfred Cobb passed away in December, but George Engebretsen and Leonard Hollenberg have barely been conscious, let alone attentive, for far too long. I would've been pleased about Jack Blackwell's appointment to fill Alf's vacancy, being as he's a younger man with solid business experience running his mill. However, his personal life is deplorable. Talk about silly women! Patti Marsh has taken him back after his latest short-lived affair with Tiffany Rafferty. No doubt Jack is already beating up on Patti again." Vida shook her head. The duck seemed to nod.

Mandy stopped off with our separate bills. "No dessert, Aunt Vida?" she asked.

"Heavens no!" Vida cried. "I really am watching my weight. Easter, I fear, always means too many sweets."

Mandy's blue eyes twinkled. "From the colonel?"

"Why, yes," Vida said coyly at the mention of Buck Bardeen, her longtime companion. "He's a very considerate *gentleman.*"

I didn't know if the emphasis on the word was for Mandy, lest she get some erotic notions about her aunt, or for me, alluding to Milo's less refined take on life and the English language.

The rest of the day passed in the usual flurry of getting the paper ready for publication. By the time I'd finished with Kip in the back shop, it was after five. Everyone else had left when I returned to my office to collect my jacket and handbag. I had two Cornish game hens in the freezer at home and didn't need any other items at the grocery store. But after Milo's complaint about strawberries being a poor substitute for dessert and the possibility that he had never eaten lunch, I stopped off on Front Street at the Upper Crust Bakery to get a pie.

One of Vida's sisters-in-law, Mary Lou Hinshaw Blatt, was coming out just as I was going in. "Well!" she exclaimed, looking disgruntled. "Are you picking up something for the birthday party, too?"

"What birthday party?" I asked, backpedaling to the sidewalk.

"For the child of that nincompoop Roger. Today's his second birthday." She stared down at me with probing brown eyes. Not only was she close to Vida in size, but she was just as opinionated and outspoken. Thus, the sisters-in-law had never gotten along. "I happened to arrive at the bakery as she was collecting the poor little nipper's cake. Thirty dollars! Can you imagine? If he's as ill-behaved as Roger was, he'll smear it all over himself and the walls. And don't think I didn't tell that to my self-righteous kinswoman!"

I've never exactly warmed to Mary Lou, having spent very little time in her company. But despite my loyalty to Vida, I couldn't play the hypocrite. "I'm afraid Vida has a problem seeing Roger in anything but a good light. It's her blind spot. Are you going to the party?"

"Ha! I wasn't asked, and I wouldn't go if she *had* invited me," Mary Lou asserted. "Vida's daughter Amy is a spineless creature, and her husband, Ted, is a mere cipher. Count yourself lucky that you weren't included in the Hibbert family celebration. It's the little boy I feel sorry for. He's an innocent child being raised by a passel of fools. All I can say is I hope he doesn't turn out like Roger. I volunteer at RestHaven and observed that lazy obnoxious lout lolling around instead of pitching in like the rest of us do. Outside smoking half the time and inside tagging along after that Sigurdson girl. Mark my words, her parents will quash that romance before it's too late. Good night, Emma." Mary Lou started to turn away, then stopped. "Oh! I haven't offered congratulations on your marriage. I'm relieved that you and the sheriff made yourselves legal. You're both old enough to know better than to set a poor example for young people. Have a pleasant evening."

She swerved on her own pair of chunky heels and clomped off down the street.

At least Mary Lou was one step ahead of Vida with good wishes. I would, of course, have preferred it to be the other way around.

After buying a blackberry pie and a half dozen French rolls, I headed home. Driving my Honda into the carport, I could see a pile of logs out in the backyard. I grimaced, wondering if my cozy little cabin would feel chilly. The fitful April showers had ceased, though clouds still hung low over the mountains, drifting slowly to the west.

I'd been inside just long enough to turn on the oven and put the game hens in the microwave to defrost when the phone rang. Dashing out into the living room, I snatched up the phone from the end table.

"Scratch Tanya for dinner," Milo said. "She's going out to eat with an old pal, Deanna . . . I forget her married name. She'll be back around seven, seven-thirty. I'm in touch with the Yakima County sheriff's office, so I might not get home until six or so."

"Okay," I said — and realized that the sheriff had already disconnected. Maybe he thought he was talking to my voice mail.

I wondered if I should hold off cooking one of the game hens, but given Milo's prodigious appetite, I put both in the oven. If there was anything left over, I could take it to work for lunch. By the time I'd prepared a mixture of white, wild, and brown rice out of a box and readied the asparagus for steaming, I considered making a drink but decided to wait for Milo. I sat down on the sofa, opened my laptop, and started an email to Adam. He'd returned to St. Mary's Igloo Sunday night after attending a conference in Fairbanks. I'd received a brief message from him saying he'd arrived safely — details to follow. I hadn't heard anything further, so I assumed he was busy with his villagers. As ever, I wished he'd be assigned somewhere that wasn't so isolated and remote. Like Ben, he had to go where he was sent.

I told him how the remodel was progressing and that I'd decided to keep my old double bed in the expanded spare room. "I've moved all of your stored belongings to the so-called den, between the living room and your old room. As you may recall, that area was so small that there wasn't enough space for a kid's school desk. Scott Melville suggested we also rip out that wall to double the bedroom's size."

I paused. For all I knew, the church and rectory where Adam lived wasn't as big as my little log cabin was now. I wondered if he thought his mother was bragging. Or cajoling. Or . . .

I gave a start when I heard the kitchen door open and bang shut. "Milo?" I called, closing the laptop and hurrying into the kitchen.

"It's not Mother Nature," my husband growled, taking off his hat and tossing it on top of the dishwasher. "All I can get out of Yakima is the drought that's predicted over there. The fruit crop's heading for disaster and the governor is already worried about forest fires. Worst water shortage in the state's history."

"We've had some rain here," I said in an unnaturally meek voice.

Milo shrugged out of his regulation jacket. "Not enough. Besides, we're on the so-called wet side of the Cascades, in case you forgot." He grabbed his hat and stalked out of the kitchen.

"Hey," I yipped, chasing after him as he hung up his hat and jacket on a peg by the front door. "How many times do I have to remind you I'm your damned wife?"

"Oh . . . hell." Milo's broad shoulders sagged before he took me in his arms and kissed me. "Damnit, Emma," he said, resting his chin on top of my head, "I don't deserve you. I told you that before we got engaged."

I rested my cheek against his chest. "Hey, big guy, I knew what I was getting into. You deserve something better than a bitchy homecoming." I managed to pull away to look up at him. "What's wrong?"

"Wait until we sit." He glanced over at the end table. "You don't have a drink?"

"No. Now that we're married, I don't like drinking alone."

He leaned down to kiss my nose. "I'll make the drinks. I can change later. How soon is dinner?"

I followed him out to the kitchen to check the game hens. "You're a little earlier than I thought you'd be, so at least twenty minutes." *More like half an hour,* I thought, but maybe Milo wouldn't check his watch. The game hens were only now starting to brown.

He didn't speak while he fixed my Canadian and his Scotch. I turned the heat on low under the rice. He handed me my glass, his hazel eyes troubled. I touched his cheek before leading the way back to the living room.

Milo sighed in relief as he sat down in the easy chair before taking out his cigarettes. "You want one?"

"You know I've been trying to quit.

Again," I said, but decided maybe I should go ahead and smoke anyway. "What the hell." I got up and let him light a cigarette for me.

"Something's not right," he stated after I'd sat back down on the sofa and he'd taken a sip of Scotch. "I had to listen to all the dire predictions about drought and the eastern half of the state burning up this summer." He paused to take a drag of his cigarette and another sip of Scotch. "Hell, I'm not unsympathetic. I worked with the Yakima crew back in December. They're good people. My counterpart wasn't in, so I talked to a senior deputy. He didn't exactly stonewall me, but he was evasive. In fact, he sounded downright uncomfortable."

After a couple of puffs on the cigarette, I felt a bit lightheaded. "Uh . . . about tracking down a guy with a common Hispanic name?"

Milo leaned forward to peer at me. "You sure you didn't start drinking before I got home? You look kind of goofy."

I laughed and shook my head. "I don't think I've smoked in almost a month. I feel woozy."

"Oh. I've cut down, too, at least around Tanya." He sat back in the chair. "The deputy's first reaction was that there had to

100

be a ton of Fernandezes in the county. Then I prodded him a bit, asking if they had any missing persons reports. They did, but no one by that name. That answer came too fast. It's a relatively big and fairly mobile population. I figured he was putting me off. But why? It makes me think they know damned well who the stiff is."

I gave Milo a curious look. "Are you sure you're supposed to be telling me this, Sheriff? Do I need to remind you I'm the press?"

Milo waved the hand that wasn't holding the cigarette. "I'd tell Vida if she were here. Of course, she isn't speaking to me. But this is one of those quirky things that you women are good at. Besides, by the time I finished the Yakima call, Jack Mullins was the only one left in the office. You know what kind of smart-ass remark he'd make. Not helpful." Milo took another sip of his drink. "You can't use this in the paper anyway."

I agreed. "Unless, of course, it escalates."

"It better not. I'll raise hell if it does."

"Do you think the dead man might be one of their own?"

"It crossed my mind," Milo replied slowly, "but there was nothing on the guy to indicate he was with the sheriff's department."

He paused, stroking his long chin. "It could go one of two ways, though. Either he *is* some kind of law enforcement type — or he's on the wrong side of the law and they want to do some checking before they say anything."

The phone on the end table next to me rang. Kip was on the line. "Hey," he said, "do we have anything new on the guy who got thrown from the sports car? Mitch didn't update me before he left."

"Let me ask the sheriff." I put my hand over the receiver. "Sports car guy — dead or alive?"

Milo shrugged. "Don't ask me. They took him to Valley General hospital, in Monroe."

I spoke again into the phone, relaying what Milo had told me. "Mitch may have forgotten. Brenda was ailing this morning, so he was probably preoccupied. Have him call Monroe. Doobles, or whatever his name is, isn't local, but we should at least find out if he's dead."

"Will do. Otherwise, we're good to go." Kip paused. "I take it you don't have ID on the corpse in the river?"

"No. It's aggravating, but there's nothing we can do about that."

"Isn't that sort of weird?" Kip asked.

"Yes."

"Okay. I think I get it. The sheriff's not talking."

"Right. If that happens, I'll let you know." I rang off.

Milo was grinning. "You talking in code?"

I got off the sofa. "My staff — and Spence — have a problem figuring out why you don't unload about your job when you come home."

"I just did."

"But it's not news. Venting doesn't count." I went into the kitchen to peek at the chickens. They still weren't quite done. "Five minutes," I called to Milo as I turned on the asparagus.

"Good. I missed lunch."

As the days ahead would prove, there was a lot more missing in Alpine than the sheriff's lunch.

SIX

Milo ate an entire game hen by himself. That was no surprise. Despite his expressed displeasure over being forced to eat rice instead of potatoes, he was placated by the blackberry pie. Or almost.

"No ice cream?" he asked, looking disappointed.

"If you want ice cream, why don't you tag along with Bill Blatt when Vida treats her nephew so she can inveigle information about your latest investigation?"

"And have her *not* speak to me? That'd be a relief, I suppose. I'm surprised she doesn't make Bill sit in a booster seat."

"Maybe that's because he's almost six feet tall."

"Five-ten," Milo said, loading his fork with pie. "That's what it says in his personnel file."

I glanced at my watch. "It's going on eight. Kip hasn't called with any more problems, so the paper must be almost set to print."

"I don't know why," Milo said after eating another mouthful of pie, "if you print the paper tonight, you can't get it on the street in the morning instead of the afternoon."

"Because it takes a while to print," I replied. "I can't afford to hire drivers or carriers to deliver a morning paper. That's why. Marius Vandeventer had to send the paper to a printer in Monroe, and so did I before we started our own back shop operation. That's also why we have a five o'clock deadline. Unless, of course, there's breaking news before the paper is ready to go to press."

Milo reached out to brush at my lower lip. "Crust crumb. Makes sense. Maybe I should try to remember that about your deadlines."

"You won't."

He shrugged. "Probably not."

I narrowed my eyes. "Why do I suspect you *do* know about our deadlines?"

Milo's expression was innocent as he devoured more pie. "No clue."

I didn't believe him, but I decided not to argue. I concentrated on my pie, then suddenly remembered Janie Engelman's visit. "She thought Fred might like earning extra money as your handyman," I explained. "You told me he did a decent job when he used to spend the weekends in jail."

"He was okay," Milo said without enthusiasm. "Frankly, Fred's kind of an alarmist. He sees problems that don't exist."

Before I could respond, the doorbell sounded. "I'll get it," I volunteered. "It must be Tanya." I took a last bite of pie and hurried out to the living room.

I was right. Tanya stood on the porch with a young woman I didn't recognize. "Hi, Emma," my recently acquired stepdaughter said. "Dad's here, right? I saw his Yukon in the driveway."

"Yes," I said. "We're late with dinner tonight."

Tanya beckoned for her companion to follow her. "This is Deanna Engstrom. We went to school together when I lived here."

Deanna put out a plump, freckled hand. "Hi, Mrs. . . . Dodge."

"Hi, Deanna." Her grasp felt very soft and tentative.

Milo came into the living room, saluting Tanya. "Hi, kid," he said before looking at Deanna. "I think I remember you." His big hand swallowed up her much smaller one. "You married a guy from . . . Startup?"

"Gold Bar," Deanna said, trying not to

wince as Milo shook her hand. The first and about the only time he'd shaken my hand I'd thought all my fingers would break.

Tanya was taking off her tan suede jacket. "Deanna needs to talk to you, Dad. Is that okay?"

"Sure." He frowned slightly, darting a glance at me. "Is it anything I need to hear in private?"

"Ah . . ." Tanya looked at me, then at Deanna, who simply stared back with wide blue eyes. "I guess not." She turned again to her friend. "My stepmom owns the newspaper. She finds out everything anyway."

I accepted that oversimplification without comment. "Make yourselves comfortable," I said. "Can I get anything for you two?"

"I'll grab us both some bottled water," Tanya responded, her plain, yet mobile face showing compassion for her companion. "Go ahead, Dee. Take a seat."

Deanna hesitated before sitting down at the far end of the sofa. She was wearing a thick navy sweater over what looked like a mock turtleneck of the same color. Milo settled into the easy chair, while I assumed my usual place at the other end of the sofa.

Over the years, I'd had some opportunities to see how Milo dealt with witnesses and suspects. He had a knack for reading

107

people. The sheriff could bulldoze, intimidate, befriend, or — his favorite ploy — play the small-town hick lawman out of his depth. That last guise had actually fooled me until I got to know him better.

"My son, Bran, likes to white-water-raft out of Gold Bar," he said as his opening gambit. "He goes with an old pal from Alpine."

Deanna nodded. "A lot of people like doing that, but Dave and I think it looks kind of scary."

Tanya returned with the bottled water. She handed one to her friend, but though there was room on the sofa, she sat down in the armchair on the other side of the fireplace hearth from her father.

"We've got white-water rafting here, too," Milo remarked. "I'm guessing you're not here to talk about outdoor hobbies."

"Well . . ." Deanna's fair, freckled face darkened. "No. It's my sister, Erin. She's missing."

Milo nodded once. "Yes. We heard about that." He looked at me. "Emma's reporter noted it in our log. It'll be in the paper tomorrow. Do you know why she'd run away?" His voice remained casual as he stretched out his legs on the ottoman.

Deanna shook her head. "No. I hadn't

108

talked to her for maybe a week or so, but she seemed fine. Erin doesn't like school much, but she gets decent grades. Anyway, it's spring vacation."

"Has she got a boyfriend?" Milo asked.

"She did for a while, but I think they broke up."

"You talked with any of her other friends?"

"Mom did. They're clueless."

Milo looked thoughtful. "How long has it been since your dad died in that hit-and-run in Everett?"

"Six years last January," Deanna replied, turning the unopened bottle this way and that in her hands. "They never caught who did it."

Milo nodded again. "It was dark. No credible witnesses. I worked with Snohomish County on that, but they came up empty. Your mother remarried, right?"

"Yes. Vince Moro from Wenatchee. He walked out on her almost two years ago. That's how Mom and Erin ended up in the trailer last November. Vince cleaned her out."

"I didn't know that," Milo said quietly. "I'm sorry. Where did your brother go? He was younger, right?"

"Duane's married with two kids and lives in Marysville. He works at Paine Field as a mechanic."

"I take it Duane hasn't any idea why Erin might have gone off?"

"No." Deanna bowed her head. "None of us can think why."

"She and your mom got along, didn't they?"

"Most of the time." Deanna looked up. "She's the baby of the family. If anything, she got spoiled. There was a big gap between her and Duane — kind of a menopause baby, I guess. At least that's what Mom said sometimes. But in a funny way, not mean."

I couldn't help but wonder if perhaps Deanna's mother wasn't secretly resentful. But, like Tanya, I was a mere observer.

Milo started to reach for his cigarettes, caught a sharp glance from his daughter, and put his hands on the easy chair's arms. "Your mother's report stated that Erin went out Friday night to see a friend, but didn't say who. Mrs. Moro didn't contact us until Sunday morning. Why did she wait so long?"

Deanna's face not only turned bright red, but she began to cry. "I . . . don't . . . know," she blubbered.

I could tell that Milo was getting impatient, but when he spoke, his voice was still casual. "That's okay. Do you know Samantha Ellison?"

While trying to control her tears, Deanna shook her head.

Tanya spoke up: "Who's Samantha Ellison?"

Milo shifted around to look at his daughter. "She was reported as a runaway a few weeks ago. It turned out she'd gone off with her boyfriend. You wouldn't know the Ellisons. They moved here last fall."

"Maybe," Tanya said, faintly chagrined, "I should check the log once in a while."

"Not your problem." The sheriff kept quiet while Deanna wiped her eyes with a couple of tissues and finally opened the bottled water. "Dustin Fong took the original report about your sister," he finally said when Deanna seemed to have composed herself. "He was off yesterday and we were shorthanded today, so I'll check with him tomorrow. If you think of anything or anyone who might be able to help us — especially from your sister's friends — let us know, okay?"

Deanna nodded dumbly. She might not have realized she'd been dismissed, but Tanya did. "Dee's spending the night with me at the house, Dad," she said, standing up. "I don't want her driving back to Gold Bar tonight. Besides, maybe she can talk to some of Erin's friends."

Milo had also gotten to his feet. "Good idea." He hugged his daughter before helping Deanna get up from the sofa. "Try not to get too worked up over this," he said. "It's spring break. Teenagers get some crazy ideas. One year Tanya ran off with the Easter Bunny."

"Dad!" Tanya shrieked, but she laughed. "That was Robbie Anderson. He'd been the bunny for the Baptist church's egg hunt. We only went to Skykomish."

"Your mother and I didn't know where you'd gone," Milo said. "You didn't come back until after midnight."

I had gotten up from the sofa, standing off to one side, still being an observer. Deanna's face was blotchy, but she seemed in control of her emotions. "Thanks, Mr. Dodge. I mean . . . *Sheriff.*" She glanced at me. "You, too, Mrs. . . ."

I moved to touch her shoulder. "Take care," I interrupted in my kindest voice, lest she call me Mrs. Sheriff and start blushing all over again. "I'll keep you and your family in my prayers."

The offer seemed to flummox her, but she merely nodded before heading out the door with Tanya.

"Holy shit!" Milo exclaimed after they'd gone. "How did Tanya get mixed up with some poor little twit like that? I don't remember Deanna as one of her chums while she was still at the high school here."

"Maybe," I suggested as Milo fell back into the easy chair and I collapsed on the sofa, "Deanna wasn't. I mean, she *knew* Tanya and figured it was the best way to get some help in finding her sister."

"Probably," Milo replied after lighting a cigarette. "Hell, I can't blame the girl for being upset because this . . . Erin has taken off, but she hasn't talked to any of the high school crowd she hung out with. Yeah, Mrs. Moro asked some of them, but if they knew the girl had pulled some crazy-assed stunt, they wouldn't tell her mother. Maybe the ex-boyfriend's got an idea. I'll talk to Tanya tomorrow."

"If Deanna wasn't a close buddy of Tanya's, how come you remember her?"

"Good point," Milo said, gazing up at the ceiling. "I was trying to think why I did know who she was." He stopped looking upward, took a last puff on his cigarette, and grimaced. "I went to high school with her mother — Wanda Everson, Roy's sister. She got involved with our favorite fixated postmaster in their wacky search for their mother's remains. And don't remind me I haven't acted on your theory about where

Myrtle's bones might be found. I've been kind of busy."

I'd almost forgotten about Myrtle Everson, too. My new role as a wife had put a lot of things on the back burner. But I was sure the Everson family hadn't forgotten. Myrtle had disappeared sixteen years ago, presumably while berry picking on a fine August day. Family members, especially Postmaster Roy Everson, had become obsessed with trying to find any sign of her. I'd done some conjecturing that she might be buried at the dump site near the Everson family home on the Burl Creek Road. Back in December, the ground had been too frozen for digging. Since then, my life and Milo's had been focused on more pressing matters, both personal and professional.

"If," I said, "Myrtle is where I'm guessing she is, she hasn't moved."

"Don't be too sure," Milo said. "Burl Creek's flooded a few times over the years. Part of the dump site may've washed away. Why don't you come over here and sit on my lap?"

"Because," I said primly, "I have to clean up the kitchen. I should've done it while Tanya and Deanna were here. I felt like a ventriloquist's dummy."

"You're right. You usually talk more even

in your sleep."

"If you say so. I've never heard me." I headed for the kitchen.

By the time Milo ambled out from the living room to join me, I was almost finished. "Did you look at that kitchen plan Scott drew up?" he asked, leaning against the fridge.

I scowled at him. "What kitchen plan?"

Milo scratched at the graying sandy hair behind his right ear. "Maybe I left it at the office. I got kind of busy by the end of the day."

"Dare I ask for a brief summation?"

"It'll be longer and maybe wider after the carport is enclosed for both our cars." He stopped leaning and reached out to pull me close. "Hey — why don't you try to get me to open up about the details in bed?"

I gave him a flinty look. "Would it work?"

I felt him shrug. "Let's find out."

"We don't need granite counters," I declared an hour later. "We don't need to close off the washer and dryer. We don't need a nook in . . ."

Milo put his hand over my mouth. "Okay, skip the granite stuff. Pick out something else. But aren't you tired of having to walk around the little table and chairs in the middle of the kitchen?"

He'd removed his hand so I could speak. "Well . . . yes. I do bump into them a lot. So do you. As for enclosing the . . ."

"Stop. That's about a hundred-dollar idea. The whole thing only adds about five grand to the total cost, okay?"

I rested my head on his bare shoulder. "It's your money."

"You bet it is. This place can only be ours instead of just yours if you let me pay for the remodel." He kissed the top of my head. "When I sell my house, it'll cover most of this job. You fuss too much."

"I feel guilty, though, being an impecunious journalist."

"Don't." He hugged me tight. "You've done your own remodel on me. You've made me happy."

"Oh, Milo! I was such a pain in the ass, as you put it, for so long."

"Damned right," he said in an amused tone. "But you were so cute. Even when you walked into walls and fell over your own feet. I couldn't resist somebody who was even clumsier than I am."

I laughed. And went to sleep in Milo's strong, safe arms.

The first bad news of the day came when

Amanda informed me that Mitch had called to say Brenda was still sick. "He's taking her to see Doc Dewey this morning," our receptionist explained. "Maybe it's not just an emotional crisis this time."

"Or both physical and mental," I said, wishing my voice didn't sound so churlish. Repenting, I paused by the counter to offer Amanda a rueful smile. "A noisy start at home. I thought they were done, but the Bourgettes are taking out more logs. It sounded as if they're rolling them into the house instead of away from it."

"That's okay," Amanda said. "I still have some ups and downs with being pregnant. Speaking of houses, Walt and I are thinking of looking for one. When the baby arrives, the condo at Parc Pines will be too crowded. I wonder if we can afford what Dodge is asking for his house."

"It's too much," Vida asserted, suddenly appearing in the doorway between the front office and the newsroom. "Milo hasn't kept up that place the way he should."

I turned to glare at Vida. "He's always done basic maintenance, and lately he's been making sure everything else about the house is in good order. He's never been much of a housekeeper, except for his workroom downstairs, which is in perfect order."

"The garden is a disaster," Vida shot back. "I thought you were going to help with that."

"I did," I retorted. "I've done quite a bit, but you know that this time of year everything grows like crazy. Besides, he's asked Mountain View Gardens to landscape it."

Vida harrumphed before veering around to head to her desk. Amanda and I exchanged puzzled looks, but neither of us spoke. My House & Home editor had such keen hearing that she could probably get messages from one of Averill Fairbanks's alleged UFOs.

To avoid any further remarks from her, I headed straight to the back shop. Kip was eating a chocolate doughnut and checking a list of subscribers who lived outside of our delivery area.

"No problems?" I asked.

He shook his head. "But we need to update some of our programs." Knowing I'd beg him to spare me details I wouldn't understand, he grinned. "No big deal. Technology moves so fast these days. It'll probably cost only about two hundred bucks."

"Go for it," I said. "Any idea why Vida

seems, as she would put it, to be on the peck this morning?"

"No. She was on the phone when I got here. In fact, I think she arrived early, even before Amanda. What's up with Mitch?"

"Brenda," I said. "He's taking her to see Doc Dewey. Apparently, some bugs are still going around. We need more rain." I glanced at the *Advocate*'s front page. "Looks good, Kip. I'll check out the rest of it at my desk."

I entered the newsroom via the back hall, noting that Leo had just arrived. He was talking to Vida, so I assumed she hadn't yet verbally assaulted him. Taking my time to skim the newspaper, I didn't find any glitches, though the retirement home photos were mediocre. That couldn't be helped. Vida took decent pictures, but she didn't have time to cover all of their numerous events.

Finally deciding I was a chicken, I went to get coffee and a pastry. Amanda had chosen two kinds of cinnamon rolls along with several varieties of doughnuts. I opted for a raised sugar doughnut, turned around to greet Leo, and marched over to sit in Vida's visitor chair.

"Are you feeling sick, too?" I asked in a serious tone.

Vida stared at me from under a purple

cloche adorned with a bright yellow bow. "Of course not. Why do you ask?"

"You don't seem very cheerful," I said. "There must be something bothering you."

She looked away. "Certainly not. I was merely trying to give Amanda some guidance about real estate. It's a big decision. At almost two hundred thousand dollars, Milo should arrest himself for attempted robbery. His house is basically a fixer-upper. The Hansons don't need to take on such a burden with a new baby."

"It is *not* a fixer-upper," I declared, practically speaking through clenched teeth. "Face it, Vida, you have no idea how much work Milo has put into that house, both inside and out."

She shrugged but still didn't look at me. "If you say so."

I may have been talking through my teeth, but Vida was talking through her hat. *Something* was bothering her, and it wasn't Milo's house. I wasn't giving up.

"I meant to ask," I said, hoping I looked more pleasant than I felt, "how was the birthday party?"

Vida finally favored me with eye contact. "Very nice. Dippy adored the lovely cake I bought. Especially the frosting."

I felt like saying that was Ed Bronsky's

favorite part, too. Instead, I asked if Roger was still volunteering at RestHaven.

Vida frowned slightly. "He's taken some time off to mull his future."

I kept a straight face. "Is he considering going back to college?"

"Among other options." She looked away again. "Making life choices is so difficult for young people these days."

In my opinion, life's biggest choice for Roger was getting out of bed in the morning. "It took Adam a long time to figure it all out," I said, standing up. "He was the same age as Roger is now — twenty-four — when he realized he had a religious vocation."

"Roger is barely twenty-three," Vida said — and seemed to wince.

Or maybe I did, with a vision of Roger becoming a Bible-thumping preacher. "He'll find . . . something," I said before heading back to my office.

After finishing the doughnut and drinking most of my coffee, I headed out to assume Mitch's duties at the sheriff's office. The sun was rising over Cowboy Mountain, to the east. I could hear a freight train whistling as it approached town from the other direction. Front Street was doing its best imitation of a morning rush hour. I counted ten cars, four trucks, and a bicyclist in the little over a block between the *Advocate* and the sheriff's headquarters.

When I arrived, the receptionist, Lori Cobb, was seated in place behind the curving mahogany counter. The taciturn Dwight Gould looked as if he was about to go off on patrol. Dustin Fong wore an unusually gloomy expression. Even the usually cheery Lori seemed to droop in her chair, though she did attempt a weak smile.

"Hi," she said in a wispy voice. "Do you want to see the sheriff?"

"Not really," I replied. "Mitch will be late today, so I'm checking the log." I glanced at Milo's closed door. "Is the boss incommunicado?"

Dwight walked out of the office without saying a word. Lori and Dustin exchanged quick looks. The deputy spoke first: "Go ahead. He'll probably talk to you."

I took a deep breath, entering through the swinging half door and walking purposefully into the sheriff's lair. Milo was doing some paperwork. As I closed the door behind me, he looked up.

"If you've got a problem, save it for after hours," he growled.

"My only problem is that Mitch isn't at work today," I said, sitting down in one of his visitor chairs. "I gather you're the one with a problem. Do you want to tell your wife, or is it a state secret?"

Milo expelled a deep breath and leaned back in his chair. "Sam Heppner's taken off."

I stared at the sheriff. "What do you mean?"

"He's gone." Milo took out his Marlboro Lights and offered me the pack. Like a fool, I took one and let him light it for me before he spoke again. "Sam rarely takes vacation, unless it's for a fishing or hunting trip. Yesterday he called in sick. He phoned this morning right after I got here to say he needed some time for himself. I was kind of puzzled, but I said go ahead. I asked if he was still sick. He said no." Milo paused to sip from the Seahawks mug Tanya had given him for his March birthday.

"Where *is* Tanya?" I asked, realizing she hadn't been out front.

"Still holding Deanna's hand, I guess." He made a dismissive gesture. "That's the least of my worries. Heppner said he didn't know when — or if — he'd be back and hung up on me. I had Lori try to call him, but he didn't answer. I checked in with his sister in Sultan. She hasn't talked to him for two weeks. Mullins had just come off patrol, but I told him to go out to Sam's place on River Road and see if he was there. He wasn't. His Jeep was gone, too. By the way, this doesn't go public. I don't want would-be perps finding out we're short-handed." Milo paused to puff on his cigarette. "If anybody asks, Sam's taking some vacation time."

"Has he been acting any weirder than he usually does?"

Milo shook his head. "Not that I could tell. Face it, he's grim by nature. I'll admit that over the years, he's gone deeper into his shell. Looking back to Monday, I don't remember him saying much of anything the last couple of hours before he went off duty. I didn't think more about it, especially when he called in sick the next day." Again, he paused to sip coffee and take another puff on his cigarette.

"You're right," I said. "When I first knew Sam, he was at least civil. Even Mitch has noticed how surly he is."

"Sam knows better than to give me any lip." Milo put out his cigarette. "This is all wrong. I don't like it. He's an odd duck, but he's steady. Frankly, I wonder if he's gone 'round the bend. The only thing I know for sure is that he's gone."

I didn't know what to say. I noticed I'd let

my cigarette burn down in the ashtray. Just as well. "Does Sam have *any* friends?"

"Not that I know of." Milo took another drink of coffee and pushed the mug aside. "I asked his sister, Ruth, about that. She kind of brushed me off, saying I ought to know Sam didn't socialize much. No kidding."

"Are you going to search his house?"

Milo leaned his elbows on the desk. "It crossed my mind. But hell, if Sam's just in some kind of temporary funk and finds out we've been poking around in his private life, I wouldn't blame him for getting really pissed off and quitting. I might do the same thing in his place."

I didn't speak right away. "What's wrong with everybody? Vida's being a pain again and Mitch took Brenda to the doctor's this morning. What ever happened to *normal*?"

Milo smiled wryly. "Doe Jamison swears it's the lack of serious rain. The drizzle we've had off and on doesn't get down to our roots. I won't argue with her. Being part Muckleshoot, her tribal roots go a hell of a lot deeper than the rest of us. I asked if she could do a rain dance. Luckily, she laughed. I thought she might slug me instead. Doe's one tough mama. I wish I had another one like her, but I can't afford it."

"Maybe," I suggested, not without irony, "after the *Advocate* comes out today and everybody reads what Fuzzy and I have to say about reorganizing the county, people will be clamoring for change."

"Right." Milo sat back, arms folded. "Go away. I have to work."

I got out of the chair. "No official ID on your corpse?"

"Nope."

"Body still at the SnoCo lab in Everett?"

"Yep. Now we wait. As usual."

I left my husband in peace and almost forgot to check the log. Two minor vandalisms of private property, bear sighting not far from the ranger station, stolen car from Ptarmigan Tract, minor collision of a Ford pickup and a Honda Civic at the intersection of Spark Plug and the Icicle Creek Roads' intersection by First Hill — no injuries. In short, there was nothing startling — such as a missing sheriff's deputy.

SEVEN

As I walked back to the office, it dawned on me that Vida hadn't made any inquiries about the dead man. That wasn't like her. No one in Skykomish County had a more rampant curiosity than my House & Home editor.

To test her, I stopped by her desk. "No word on the corpse," I said.

Vida looked up from a news release she'd been perusing. "I believe he's not a local." She turned back to her reading.

Irked, I went into my office. Wednesdays were usually down time that I used for planning the next issue while waiting for the paper to hit the streets and mailboxes. Having editorialized the past two months to pave the way for the mayor's restructuring plan, a follow-up would be due next week. But that was on hold until I got reader response.

There was nothing I could do about the

dead body. More waiting, in this case for Milo and Yakima's law enforcement personnel.

But I could tackle the runaways. There was something about having two girls run off within such a short time that bothered me. Journalists get hunches, and I'd had my share. I decided to take a chance that my latest hunch was worth pursuing.

New SkyCo phone directories had been distributed the first week of April. I looked up the Ellisons' listing. Charles and Janice Ellison lived up on the Icicle Creek Road, not far from the ranger station. I dialed their number. A young female voice answered on the second ring.

"Samantha?" I said.

"No," the voice replied. "She's not here. Who's this?"

"Emma Lord, from the *Advocate.* You are . . . ?" I let the query dangle.

"Chelsea. Did you want to talk to my parents? They aren't here."

"That's okay," I replied. "I'm doing some background for an article about high school students. What grade are you in, Chelsea?"

"I'm a sophomore," she replied.

"Is Samantha there?"

"No."

"What grade is she in?"

128

There was a long pause. "Well . . . she'd be a senior."

"I'm sorry. Do you mean she dropped out of school?"

"Um . . . kind of. I mean, she . . . moved."

"Samantha left Alpine?"

A shorter pause. "Yes. She went somewhere with her boyfriend."

I thought fast. "That's fascinating," I said. "In fact, it's exactly the sort of information I can use in my article. I want to focus on how today's teenagers have more choices with what they can do with their lives. It's all rooted so deeply in technology," I asserted, wondering when my nose would start growing like Pinocchio's. "You know, the unlimited access they have to family and friends, no matter where they are. Have you got a phone number or an email address for your sister? I'd love to talk to her."

"Ah . . . no. Sammy calls here every week, but she uses a pay phone."

So much for the technology angle. I was undaunted, however, if only because Samantha hadn't gone the high-tech route. "I'm even more curious about that," I said in my friendliest tone. "Your sister must be one of the few teens I know who isn't glued to a cellphone."

"I guess she lost hers," Chelsea said

vaguely. "Hey, I have to go. My brother's gone outside and I can't see where he is. 'Bye."

To my surprise, Vida was coming toward me. "What," she asked, "was that all about?"

Relieved that she was at least being civil, I unloaded on her after she sat down in one of my visitor chairs. I concluded by asking if she'd interviewed the Ellisons when they'd moved to Alpine last fall.

For once, she looked stumped. "I *think* I did," she said, frowning. "In October, which you may recall was a hectic time for me." Her admission was strained.

"I know," I said, hoping to sound sympathetic about her reference to the trailer park disaster that had temporarily derailed Vida's delusions of Roger as the ideal law-abiding grandson. "Do you recall mentioning the Ellisons at all?"

"Yes," she replied reluctantly, "but only in a monthly wrap-up."

I shrugged. "No big deal, except, as you might have heard me on the phone, their daughter Samantha was reported as a runaway but later contacted her parents. Now that the Johnson girl is missing, my curiosity's piqued. Frankly, the younger Ellison daughter didn't do much to reassure me about her sister's well-being."

Vida shifted from chagrin to curiosity. "How so?"

I went back over the conversation. "Samantha's still a minor. I'm wondering who the boyfriend is. Maybe it's time you called on the parents and did a bigger story about why they moved to Alpine."

Vida nodded. "Very wise of them to settle here, of course. The one thing I do recall from a very brief phone conversation with Mrs. Ellison was that her husband had been hired by the railroad. She was hoping to get work in town as an LPN. I assume both parents aren't home now?"

"That's right. There's a younger brother, too." I handed her the phone number I'd written down on a Post-it note. "Maybe you could call them this evening?"

"Of course," she agreed. "There's a potluck at the Presbyterian church, but I'll do it after I get home. We never stay late. I made a sausage casserole that sounds very enticing. It came out of my file."

Vida might have added the file — or made the dish *with* a file. Her talent for cooking ended with "Face the stove."

"By the way," I said as Vida appeared to be getting out of the chair, "Tanya stopped by last night with the Johnson girl's older sister, now Deanna Engstrom. Do you know the mother? Her current married name is Moro." For the sake of Vida's feelings, I avoided mentioning that she lived in the trailer park. "She's Roy Everson's sister."

"Yes," Vida murmured, "so she is. I'd forgotten that Wanda made an unfortunate second marriage. When they were young, my eldest daughter, Meg, and Wanda were rather close." She paused, looking thoughtful. "My, my — it's no wonder you're following up on the Ellison girl. I do see a pattern, faint as it is. I can't recall any runaways reported for some time. Before you arrived, when logging had been curtailed and so many families were devastated by the loss of work, there was quite a rash of runaway teens. Some came back, some never did. Very sad."

"Alpine was still trying to recover when I got here," I reminded Vida. "Any chance you might pay Wanda a call?"

Vida stood up. "Well . . . I'll think on that." She exited my office.

At least I'd distracted her from whatever was on her mind. Vida used everything short of waterboarding to elicit information from other people, but when it came to her own life, she was agonizingly discreet.

Mitch showed up shortly before eleven-thirty. "Some kind of virus," he said, standing in my doorway and shrugging out of his jacket. "Doc Dewey told us there isn't much he can do. It just has to run its course."

I nodded. "How is she feeling otherwise?"

Mitch brightened a bit. "Better, I think. She's been weaving more lately and has taken a couple of orders. Of course, she's fretting about the virus keeping her from finishing the projects on time. I hope she's feeling good by the weekend. We plan on driving to Monroe to see Troy."

The subject of the Laskeys' imprisoned son was touchy, so I merely said I hoped they could do that. I followed up by telling Mitch that Vida was doing background on the alleged runaways. If there was more to it, he'd take over the hard news. I'd already zapped him the items from the sheriff's log.

I suddenly remembered to ask about the sports car driver who might or might not still be alive in Monroe's hospital.

"I checked while I was waiting for Brenda at the clinic," Mitch replied. "He's been upgraded to stable. Maybe he'll make it."

"Good," I said, not admitting that Milo hadn't known — or cared. For the sheriff, the accident victim was just another non-local who didn't understand the hazards of driving on Highway 2.

A few minutes later, Milo called me. "You

won't believe this," he said, "but your idiot neighbor Laverne Nelson filed a complaint about the noise from the construction going on at your house."

"What?" I shrieked. Before he could respond, I kept talking: "In case you've forgotten, that's *our* house, you jackass!"

"That's my point," he said in a relatively calm voice. "Apparently, the wife and mother of the tree poachers, arsonists, and perps of some other felonies has been on the lam, so she doesn't know you're Mrs. Dodge. Her complaint is only against Emma Lord."

"Crap," I said, holding my head with the hand that wasn't holding the phone. "What do I . . . what do *we* do now?"

"Not a damned thing," Milo replied. "But I wanted to warn you in case she shows up when I'm not around. You gave the deposition about the two younger Nelson kids trying to burn down the house in December. Meanwhile, I'm sending Gould to enlighten Mrs. Nelson. This is right up his alley. Dwight's complete lack of tact is a plus in this situation. He enjoys badgering people. I think the daughter-in-law and her kid are probably living in the house, too. Mrs. Nelson reported that her grandchild couldn't nap because of the noise."

"I wonder if Laverne and the other two have been holed up with her cousin in Index," I said. "Any word on when the two younger kids who started the carport fire will get out?"

"Next March," my husband replied. "Doyle and the oldest son each got a year in Walla Walla, but they still have a hearing on reimbursing the county for cutting down those maples in the first place. You watch out for yourself when you go home, Emma. I mean it."

"I will," I promised. "Are you going to be late?"

I heard him sigh. "You know I can't be sure. Let's hope not."

Leo was standing in the doorway. "Okay," I said. "See you later."

My ad manager chuckled. "I assume that was your better half. I'm not used to thinking of you as a wife."

I laughed. "I'm not, either, never having been one until lately. On the other hand, I feel as if Milo and I have been together forever."

"You have," Leo said seriously. "That's why you'll make it. No surprises. Would he mind if you ate lunch with your aging ad manager?"

"He's never minded," I said, looking

135

around Leo to see if Vida was at her desk. She was nowhere in sight, and her coat was gone. "You choose. Not that we have a lot of options."

"How about driving down to Skykomish, to the Cascadia? I'd like a change of menus."

"Sounds good. I haven't been there in ages."

"Shall we?" Leo asked, making as if he were offering his arm.

It was a quarter to twelve. "Why not? It *is* Wednesday."

We took Leo's Toyota, which was even older than my Honda. The sun now shone almost overhead as we crossed the rusting green truss bridge over the Skykomish River before reaching Highway 2.

"It definitely feels like spring," Leo remarked as we passed the road to Alpine Falls. "I can't complain about rain this year."

"I can," I said. "I'm a native. Not getting rain is bothersome."

Leo grinned. "Tell me that when we haven't had any in June."

"I know," I admitted. "June can be wetter than May some years. But they're talking drought east of the mountains."

"Maybe it's all a plot to keep me in Alpine instead of going back to sunny South-ern California," he said as we passed the Skykomish Ranger Station. "I've never quite adjusted to those endless weeks of gray skies."

"Stop reminding me that you're going to retire in the not-so-distant future," I re-torted. "Take a few days for your birthday in May and go see your grandson. What's his name? I forget."

"Austin." Leo made a face. "Liza and I weren't pleased. All I can think of is Texas, and she bitches because she never heard of a Saint Austin. What kind of nickname do you give the kid? Aussie? Tinny?"

"Don't ask me. I'll never be a grand-mother."

"Yes, you will," Leo said. "A step-grandmother, anyway. One of Milo's kids is bound to produce some offspring."

I nodded faintly. "His son, Bran, and his girlfriend are talking marriage, maybe in the fall."

Traffic was fairly light as we wound our way along what was also known as the Stevens Pass Highway, with its glimpses of the green-colored Sky rippling and rushing westward. I missed the little waterfalls that usually trickled down the steep rocks on the northern side of the road. The snowpack at the higher elevations had already diminished.

Leo slowed to turn off for the bridge that led back over the Sky and into the little community that bore the river's name. Like Alpine, Skykomish had its own Railroad Avenue. The town's history was rooted in the building of the Great Northern Railway when one of the surveying engineers, John Maloney, homesteaded on the site in 1892. First called Maloney's Landing, the original depot had been a boxcar on a siding. The town grew, but even as Carl Clemans's mill produced the timber for the new Cascade tunnel, the die was cast not only for Alpine, but for Skykomish. The railroad had been Clemans's major customer. When the tunnel was finished, he was forced to close his mill. Skykomish endured as a railroad town until 1956, when diesel engines replaced the old electric trains. The town's usefulness was over. Only some two hundred people remained, determined to preserve the spot as a historic landmark.

One of those landmarks was the venerable Cascadia Hotel, with its café and lounge. The bar didn't open during the week until after five, so Leo and I sat in the dining area. The menu was far more extensive than the Burger Barn's — and more inventive than the Venison Inn's. Leo chose the Maloney chicken sandwich, and I asked for the Great Northern hamburger dip.

"Why," I said, after coffee was poured for us, "do I think you have a reason for coming here other than that it's a nice change of pace?"

Leo's leathery face crinkled with amused irony. "The Duchess — what else? As you've noticed, she's off her feed again. Any idea why?"

"I assume it's Roger," I replied. "I'm not sure he's volunteering at RestHaven anymore. I always thought he did that only to be within the proximity of the buxom Ainsley."

"Maybe the romance is kaput," Leo suggested. "What does Ainsley do there? I assume she's not their consulting brain surgeon."

"She's an aide in the rehab wing, working for Jennifer Hood, the RN in charge of the unit."

Leo frowned. "Weren't there some rumors about Nurse Hood going around a while ago?"

I laughed. "Yes. Remember when Jack Blackwell kept reporting that someone was trying to kill him?" I saw Leo nod, and continued. "It turned out that Jennifer was

Jack's first wife, years ago in California. She'd never quite gotten over him, despite his inclination to beat up on the women in his life. According to Milo, Jack dropped the charges because he was embarrassed. For all I know, he's still seeing Jennifer when Patti Marsh isn't looking."

"He's a strange guy," Leo said, but paused as our side salads arrived. "I haven't dealt with him much over the years, because he runs a standing ad. When I have met with him, he's all business. If we had two more county commissioners like him, we might not be stalled in SkyCo."

I narrowed my eyes. "You haven't read this week's *Advocate.*"

"Ah! I plead guilty. Sorry. I've been too busy this morning seeking revenue to keep said *Advocate* in the black. I gather you have a plan."

"Incredibly enough, it's Mayor Baugh's plan. Or his wife's. But it's a good one."

Leo looked bemused. "I'll check it out when we get back to the office. I take it there's nothing in this plan that'd set Vida on her ear?"

"Not that I can think of. I'll stick with Roger being the cause of her current mood. I'd ask her about him, but it's hard to do without showing my disgust."

Our entrées were delivered. "Let me tackle that one," Leo said. "I assume she's still pissed at Milo, Rosie Bourgette, and Judge Diane."

"She is. Maybe," I suggested, "Dippy, as he's called, is two and he's probably a handful for Amy and Ted, who've both reached middle age. They celebrated the kid's birthday this week. It should come as no surprise that I don't think Roger takes fatherhood seriously."

Leo snorted. "Did that kid ever take anything seriously except drinking, eating, and doing drugs?"

"He did seem interested in acting at one point, but that requires effort and study and focus. None of those things suit Roger very well."

Leo looked unusually solemn. "Here's how I see it in the office. Mitch is up and down with his wife's breakdown and a son in prison. Amanda will be around for another couple of months before she has the baby. With Vida often being a prima donna, the newsroom is not always a pleasant place. You know that, if only from when she makes some crack about the sheriff. Don't get me wrong — I appreciate what you've done to get me out of my drunken stupor. Working on the *Advocate* has been good. But the ups and downs of the past few months are turning me sour. Santa Maria's looking better and better all the time."

I set down the French fry I'd been about to put in my mouth. "Oh, Leo, I hate to hear that!"

He shrugged. "I have to be honest with you. I'd *like* to stay on for another year or so. Frankly, I'm still not sure if Liza wants me back on a permanent basis. But if she does . . ." He raised both hands in a helpless gesture. "I may be gone when I turn sixty-two in May."

We lived in an era where newspapers were an endangered species, just like the loggers and the spotted owls. The food at the Cascadia was very good, but my appetite was ruined. Worse yet, Leo's defection could ruin the *Advocate.*

EIGHT

My ad manager apologized profusely for upsetting me. I tried to put on a blasé face. He knew me better, though. Of course, I couldn't blame him for wanting to reunite with his family. But after the disaster that had been Ed Bronsky, Leo had single-handedly turned the newspaper from borderline red into solid black.

"Damn," Leo said, shaking his head and gazing at a hand-painted wooden train on the nearest wall. "I swear I didn't intend to dump all that on you now. I only wanted to find out what was up with Vida."

I nodded faintly. "What's up with Vida is often what's up with the *Advocate*. I'm the editor and publisher, but most people think she's in charge, just as she exerts her influence on the town itself. She not only loves Alpine, but considers it her fiefdom." I managed a small smile. "She reminds me of the Dame of Sark, who ruled over the small

143

island in the English Channel. Even when the Germans occupied it, they were forced to respect her. As I recall, she also wore some amazing hats."

"Good thing we Californians who've invaded Alpine keep a fairly low profile," Leo said.

Our conversation turned to less depressing subjects. I managed to eat a bit more food, though I still felt glum. I didn't like contemplating life without Leo.

Back at work, I had a message from Edna Mae Dalrymple, the town's head librarian. Maybe she'd already seen the *Advocate* and was calling to cheer or jeer. But the first words out of her mouth pertained instead to our bridge club.

"Emma, dear," she chirped in her birdlike voice, "we are muddled about which night we play, even if it's only twice a month. It's very confusing since we switched dates the first of the year. Anyway, it *is* this evening at my house. But we forgot that Charlene Vickers and Darlene Adcock have other commitments. Can you play?"

During January, when the night was switched to a Tuesday, I'd bowed out, and not just because it was our deadline. Certain members weren't numbered among my fans. After what Milo and I had gone through in late December, I didn't feel like putting up with their intrusive and often snarky comments. I'd played bridge once in February, substituting for one of my detractors, high school gym teacher Linda Grant. In March, the members had become so mixed up that they'd met only once — on another Tuesday. Again I'd begged off. They'd switched to Thursday in early April, but the hostess, Mary Jane Bourgette, had called at the last minute to say their dishwasher had flooded the kitchen. When no one leaped into the breach, the get-together was canceled. As I was trying to think of a viable excuse, I saw Fuzzy Baugh in the doorway. I told Edna Mae I'd play. I'd have to wait until the mayor left to kick myself.

"Emma, darlin'." Fuzzy greeted me in his Bayou baritone as he gingerly sat down in a visitor chair. "Your editorial has stirred my very soul. I had to come in person to congratulate you."

"It was your idea," I said. "All I did was run with it. Have you heard from any of the county commissioners?"

"Not yet," Fuzzy replied. "Due to the consideration of your predecessor, the venerable Marius Vandeventer, I am always the first to get a copy of the *Advocate.*"

Somewhere along the way I'd forgotten about that courtesy. The mayor was mainly a figurehead, while the commissioners ruled supreme. "You might not like what you hear from Engebretsen, Hollenberg, and Blackwell," I warned him.

He ran a hand through his thinning dyed red hair and chuckled. "I'm a product of Louisiana politics. I remain unafraid. How can they protest too much when I'm eliminating myself?" He chuckled some more.

"I'm prepared for some flak," I said. "Not just from the commissioners, but readers, too. You know how people around here dislike change, even if in this case it's intended to save them money."

"Ah," Fuzzy responded, with a sly look, "that's where we have them by the short hairs. In the long run, they'll come 'round. If not, I shall request a bond issue and perhaps a levy or two just to show them the alternatives. I'm anxious to hear what your stalwart husband will have to say about all this."

Fuzzy didn't know that I'd broken my word to him and blurted out the whole plan to Milo only hours after the mayor had confided in me. "He'll back you," I replied. "The sheriff knows what's best for SkyCo."

"I'm grateful for his support," Fuzzy

declared, taking his time to rise from the chair. At eighty, or close to it, he moved as slowly as a southern breeze. "The only fierce opposition I expect would be from Blackwell. But I must take the liberty of saying I would have the redoubtable sheriff on my side. I'm from Louisiana, but I don't want to end up like Huey Long. I was only a lad when he was gunned down at the capitol in Baton Rouge, but I remember it well."

"I don't think Jack would shoot you," I said, getting up to walk the mayor out through the newsroom. "I'd worry more about him wanting to become the county manager. He does have business experience."

For a split second, Fuzzy's faded blue eyes seemed to snap. "He wouldn't. He may operate a fine mill, but that's very different from running a government. If my aging memory serves, your valiant mate gave him a sound whopping in his futile attempt to become sheriff when that position was an elected office."

"True." I glanced at Vida, who was on the phone, but her posture indicated that she wanted to hang up and pounce on the mayor. "Let me know what you hear from the voters."

Fuzzy assured me he would, paused to make a courtly bow to Vida, and went on his way. It was another five minutes before she tromped into my office to interrogate me about the mayor's visit.

"Hey," I said, "don't tell me you haven't read Mitch's front-page article or my editorial."

She looked somewhat taken aback. "I saw the headline indicating Fuzzy had done something, but knowing him, I assumed it was self-serving. It often is."

"Not this time. In fact," I went on, hoping to placate Vida for whatever fault she was mentally accusing me of now, "you can be a huge help making Fuzzy's plan work. I assume you're still at the top of the Presbyterians' telephone tree?"

"Well, of course! You'd think I'd abdicate that responsibility?"

"No," I said with a straight face. "Someone has to spread the news down the line, and you *are* a journalist."

"Well now. I must learn what this is all about." I could almost hear a blare of trumpets as Vida marched off to her desk.

My phone rang a few minutes later. "Do I want you or Mitch?" the sheriff asked in a beleaguered voice.

"Gosh," I said in a mock-injured tone, "I

148

never thought you cared that much for my reporter. I'm jealous."

"Cut the crap," Milo barked. "I mean in terms of handling the ID on the body. It's tricky."

"You have an ID?"

"Yeah, in a way. Maybe you better get your cute little butt down here. I'll let you figure out how to do this in the paper. You *are* the boss."

"Don't say that in front of Vida," I said in almost a whisper. "Okay, I'll be there ASAP."

I walked casually through the newsroom, not wanting Vida to pick up even a faint scent of urgency. Nevertheless, when I turned to exit through the front office, I could feel her eyes boring into my back like laser beams. Once I hit the sidewalk, I moved faster. By the time I reached the sheriff's headquarters, I was out of breath.

A frazzled-looking Lori gestured at Milo's closed door. "Enter at your peril. He probably won't try to take your head off."

"If he did, the cook would quit." I went through the swinging gate and didn't bother to knock. Milo was on the phone, acknowledging my arrival with a raised hand. I closed the door and sat down.

"No," he said, "I don't need to mix it up

149

with the Feds. That's your call, not mine."
He grew silent, listening to whoever was at
the other end of the line. "Okay. If that's
the way it is, you handle it." He started to
slam down the receiver, thought better of it,
and carefully set it in the cradle. "Freaking
red tape," he muttered, taking out a cigarette
and lighting it. "You want one?"

"No thanks. I'll just watch smoke come
out of your nose, mouth, and ears."

"Fire and brimstone should be more like
it," Milo muttered. "Okay." He leaned back
in his chair. "The deceased may or may not
be José Carlos Fernandez of Wapato. He
may, in fact, be an undercover agent for the
Feds or he may be a crook. You and I are
both in a bind."

"You mean," I said after absorbing Milo's
revelation, "that the Yakima sheriff's office
doesn't know? Or that they won't tell?"

"I don't think they know." He leaned
forward, elbows on the desk, and fingered
his long chin. "Yakima's a hell of a lot bigger county than SkyCo, but when it comes
to a federal issue, a local sheriff doesn't have
much clout in D.C."

"I guess not." I paused, trying to wrap my
head around the situation. "No word yet
from the SnoCo ME?"

"No. I'll call later this afternoon if I

haven't heard by then."

"Can I use the victim's alleged name online?"

Milo shrugged. "Why not? It's what's on his driver's license. I'll have to release it to Fleetwood, but without filling in the background. Same with Laskey. I'm only telling you because . . ." He grimaced. "Damnit, I guess I had to tell somebody. Why not my wife? You've liked calling me 'baffled' over the years. Now I am. So's Yakima."

I smiled. "I've never called you 'baffled' in print. But you know we can't use it in the paper anyway. Does your Yakima contact believe the license may be phony?"

"We're not supposed to know that."

"Have you found a vehicle?"

Milo shook his head. "The only thing I know is that he didn't walk here from Wapato. If he was ever there in the first place." He took a last drag on his cigarette.

"I don't get it," I said. "Why does your vis-à-vis in Yakima think Fernandez could be a crook? I mean, why would anyone think he was a crook just because he isn't some kind of federal agent?"

"I asked that question," Milo replied. "It appears there *is* an agent by that name, but he's not supposed to be anywhere near this state. He operates out of Southern California. If he's undercover, I suspect they can't find him. That's not unusual. Those types go deep into their roles."

"So we can ID him?"

"Sure." Milo stood up and stretched. "It might bring somebody out of the woodwork. I doubt it, but it can't do any harm."

I got to my feet, too. "By the way, I'm playing bridge tonight."

The sheriff didn't look pleased. "How come? I thought you decided to bail from that bunch."

"I resigned from Marisa Foxx's poker group. I can't afford playing with her fellow well-heeled attorneys. Besides, some of the games are too far out of town. Edna Mae Dalrymple caught me in a weak moment."

"Would she yank your library card if you turned her down?"

I laughed. "No. Why don't you round up a poker game with your own crew? You've only played once in the last few months."

"I know. I've been too damned busy and Doc Dewey is as overworked as I am. Gerry and I are usually the ones who get the rest of them together." He looked a bit chagrined. "Maybe I'll give him a call. Now go away before I start messing with your face."

I went — but not before advising him to call Mitch. If my reporter didn't get the news directly, he might plunge into one of his moods. When it came to turf, Mitch was hypersensitive.

Half an hour later, he was also confused. "What was the big holdup releasing the dead guy's name?" he asked from my office doorway.

"There are a lot of Fernandezes in Yakima County," I hedged. "Their sheriff wanted to be sure they had the right one."

Mitch looked thoughtful. "I suppose that's true. I keep forgetting how much agriculture there is on the other side of the mountains. I shouldn't — not after Troy got arrested in Yakima for drug dealing." Shoulders slumping, he turned away and went back to his desk.

Except for fielding two dozen phone calls about Fuzzy's proposal and my editorial — seven against, five for, and the rest confused — I spent the next two hours going through notes I'd made in February while researching some of the less savory aspects of local history. Admittedly, until then my knowledge had been limited to the town's founding and its near demise before Rufus Runkel and Olav the Obese injected new life into Alpine. The retrospective had been triggered after Vida interviewed Clarence Munn, a former mill owner who was now confined to RestHaven with something akin to Alzheimer's. While Clarence might not recall what he'd had for lunch or even what lunch was, his memory seemed quite keen when it came to the distant past. He cited various forms of corruption, some of which came as news even to Vida. Whether his recollections were worthy of publishing was dubious. Milo had suggested holding off at the time, but to save the long-ago dirt until we announced Fuzzy's proposal. Still trying to get back into my House & Home editor's good graces, I sought her opinion.

"I believe," Vida said, adjusting her glasses, "that you decided to withhold Clarence's revelations to show opponents what happens when government is in shoddy hands. That was probably wise."

I nodded but wouldn't let on that the advice had actually come from Milo. "I have no idea if we'll need to resort to that, but the phones aren't ringing off the hook with unbridled endorsements."

"No-o-o," Vida said thoughtfully. "I wouldn't expect that to happen. People here tend to take their time making up their minds. Prudent, of course. Knee-jerk reactions are often later retracted."

I heard my phone ringing but decided to ignore it in deference to Vida. "I suppose you'll start rallying your Presbyterians tonight before you get on your telephone tree."

"I certainly will. Perhaps the new minister, being young, will be of help. Pastor Purebeck tended to hold more conservative views. Except," she added with a look of disgust, "when it came to Daisy McFee."

Amanda called my name from the front office. "It's the sheriff," she said. "Are you or Mitch available?"

"He must be in the back shop," I informed her. "I'll take it in my office." Despite Vida's sour look, I excused myself to beat a hasty retreat.

"We just got the ME's report," Milo said. "Four stab wounds to the chest and abdomen. No sign of a struggle. Death occurred between two and six A.M. Vic was a healthy male and if his driver's license is real as well as accurate, he was twenty-seven years old. What's for dinner?"

"Chicken," I said, though I hadn't given it a thought.

"Chicken again? What ever happened to steak?"

"I'm in a rut, okay? Back up. This guy was stabbed in the chest and abdomen but he didn't put up a fight?"

"Neal Doak doesn't elaborate in his reports. If you want a story, ask Edna Mae Dalrymple to bring you a book at bridge club tonight." Once again, the sheriff hung up on me.

I met Mitch coming out of the back shop and relayed the information to him. He turned around to have Kip put the news online. Finally reaching my desk, I noticed it was ten to five. Not knowing if Tanya was coming to dinner, I called the sheriff office's main number.

"Tanya didn't come in today," Lori said. "Dodge told us she had out-of-town company. You have her cell number, right?"

I did, though I had to look it up. I still wasn't fully immersed in my role as stepmother. Tanya answered on the first ring. I inquired about her dinner plans.

"I'm in Bellevue, at Mom's," Tanya said. "With the weather getting warmer, I decided to drive down here to get some of my spring clothes. I'm spending the night so I can go shopping at Bellevue Square with Mom. Didn't Dad tell you?"

"No," I replied, deciding to make excuses for her father. "He's been busy." That much was true. "Enjoy your fashion frenzy. Are you coming back tomorrow?"

"I'm not sure. I might stay over again to catch up with some of my friends here. I haven't been in Bellevue for almost two months. I'm out of the loop, despite texting. You can't get all the juicy details that way. I'll let Dad or you know tomorrow."

I wished her luck and rang off. Given her aversion to all things Bellevue, with its horrific memories, I viewed her visit as an encouraging sign. Maybe Tanya wasn't going to make Alpine her permanent home. On the other hand, Bill Blatt wasn't on Seattle's Eastside. I wondered if Tanya wanted to perk up her wardrobe for his benefit.

I had time to make one last phone call. Not wanting to pester Tanya while she was out of town, I'd decided to go to the primary source, Deanna Johnson Engstrom. I found the number for David Engstrom in the SnoCo directory, but got a recording. She hadn't mentioned having children. Maybe Deanna worked. I hesitated before leaving a message, then figured the *Advocate*'s number had shown up.

"Hi, Deanna," I said, "this is Emma Dodge." Damn, I'd forgotten — my office phone came up as Emma Lord. But Deanna knew me as Emma Dodge. Maybe she could sort it out. "I was wondering if you'd found out anything from your sister Erin's friends. We're all concerned about her."

Double damn. She'd think the sheriff wasn't doing his job. "My husband and his staff are involved in a murder investigation." Great. Deanna might worry that he'd found Erin's body. "If you can, could you call me back" — I hesitated, realizing I'd be gone most of the evening and Milo might be playing poker — "tomorrow at this number? Thanks."

Suddenly, being Mrs. Dodge and Ms. Lord at the same time didn't seem like a good idea. I decided to go home and forage in the freezer. At least I knew how to deal with cooking chicken.

My biggest anxiety was that someone had cooked Erin Johnson's goose.

NINE

When I arrived at home, the first surprise was that I couldn't put my Honda in its usual spot. That was because the carport was gone. The Bourgette brothers were still at it when I parked in the driveway.

After greeting me, John offered an explanation: "We figured we should begin with that because once work starts on the cabin itself, the weather will be warmer. Maybe you and Dodge can move into the other bedroom while we're adding on to yours. The existing bathroom will be fine, but the kitchen will be out of commission for two, three days. By then you could be barbecuing if the weather holds." He grinned in his affable manner. "Or maybe you'd both like to go on vacation."

"What's a vacation?" I mumbled. "How long is all this going to take? Milo originally thought it'd be under a month."

Dan had joined his older brother. "That

was before he and Scott Melville made additions to the project. The second bathroom, along with the kitchen and laundry area alterations, will require new plumbing. That's another two, three days of work right there."

I kept my exasperation in check. "Okay. I guess I missed something along the way." *Like the dunderhead I married not keeping me informed.* "Are you two off the clock now?"

"Almost," Dan replied, still chipper. "We'd like to polish off the carport first. Don't worry. We'll haul everything away when we're done."

It was impossible to get annoyed with the Bourgettes. I forced a smile and went inside through the back door. Luckily, they hadn't yet removed the steps.

I didn't need to change clothes since I'd be going to bridge club, so I found some chicken breasts in the freezer, put them into the microwave to thaw, and searched for the rest of the ingredients I needed to make a longtime favorite I usually reserved for company dinners. It was easy to do, but I couldn't recall if I'd ever served it to Milo. About now I felt like feeding him gruel. Or one of Vida's loathsome casseroles.

After forty more minutes of pounding, the

sheriff literally vaulted in through the kitchen door. "What on earth . . . ?" I asked before I saw that the carport steps were gone.

"What?" he barked, taking off his regulation hat.

"Nothing," I snapped. "Damnit, you're a real jerk when it comes to letting me know what's going on with this remodel. Why didn't you tell me the carport was coming down today?"

Milo shrugged. "I didn't know it was. I'm not supervising the project. That's Dick Bourgette's job." He opened the liquor cabinet.

"Hey," I yipped. "Don't I get a kiss? And how come you're not changing your clothes before you make a drink?"

"Oh." The sheriff looked pained before he took me in his arms. "Damnit, it's a wonder you don't walk out on me like Mulehide did."

"Too late for that," I said, looking up into his face.

"You're too damned softhearted." His kiss lingered until we both needed to breathe. "I'm still on duty," he said, letting me go.

"What? No poker game?"

Milo took the liquor bottles out of the cupboard. "Doc's delivering a baby — or will be in about ten minutes. Then he has to back up Sung, who hasn't gotten out of surgery. This was Heppner's night to hold down the desk. I made Mullins stick around until I had dinner."

"Can you wait twenty minutes to eat?"

"Sure. Mullins can probably use the extra money. Jack Junior's going to be sixteen in May. He wants a car for his high school graduation present. Speaking of cars, some kids came across an ATV by Anthracite Creek. No registration, but Jack's checking the plate."

I stared at Milo. "Gosh. That sounds like something akin to news. Is the only reason you mentioned it is because J.J.'s hankering for his own wheels, *you big dolt*?"

Milo's expression was innocent as he handed me my Canadian Club. "Hell, I only got the news from Dwight when he came back from patrol as I was leaving. I haven't seen the damned thing. Cal Vickers is towing it to headquarters. I'll check it out when I get back to work. What's the rush? Fleetwood won't hear about it until we tell him."

"I know, but . . ." My shoulders sagged. "I've never figured out if you and your crew really don't recognize news or if you just like teasing me."

"You want to come into the living room

162

and sit on my lap while I explain that to you?"

"I'll come into the living room, but I won't sit on your lap. I have to check the rice and the broccoli."

"Rice again?" Milo said as we left the kitchen. "You got something against Idaho and their spuds?"

"No. Stop asking that. Besides, some of the Grocery Basket's potatoes come from the Moses Lake Basin in this state. This chicken dish is better with rice." I paused to look out through the picture window. "There go the Bourgettes. Are we paying them overtime?"

Milo sank into the easy chair. "They're charging for the overall project. Jesus, stop fussing. You're tying yourself into knots over this."

"That's because you're very lax at keeping me informed. Besides, you didn't let me know Tanya was going to Bellevue today."

"Oh. Guess I forgot." He lighted a cigarette before continuing. "She told me some of the stuff she and Deanna heard from Erin's pals."

"Gee," I said, leaning forward and propping my chin on my hands, "I don't suppose I'd even be remotely interested in what it was."

"I don't know if I should tell you. It could violate father-daughter confidentiality." Milo's eyes strayed to the beamed ceiling. "I wonder if we need a new roof. It must be at least twenty years old. If we do that, we might replace the beams or redo them. They look kind of smoky."

My head sank almost to my knees. "I can't stand it. I really can't."

Milo kept looking at the ceiling.

I sat up straight. "You're drinking on duty. I should report you to the county commissioners."

"Go ahead." He finally made eye contact. "You want to get me fired and end up paying for the remodel all by yourself? God, but you're a perverse little twit. Changed your mind about sitting on my lap?"

I stood up. "No. I have to check the rice." I detoured to kiss the top of his head. "I hate you."

"Right. I'm used to it." He picked up *The Seattle Times* and pulled out the sports section.

I continued on into the kitchen. The rice was done. So was the broccoli. The chicken needed only another five minutes, so I started to dish up. It'd take my aggravating mate that long to finish whatever sports story had caught his eye.

164

"Okay, big guy," I said, leaning against the doorjamb. "Dinner's ready. You through underlining all the words as you go along?"

Milo tossed the paper aside and stood up. "What the hell kind of crack is that? I was reading the box score of the Mariners game against the Angels. You're the one who can't do numbers. I read just as fast as you do. I know that. I've timed you."

"What?" I shrieked as he barged past me. "You did not!"

"The hell I didn't," he shot back, sitting down. "Where's the chicken?"

"Right here," I said, opening the oven. "You want cold food?"

"See what I mean? You can't read a clock."

I placed the baking dish on the table and plopped down in the chair. "Cooking isn't an exact science," I muttered.

Milo helped himself to a chicken breast and heaped sour-cream sauce over his rice. "I was good at science in school."

"I wasn't," I admitted, suddenly feeling childish. "Why are we arguing?"

Milo paused before taking a bite of broccoli. "Because we can."

I reached out to touch his free hand. "You're right. It doesn't matter, does it?"

He shook his head but finished chewing before he spoke again. "Even when Mulehide and I were first married, every argument escalated, no matter how dumb. At least back then, we could make up later on. Then it got to the point where we couldn't do that. She'd go into her deep-freeze mode, I'd go fishing or she'd tell me to sleep on the sofa. Finally, I gave up arguing and just let her badger me. It wasn't worth it anymore. But I never saw it coming when she ran off with Jake the Snake and took the kids with her." His expression was rueful. "That won't happen to us, little Emma. Not after almost sixteen years."

I smiled. "You and I've had time to get to know each other on so many levels. I never really knew Tom very well and Rolf was unknowable by design."

My husband shrugged. "I'll bet neither of them ever bothered to time you while you read a book."

"Milo! Did you really do that?"

"Hell, yes. A couple of weeks ago you were reading in bed and told me you only had three pages to go before you finished and could turn out the damned light. It took you six minutes and forty seconds. Was the print that small?"

I winced. "I kept nodding off."

"I thought you were meditating on what you were reading."

"Let's say the ending wasn't packed with suspense. Now tell me what Tanya had to say about Erin Johnson."

Milo tugged at his left ear. "The boyfriend was of the most interest. One of the girls said he was older, a college student who was transferring to another community college. All she could remember was that his first name was Rick. I had Dustin Fong check the SkyCo Community College records, but among the dropouts from the past year and a half, they found three Richards, four Erics, one Erik, and a couple of last names that began with Rick or Rich. Only three of them could be accounted for in the county. The rest came from somewhere else. We'll keep checking."

"He may never have been enrolled at all," I pointed out.

"Right. It'd be the kind of thing a guy might make up to impress a high school girl." Milo jabbed his fork at his plate. "This is pretty good."

"Chicken is very versatile," I said in a tone that would have done Vida proud — if she could actually cook a chicken that didn't taste like a bald tire. "Did this girl have a description of Rick?"

"She thought he was okay but no hottie, as she put it. One of the other girls thought he was on speed. Tanya figured they were both jealous or some damned thing."

"I meant what he *really* looked like."

Milo grimaced. "Tanya and Deanna talked to three girls, but not at the same time. One said he was six feet, average weight and build, dark eyes, and had a black mullet. I asked Tanya if that was his dog. She told me I was hopelessly uncool. Hell, it sounds like Mullins's hair when he lets it grow too long and it goes all over the place."

I laughed but kept on track. "Did the other girls agree?"

My husband shot me an incredulous look. "Are you nuts? Since when do witnesses ever agree on a description? The second one said he had medium-length light brown hair, bad complexion, sketchy mustache, about five-nine and stocky. Number Three just shrugged and said she thought he looked a lot like Christian Bale. I asked Tanya if that was the new guy at the PUD, but she told me he was the new Batman. Guess I got him mixed up with Chris Bailey, who was hired after Wayne Eriks got killed. I guess if we find somebody in a cape and tights, that's our man."

"It sounds more like Crazy Eights Neffel," I remarked. "He trashed his unicycle, so maybe he'll get a Batmobile. Anything else the teenagers had to say that might be of interest?"

"Not really," Milo said after eating a bite of chicken. "The Ellison girl's boyfriend wasn't a high school student, either. He was supposed to be working for the forest service. Cameron — Cam — Frazier. We checked him out. They never heard of him."

I was taken aback. "You never told me that."

"You never asked. Besides, Blatt — or was it Fong?" He shrugged. "That came to light while I was away from headquarters, working on my house." Milo checked his watch. "Damn. It's going on seven. I'd better go hold down the fort." He took one last bite of his dinner and stood up. "No dessert for me tonight. Of any kind," he added ruefully, leaning down to kiss the top of my head. "Good luck with the bridge bunch."

I started clearing the table. Strange, I thought, how I'd lived alone for so many years and had never minded it. Of course, I'd missed Adam when he went off to college in Hawaii, but he'd only spent a short time with me in my little log cabin after the move from Portland. Now that Milo and I'd been living together — at least off and on, except when he had to stay with Tanya at his house — my home seemed empty without him.

Luckily, there wasn't much time to dwell on such things. I had to be at Edna Mae Dalrymple's house by seven-thirty. She lived less than two blocks away, so I didn't need to drive. As I left my ever-expanding log cabin, I could see the sun sliding down behind Tonga Ridge. The last of the clouds had lifted by the time I'd gotten home, but I'd been too distracted by the Bourgettes to notice. I could smell new-mown grass after I crossed Fir Street. Maybe Edna Mae had spruced up the lawn for her guests.

My hostess greeted me in her usual twittering, friendly manner. "How nice! I was so glad you agreed to fill in for our absentees. Almost everybody is here except Janet Driggers. Do sit and have some wine."

I exchanged greetings with Mary Jane Bourgette, Dixie Ridley, Linda Grant, and the Dithers sisters, Judy and Connie. I was always a bit surprised that they played cards or did anything that didn't involve their beloved horses. Maybe at home they honed their bridge skills by having a couple of their mares sit in. I suppose it wouldn't matter if they had two dummies instead of only one.

I'd just accepted a glass of Riesling that I'd nurse for most of the evening when Janet staggered through the door. "Holy crap!"

she gasped. "Wouldn't you know Al would get horny just as I was changing clothes to come here? When he said he wasn't getting any lately, I thought he meant dead people at the mortuary. Quick, Edna Mae, hand me a bottle of that stuff you're pouring."

Given that we were all accustomed to Janet's big, bad, bawdy mouth, nobody seemed shocked. Whether or not she was telling the truth about her husband was another matter. Al Driggers looked as if his own veins might be filled with formaldehyde. But if nothing else, nobody could call Janet dull.

She zeroed in on me. "Your big stud's got a stiff — as in corpse, that is — stashed someplace, but I hear he's not local. Any way you can coax him into making the dead guy an honorary SkyCo citizen so we can do the funeral? Better yet, can I borrow Dodge for an hour so I can try to have my way with him?"

"The sheriff," I said calmly, "is on duty tonight. You're out of luck, Janet. He's a one-woman kind of guy."

"You mean one at a time," she shot back. "Hey, I don't want to marry him, I just would like to . . ." She broke off as Edna Mae handed her a glass of wine and announced that we should sit at the card tables in order to draw for partners.

"Partners?" Janet echoed. "I already . . ."

I kicked her. Not very hard, but at least she shut up. I drew Connie Dithers as my partner, facing off with Linda Grant and Edna Mae. We cut the cards to see who'd deal. Our hostess got the ace of hearts, causing her to flutter a bit.

"I shouldn't be first," she declared. "It doesn't seem right when you're my guests."

Linda smirked, her cool blue eyes veering in my direction. "Emma should've gotten the ace of hearts. She's the new bride. By the way, congratulations to you and the sheriff. We were all so surprised."

I recalled that before I arrived in Alpine, Linda had made a play for Milo after losing Jake Sellers to Tricia Dodge. Apparently, Linda and Tricia had similar tastes in men. I'd never asked my husband about what had gone on with Linda. That had been then, and this was now.

"Thanks, Linda," I said. "It was a surprise to me, too."

Linda's angular face evinced puzzlement. "You mean you were reluctant after *all these years?*"

"No," I replied calmly. "We'd been engaged for almost two months. I merely didn't expect it to happen at the end of the lunch hour, but it was better than waiting for Tuesday. That's deadline for the *Advocate*. I tend to get distracted, especially if we have breaking . . ."

"Oh, no!" Edna Mae squealed. "I'm short two cards. These decks are new, and I . . . well, perhaps they may stick together."

"Hu-u-u-nh," Connie remarked in what sounded like a whinny. "I had opening points. Shoot."

If Linda had looked puzzled before, she now seemed downright mystified. "That doesn't sound very romantic," she said.

"It was the best we could do," I responded, moving my feet while Edna Mae got under the table to see if she'd dropped the missing cards. "We had to have Judge Proxmire marry us before traffic court started."

Linda looked askance. Edna Mae had scrambled back into her chair and was dealing from the unused deck. For the next few hands we all settled into full-fledged bridge mode. It probably helped that everybody but me seemed to be on their second or even third glass of wine. While we were waiting for the other table to finish, I asked Linda if she knew the girls who had originally been reported as runaways.

"Of course," the high school PE teacher

replied, with only a trace of asperity. "I had them in class. Why do you ask?"

"Background for the paper," I replied. "Tanya Dodge knows the Johnson girl's older sister, Deanna."

"Isn't it up to your *husband* to find out that sort of thing?" Linda didn't exactly sneer, but she came close.

"The last time I looked, Milo wasn't on my payroll," I said pleasantly. "As you may recall, my reporter, Mitch Laskey, and I did a series on child abuse last February. Vida Runkel also featured the subject on her radio show about that same time. The media has to keep on top of social issues. And that includes runaways."

Linda tossed her head, making her blond page-boy hair swing. "I already told Deputy Jamison everything I know about those girls. Surely she or the sheriff shared that information with you."

For some reason, I loathe the word "share" when used in certain contexts. "So," I said, politely, "you agree that the Johnson girl's boyfriend is a speed freak?"

Linda bristled. "I've no idea. I never saw her boyfriend. I don't believe he was a local."

"Rick was attending the college," I noted — and feigned confusion. "His last name

174

was . . . oh, drat, I can't remember."

"Morris," Linda said, looking as pleased as if she'd trumped my trick. "I remember it only because that was my mother's maiden name. No relation, of course," she added hastily.

"Of course," I said as the players at the other table stood up and announced that we should shift places.

I was relieved to have Mary Jane Bourgette as my partner, with Janet and Dixie as our opponents. Naturally, Mary Jane's first question was if Milo and I were pleased with the work her husband and sons were doing. I told her we were. It wasn't her fault — or her family's — that so much noise was involved.

But Mary Jane's pretty face turned puckish. "You haven't run out of earplugs yet?"

I laughed. "Not quite. But we know it can't be helped."

"You could've gone to Milo's house for the duration," she said.

"We might do that when they start on the bedroom," I replied. "I'd rather not. My husband's a poor housekeeper."

"Hell," Janet said, dealing the cards, "if I were you, I wouldn't care if I had to sleep on the frigging floor." She narrowed her emerald eyes at me. "That's assuming you

175

two ever sleep once you hit the sheets."

"Janet," I said firmly, "if you make one more crack like that, I'm going to have to hit you."

"Damn, Emma," Janet murmured, assuming a mock-sulky expression, "I thought you'd enjoy a little teasing after playing the first round with the grim and green-with-envy Linda Grunt."

Dixie sat up very straight and glared at her partner. "Don't talk that way about a member of our high school faculty. You have no idea how hard teachers work. Every year gets more stressful dealing with students. So many of these poor kids are almost illiterate."

Janet fluttered her eyelashes. "That's odd. Not long ago I heard they were reading porn at the high school. Sure, most of it was pictures, which made it easier for your husband's athletes. Wasn't a lot of it found in his basketball players' lockers?" Janet ignored Dixie's outraged expression and kept on talking. "What the hell. I'm bidding three hearts."

That took Dixie's breath away. In fact, I thought she'd pass out when Mary Lou doubled. I felt like I might have a stroke, holding only a lone jack of clubs and even distribution. Janet ended up going set by two tricks. I wondered if she'd done it on purpose to annoy her partner.

While Mary Jane dealt the next hand, I asked the coach's wife why she felt literacy was a growing problem in Alpine. Dixie's answer was predictable: fewer parents who read books, lack of encouraging their children to read, a decline in literacy across the country. She reminded me — as if I needed to be told — that high school librarian, Effie Trews, had addressed the problem on "Vida's Cupboard" back in February.

"I wonder," I said, "if the rise in divorce stats and dysfunctional families has contributed to the situation. For example, we haven't had two runaway girls within such a short time since I moved here."

Dixie, who had spent much of her married life trying to shed the Miss Pasco image that had attracted her football player husband, looked genuinely thoughtful. "The family unit isn't what it used to be," she conceded. "I don't know the Ellisons very well because they're newcomers. Maybe Samantha — that is her first name, isn't it?" She saw me nod. "Maybe she didn't want to move. This was her senior year. I can only guess that she wanted to finish school with her former classmates. That's a big thing for a girl her age. It's possible she simply rebelled. Anyway, she contacted her family to say she was all right, so I suppose they have to take her word for it."

"That makes sense," I agreed, but I couldn't ask anything else because Mary Jane had finished dealing.

The rest of the evening moved along without much conversation except for the usual griping over poor cards, lashing out at opponents, and outraged exchanges between partners. In other words, there was enough drama to fill the time before the party broke up at ten-thirty. I seemed to be the only one who was sober enough to drive, but I was also the only one who could walk home — unless I counted Edna Mae, who wasn't exactly sure *where* she was when we left.

As soon as I took off my jacket, I went into the kitchen to set up the morning coffee while I called Vida. "I hope you learned more from your phone chat with the Ellisons than I did at bridge club," I told her as I ran water into the coffeemaker.

"You people spend too much time playing cards instead of talking," she said. "That's why I've never cared for that sort of thing. It's too distracting. However, Janice Ellison — who did get on as a nurse at the hospital — was reasonably helpful, if vague. She didn't seem overly concerned about her daughter, saying Samantha's always been willful. Contrary to what you may have heard, her mother didn't think the young couple had broken up. A mere tiff, perhaps. Indeed, she thinks they probably ran off together. His name is Cam Frazier. I've never heard of him," she stated in a tone that suggested he probably didn't exist.

"Nobody else has, either," I said, though I didn't want to quote Milo for fear of Vida scoffing at the mere mention of my husband's name. "Have they met Cam?"

"Once or twice," Vida replied. "They thought he had very nice manners. He usually picked up Samantha at the high school. She turns eighteen next month, the legal age of consent to marry. That doesn't faze her mother, who told me, and I quote, 'If it's true love, age isn't important.' I wanted to gag at that comment, but I refrained."

"I don't blame you," I said as Vida paused for breath. "I wonder if the Ellisons married young."

"Perhaps," Vida allowed. "Mrs. Ellison has a rather youthful voice, though you can't always tell over the phone. The third child is only nine, and is named for his father. I suspect Mrs. Ellison is the romantic type. Frankly, I was put off by her rose-colored view of Samantha's defection."

"I don't blame you," I said. "Do the Ellisons have any idea where Samantha and Cam may have gone?"

"No," Vida replied, "though if she had to guess — *guess,* mind you — it would be back to where the family came from — Chehalis."

"Chehalis," I repeated softly and felt a tingling along my spine. Then I realized it wasn't due to the mention of the town midway between Seattle and Portland, but was caused by the doorbell chiming. It was late for a visitor. I wondered if I'd left something behind at Edna Mae's, though I couldn't think what it might be, unless it was my wallet. I'd taken it out to pay my penalty money for going set three times during the evening.

"Got to go," I said to Vida. "Somebody's at the door."

"Who?" Vida demanded, apparently assuming I'd acquired X-ray vision. Why not? I almost believed she had eyes in the back of her head.

"I don't know," I replied, heading for the front door.

"Let Milo answer it," she said. "Oh, I must hang up. Cupcake is carrying on in his cage. Maybe his cover fell off. Canaries can be so capricious. Good night." She hung up just as I got to the door.

I peered through the peephole, but over the years the little glass had become murky. All I could see was a blurry form. When I opened the door, I didn't recognize the stocky, dark-haired man on my porch.

"Mrs. Lord?" he said.

"Yes?" I responded, holding the phone more tightly.

He grinned, revealing crooked teeth. "You want to party?"

"I already did that," I replied, using my free hand to close the door.

But he stopped me by putting his booted foot down to keep the door open. "That's too bad. We're gonna party all night over at Laverne Nelson's place. Hell, why not? All that fucking noise you make during the day gets us in a party mood. You oughta come over. You won't be able to sleep." He laughed in a wheezy sort of way. I could smell liquor on his breath. "We got fireworks, too."

Apparently Dwight Gould hadn't made any impression on the Nelson gang. My first reaction was to tell him I'd call the sheriff, but I was afraid he'd grab the phone. "Go ahead," I said, trying to calm my nerves. "It's a free country."

I tried to close the door, but the jerk wasn't budging. "Aw, shit," he said, "you should come along. You might be kinda fun to party with." He lurched over the threshold and almost knocked me down. "Well? You wanna party with us or party with me here first?"

"Ohhh . . ." We were only a couple of feet from the open door. I hoped he couldn't see the fear in my eyes. "Should I bring some booze?"

The query seemed to surprise him. "Hell, why not? You're a good sport," he said after kicking the door closed and walking behind me to the kitchen. "Whatcha got besides a cute little ass?"

I'd left the kitchen light on. "See for yourself," I said. "Top cupboard to your left."

As he turned his back, I frantically dialed 911, wondering how close Milo's patrol deputy was from my now not-so-cozy log cabin. Mr. Party Dude took out a new bottle of Scotch, a half-empty fifth of Canadian Club, a pint of vodka, and the leftover Christmas holiday rum. "Good stuff," he murmured as I heard the faint voice of 911 operator Evan Singer on the phone.

I didn't dare respond to Evan. "Let me

get my jacket," I said.

"Oh, no," my unwanted visitor declared. "You might take off. We're only going to Laverne's. We'll go this way." He nodded at the kitchen door.

I shrugged, aware that I could no longer hear Evan. "Okay, but give me the Scotch and the C.C. Go ahead, I'll lock the door behind us."

He complied, but his dark eyes narrowed with suspicion. "You pulling a fast one?"

"Do I look like it? I'm loaded down. Let me turn on the carport light." I set the bottles on the counter as I reached for the switch plate by the sink.

"I'm not taking my eyes off of you," he warned.

"Fine," I said. "Just do it."

He did — just as I turned off the kitchen light and plunged the area into darkness. Never was a sound so miraculous as that of the heavy thud on the concrete carport floor and the obscenities that erupted from the jerk's foul mouth. I slammed the door shut and ran to lock up the front. Catching my breath, I leaned against the wall and re-dialed 911.

"Emma!" Evan Singer exclaimed. "What's going on? Dodge is on his way. Can you hear the siren?"

"I . . ." My voice seemed to have been sucked dry by momentary relief. "Yes, I can now," I finally said. "I had a guy force his way into the house and . . ." I staggered to the picture window, pushing aside the drapes I'd closed before leaving. "Milo's here. Thank God. I'll hang up."

The sheriff had pulled into the driveway. I couldn't see him, but I could hear him bellow. Apparently, Mr. Party Dude had managed to get to his feet after falling down the stairs that were no longer there. Milo's voice had grown faint. Maybe he was chasing the would-be perp. Still afraid to open either door, I stood frozen in place until I saw a cruiser pull in behind the Yukon. Dustin Fong got out and immediately headed in the direction of the Nelson house.

The effort to stay calm had taken its toll. Suddenly weak in the knees with a delayed reaction, I managed to stumble to the sofa and collapse. Only then did I realize I was holding the Canadian Club. If I hadn't been shaking so hard, I'd have tried to open it and slug down enough to quiet my nerves. But I didn't have the strength to do even that. Instead, I stayed in a half-sitting position until what seemed like forever, but was probably not more than five minutes before Milo came through the front door.

"Jesus, Emma!" he cried, crossing the room in three long strides and flopping down to put his arm around me. "Are you all right?"

"Yes. I'm just . . . upset." I looked up at him, seeing the distress in his hazel eyes. "He didn't touch me. He was just . . . an asshole."

Milo didn't say anything. He leaned down to press his face against the top of my head for a moment. Then he just held me close and caressed my back. When he finally spoke, his voice was all business.

"I have to go back to headquarters. You're coming with me. I won't leave you alone. Can you manage that?"

"Okay. But . . ."

He put a finger to my lips. "No buts. Those Nelsons are damned dangerous. Gould never got to talk to them today. They either weren't home or they wouldn't come to the door. I should've guessed that would happen. Besides, I busted your intruder, so I have to take your complaint." He finally let go of me and stood up. "I'd tell you to take a swig of that booze, but I don't want anybody to think you were under the influence. Or did you already guzzle a lot of wine at bridge club?"

"I had one glass," I asserted as Milo took

my hands and brought me to my feet. "I nursed it all evening. Damnit, I don't even know who this jerk is."

"I do," the sheriff said as he walked to the door while I put on my jacket. "He had ID. His name is Vince Moro. Does that ring any bells?"

TEN

"Vince Moro?" I repeated as we went outside. "Isn't he Wanda Johnson's ex-husband?"

"He sure as hell is," Milo said, opening the Yukon's passenger door for me. "You're not going to throw up or something, are you?"

I glared at him. "No. I think I've recovered from the shock of it all. But there's a hell of a mess out in the carport."

Milo shook his head and closed the car door. "How," he asked after he was behind the wheel and backing out of the driveway, "did you manage to get rid of him? He was covered in booze and broken glass when I ran him down before he got to the Nelson house."

"It was a long shot," I admitted, "but it worked. Stupid people fall for stupid tricks."

"He fell, all right," Milo said as he turned onto Fir. "I take it he didn't break in. Why did you open the door in the first place?"

I winced. "I almost didn't. But it could've been Edna Mae or one of the Marsdens from next door or . . ." My voice trailed away.

"We're getting a new door with a bigger peephole you can see through," the sheriff informed me. "You've had problems with the doorbell and the lock, too. You complain about my housekeeping, but your home maintenance sucks. Hell, I've done most of it for you over the years, but that was only because I wanted to sleep with you."

"Milo! That's mean!"

He laughed. "Hey, it worked. Don't worry. I still want to sleep with you. You do the housework, I'll do the maintenance. Maybe eventually we'll get used to each other."

I leaned over and grabbed his arm. "You really are awful."

"And you really are an idiot," he said, turning onto Front Street. "Don't *ever* let anybody in when I'm not around."

"What if it's Vida? She'll only come to see me if you're *not* around."

"That's her problem, not mine." Milo pulled into his usual parking spot. "Now I can let Fong go back on patrol."

"How come you showed up? I thought you were working the desk."

Milo looked at me as if I were about as goofy as I felt. "My wife calls 911, can't tell Singer what's going on, and I sit on my dead ass wondering what's happened to her? I didn't give a damn if a freaking fleet of state patrol cars showed up. It scared the hell out of me."

I lowered my eyes. "It scared me, too."

"It should." Even with his face in shadow, I could see how stern he looked. "Damnit, Emma, how many times over the years have I warned you about being reckless? Okay," he went on, seeing that I wanted to defend myself, "never mind that you didn't go looking for trouble tonight — it came to you. But you sure as hell didn't have to open the door."

I hung my head. "I'm sorry. Really."

He sighed. "Right." My husband didn't sound convinced as he opened his car door. "Can you get out without breaking your leg?"

"Yes!" My remorse had turned into anger. I opened my door and was in the street before Milo loomed up on the other side of the Yukon.

He still managed to get to the entrance before I did, but he paused to open one of the double doors for me. "Twit," he said under his breath as we went inside.

Dustin Fong was on the phone, but he hung up just as his boss was opening the half door that led behind the counter. "The perp's locked up," he said after greeting me. "Shall I go back out on patrol?"

"Sure," the sheriff replied. "Keep an eye on the Nelson house. They plan to party. When Blatt comes on duty, pass the word on to him."

"Yes, sir," the ever-polite deputy replied. "Good night, Ms. Lord."

I shook my head as Dustin left. After eight years on the job, he still rarely addressed me as Emma. Since I retained my maiden name in my professional capacity, he wouldn't dream of calling me Mrs. Dodge.

Instead of going into his office, Milo sat down at Lori Cobb's desk. "It's after eleven. We might as well do this here. Do you want to fill out the complaint form or would you like to bang it out on the computer first? I know you screw up when you fill in any kind of form."

I glared at my aggravating better half. "Stop pissing me off or I'll file a harassment complaint against *you.*"

"You would," he said, taking out his cigarettes and lighting up. "I'd offer you one, but we have a No Smoking sign in here."

"Then why don't you arrest yourself?"

Milo just looked at me and blew smoke in my face.

"Give me a pen," I demanded, "and I'll fill out your stupid form."

"You haven't got a pen?"

"I don't have my purse. I left it at home."

He leaned back in the chair and gazed at the ceiling. "Jesus. The rest of the Nelson mob may break in and steal it."

I spotted a pen on the counter and grabbed it. "Give me the frigging form."

Milo acquiesced. "You're so damned ornery. Are you sure Moro wasn't asking to borrow a cup of sugar and you threw him out the back door just for the hell of it?"

"I'd like to throw you out the back door about now," I snapped, starting to fill in my name and address. "Instead of Emma Lord Dodge, can I put Emma Lord Jackass instead?"

"You could, but that would nullify the complaint."

Aware that I couldn't rile the sheriff with an AK-47 when he was reining in his emotions, I complied without another word until I was finished. "There," I said. "Satisfied?"

He read through the form without comment until he'd finished. Too late, I realized

I should've timed him.

"Looks good," he said. "Want to sit on my lap?"

I opened my mouth to yell at him, but stopped. "Damn," I said softly. "Why can't I stay mad at you?"

Milo glanced at his watch. "You did better than usual this time. You stayed mad for eleven minutes."

"Would you stop timing mc?"

"Can't help it. I do it with my deputies. It takes Dwight Gould twenty minutes to fill out a simple two-car-accident report. It only takes Doe Jamison six. Sam Heppner's almost as slow as Gould." He grimaced. "Where the hell *is* Heppner?"

"Where's he from?" I asked. "I've never heard him — or you — talk about his background except that his sister lives in Sultan."

"Neither of them are from here," Milo replied, moving the chair back so he could put his feet on the desk. "Ruth moved to Sultan twenty-odd years ago, when her husband, Phil, went to work for the state highway department. Ruth and Sam grew up in Eastern Washington. Toppenish, I think. After Sam went into law enforcement, she suggested he move over here. He was my first hire as sheriff."

"But you and Sam have never been friends, right?"

Milo shook his head. "I don't want to be friends with my deputies. I've gone fishing a few times with both Sam and Dwight. In fact, I went hunting a couple of times with Sam. Sometimes one of them will play poker. But that's different. Those aren't the kind of situations where you sit around and talk much except about what you're doing."

"Would it help to dig a little into Sam's background?"

"Oh . . . I thought about it, but as I mentioned before, I don't want him to feel as if we're snooping into his private life. Still, if he doesn't show up by Monday, I might have to do some checking." He frowned at me. "I suppose you're already doing that."

"No," I assured him. "I haven't had time. Mitch doesn't know Sam's missing, as opposed to being on vacation."

"Vida might've found out from Bill Blatt."

I shrugged. "If she has, she hasn't mentioned it. Which would be most unlike her. I think Vida has some personal problems of her own. As usual, I suspect whatever it is probably relates to Roger."

"Damn that kid." Milo put out his cigarette. "It's quiet around here. Your intruder must have gone to sleep."

"What happens next with him?"

"He can post bail tomorrow," Milo said with a pained expression. "I didn't know Moro was still around. I thought from what Deanna told Tanya, he'd gone back where he came from after walking out on Wanda, who's gone back to using Johnson as her last name. As I recall, Moro moved here from Wenatchee."

Neither of us spoke for a few moments. "I wonder how he got hooked up with the Nelsons," I finally said. "Maybe he's a drifter and latches on to whatever currently unattached woman is available. With the Nelson males doing time, Laverne and her daughter-in-law may not be the type who can survive without a man for very long. I assume Moro didn't break anything when he fell into what's left of the carport."

"Fong asked if he wanted to see a doctor," Milo replied. "He didn't. The only thing he broke was our liquor bottles. He sure as hell was mad, though. He called you all sorts of names. Then he called me all sorts of other names. But I never let on you were Mrs. Dodge."

"He'll find out from the complaint."

"Good. That should make him think twice about bothering you." Abruptly, Milo swung his legs off the desk and leaned closer. "That does *not* mean you can let your guard down. You got that?"

"Yes, big guy, I've got it. Frankly, I was terrified."

"You should've been." He sat up straight again. "Dustman's taking over the desk while Blatt goes on patrol. I'd better check on our prisoner. He's the only one we've got here at the moment, thank God."

As soon as Milo went off to the cells, I stood up to stretch. I'd been sitting for most of the last five hours — except for the encounter with Vince Moro — and I needed to get my circulation flowing.

Looking out onto Front Street, I could see almost nothing moving. Not a pedestrian in sight, and only two cars and a pickup drove by on this typical late weeknight in Alpine. It was so quiet that I felt as if I stepped outside, I could summon up the past, echoing across the Valley of the Sky from Alpine Baldy to Mount Sawyer. If I listened closely, maybe I could hear the buckers following the instructions of their chaser before a freshly cut tree's choker noose was removed to send it to the holding pond. I'd learned the language of logging late, but it was magic on the old-timers' tongues. Off-bearer. Splitter. Rigger.

Setter. Tallyman. Edgerman. Vida could recite those titles of the trade as if they were poetry and attach names to each job. Clemans. Duell. Engstrom. Bassen. Napier. Jersey. Deveraux. Duffy. Rix. She knew them all, even if most had come and gone before her time. And be damned to the danger of working in the woods. The death whistle sometimes made its mournful cry, but Alpine's early settlers were as strong as they were hardy, almost as mythic today as the Norse gods and goddesses in King Olav's bar.

"He's out like a light," Milo announced, making me jump before I turned around to look at him. "We still have almost half an hour to kill. You want to sit on my lap now?"

"Uh . . . no. What if somebody shows up?"

"They probably won't, but Evan Singer may be ready to take off. He leaves a little early if the movie lets out before midnight. He still closes up the Whistling Marmot. That guy sure knows his movies. Maybe I should pay more attention and get caught up before I embarrass Tanya in public and admit that the last movie I saw on a real screen was *Star Wars*."

"I'm no better," I said. "I saw *Mystic River* on TV and fell asleep."

The phone rang. Milo picked it up, and

instead of his usual "Dodge here" response, he answered with "Skykomish Sheriff's Department." Then he grew quiet, looking resigned. "I'm sorry, Mrs. Grundle," he finally said. "If the Iversens' dog's barking, call them, not . . . Okay, since you've talked to . . . If the barking bothers your cats that much, call Jim Medved. He's the vet. . . . Yes, I know you don't want to bother . . ." He flinched as I heard a high-pitched voice at the other end of the line. Then silence. Milo slammed down the phone.

"Grace Grundle with another complaint about her damned cats. She hung up on me. Are you sure you don't want to sit on my lap?"

I laughed. "Yes, I'm sure. It's almost time to go home. But for some reason, your latest offer reminds me of when I was dithering about marrying Tom and came to ask for your advice."

Milo chuckled. "You were afraid he'd make you give up the *Advocate* and move to San Francisco."

"Right. You suggested I ask if he was willing to move to Alpine — and he was. But before you and I even started talking, I realized I could solve the problem by leaping across your desk and landing in your arms, where I always felt so safe. Why didn't I do that?"

My husband looked stunned. "You're serious?"

"Yes," I said sheepishly. "How dumb was that?"

"The *not* leaping part?" He saw me nod. "You were fixated on the guy. Nothing I could ever do — or did — could change that."

"True," I admitted. "It took him getting killed to destroy my dream. Or delusion. Even then, I had trouble realizing I'd been a fool. But he was my son's father, and Adam wanted to see his parents married. Of course he didn't know Tom was involved with Irish gunrunners. Acknowledging that he was a criminal wasn't easy, either."

"Hell, Cavanaugh thought he was shelling out money for a worthy cause," Milo said. "Misguided, but I figure he needed something all those years to keep from letting his nutty wife make him as crazy as she was. Ah!" he said, standing up. "Here's Fong, with Blatt right behind him. We're out of here."

But we weren't.

"Sir," Dustin said, "do you want me to stick around to process the ATV we found out by Anthracite Creek?"

Milo hesitated. "You're expecting over-time?"

"No," Dustin replied. "But we're short-handed, so I thought if Bill and I had time, we could do it now when it's quiet."

"Oh, hell," the sheriff said. "Mullins is already getting his extra buck-fifty an hour for this evening. I checked it out while I was here, but go ahead, finish the job." He grabbed my arm and we were finally out the door.

"Tell me about that ATV," I said after we were in the Yukon. "Between bridge club and the nasty Mr. Moro, I forgot it had been impounded. Did you say it was found by Anthracite Creek? That's way beyond Alpine Falls and Cass Pond."

"Some college kids found it." Milo paused to eyeball an older Chev that had made a California stop at the arterial on the corner of Fourth and Front. "Damned teen drivers. They shouldn't be out this late, even if it is spring break."

"Are you going to bust them?"

He shook his head. "If they keep cruising, Blatt can nail them. I'm off the clock. What did you . . . oh, the ATV. Yeah, it was less than fifty yards off of Highway 2. A road goes off almost across from the Skykomish Ranger Station. You know where it is, right by the landing strip."

"It's not really all that far away from where the body was found," I said as we climbed the steep hill up to Fir. "Do you think the victim could've driven it?"

"That should be easy enough to find out after we compare any DNA with the vic's. I can't release the body anyway until somebody claims it." Milo had turned the corner by Edna Mae's house, which was now dark. He glanced at me. "The scene of your recent bridge bash. I suppose you grilled whichever faculty members were there."

"I tried," I said. "It's not easy because they're serious about their cards. But I did find out that Erin Johnson's boyfriend's name is Rick Morris. Linda Grant condescended to tell me that much." Just for the hell of it, I shot Milo a sidelong glance to see how he reacted to her name.

"Interesting," he said, pulling into the driveway. "If he's not another high school kid, Erin must've talked about him a lot at school. Maybe we should be interviewing more of the faculty instead of the students. But at least we can now check him out at the college. Are you going to get out, or do I have to carry you?"

My dropping of Linda's name had no apparent effect on Milo. Maybe they'd never been a hot duo. Maybe it was so long ago that he'd forgotten. Maybe I was nuts.

I got out of the SUV and went into the house with my husband. Suddenly my log cabin felt like home again.

ELEVEN

Milo and I both crashed immediately upon arrival. He'd put in over a sixteen-hour day, and I was tapped physically, mentally, and emotionally. I awoke to sunlight seeping through the window shades, the nearby sound of hammering, and the faint smell of bacon. I rolled over to look at the clock. It was 9:08.

I hurtled out of bed, rushing through the hall, the living room, and into the kitchen. Milo was drinking coffee and taking a last bite of toast.

"What's going on?" I shrieked. "I never heard the alarm go off!"

"I didn't set it. I'm not going to work until ten." He leaned back in the chair and stretched. "How do you feel? Besides pissed off, that is."

"I'm late for work," I shot back. "I haven't ever been this late to the office. Why didn't you get me up?"

"Calm down. I called MacDuff and told him you wouldn't be in until ten. If you hadn't been worn out, you wouldn't have slept this late. Go pull yourself together and relax." He calmly lighted a cigarette and picked up *The Seattle Times*.

I didn't have much choice. Twenty minutes later, I'd showered, dressed, and made myself presentable despite the hammering that seemed to be coming through the bathroom wall. Now that I was almost fully awake, I realized I felt refreshed. Having lived together for less than three months and been married for only two, I still wasn't used to having someone looking after me. Not that Milo hadn't tried over the years, but between my fierce streak of independence and my refusal to realize that I needed him as much as he needed me, I'd often balked at his good intentions. Arriving in the kitchen, the first thing I did was to lean down, put my hands on his shoulders, and kiss his forehead.

"Thanks," I said.

I felt him shrug. "You were one little beat-up kitten last night. Luckily, you only walked into the bedroom wall once."

"I vaguely remember that," I said, pouring a cup of coffee. Oddly enough, I didn't feel hungry. Maybe I was still full from all the bridge mix Edna Mae had served. "Speaking of walls, what's happening to the ones on the east side of the house?" I asked as I sat down.

Milo put the paper aside. "Hey," he said, grinning, "you *can* talk when you first get up. You usually cuss and make weird noises."

"You're not any better," I retorted. "Maybe both of us don't sleep enough during the workweek."

"Could be." He looked thoughtful. "Oh — the Bourgettes are starting on that side of the house because you haven't picked out the new appliances. No rush, but it'll mean the bedrooms' wall will have to come down next week. They can do some of the framing first because they want to have all the plumbing done at the same time. Cheaper that way. Want to go on a honeymoon?"

I was taken aback. "I . . . I suppose I could take some time off. But you've got a homicide investigation. That means I've got a big story. Could we wait to see how everything unfolds before making plans?"

"I wasn't thinking of going to Europe," Milo said. "Maybe up to Vancouver. It'll only take the Bourgettes two, three days to enclose that part of the house. Think about it. We don't have to decide right now. You always take forever to make up your mind."

"Where did you go the first time?"

"A dude ranch in southern Oregon." Milo chuckled. "It was Mulehide's idea. She was nuts about horses. Luckily, I knew how to ride, but neither of us had done much of it in a long time. Let's say it wasn't the most comfortable honeymoon we could've had."

I burst out laughing. "Oh, Milo! I've only ridden a horse two or three times in my life, and I was utterly miserable afterward."

"Tell me about it," he said. "Remember how Fuzzy Baugh got a notion to have a sheriff's posse ride in the old Loggerama parade and later in the Summer Solstice shindigs? The first time I did that, I ached for three days. Ever since, I take time out to ride one of the Overholt or Dithers horses, just in case Fuzzy has another crazy idea."

"That reminds me — I should be getting letters today about the mayor's proposal. You never told me what you thought about how Mitch and I handled it in yesterday's edition."

Milo made a face. "I didn't have time, but you'd already told me what you'd write. I'll remember to act surprised when I see Fuzzy."

"He plans to call you and the county commissioners together in the next day or so," I said.

"Damn. I'll have to sit down with those two old coots, Engebretsen and Hollenberg. That I can handle, but it also means I'll have to be almost civil to that asshole Jack Blackwell. He's not going to like Fuzzy's plan."

"You can do it," I said. "It may take some time, but I really believe the voters will come around to the idea as long as they can be convinced it'll save them money."

"Guess I'd better read what you and Laskey wrote," Milo said a bit sheepishly. "Are you going to eat something, or should we saddle up, to borrow a phrase from my ill-fated honeymoon days?"

"I'll grab whatever pastries are at the office," I replied. "Unless Ed Bronsky's shown up, there should be some left. By the way, did you clean up the mess my intruder made out in the carport?"

Milo shook his head. "The Bourgettes did that. They thought we must've had one hell of a party here last night."

"Some party," I muttered, getting up to unplug the coffeemaker. "Let's ride, cowboy."

"You might as well ride with me," Milo said. "No point taking two cars. I'm not putting in more overtime, even if a bomb goes off at the courthouse." He put his arms around me. "Hey, we've never made love in the morning. Want to try that?"

I looked up at him. "With the Bourgettes playing the Anvil Chorus outside of the bedroom? No thanks, big guy. We have to earn a living."

Milo kissed the top of my head and let me go. "What the hell. It was worth a shot."

I smiled at him. "By the way, I like being married."

He smiled back. "So do I. It's a lot better the second time around. And somehow I can't picture you riding a horse."

Amanda's greeting was friendly, as usual. Kip was in the back shop, and both Leo and Mitch were out on their rounds. Vida, however, looked fit to spit when I entered the newsroom.

"Well? What on earth happened to make you so late?"

Just to remind her that I was the boss, I ignored the question. My priority was getting a cinnamon roll and a mug of coffee before I sat down in her visitor chair.

"Has Mitch checked the sheriff's log yet?" I asked.

"Probably," Vida replied, tight-faced. "He was going to interview Fuzzy about reaction to his proposal regarding our government. Well?"

I felt smug, knowing that Vida wouldn't have been able to coax even a small scrap of information out of Bill Blatt because he'd been on all-night patrol. "I had an intruder," I said matter-of-factly. "I had to call 911. You should have stayed on the phone with me instead of tending to Cupcake."

"What?" Vida squawked, sounding like a much larger bird than any canary. "Where was Milo? Out drinking beer with Doc Dewey?"

"My husband was on duty. They're short-handed with Sam Heppner taking a few days off. Surely Bill must've told you that."

Vida looked briefly flummoxed. "He did not. I don't insist on Billy telling me every whim of the other deputies. I only inquire about more pressing matters, given that his superior is so tight-lipped about the public's need to know."

I shrugged and stood up. "You'll see all about it when Mitch gets back with the log. I have work to do." I stalked off to my office.

And immediately felt ashamed of myself, though I wasn't sure why. I was fed up with Vida's negative attitude about Milo. She'd put our long-standing and close friendship to the test. Did she really expect me to choose between her and my husband? There was no one I could ask about changing her mind. Her three daughters were cowed by their mother, and Buck Bardeen had previously shown that he didn't dare risk offending her. As long as she would never admit that Roger was a worthless jerk, I was sunk. And so was our friendship.

Over the long years of being a single mother while working in Portland on *The Oregonian* and later when I'd unexpectedly inherited enough money to buy the *Advocate* and a used Jaguar, I'd had little time to make close friendships or long-term romances. The only real friend I'd had in Oregon was one of my co-workers, Mavis Marley Fulkerston. Ironically, her reaction was negative when she found out Milo and I were engaged. But she only knew of the sheriff from the befuddled state of mind I'd been in when I'd broken up with him a decade ago. I'd finally managed to set her straight. Vida was a different matter. Thus, I did what I've always done when faced with personal problems. I threw myself into my work. It was my armor against an often hostile world.

And there was plenty to do this Thursday morning, in the wake of Fuzzy's bombshell.

The mail had arrived, with over two dozen letters. Phone messages totaled another fifteen, with at least as many emails. It'd take much of the day to respond. Happily, the first four phone calls turned out to be positive. I was about to dial the fifth number when Mitch showed up, a little after ten-thirty. For once, he didn't look glum.

"Baugh's getting some positive feedback," he informed me. "The only negatives are from Engebretsen and Hollenberg. But you'd expect that, right? Why do they care? They're both way beyond retirement age. They can bow out in a blaze of glory."

"Ego," I said. "They've been commissioners since before I came to Alpine. Nothing from Blackwell?"

"Not yet." Mitch had draped his lanky frame over one of my chairs. "He won't like it. But how do we handle the log? Mullins told me that one of the calls was from you. Is that why you came in late this morning? Dodge wasn't there when I checked in, but Mullins told me he'd pulled night duty. I gather Heppner's on vacation."

"It was no big deal," I said. "A drunk partying with my awful next-door neighbors barged in and I couldn't get rid of him. Run it like we always do — no name, just an address and the complaint."

Mitch looked puzzled. "But the guy's locked up. Are you intending to file more serious charges against him?"

"No. I hope spending overnight in a cell will teach him a lesson. As far as I know, he doesn't live at the Nelson house. It's no big deal."

Mitch didn't look convinced. "I know you're married to the sheriff, but still . . . it seems like more than a drunken prank. You've had trouble with those Nelsons before, right?"

"Yes," I admitted. "Their two younger kids tried to set my house on fire last December while you were gone. But they're locked up, and so are the father and the eldest son. They were the maple tree poachers."

Mitch was like a dog with a bone. He didn't let go easily — an attribute of a good reporter. "Do you know this Moro other than from when he showed up last night?"

"No, but he used to be married to the mother of the missing Johnson girl." I suddenly realized where Mitch was going with his questions. Or at least in what direction I could steer him. "Moro supposedly left town after Mrs. Johnson divorced him. Maybe you could do some checking. I think he's being released today. What did Mullins tell you?"

211

"He was waiting for Dodge. You're sure the guy's not a threat?"

I frowned. "I think it was retaliation. Laverne Nelson filed a complaint against me about all the construction noise. I don't think she knows Milo and I are married. I suspect Vince Moro was showing the Nelson women what a macho stud he is. Maybe he's more dangerous than I think. See if he's got a rap sheet."

Mitch went away with a gleam in his eyes, the kind that serious journalists have when they smell a story. He'd mastered his craft with twenty-five years on the *Detroit Free Press*. While his moodiness might be irritating, he was the only seasoned reporter I'd ever had on the staff. The others had all been young and relatively fresh out of college. If there was any spare cash in the *Advocate* account, I'd give him a raise.

As soon as he left, Vida tromped into my office. "I couldn't help but overhear. I thought I was helping with coverage of the runaways."

"You are. You're doing background. Hard news takes away from your House & Home page." Thinking fast to dig myself out of a hole, I continued: "My intruder last night was Vince Moro, Wanda Johnson's ex. You mentioned that she and your Meg were close at one time. Now that you've talked to Mrs. Ellison, do you have time to call on Wanda?"

To my surprise, Vida didn't look appeased. "If I do, I'll phone," she said. "By the way, I've invited Helena Craig, the high school counselor, to be on my radio program tonight. I shall be asking her some questions about the problem of runaway teens."

I tried to keep my tone light. "Good. Just remember the rule: no news that should appear first in the *Advocate.*"

Vida's face was expressionless, but her gray eyes were cold. "I'm not responsible for what the people on my program say." She turned around and made her imperial exit from my office.

By noon, I was tired of talking to callers and reading letters and emails — even if a slight majority was in favor of the mayor's proposal. The phone calls had ended up fifty-fifty so far, with several on the fence. Of course, the undecided asked questions I couldn't answer, so I directed them to Fuzzy's office. Predictably, the letters tended to be against the idea, while the emails, from computer users, favored change.

At a few minutes after noon, the newsroom was empty. On a whim, I opened the phone directory for Sultan listings — and realized I didn't know Ruth Heppner's married name. I recalled that her husband was Phil. Sultan's population wasn't much larger than Alpine's. It didn't take long to find Philip and Ruth Bowman. The hard part was figuring out what I'd say.

Inspiration struck when I scanned the latest edition of *The Monroe Monitor.* I dialed the number and, as I hoped, a woman answered. "Ruth?" I said. "This is Emma Lord at *The Alpine Advocate.* I don't suppose your husband, Phil, is around, but I have a question for him that maybe you can answer. How close to being done are they on Highway 522 outside of Monroe?"

"Well . . . about halfway, I guess." Her voice was wary. Maybe she'd never heard of me. "Phil's not working on that. He's tied to a desk these days. Do you want his number?"

"Yes, thanks," I replied. "There was another big pileup here this week. We keep hoping the state will make this stretch less hazardous. Did Sam mention the wreck?"

"No," she said. "I haven't talked to Sam lately."

"That's okay. Say, I heard he took some time off. Do you know what his plans were? We always do a feature on Alpiners who take trips out of town. Last month one of the other deputies went to Cabo San Lucas." That was an outright lie, but Ruth wouldn't know it.

"Sam didn't tell us what he was going to do." She paused, and I suspected she was about to ring off. "He hardly ever leaves the area," she said to my mild surprise, "but I guess he's gone somewhere this time. I tried to call him last night and he wasn't home."

"So I understand from the other deputies," I said. "That makes his vacation story all the more interesting. Is there any chance he went back to Toppenish to visit old friends and family?"

"No!" Her voice had turned sharp. "That's the last place he'd go." Another pause followed. "There's someone at the door. Sorry I can't help you." She rang off.

Ruth wasn't half as sorry as I was.

I decided to eat lunch after all, so I headed for the Burger Barn. Once inside, I wondered if the sheriff had nipped across the street from his office to refuel. As usual, the restaurant was busy during the noon hour. My husband was nowhere in sight, so I got in the take-out line behind three teenaged boys — and suddenly felt a hand on my shoulder.

"What are you doing, little Emma?" Milo asked.

I slumped against him. "You scared me. I was looking for you."

He put his arm around me. "I ate a late breakfast, so I wasn't hungry until now. Let's grab a booth."

We found one toward the rear that had just been vacated. "I did something on a whim," I said a bit sheepishly.

Milo waited for the pretty redheaded waitress whose name was Cindi to bus our table. "Okay," he said. "Will it make me mad?"

"Well . . ." I took a deep breath. "I called Ruth Bowman."

The sheriff looked puzzled. "Ruth . . . ? Oh, you mean Sam's sister?" He grimaced. "Why the hell did you do that?"

"Because I was tired of dealing with responses to Fuzzy's plan and fighting an urge to can Vida's ass, that's why."

Milo paused again, this time for Cindi to bring mugs and pour our coffee. "Jesus," he said after we were alone again, "maybe you should fire her. That's about the only thing you can do that'll make her stop acting like a horse's ass. She'd have to finally choose — between the *Advocate* and Roger. If there's one thing she loves as much as that jerk, it's having her own platform in the paper."

"She's got 'Vida's Cupboard' and she's hosting the high school counselor tonight about the runaways," I said. "I already warned her to make sure to avoid hard news that should go in the *Advocate* before it's broadcast over KSKY. She was snarky about that, too."

"It's your call," Milo responded. "Vida's always acted as if she runs the paper. I don't know how you've put up with her all these years. Sure, I know you like her, but lately . . ." He shook his head. "I don't give a shit what she thinks about me. I know you two have been friends from the get-go. Do what you have to. I shouldn't give advice. I've got my own crew to run. Tell me why the hell you called Ruth. That *is* my problem."

I couldn't answer right away because Cindi returned with our cutlery and napkins to ask for our orders.

"I told you," I said as Skunk and Trout Nordby, the GM dealership owners, acknowledged us from across the aisle. "It's a story. I mean, if Sam doesn't show up."

Milo leaned closer and lowered his voice. "It's not a story. It's an internal problem. Now Ruth may figure I put you up to it.

The last thing I want is for Heppner to think I'm prying into his private life. That was a damned stupid stunt for you to pull."

The sheriff was right. I'd acted on a whim. Milo had confided in me not as the local media, but as his wife. It was one of the many pitfalls in our professional lives. I'd crashed and burned on the first stretch of the learning curve.

"I'm sorry. Really," I said. "If it helps, I don't think Ruth knew who I was. Even if she did, would she know we were married?"

Milo considered. "Maybe not. Sam isn't the type to talk about stuff like that. He's even worse than Dwight when it comes to being interested in other people. For all I know, he still thinks I'm married to Mulehide."

The hint of humor in my husband's voice made me feel a little better. "I won't do it again."

"Yes, you will. It's your nature." He shut up as Cindi delivered his cheeseburger, fries, and salad and my plain burger with the same sides.

"I mean it," I asserted after Cindi had left us. "I really will try."

"Hell, Emma, you can't. It's built into your own job. Just don't expect me to like it." He took a bite out of his burger that would have done justice to a shark.

"Ruth told me he'd never go back to Toppenish."

Milo's hazel eyes snapped. "She did?"

I nodded. "I wonder why."

"See? That's what I mean. You can't help it."

"Come on, big guy. You're curious, too."

The sheriff didn't comment. When he spoke again, it was on a different topic. "I had to let Moro go this morning. All I could nail him for was a trespassing fine."

"He didn't have to post bail?"

"You filed a complaint that stated he intruded and scared you. The dink started to give me crap because I had him locked up. I told him he needed to get sober. He couldn't argue that point."

"Did he give you an address?"

"Yeah." Milo looked irked. "The trailer park. It was the one on his driver's license from two years ago when he and Wanda were still together, but my bet is he's shacked up with the Nelsons."

"Great. Does he know we're married?"

"I doubt it. He didn't look at your complaint. But I don't want you going to the door when you're alone. I never know when I'll be called out, including the middle of the night, and especially now when we're short-staffed. I don't want to put Blatt on extra duty if he's getting serious with Tanya. It's good for both of them. And she's not hanging out with us."

"Amanda and Walt may be interested in your house," I said.

"Oh? He makes a decent salary at the hatchery. They could afford it even if she doesn't work after the kid gets here." He grimaced. "Then what do we do with Tanya? Bill still lives at home."

I looked helplessly at Milo. And wondered if we'd ever lead a normal married life. What *was* "normal"? Never having been a wife, I really didn't know.

Back at the office, Vida seemed somewhat more cheerful. I decided to take advantage of her improved disposition by asking if she'd like to do an interview with Clarence Munn about the heyday of logging.

"Well now," she said, "if he makes sense, that might be interesting. Shall I inquire about the less savory things that went on back then?"

"Sure. You can determine if they're worthy of publication. They just might goad readers into realizing that a firm hand on the reins of government can prevent any repeats. After all," I went on, trying not to sound ingratiating, "you know enough about Alpine's history to discriminate between idle gossip and just plain fiction."

"True," Vida allowed, "though apparently there were some things I missed, being too young and naïve to realize the illicit activities that went on. My parents could be closemouthed when it came to such delicate matters. Rather foolish in retrospect, perhaps."

Rather incredible, I thought, that Vida hadn't learned how to apply thumbscrews at an earlier age. It was more likely that the Blatts had turned a deaf ear to unseemly behavior, though I recalled that her father was rumored to have been less than saintly, at least when he was away on business. If true, that might be the reason for discretion on the home front.

"I'll call on Clarence tomorrow," she said. "I have to go through the latest letters for my advice column. Spring causes romantic follies. So many people fall in and out of love, especially this year. I suspect it has to do with the lack of rain."

"Possibly," I conceded. "Anybody we know?"

Vida looked vaguely affronted. "We're not supposed to know, since the letters are

221

unsigned. But of course one can often guess."

"Speaking of spring," I said, "now that I've finished paving the way for Fuzzy's proposal, I think I'll do an upbeat editorial about the recent improvement in the local economy. There've been a lot of new jobs created by RestHaven's impact along with the Alzheimer's wing they plan to build and the opening of the fisheries building at the college next week. The timing on that one is especially good, since Mitch will cover the dedication. The best news is that we have the lowest number of the unemployed since I got here."

"Indeed," Vida agreed — and beamed. "Roger is one of the newly employed. I'm so proud of his ambition."

I hid my surprise — or maybe it was shock. "What's he doing?"

"An out-of-town firm is hiring delivery people in this part of the state," Vida said. "As you know, we've lost at least two of our truckers in the last few months. I assume it's rather like a freelance job, to fill in for whoever needs short-haul trucking."

"That sounds very good," I stated with what I hoped was sincerity. "Does the company supply the trucks?"

"No," Vida replied. "Amy and Ted bought

him a nice secondhand van from the Nordby Brothers. He has his first assignment tomorrow. I'm glad he won't be driving one of those big eighteen-wheelers. They can be quite dangerous."

"Where's the company located?" I asked. "We should do a story on it, since it's a new service for SkyCo."

Vida laughed self-deprecatingly. "I was so thrilled that I forgot to ask Roger. But I will. In fact, perhaps we could feature him in the story. As far as I know, he's the only one they've hired from Alpine."

Me and my big mouth. Images of Roger posing all over the front of the *Advocate* leaped into my mind's eye. Talk about doing a spread — Roger's rear end could fill up four columns. The newspaper term "double truck" suddenly had new meaning. But the story itself would fit nicely into my proposed editorial about the local economy. In fact, "Roger Gets A Job" should be a banner headline.

"Just let me know by the first of the week," I said, wondering how low I could go to restore Vida's goodwill. Maybe things really were looking up on the local scene. If Ed Bronsky became fully employed, I might have to put out a special edition.

I left Vida still smiling. That was worth a

little fawning and even a few inches of copy about Roger.

Later, I'd look back on this moment and wonder how I could have been so blind.

TWELVE

Mitch was still sniffing news when he returned around two-thirty. "I got Doe Jamison to run Moro through the system for me. Nothing major — check fraud a couple of times, two minor assault charges, a few DUIs, but not close enough together to get his license pulled. The only local crime he committed was using somebody else's credit card in Gold Bar, but he talked his way out of that one."

He'd paused, and I assumed he was waiting for my comment. I started to open my mouth to oblige, but he'd sat down in one of the visitor chairs after glancing out into the empty newsroom, apparently to make sure we couldn't be overheard. "There were four calls to his previous address on Cedar Street for domestic violence when he was married to Wanda Johnson. No charges filed. Typical. Battered wives make a big mistake not nailing the guy."

225

"She dumped him," I pointed out, "but he left her broke, forcing her to move to the trailer park. Now her daughter is our latest runaway."

Mitch nodded. "Makes you wonder, but that's not my point. Yet. Mrs. Johnson had to learn the hard way. I noticed the trailer park was the address on his driver's license last night when Fong brought him in after he barged into your house. Did you scc that?"

"Milo mentioned it. He thought it was because the driver's license was issued two years ago. Oh!" I clapped a hand to my cheek. "I see what you're saying. If Wanda moved there only last fall, then Vince never lived at the trailer park. That's odd."

"That's not the only thing that's odd," Mitch said, a wry smile tugging at his mouth. "My first big story here was the Holly Gross disaster, when she offed the leader of the local drug ring while they were holding Vida hostage. I got there after all the action was over, but I worked on the coverage with you. Wanda is living in Holly Gross's trailer. She must've moved in there after Holly was arrested. Go ahead, Emma. You can add two and two."

"Barely," I admitted, but realized where Mitch was going. "Moro was another one of Holly's customers, either for drugs or prostitution. Maybe that's where the creep felt at home."

"That occurred to me," Mitch agreed. "He got that license renewed either just before or after his wife filed for divorce. He wasn't there the night everything came down. Now he's hanging out at your neighbor's place while the menfolk are locked up. I can't help but wonder."

"Wonder what?" I asked.

Mitch's thin face turned grim. "That's the problem. I don't know. But I think it's worth thinking about, don't you?"

As Mitch left my office, I realized why Vida wasn't eager to call on Wanda. Last October's trailer park tragedy had revealed not only Roger's fathering of a child by the town hooker, but that he was doing drugs purchased from Holly. Vida had removed her rose-colored glasses and seen Roger for what he really was. But that reality check bounced. It had taken only a month before she began regarding him as a hero for giving the sheriff valuable information on the drug operation. If Milo hadn't grudgingly gone easy on the kid, he'd have been busted, too. After Holly was later let out on bond and tried to reclaim Dippy, my House &

Home editor had revoked any gratitude she might have felt toward the sheriff.

If Vida wouldn't visit the trailer park, I would. Grabbing my purse, I stood up to put on my jacket — and remembered I didn't have my car. Spruce was all uphill, the street just north of my house. I wasn't in the mood to walk that far. Maybe I was still worn out from last night's unpleasant activities. I'd take the easy way out and call the sheriff.

Lori Cobb answered. "The boss went to Monroe," she informed me in her pleasant voice. "Can we do anything for you?" She sounded dubious, perhaps thinking my call was domestic instead of business.

"Maybe," I replied. "Who's on patrol?"

"Doe Jamison. Do you have something to report?"

"No, but I wondered if Wanda Johnson has been interviewed again about her runaway daughter. She's living at the trailer park, you know."

"Sam Heppner talked to her Monday morning," Lori said, "but she couldn't add anything except that maybe Erin had gone off with the guy she'd been seeing. Mrs. Johnson thought they'd broken up."

None of that was news to me. Even when Sam was on the job, his people skills weren't finely honed. I was tempted to make a suggestion that Doe interview Wanda but realized she had other duties to perform. As shorthanded as the sheriff was, the patrol deputy might be covering the whole county and even some of the highway.

"I'll try to pay Wanda a call tomorrow," I said — and suddenly wondered why Milo had gone to Monroe. He wasn't just my husband, but my ride home. "When do you expect your boss to be back?"

"I don't know," Lori replied. "He only left about fifteen minutes ago. It's a fairly long drive, at least an hour round-trip. Are you sure there isn't something we can do for you?"

"No, I was just curious — about dinner. Thanks, Lori." I hung up. If Milo didn't get back by five, maybe I'd ask Leo to take me home. My house was just five blocks up from his apartment on Cedar Street.

My phone rang, and to my delight it was Adam. I hadn't talked to him in over two weeks. The connection between St. Mary's Igloo and Alpine was iffy at best, so we usually emailed instead. Thus, I was startled when his voice came through clear, if not loud.

"Where are you?" I asked, wondering if he'd miraculously come down to the Lower

Forty-eight.

"Nome," he replied. "I had to fly here with a new mom from the village who had twins — and complications. I was lucky to get a bush pilot to collect us in time."

"Is everybody okay?"

"Yes, everything's fine, but I guess I missed the seminary class on delivering babies. Our midwife got a bad case of flu and couldn't help except to tell me what to do."

"You . . . ?" I was speechless.

"We had to leave the dad behind. Not enough room on the plane. He's probably a nervous wreck, but we'll head back tomorrow. What's up with you, pretty and wise mother of mine?"

"What do you want? Or is it a need?"

"If you call clothing a need, then it is. A nude priest makes a poor impression. Besides, summer's coming, and that means mosquitoes the size of a 747. I'll email you my list. How's the annulment going?"

"Well . . . Milo's been busy with readying his house for sale and the remodel here. He planned to see Father Den to get some advice, but our pastor went to visit family in Houston."

"Has Dodge talked to Mulekick?"

"Mulehide," I corrected him. "Try to call

her Tricia. I'm working on that, too. No. He hasn't been down to Bellevue since February."

"Do I hear the sound of dragging feet?"

"No. I mean . . . really, we've been up to our ears. You forget we both have jobs. Don't worry, we'll do it. How could we not with you and your uncle nagging us?"

"Hey, I should call that rascal while I'm in Nome. I want to hear about his new assignment in El Paso. I better go, Mom. Got two small mouths to feed. Bet you never thought I'd say that."

"You're right. I had no idea where your vocation would take you. Delivering babies was never on the list of duties I thought you'd be carrying out."

"Me neither. But it's kind of a hoot, now that I did it without bouncing one of the kids off the floor. Prayers, Mom. Love you. The list is yet to come."

I sat back in my chair and smiled. Who knew? My irresponsible son who couldn't make up his mind about anything except which girl to take out or which kegger to attend had made me proud. Not that I'd had much to do with it. He was more Ben's son than mine. I'd resented that for a while, but now that I was married and had a man of my own, I could take a certain amount of pride in having kept Adam out of jail for the first twenty years.

I spent the rest of the afternoon sorting through more of the responses to Fuzzy's brainstorm. The most outlandish of these came from an unknown source who had written that we should abolish Skykomish County altogether and throw in our lot with King or Snohomish County because they had money to burn. Knowing that both those huge entities were growing so fast that they, too, were strapped for cash, I figured this reader hadn't done his or her home-work. At least that was one letter I wouldn't print in the *Advocate*. Unsigned missives were never published, which saved me from being called a wacko left-wing dirtbag — or worse.

Just before five I called to ask if the sheriff had returned from Monroe. Lori informed me he hadn't, so I told her I'd get a ride home from someone on my staff. Vida had already left to prepare for her radio show, Kip had a four o'clock dental appointment, Mitch was always anxious to get home to Brenda, and I didn't want to bother Amanda, who seemed more and more tired by the end of each workday. Luckily, I still had my first choice of Leo.

"Damn, babe," he said, "I can't. My car's

in the shop. The fuel pump went out, and it won't be ready until tomorrow. I planned to walk home. It's only two blocks, and it's nice out."

"That's okay," I said. "I'll wait for Milo at his office."

"I'll walk you to the corner," he said, putting on his sport coat. "Hey, the Duchess seemed in a better mood this afternoon. How come?"

"You won't believe this, but Roger has a job." We both paused to say good night to Amanda, who was about to leave, too. "He's going to be making short-haul deliveries."

"Of what?" Leo asked, opening the door for me.

I shrugged. "Whatever anybody wants delivered. It's an out-of-town company. When Vida tells me who and where they are, you should hit them up for an ad."

Leo frowned as we passed the dry cleaners. "If they've been around for a while, I wonder why I haven't heard of them already."

"I gather SkyCo is new territory for them. For all I know, they're located in Everett or even Seattle."

"Could be," Leo said we got to the corner. "It's not a bad idea. Competition for UPS and FedEx, maybe with cheaper rates. If they've been in business awhile, they probably know what they're doing. They've got a lot of those smaller delivery services in the metro areas. See you tomorrow — and don't forget 'Vida's Cupboard.' "

"Required listening for all of SkyCo," I asserted, waving Leo off and continuing along Front past the hobby shop and Parker's Pharmacy. I nodded to an older couple from St. Mildred's that I knew by sight if not by name. The Yukon wasn't parked in its usual place, so I assumed Milo wasn't back from Monroe.

Lori came out as I went in. We exchanged a brief greeting in passing. Bill Blatt was behind the counter, looking as if he'd just come on duty. "Two nights in a row?" I said. "How'd you get so lucky?"

"Well . . . I don't mind," Bill said. "We're all doing extra with Heppner gone. Anyway, I have nothing better to do."

I smiled. "You mean Tanya's still in Bellevue?"

Bill's ruddy complexion darkened. "She'll be back tomorrow. I made dinner reservations at Le Gourmand. She's never been there. It wasn't around when she lived here before. Do you think she'll like it? I mean, she's used to those fancy places in Bellevue."

I leaned my elbows on the counter. "Tanya isn't exactly a high-flying Eastsider. For all you know, her favorite eatery is Guido's Pizzeria."

Bill grimaced. "Maybe so, but she's not used to small towns anymore. I know she insists she can't stand living in Bellevue because of all the bad memories, but she'll get over that. Heck, she's there now. I've never liked big cities. I feel like a rube compared to her. What would she see in a guy like me?"

"Gosh," I said, "I actually know some other guy who had that idea about a city girl. Guess what? He was wrong."

"You mean . . . ?" Bill's gaze had moved beyond me to the entrance.

I turned around as Milo came through the door. "Yes," I said under my breath. "That guy."

"What guy?" my husband asked, putting a big paw on my shoulder and looking at his deputy. "Mullins just pulled in. You better hit the road."

"Yes, sir," the deputy replied, grabbing his regulation hat. "I'm out of here."

"Stay put," Milo said to me. "I've got to go into my office." He loped off through the open area to his inner sanctum — and closed the door.

"No girls allowed?" Mullins said with his puckish grin as he settled in behind the counter at the desk.

"I guess. What's up?"

"Don't ask me," Jack replied, running a hand through his untamable red hair. "I just got here. Man, I hope Heppner shows up soon. This extra duty is killing me. I'm even starting to miss my wife."

"How many times do I have to tell you to stop talking that way about Nina? Why is it so hard to admit you're crazy about her?"

"Because she drives me crazy? Hey, speaking of spouses, I've been meaning to ask," he went on with a glance over his shoulder and lowering his voice, "how did you get your big stud to Mass on Easter?"

"I told him my immortal soul depended on it. Besides, I played on his vanity by saying I wanted to show him off in that sport coat I bought him for his birthday."

"I've never seen the boss dressed up like that. Nina told me that was one expensive jacket. He looked damned sharp. At first, I thought you'd taken a lover."

"He bitched and moaned when I gave it to him, but I insisted he get new slacks from Warren Wells to go with it. I told him I bought the sport coat from Penney's through their sale catalog. Warren didn't let on that it came from his store."

Jack laughed and shook his head. "I didn't know Dodge had any vanity. That almost makes him human."

My expression may have conveyed that I was the only one who knew how human Milo really was. I'd seen him at every extreme of human emotions since I first met him on an overly warm day in August 1989. His self-esteem was still at a lower ebb after his wife's betrayal, though he hid it well. He was a different man back then — much quieter, less vocal, and seemingly laid-back. It took me a long time to figure him out — and when I did, I'd almost lost him. It was only recently that I'd realized he'd known me much better than I'd ever known him.

I changed the subject. "Jack, did you ever get called to any of those domestic disturbances when Vince and Wanda Moro were still married?"

Jack grinned at me. "You doing background on your intruder?"

"I'm doing background on why his ex-stepdaughter ran away," I replied. "I'd heard Moro had gone back to Wenatchee, but now he's here. I wonder if he's been pestering Wanda and maybe Erin."

"If he has," Jack said, "we haven't had any calls lately. Wanda took her previous name back, you know."

"I gathered that," I said, frowning at the sheriff's closed door. "What's he doing in there?"

Jack looked down at the telephone console. "He's talking to somebody. Don't ask me. I wasn't here when he took off. I don't even know where he went."

"Monroe." It wasn't a secret mission, since Lori had told me where he'd gone. "What's in Monroe besides the correctional facility?"

"Maybe you can wheedle it out of him at home," Jack said, then held up his hands. "I know, I know. If the boss man doesn't feel like telling you everything about his job, he won't. Does that bother you?"

I shook my head. "I'm used to it."

Jack nodded absently. "As for the Moro dustups, I was only there for one of them. It looked to me as if Wanda had some bruises, but there wasn't any blood. They'd both calmed down by the time Dwight and I arrived, and it was the usual bullshit. Just a difference of opinions, no harm, no foul. You know how that goes."

"Sad," I remarked, looking up as Milo finally appeared.

"You're on your own, Mullins," he said. "Don't screw up."

Jack feigned innocence. "Gosh, boss, did I ever?"

"How high can I count?" the sheriff murmured before grabbing my arm. "What's for dinner?"

"Chicken," I said.

"If it is," Milo said, looking back over his shoulder at Jack, "the next domestic brawl you'll get is from our house."

Once we were in the Yukon, I refrained from asking my husband why he'd gone to Monroe. In fact, we drove up Fourth Street without either of us speaking. I could tell he was preoccupied, but I decided to wait until we were home and he had a drink in hand.

"Well?" he finally said as we turned onto Fir. "How come you're so quiet? Did you fire Vida?"

"She improved this afternoon," I replied. "Roger has a job."

Milo snorted. "The hell he does. What's he doing? Testing new brews at Mugs Ahoy?"

"I'll tell you after I've foraged for steaks in the freezer. If I get frostbite, you can take me to the ER."

"Don't forget the spuds," he said, pulling into the driveway.

"I won't. Hey — where's my car? It's gone!"

"The Bourgettes had to move it to roll the logs out of the way. It's parked over at the Marsdens' house. I told them to take your extra set of keys. I'll go get it after dinner."

I glared at Milo instead of getting out of the SUV. "I really would appreciate it if you'd keep me informed about what's going on around here. Every day seems to bring a new surprise."

"You'd just fuss even more than you do already. Are you going to sit there and stew or should I go look for those steaks?"

"Ohhh . . ." I exited from the Yukon and all but ran to the front door.

Naturally, I had trouble with the key.

"Give me that," Milo said, grabbing my wrist. "How the hell you ever got along without me I'll never know."

"Well, I did," I declared, but I refused to look at him after we entered the house.

My husband kept his mouth shut for once, and ambled off into the hall, presumably to change clothes. I found two rib steaks in the freezer, thawed them in the microwave, and made our drinks. I was peeling potatoes when the sheriff showed up in the kitchen.

"I could've made the drinks," he said, coming up from behind and putting his arms around my waist.

I leaned against him. "You had a long

drive. Was traffic a pain?"

"Just the usual morons who don't know how to drive Highway 2. They haven't replaced the busted milepost sign yet. They should put up a skull and crossbones instead. Hey, you found the spuds."

"They never disappeared," I said as he let go of me. "Once I finally got you to eat rice, you seemed to like it."

"It's okay. Mulehide's was always soggy, kind of like oatmeal. Yours isn't. She insisted that's the way it should be cooked. At one point, she tried to teach us to use chopsticks. Bad idea."

"I don't even want to think about it," I said, trying to picture my husband coping with those two slim sticks in his big hands. "Are you going to sit down in the living room now that I've got dinner started?"

"Sure," he replied, swatting my rear as he headed out of the kitchen. "I'm waiting for you to interrogate me."

I made sure the potatoes had started to boil before I joined him. "Well? Why did you go to Monroe?" I inquired, sitting on the sofa.

Milo had lighted a cigarette and took a puff before replying. "I can't tell you. I just wanted to get that part out of the way so it didn't ruin dinner. Now I suppose you don't want to sit on my lap."

"Well . . . it's not because I'm mad, but I have to keep an eye on dinner." I checked my watch. "It's ten to six. Don't forget, we have to listen to Vida's show at seven."

Milo made a face. "Is she interviewing Roger about his new job?"

"No, but she probably will at some point. She's talking to the high school counselor, Helena Craig. Do you know her? I don't."

"I think she's fairly new," Milo replied. "You must've run something about her in the paper when she got here."

I thought back to recent faculty assignments. "We did. It's her second year. Scott Chamoud wrote a feature on her before he and Tamara moved to Seattle. Helena is from Blaine, up in Whatcom County."

"Scott was that good-looking dude," Milo said after sipping from his drink. "I think half the women under sixty had their eye on him. I was always afraid you'd go through some crazy older woman–younger man phase and nail him."

"Milo! That's terrible! I had enough trouble fending off the older Leo when he first came to work for me." I lowered my eyes. "I'll admit, I had to fight a fantasy now and then about Scott. I was always afraid Janet Driggers would snatch him off the street as he walked by Sky Travel when she was working there instead of at the funeral home."

The phone rang. I automatically reached for it on the end table, then realized it was the sheriff's cell.

"Dodge here," he said.

I got up to start his steak, which he preferred medium-well, while I liked mine rare. The clatter of frying pans drowned out whatever he was saying on the phone. By the time I came back into the living room, he was putting the cell back in his shirt pocket and looked worried.

"What's wrong?" I asked, going over to sit on the easy chair's arm.

"I'm not sure," he replied slowly. "That was Mullins. Some woman just showed up at headquarters looking for Heppner. Jack couldn't help her, so she's coming over here. Now, what the hell is that all about?"

THIRTEEN

"I'd better put dinner on hold," I said, getting off the easy chair's arm. "Did Mullins say what this woman wanted?"

"No. She's fairly young and didn't give her name." Milo frowned. "Maybe you should make yourself scarce."

"You're expecting her to get violent?"

"I'm expecting her to want the sheriff, not Emma's husband," he replied. "Would I sit in with you on an interview for the paper?"

"Good point," I murmured. "Maybe I should go next door and party with the Nelsons."

"Funny Emma. Why don't you go next door to the Marsdens and get your car?"

"Good idea," I said and went into the kitchen to turn off the stove.

"Quit stalling," Milo called to me.

"I'm not," I asserted, racing through the living room to grab my jacket. "Do you want to set the house on fire?"

"That's already been done." His expression grew serious. "Be careful. Have you got your cell?"

"No!" I backtracked to snatch up my purse. "I think I liked it better when I was living alone and dangerously," I muttered as I went through the front door.

I was almost down the drive when I saw a midsized blue sedan approaching slowly. Not wanting to be spotted, I cut across the grass and edged my way to the end of the fence separating my yard from the Marsdens' property. As the car turned into my driveway, I ducked down to peer through an opening between the cedar fence posts. A woman in a hooded blue jacket that almost matched the car headed for the front door. She seemed anxious, fidgeting with the strap on her shoulder bag. After a few seconds I could see her disappear inside. I supposed the good news was that she hadn't fallen into Milo's arms.

Only as I started to walk toward my Honda did I realize I couldn't park it in the driveway because I'd block the visitor's exit. I trudged up to the Marsdens' front door to ask for asylum.

Viv came to let me in. "Emma! What's going on now at your place? We heard sirens there last night."

"One of the Nelsons' guests came calling uninvited," I said. "I'll explain after I ask if I can impose on your hospitality. The sheriff is doing business in our living room, and I've been exiled."

Viv looked surprised, but Val, who was sitting in a leather recliner, laughed. "The neighborhood's more interesting since he moved in. Should we arm ourselves, or is he taking somebody into custody?"

"That was *last* night," I replied, sitting down next to Viv on the sofa. "This is something else, but don't ask me what."

"Can you tell us what happened last night?" Viv asked. "It sounded as if the siren was at your place."

"It was," I said. "Unfortunately." Then I explained about the confrontation I'd had with Vince Moro.

Viv shook her head. "I feel so sorry for you having to put up with those people all these years. No wonder you married the sheriff!"

"Uh . . . well, that's not exactly the reason I married him," I said.

Val chuckled. "Hey, I feel better having him around. But I still can't get over the body that was found down by the forks. I wonder if the poor guy was killed at the hatchery wetlands. We haven't heard much more about that. I've checked your online site and only saw who he was. Fleetwood hasn't had anything new, either."

"You're fishing," I said. "You'll come away skunked. The sheriff is still investigating. Milo has always been very tight-lipped about his job and marriage hasn't changed him."

"Sorry," Val murmured, though he didn't really look it, since he was smiling. "I guess we feel kind of left out. Some poor guy bleeds all over our property and nobody even knew he was there. I have to wonder what he was doing at the hatchery after dark. Derek Norman worked late that night, until almost ten, and he didn't see or hear anything."

"He was inside?" I asked.

"Not the whole time," Val replied. "He smokes, but he never does it in the lab. He went outside once or twice but didn't see anyone. Nobody was around when he left, either. Sure, people stop by to look around at the holding ponds, but they don't do it after dark."

I considered the time of death based on Neal Doak's estimate of between two and six A.M. "I guess there's no way to be certain that the victim was actually stabbed at the hatchery site. Whoever attacked him may have done it somewhere else and . . ." I'd lost the thread of my theory. "I don't know how to explain any of it. Obviously, Fernandez wasn't dead when he was bleeding in the wetlands or he wouldn't have ended up being found by the river."

"I'm glad it's no one we know," Viv said. "Wasn't he from Wapato?"

I confirmed that was what his driver's license stated. And, like a dunce, I'd forgotten to ask Milo what, if anything, he'd found out about the abandoned ATV. I'd been too distracted by being irked at my husband on the way home. For all I knew, our resident UFO spotter, Averill Fairbanks, might be right if he told me Fernandez had been killed by purple-clad Martians who'd landed in an ATV from outer space.

"Let me see if Milo's guest is gone," I said, going to the window that looked out onto my ever-changing log house. The blue car was still there. "You're stuck with me," I said. "Am I interrupting dinner?"

Viv looked at the wall clock with hands shaped like big and small fish. "My casserole needs ten more minutes. Would you like some wine?"

"No thanks," I responded. "I left my cocktail on the end table. Maybe Milo's guest is drinking it."

Viv smiled. "I forgot that you're not a wine drinker. It didn't take us long to go through those wonderful bottles that you received from Paris last fall. Val's allergies to alcohol have diminished over the last year or so. He can now tolerate wine if not the hard stuff. But we felt guilty drinking them. Is your friend still living over there?"

"I've no idea," I said. "I haven't heard from him in months." And probably never would, since Milo had told Rolf Fisher that he'd arrest him for harassment if he so much as blinked in my direction. That was fine with me. Rolf had charm and brains, but he was a riddle I'd never been able to solve.

I'd no sooner spoken than I heard a car start up. "I think that's my cue," I said.

Val was already out of his chair. "Let me check. It might be one of the Nelson gang stealing your Honda."

"Val!" Viv cried. "Don't tease Emma. She has enough problems."

"All clear," Val said. "I can only see the Yukon."

I headed for the door. "That probably means Milo didn't arrest her. Or else she kidnapped him."

Val laughed. "She'd have trouble doing that unless she drugged him first. He's almost as intimidating as my mother-in-law."

Viv shot Val a dirty look. "Ignore him. He adores my mom. Though," she added, "she does have his number."

I thanked my hosts, got in my car, and pulled into the driveway. Milo was waiting for me on the porch.

"I was going over to the Marsdens' to tell you the coast was clear," he said. "Then I figured maybe you were lurking outside trying to listen through the bare walls."

I took off my jacket. "Damn. I never thought of it. Dare I ask what that was all about?"

"Hell, no. I'm starving. What ever happened to dinner?"

"It won't take long," I assured him. "I never got to finish my drink. Get us both a refill. My ice has probably melted."

"I put both our drinks in the fridge," he said, following me into the kitchen. "I don't drink on the job."

I turned up the potatoes, opened a can of string beans, and started frying Milo's steak. "Did you ever bring your work home when you were married the first time?"

My husband was topping off our drinks. "Don't get cute. I'm not sure my kids knew I had a job. I think Mulehide told them I went fishing every day. When Bran was about six, he asked why he couldn't go fishing with me all the time. I explained it was because I never caught anything and asked him how often I brought home a mess of fish. He said he thought I ate them before I got to the house."

"I'd believe you," I said as we resumed our usual places in the living room, "if I didn't think you were fobbing me off about your visitor."

"You got that right. I can't tell you because it's not official."

"A strange woman comes to our house on unofficial business? Should I get jealous?"

"She doesn't want my body, if that's what's worrying you." Milo paused to sip from his drink. "Do I smell steak burning?"

"Oh!" I jumped off the sofa, spilling some of my drink on the rug. "Damn!" I cried, racing into the kitchen. Sure enough, I'd forgotten to lower the heat under Milo's steak. It was only singed on one side, so all was not lost. I flipped it over, added my steak, and waited until the burner had cooled down. I returned to the living room with a rag to soak up the liquid on the rug. "Pretend I broiled one side of your steak, okay? Now tell me more about whatever you can't tell me."

Milo shot me a disgusted look. "You know damned well I won't. As sheriff, I often get stuck listening to people with weird problems that aren't necessarily related to law enforcement. You do, too. We both have the kind of jobs that make the clueless think we can advise or help them. She came, she talked, she left. Forget about it." He paused to sip his Scotch. "Anything else about to explode in the kitchen, or can I relax?"

"Everything's fine. Dinner should be done in seven minutes. Why did she ask for Heppner?"

"She'd called earlier in the week, and he'd answered the phone. When she found out today he wasn't around, she came to see me." Milo turned in the direction of the kitchen. "Are we going to eat now or wait until Vida's show comes on?"

I looked at my watch. "It's just after six-thirty. We've got time. I'll turn my steak and mash the potatoes. Two-minute warning." Taking my drink with me, I returned to the kitchen.

Milo was right on my heels. "Your steak's still bleeding to death."

"I haven't turned it yet. Jeez, give me time! And move it, big guy. I have to dump the potato water in the sink."

"Oh — what kind of new sink do you

252

want? Double sink, ceramic, stainless steel, garbage disposal — the Bourgettes are asking you to pick out that stuff by the end of next week."

"Right now a wooden washtub would suit me fine," I retorted. "Have the Bourgettes make me a list. I can't keep track of all this stuff."

"I thought women got all thrilled over buying things for the house. Mulehide sure did."

Dumping out the potato water, I glared at him. "I'm not Mulehide."

I almost dropped the kettle when Milo put his arms around me. "Did I forget to tell you I'm damned happy you aren't?"

Managing to set the kettle down, I leaned against him. "I'm still getting used to so much all at once. Maybe I'm overwhelmed. Everything seems to have happened so fast. Don't you feel like that?"

His hazel eyes were intense as he looked down at me. "After waiting so many years for you to come around? No. I almost gave up on you a year ago last January, when you were still running off to be with Fisher in Seattle. But when I had the gall bladder attacks and didn't know what they were, I saw how scared you were. Mullins told me you almost passed out when you heard I was in the hospital with chest pains. Oh, you tried to be brave when you came to see me, but you were as white as those damned hospital sheets. I can read you pretty well. I figured you cared a lot more than you admitted."

I smiled feebly, the memory still jarring me. "I couldn't imagine my world without you in it. But you didn't make any serious moves."

He shrugged. "You know how I work a case. I take my time. I wanted to make sure everything was in place."

I was appalled. "You treated me the same way you'd solve a crime? That's not very romantic, you big jerk."

"You're not very romantic. Oh, you liked to pretend when it came to Cavanaugh, but you were delusional. I told you that ten years ago."

I tried to pull away from Milo, but he tightened his grip. "Tom and I were going to be married," I said stubbornly.

"It didn't happen. I never thought it would." He had the nerve to chuckle. "Go ahead, tell me you hate me. Again."

I shook my head. "No. I want to find out how *much* I hate you after you finish your spiel about wooing me for almost an entire year."

"I didn't. I'm not the wooing type. Fisher

was still in the picture. It didn't help when Tom's kids showed up later. Then Fisher took off and you fell for the rumor about Mulehide and me getting back together. When I told you it was bullshit, you looked . . . not just relieved, but happy. I finally decided to hell with it and stopped treating you like some dainty little porcelain doll. It worked."

I couldn't help it. I laughed. "Oh, Milo, that was the one thing that was missing — passion. I never realized you were afraid to let loose. But when you did, it was amazing. I couldn't believe it!"

"Neither could I." He laughed, too. "It's a wonder I didn't run the Cherokee off the road when I left that night. In fact, I wondered why I left in the first place."

"I wondered, too. I felt so alone after you were gone. When I didn't hear from you the next day, I thought it hadn't meant anything to you."

"It meant so damned much that I decked Fleetwood and Mullins for making cracks about us. I was so bowled over by the change in you that I lost my sense of humor." He glanced at the stove. "You never turned your steak, but I think it must be done anyway."

"That's okay," I said. "I can eat it almost

well-done."

Milo kissed me gently. "Then let's do it before Vida opens her damned cupboard."

"You never told me about that ATV," I said, hurriedly mashing the potatoes. "Did it belong to Fernandez?"

Milo sat down at the table. "We don't have any of the test results back from Everett except that the blood from the wetlands is human."

I handed him his dinner, but my brain was buzzing. "May I conjecture?" I said, filling my plate and sitting down.

Milo shrugged. "You often do."

"Naturally, I'm curious why you drove to Monroe. If it had something to do with the correctional facility, it'd probably be official. I'm guessing you went to the hospital to see the guy who was critically injured in the car crash Monday." I paused, waiting for Milo's reaction. There wasn't any. He kept eating and looking somewhere beyond me.

I persevered. "When I first asked about Erinel Dobles's condition, you expressed indifference. I figure you made a seventy-mile round-trip to talk to him today. That indicates there's more to all this than just another Highway 2 wreck."

Milo heaved a sigh. "Those other people involved were banged up pretty bad, too.

256

There could be charges brought and a potential lawsuit."

"You couldn't spare a deputy to do that?"

"Stop asking questions. You're spoiling my appetite."

"I already spoiled dinner. My steak tastes like a catcher's mitt."

"The spuds and the beans are fine. But you didn't make gravy."

"That's because there wasn't enough juice left in the steak. Jeez, I work all day. Every meal can't be a gourmet delight."

"Let's go out to dinner tomorrow night. The French place?"

"Sure. Or should we wait until the kitchen's unusable?"

"We could go twice. Hell, we could drive over to Everett."

I laughed. "Do you realize we haven't gone anywhere out of town together since we were dating way back when?"

Milo frowned. "Hunh. Too bad you didn't go to Monroe with me today. We could've stopped at Jack in the Box."

"That sounds about right. Was Mr. Dobles able to speak to you?"

"Yeah. He's the voice at Jack in the Box who asked for my order."

"Milo . . ."

"He's improving, listed as satisfactory. His

257

wife arrived late Tuesday. I never reveal an interview unless it's official — and pertinent."

"Well," I said, after being forced to chew my steak about twelve times before I could swallow it, "I assume you wouldn't talk to him about paying to replace the milepost sign."

Milo nodded absently and forked up more potatoes.

"You could've sent a deputy to cite him for vehicular negligence or whatever, but you went in person." I paused to watch my husband's reaction, but again there wasn't any. "That tells me you had other questions for him." I fingered my chin. "Now, what could they have been?"

The sheriff shrugged and ate some green beans.

"I doubt he knows where Sam is," I continued after washing down another bite of rubber steak with the last of my drink, "so you had a more pressing matter that took you to Monroe. Maybe it has something to do with the murder investigation you claim to know so little about."

Milo stood up. "That's it. I know how to make you be quiet." He pulled my chair away from the table and carried me out of the kitchen.

I stopped talking.

"Good grief!" I cried half an hour later. "We missed Vida's show!"

Milo stretched and yawned. "Why do you care? You have to listen to her all day at work."

"But," I protested, sitting up and pulling the sheet over my breasts, "it's almost illegal to miss her program. You should arrest us. Or at least make us pay a fine."

Milo laughed. "Relax. Want to snuggle?"

"No. Yes." I curled up next to him. "It's cozy in here, even if we don't have walls."

"How come you feel so soft?" he murmured. "You ought to be toughened up from walking into walls and furniture and Public Utility District poles."

"I've never walked into a PUD pole."

"You sure? I could've sworn I saw you . . ." The phone rang in the distance. "To hell with it. Whoever it is will call back."

"Is it your cell?"

"No. My cell's in my shirt pocket on the floor."

"It might be Adam. He called from Nome today."

"He can't call again?"

I moved my head to look at Milo. "He *is* my son. Really, I should check. He might be getting ready to go back to the village, where I can't talk to him without a bunch of interference and delays."

"He'd leave at night?"

"It's two hours earlier there. Come on, big guy, let go of me."

Milo relented. I grabbed my robe and hurried into the living room. The message light was on my phone. I picked up the receiver and dialed to retrieve the call.

"Really, Emma," Vida said, "you must be as overcome as I am by my program. I could not believe how frank Ms. Craig was. Principal Freeman must be exploding at her indiscretion. When you've recovered, do call me back. Spencer, naturally, is agog."

Gathering my robe more closely around me, I realized it was chilly in the living room. Wondering what on earth Helena Craig had said over the airways, I hesitated before dialing Vida's number. How could I fake commiseration if I didn't know what she was talking about? I considered calling Leo or one of my other staffers, but I didn't want them to know I hadn't heard "Vida's Cupboard." Before I could marshal my thoughts, Milo had gotten dressed and come into the living room.

"Well?" he asked, heading for the easy chair.

"It was Vida. Apparently her show was a shocker."

"It must've been if she called here." He sat down and picked up the latest *Sports Illustrated.*

"I'll have to call her back, but what should I say?"

"Tell her the White Sox look good this year. Cards should do pretty well, too."

"You're no help." I picked up the receiver and went into the kitchen to return Vida's call. I decided that the best defense was a good offense. "Should I be mad because you broke news on KSKY?" I asked before she could say more than hello.

"I wouldn't blame you," she said, sounding exasperated. "The reason I started by asking how she worked with potential dropouts was because I felt we'd be on safe ground. But when she went off about how so many parents don't care if their children do well in school, I couldn't help but press her. Do you think I was out of line?"

"Of course not," I replied. "Helping kids stay in school is the parent or guardian's responsibility."

"Certainly. I hope my dismay didn't show over the air. Spencer assured me I kept my aplomb, but it wasn't easy."

"I shouldn't think so," I asserted, wondering what the heck Vida was talking about. "Why was Helena so . . . candid?"

"For obvious reasons. She worries about students. Or former students, that is. Allowing them to drop out without official recognition could be illegal. When I asked if Principal Freeman had reported this to the school board, she hedged. Don't you agree?"

"It's hard for me to say." At least that was true. "You must've noticed her body language, right?"

"True. She seemed to stiffen. But given that funding is based on enrollment numbers, I can't help but think that this is cheating. Granted, only five students have dropped out this year, and that doesn't include the Johnson and Ellison girls. But it could make a difference when you consider that the high school began the year with slightly over 280 students. In the case of the Ostrom boy, he was eighteen and joined the navy, planning to finish his degree in the service. But those four girls simply left. The younger of the two Pedersen girls is only fifteen."

The names of Ostrom and Pedersen rang only faint bells. They probably lived on the fringes, perhaps out on River Road, up Highway 187 by the old mineshafts or by

Alpine Falls, west of the hatchery. While Vida rattled on, I quietly cleaned up the kitchen. But she paused, apparently expecting me to say something. Returning to the living room, I gave it my best shot. "Does Helena hold both the parents and Freeman responsible for these unofficial dropouts?"

"Surely you could tell from her tone," Vida insisted.

"I thought maybe she added details after the broadcast."

"She merely stated she hoped she'd given listeners something to think about. I must go. Calls are coming through on my other line. Goodness, I'd so hoped to stop off to wish Roger well on his job tomorrow. You'll put something on the website, of course."

"About Roger?" I said, causing Milo to look up from his reading.

"No, no. About my program, of course." She paused briefly. "It would, of course, be nice if you mentioned Roger."

"That's a 'Scene' item. As for Ms. Craig, I'll think how to approach posting anything. We can't be careless if there are legal implications."

"True," Vida allowed. "You're not angry with me for having such a bombshell on my program, are you? I had no idea!"

"I wish we'd had the story first," I hedged.

"Good luck with the callers."

I rang off. Milo again looked at me. "Is Vida's shocker that Roger got a job? That *is* damned surprising. Or is he working for Fleetwood?"

"No, it's what Helena . . . skip it. I don't know what I'm saying."

"That's not unusual." He glanced at his magazine. "The Spurs look solid for the NBA play-offs. So do the Pistons and the Heat."

"Stop distracting me. I'm going to the kitchen to call Fleetwood."

Figuring Spence had probably taken off after Vida's show, I dialed his cell instead of the station. He answered on the fourth ring, sounding less than his usual mellifluous self. "Damn," he said, "I'm going a-wooing. Rosalie awaits at Parc Pines."

"Tell the merry widow to sit tight and give me three minutes. What's your reaction to Helena's indiscreet revelations?"

"She's lucky she isn't fired," he replied. "On the other hand, if the school board has any gumption — which they probably don't — Freeman's job may be on the line. But my money's on him. Ms. Craig went public, so do with it what you will."

"Can you get me a copy of the tape?"

"Sure, if you . . . why do you need a copy?"

"Because I want to make damned sure I get it right."

"Can you wait until tomorrow?"

I told Spence I could. "I'll wait to post anything online."

He laughed. "You didn't listen to 'Vida's Cupboard'? Were you letting your favorite bear maul you instead?"

"Stop. If you breathe a word to Vida, I'll make her put you two in 'Scene.' At least Milo and I are married."

"You're a bothersome wench. Have it your way. My lips are sealed."

"Not for long after you get to Parc Pines. Good night, Spence."

"That was quick," my husband remarked when I came back into the living room. "You got everything sorted out?"

"No. I'll have to listen to the blasted tape."

Milo put the magazine aside. "Did Fleetwood ever come on to you?"

I shook my head. "His romantic history is as weird as mine — and yours. I don't care much for Rosalie, though you and I've seen her softer side. They're both superficial on the outside, but not on the inside."

Milo frowned. "That doesn't make any sense."

"You're right. But you know what I mean."

"I don't think *you* know what you mean."

"You could be right."

Of course, we were both wrong — about so many things that would happen in the days to come.

FOURTEEN

"More dropouts?" the sheriff barked at me over the phone shortly after eight-thirty Friday morning. "What the hell does that mean?"

"Just what Helena Craig said on Vida's show. Maybe you should listen to the tape, too."

Milo sighed. "Give me those names again."

"Ostrom, Pedersen, Fritz, and Kramer. The Pedersens had two daughters drop out."

"I'll skip the tape for now. I've got work to do. We got the body back a few minutes ago." He hung up.

Spence had discreetly left the tape with Amanda shortly before I'd gotten to work. I'd taken it into the back shop so Vida wouldn't overhear me listening to it. If Kip suspected I hadn't heard the original version, he didn't say so. In fact, he expressed his own concern about what was going on at the high school.

"Chili and I have a long time to wait before we worry about kids going to high school," he said, "but what's going on with Freeman? A couple of months ago, it was porn in the lockers, now it's unreported dropouts? Is he losing his grip?"

"Vida has a family member — a Gustavson — on the school board," I said. "If she ever gets off the phone, maybe she'll pin him to the wall."

Kip laughed. "Oh, she'll build a fire under him. But some of those other school board members may not have the guts to hold Freeman accountable. Will you handle the story or give it to Mitch?"

"Being from Detroit and not having local roots, Mitch should be the point man. I'll talk to him when he gets back from his rounds."

Kip stroked the red goatee that didn't quite conceal his still-boyish looks. "Karl Freeman was only in his second year when I started high school. He isn't all that old, really. Fifty or so?"

"I'm fifty or so," I retorted.

Kip's fair skin flushed. "I never think of you as that old, Emma. Honest. Maybe that's because . . . how old is Dodge?"

"Ninety-six," I said. "I'm going to dodder off now and try to find the equally decrepit Mitch. He's even older than Milo and I are."

"Well now!" Vida exclaimed, rubbing at her tired ear. "Are we having computer problems? You've been in the back shop forever."

"I wanted to listen to your show again," I said. "I'm going to let Mitch cover it."

"No! It should be my task, since my program broke the news."

I rested a knee on her visitor chair. "All the more reason for Mitch to do it. We need an unbiased viewpoint. He's only been here for seven months. His perspective will be more objective than yours — or mine."

Vida scowled while adjusting the be-ribboned mauve pillbox that seemed to be slipping off to one side. "Perhaps. But my ties to the high school go back three generations."

"I know. That's why we need an outsider's point of view."

The outsider came into the newsroom, running a hand through his thick gray hair. "Am I supposed to mention that the sheriff is not in a good mood?"

Ignoring Vida's contemptuous snort, I shrugged. "He's been in one of those off and on for over fifteen years. I'm used to it.

The only difference is that early on he was quieter about it. I don't suppose the cause of his ill humor is newsworthy?"

Mitch was pouring coffee and picking up a bear claw. "Maybe. Just as I left, he took off in the Yukon."

"Check back later," I said. "He may have news on the murder vic. They just got the body back. Meanwhile, take on Principal Freeman. It may be spring break, but I assume he's in town. If he's not at the high school, talk to him at his home. The address is in the phone directory." Unlike Vida, I didn't have every SkyCo resident's number in my head.

Mitch looked mildly surprised. "I thought maybe you or . . ." He stopped, seeing that Vida was pretending to be absorbed in a news release. "Sure. But what about the dropouts' parents?"

"Freeman's first up. I don't know these people." I winced before turning to Vida. "Do you recognize the names of the latest dropouts?"

Her head snapped up, sending the pillbox dangerously aslant. "Of course I recognize them, though they haven't lived here all that long. The Ostroms are up on Second Hill. He works for the state parks and was a career navy man, which is why their son is going into the service. Mrs. Ostrom tutors dyslexic children. They have a sixth grader named Grace. I wrote an article about them about a year and a half ago when they arrived, having lived previously in Everett."

"And the others?" I asked.

"The Pedersens are a bit elusive. They've been here only a few months. In fact, I believe Mrs. Pedersen may be a single mother. I contacted her when they came to Alpine, but she proved . . . distant. Perhaps the separation was recent and she didn't want to discuss it. Understandable, of course. I never pry."

Mitch turned away abruptly, apparently to hide his incredulity. I could hear my phone ringing, so I had to put off asking about the other two names Helena Craig had mentioned.

"Okay," Janet Driggers said, "as the sheriff's wife, can you tell me what we should do with the stiff your big stud sent us? They ran out of space at the hospital morgue, which is good news for us, but not so good for the two old coots who croaked last night. Autopsies pending, though they were both older than God. Pidduck and Nerstad obits to Vida. So do we release the dead guy to the woman who claims to be his mother?"

"His mother?" I was stunned. "Where did

271

she come from?"

"How do I know? I didn't ask, and I don't need to know until I talk to your mega-dude. He's not in, and I already heard he wants the stiff back. Dodge has priority over a mere mama." She paused while I collected my wits. "I wonder," Janet mused, "if I should meet with the sheriff, say at the Tall Timber Motel or the . . ."

"Stop!" I shouted. "When did Milo call you?"

"Jealous? Oh, come on, there's plenty of that big guy to go . . ."

"Janet." My voice turned severe. "I repeat, when did Milo call . . ."

"He didn't." Janet sounded only faintly irked. "Heppner called Al last night and asked to claim the body. I assume the sheriff wants it back for some reason."

"I . . ." Pausing, I wondered if I'd heard Janet correctly. "*Sam* called Al? Or do you mean one of the other deputies?"

"Hell, Emma, Al can tell that sourpuss Heppner from the rest of Dodge's crew. Unless it's Dwight Gould, of course, but I heard he's been banging his ex-wife. It's almost unbelievable, though it does make him semi-human. Heppner doesn't come close."

I was flabbergasted but didn't want to give

anything away about Sam's apparent defection. "Did you tell Mrs. . . . . Fernandez, is it?"

"I guess," Janet replied. "I don't need to get her ID until I know it's okay for her to claim the stiff."

"Where's Al?" My brain seemed to be recovering. "Maybe I should talk to him."

"He went to Snohomish. Cubby Pierce died during the night, and his widow wants him buried in the Alpine family plot. Cubby and Kitty retired to Snohomish, you know."

I didn't know. In fact, I didn't know Cubby and Kitty Pierce, unless they were somehow related to Vida, which was always a good guess. "Honest, Janet, I don't know what to tell you. You're talking to the wrong Dodge. Mitch told me Milo's on a call, so ask him when he gets back. I'm out of my league here."

"So am I," Janet admitted. "We're liberated women. Why can't we function when our husbands aren't around? Unless I've got my vibrator."

I ignored the remark. "We're liberated, but we aren't wizards. Now you've got me confused. Let me know what you find out, okay?" I rang off.

For a few moments I sat back in my chair and wondered if Janet could have been mistaken about which deputy had called Al about Fernandez. But while Janet might have a bawdy mouth, she had an agile brain. If she hadn't, she couldn't hold down two jobs, at Driggers Funeral Home and Sky Travel. As she often said, she had to stay sharp to figure out if she was sending people on a one- or a two-way trip.

Vida snapped me out of my reverie. "The Fritzes live outside of town, down by where the old second logging camp was located. The Kramers are in the Clemans Manor apartments, by Old Mill Park. It's well and good to let Mitch handle the story, but I feel an obligation to speak to these people. We need to find out if their children have plans to get their GEDs. I find all this very upsetting."

"Have you considered that the parents may be homeschooling?"

"Yes. I didn't want to ask Helena, because I disapprove. Even if a parent is a teacher, that person is still a parent. The lack of social contact is extremely bothersome. Can you imagine not knowing what your fellow youngsters are doing?"

Vida could never imagine not knowing what every resident of Alpine was doing, so the comment breezed by me. But she had a point. I'd known a couple of Portland families who had homeschooled their kids, and they'd seemed fairly well educated. I'd noticed, however, that they interacted well with adults but seemed awkward with their peer group. Maybe when they got out into the real world, they caught up. I'd moved to Alpine before they had come of age.

"That's fine about talking to the parents," I said, "but touch base with Mitch. He gets prickly if he feels any of us are edging onto his turf."

Vida looked askance. "So silly. It's not as if we have a large staff. Sometimes I think he doesn't realize he's not in Detroit anymore."

"That would be pretty hard for him not to notice," I said.

Vida put a hand to her imposing bosom. "I should hope so! Can you imagine what it would be like living in such a place? Rust Belt, indeed! It must be comparable to the Dust Bowl."

It was futile to argue with Vida, but sometimes she succumbed to reason. "I came to Alpine shortly after logging had been curtailed. This town was in bad shape and it didn't start getting better until the college came along. You've also told me about how rough-and-tumble it was during the Depression. When I was growing up in

Seattle, every time Boeing lost a big contract, the city was sunk into gloom. Back then, it was basically a company town. Now look at it — Microsoft, Amazon, Starbucks, Costco, T-Mobile, Nintendo of North America. I could go on, but my point is that cities can rally."

"And end up like Seattle, with all that horrid traffic and construction? Cranes everywhere, or so my son-in-law Ted told me when he attended a meeting there recently. He thought they looked like giant steel dinosaurs looming overhead. So ugly. If that's progress, I don't want to see it here."

"But we've got our own progress," I pointed out. "I just wrote an editorial about that."

"So you did." She frowned. "This morning I had to wait for three other cars before I could get to Front Street and make sure no one had taken my parking place in front of the *Advocate.*"

Then there were times when Vida *didn't* listen to reason. I gave up. "Which family will you start with?"

"The Pedersens," Vida replied, obviously having already made the decision. "Mrs. Pedersen's evasiveness irked me. Most newcomers are pleased to be welcomed to Alpine. I'd like to know why she seemed indifferent to what is basically being a good neighbor on my part."

I wished her luck. My priority was to find out why Sam Heppner had asked Al Driggers about Fernandez's body. Back in my office, I called the sheriff, but Lori told me he was still out. After I emphasized that it was business, not domesticity, she promised to relay the message to her boss.

Mitch returned around ten-thirty. "Freeman was home, but he tried to stonewall, as usual," he said, sitting down. "I persevered in my best UAW-union-local-boss-interview mode. The Ostrom boy was officially noted as dropping out, but not until last week. Apparently the kid began waffling about joining the navy when he realized he could be sent farther than San Diego."

"I suppose Helena Craig hadn't yet heard about that," I said. "What about the girls?"

Mitch held his hands up in a helpless gesture. "It was never official. The Kramer girl didn't come back after the Martin Luther King weekend in January. Her mother explained that she had mono."

"For three months?"

Mitch's expression was ironic. "That's what I asked. Freeman said the mother insisted she'd had it before a couple of times, as their doctor in Marysville could confirm. As for the Fritz kid, Freeman said that was confidential, but she'd been suspended and would probably return to school before the end of the year. Knocked up, I figure. She left in early February, so maybe she was beginning to show."

"Baby bump." I sighed. "The Pedersens?"

"Unexplained absences. After thirty days, come Monday — they don't count spring break — both girls will be considered dropouts unless the parents come up with some good reasons."

"Well . . . it doesn't sound as if Freeman has done anything illegal. Did you ask him about Ms. Craig's allegations?"

"He called them ill-informed." Mitch grinned. "I mentioned calling on her, but he told me to wait. She's very sick with a cold."

"I'll bet. Good job, Mitch. I'm getting spoiled having a real reporter around here." I leaned to one side, making sure my House & Home editor hadn't overheard, but she was gone. "By the way, I'm letting Vida talk to some of the parents. I don't want to overload you."

"And you couldn't stop her with a sawed-off shotgun." Mitch stood up. "That's fine. I don't shine at doing domestic interviews. Maybe that's because my own family situation isn't exactly ideal."

"How is Troy?" I asked, willing to bring up the Laskey son since Mitch had alluded to the subject first.

"Okay. He's got seventeen months to go. The Monroe Correctional Complex isn't as god-awful as some prison facilities. Another inmate is teaching him the electrical trade. The guy's good. He got busted for disabling bank security in Tacoma. But he'd done it a half dozen times before he got caught."

"Sounds tricky. How did they catch him?" Mitch shook his head and laughed. "Somebody hot-wired his car while he was in the bank, so he stood outside to wait for a bus and the police nabbed him. I guess the bus driver was behind schedule."

I laughed, too. "That story must've been on the wire service, but I missed it. Did the guy ever get his car back?"

"No. The thief crashed it on the Tacoma Narrows Bridge."

My reporter ambled off just as my phone rang. "What now?" the sheriff asked in a beleaguered tone.

"Are you available?" I inquired.

"Jeez, Emma, what's with you? It's not even eleven o'clock. I can't take off right now. I'm busy."

"It's business, you big jerk." I lowered my

279

voice. "It's about Sam."

"Shit. Okay, come on down."

"I'll . . ." But Milo had already hung up.

I arrived in less than five minutes and went directly into the sheriff's office. Keeping my voice down, I relayed Janet's account of Sam's request for Fernandez's body. "I assume it wasn't official, but personal."

Judging from the puzzled expression on Milo's face, he agreed. "That's damned odd." He drummed his fingers on the desk. "I don't suppose Janet had any idea where Sam called from?"

"She naturally figured it was from here."

"Right. No way to tell these days, with all the cellphones. Hell, maybe he's home. We haven't checked his place since Mullins went out there. He hasn't been spotted in town. Even Sam has to eat."

"But no matter where he is, why would he want to claim Fernandez's body? Do you think he knows this Mrs. Dobles somehow and is acting on her behalf?"

Milo was lighting a cigarette. He took a puff before answering my question. "I wonder if maybe he does. Or else he knows her husband, but I can't think what the connection would be."

"Or . . ." We stared at each other.

The sheriff sighed. "I'd better call Al Drig-gers."

"He went to Snohomish. He might not be back yet."

Milo nodded once. "Okay." He paused again, looking off at his SkyCo wall map. "I've worked with Sam for twenty years. It dawns on me that I don't know the guy. He might as well be a stranger."

"Maybe it's time to find out more about him," I said quietly.

"Maybe. But will I like what I find out?"

I couldn't answer that question.

"Okay," Milo said after a long pause, "maybe I should delegate."

"Meaning what?" I asked.

He leaned closer and dropped his voice another notch. "I don't want the rest of my staff to know I'm digging into Heppner's private life. You're good at that stuff — you've done it a hundred times. Just don't let anybody else in on it. Especially Vida. She'd blab to Blatt."

"And the rest of Alpine," I murmured. "Got it."

"If it costs anything to check into records, use my credit card. You're on my personal one anyway. Now beat it, so I can get back to whatever the hell I was doing before you showed up."

I got to my feet. "Keep in mind that if any rumors start flying, they won't be from me, but from Janet Driggers."

"Damn!" Milo held his head. "Is there any way you can shut her up?"

"Probably not," I said. "You could, but the only way I know how would cause me to shoot both of you. 'Bye, Sheriff."

I left Milo still holding his head.

"Anna Pedersen is indeed a single mother. Living on welfare, I should imagine. She told me her daughters were with their father in Maltby. Then she slammed the door in my face. Imagine!" She clutched at her hat before it slipped down over her angry gray eyes.

"Are you sure that hat fits you?" I asked. "It seems kind of big."

"Oh?" Vida stared at me before yanking off the hat and tossing it at her desk. She missed. The hat fell to the floor. "You're right. At our church TULIP festival, we have Secret John Knox presents, like Secret Santa at Christmas. My present was this hat. I suspected at the time — due to her smirking — that my horrid sister-in-law, Mary Lou Hinshaw Blatt, had drawn my name. I decided to wear it in case she asks me how I liked it. Of course it's too big. Mary Lou head's so swollen with ego that it doesn't fit me."

"You're lucky the tulips are blooming earlier this year," I remarked as Vida retrieved the hat and plopped it on her desk.

"TULIP doesn't refer to flowers," Vida said. "It stands for John Knox's five points of Calvinism. Total depravity, Unconditional . . ."

Mercifully, my phone was ringing.

Amanda leaned into the newsroom. "It's the mayor, Emma. Can you pick up?"

Saved by the Baugh. "Sure." I dashed into my office, marveling anew at how the strait-laced Knox would spin in his grave if he knew his followers were taking his name in vain to have *fun.*

"I have been remiss," Fuzzy said into my ear. "I'd intended to call a meeting between the county commissioners and your stalwart husband, but Irene and I've had a touch of the flu that's going 'round. I'm setting the get-together for Monday, being as it's an off week for the commissioners' bimonthly meeting. It might be a trifle . . . shall we say *heated*? It will be closed to the public." He paused. "You understand, Emma, darlin'?"

I thought I did. "Yes, that's fine. But Spence may not be happy."

"You *are* the sheriff's lady. To appease Spencer, I'm inviting myself to be on Vida's next program, though I haven't yet informed her."

"Can we put the meeting on our website now?"

"Hold off, if you will," Fuzzy said. "I haven't issued the invitations, though I'll do that before the day is done."

"Okay," I agreed. "I'll wait until Milo tells me he's heard from you." *Assuming he re-*

members.

"Thank you, sugah. As ever, I'm grateful for your discretion."

I rang off just as Vida charged at me like a warrior going into battle. If she'd been a medieval knight, her shield would have had curiosity rampant markings.

"So what did our mayor have to say for himself?" she asked, settling into one of my visitor chairs. "Still preening over his proposal?"

"Fuzzy was bringing me up to speed," I said. "He and Irene have both had the flu."

"Oh? That could be a 'Scene' item. I'm sure he nursed his illness with liberal doses of Southern Comfort."

"You won't mention that in 'Scene,' I trust." To divert her, I kept talking: "Did you see any sign of the Pedersen girls before their mother shut you out?"

"I did not," Vida declared. "They're supposedly in Maltby, but she opened the door only a few inches. I suspect she's not much of a housekeeper." She brightened a bit. "I did, however, find out the name of the company Roger is working for. It's called Party Animals."

I must have looked put off, because Vida hurriedly explained: "They provide party supplies for people of all ages. All sorts of themes — Hawaiian, Hispanic, Asian, English garden and tea parties, not to mention all the major holidays. Quite ingenious."

"It actually sounds like a good idea," I said, "but I thought it was a short-haul trucking company."

Vida laughed in a faintly embarrassed manner. "I guess Grams was too thrilled to take in all the details. Of course, Roger was so delighted to reveal his participation in this enterprise that he may have been a trifle inexplicit about the company's operation."

Or maybe the dumb cluck was grunting his answers in his usual monosyllabic speech. "You should tell Leo so he can get them to advertise," I said. "We don't have much in the way of party supplies, unless you count the gift shop at the mall or the stationers in the Clemans Building."

"I'll find out the details," Vida promised, still beaming. "It occurred to me that they could have a float in the Summer Solstice Parade. Roger could ride on it. Wouldn't that be special?"

The only way I could keep from looking horrified was to feign a coughing fit. "Hay fever," I gasped, not able to look her in the eye. "The pollen is worse this year. I suppose it's the lack of rain. Are you going to talk to any of the other dropouts' parents?"

"Perhaps the Kramers. They're also apartment dwellers. I haven't heard anything about a housing shortage. If Milo wasn't so greedy, he could probably get a quick sale on his place."

I ignored the barb. "I suspect that some newcomers are looking for work or haven't found jobs that pay enough to cover a mortgage."

"Perhaps. I'm wondering if Helena Craig didn't do herself a disservice by criticizing Karl Freeman on my program. Oh, he can be a stuffed shirt, as so many educators are, but it does bother me. I've always been a loyal supporter of the high school, being an alum."

"Freeman tried to cover up the porn that was found in the school earlier this year," I pointed out. "That was foolish of him."

"True, but it's a touchy subject," Vida said. "That story also broke on my program. I must find something noncontroversial for next week. Perhaps I'll ask Roger to talk about his job. If, of course, they agree to advertise. It would mean Leo should go the co-op route with Spence."

"Yes," I agreed, though not keen on listening to Roger mumble and bumble over the airways, as he'd done on previous "Cupboard" segments.

Vida stood up. "I must finish my advice letters. So many concerns about love gone wrong. People make such poor choices."

As she made her exit, I wondered if she was referring to me. It occurred to my evil side to write her a letter saying that my dearest woman friend disapproved of my husband. How could I possibly win her over? But Vida would sense that I was the writer. Unless, of course, I tossed in a lot of misspellings and poor grammar.

Shortly before noon, Vida left for lunch and Leo came into my office. "I *have* seen that Pedersen woman, now that I think about it. I was going to mention it, but Vida went off on her tangent. Too bad, because she'd like this juicy tidbit."

"Which is?" I asked.

"I've spotted her with a guy a couple of times. He looked familiar, but I couldn't place him until now. It's the former owner of Gas 'N Go, Mickey Borg. I always go to Cal's Chevron, but I've stopped at the minimart there over the years. I thought Borg left town."

"He did," I said. "I haven't seen him in a long time. His ex — Janie Engelman — indicated he'd moved away. He's always struck me as a sleaze, though he stayed out of trouble with the law."

"Being a sleaze isn't illegal," Leo noted. "I'm off to lunch with the Kiwanis Club to suck up to advertisers. Oh — they're going as a group Sunday to see the Mariners play the Indians. They'll ask to be acknowledged on the big screen at Safeco Field. Contain your excitement."

I laughed and wished Leo good luck. But for some odd reason, something he'd said niggled at my brain. Being unable to figure out what it was, I switched gears, deciding to pick up a sandwich at Pie-in-the-Sky and then go to the trailer park to interview Wanda Johnson. Deanna had never called me back. That bothered me. But not as much as I'd been bothered by Wanda's second ex, Vince.

I decided to drive to save time. Arriving at the sandwich shop, I was about to get out of the car when my cell rang.

"Want to meet me at the Venison Inn for lunch?" Milo asked.

"I just pulled up at Pie-in-the-Sky."

"Oh. Get me a roast beef sandwich with mustard, mayo, and lettuce. Potato salad, since you haven't made any lately. Chips and pie. Apple, if they've got it, and coffee. It tastes better than ours at work."

So does chemical waste, I thought. "I'm glad I drove or else I couldn't carry your order without getting a hernia." I hung up on him.

Milo was right about how I'd fed him over the years we'd known each other. The thought occurred to me as my large order was rung up for twenty-four dollars and thirty cents. When I arrived, shortly after noon, the only person on duty was Jack Mullins. "Whoa," he said when I came in the door, "you get to feed the big guy lunch, too?"

"Keep your mouth shut or he might get ideas," I retorted.

"I have to admit you have a good effect on him. He only reams us a new one twice a day now instead of every hour or so."

"No comment." I noted that Milo's door was closed. "Is he busy?"

Jack shook his head. "Not too busy for you. He shut the door because he's listening to the tape from Vida's show." He grinned and leered. "Don't tell me you two didn't catch it live last night."

I tried to look indignant. "As a matter of fact, it turns out that Helena Craig was off base about some of the things she alleged. You can read all about it on our website. I'm not sure if Fleetwood will have it on the news, unless he makes a disclaimer."

"He already did," Jack replied. "Spence

mentioned it when he brought the tape to Dodge. He doesn't want his butt sued off."

I made a mental note to ask Mitch to interview Helena. "He's not responsible for what an individual says on KSKY. If he's smart — and he is — he'll interview Freeman for a special program."

"Why not let Vida do . . ." Jack shut up as Milo opened his door.

"Where the hell is lunch?" he bellowed.

"Jack ate it," I snapped, moving through the swinging gate to thrust the large paper sack at him. "Here. It's heavy, you big pig."

The sheriff grimaced. "Watch it in front of the hired help. They're supposed to respect me. Got that, Mullins?"

"Yes, sir!" Jack responded, but he kept his back turned. I sensed he was trying not to laugh.

"Did they have apple pie?" Milo asked as we went into his office.

"Yes. I even got a chunk of cheddar to go with it."

The sheriff eased his big frame into his chair and chuckled. "You're so damned perverse. Hell, I could probably have walked across the street and asked Janet Driggers to feed me lunch."

I flashed him a dark glance. "Don't even think about it."

"I won't. I just wanted to see your reaction."

I searched in my separate, much smaller, paper bag. "Hey — you've got my chips."

"Oh." He tossed a bag to me. "I thought you'd gotten me two."

"Keep it up and you'll look like Ed Bronsky." And, feeling perverse, I told him about Ed's wacky idea.

"Sheriff Pig?" Milo groaned. "Oh, God, can I arrest him for . . . something?"

"You want him here with you in the jail? You couldn't afford to feed him. I can't afford to feed you, for that matter."

Milo reached for his wallet and threw me a twenty. "Keep the change."

"What change?"

"My stuff didn't cost twenty bucks. I listened to the tape of Vida's show. That Craig woman has a loose mouth."

"As it turns out, she's also wrong. Mitch interviewed Freeman this morning. You can read some of it on our website."

"I'll let you tell me about it at home. Frankly, I don't give a shit." He looked out into the front office to make sure Jack wasn't listening, then lowered his voice anyway. "You had a chance to do any research?"

"No. I've been busy. But I will, maybe this

afternoon when I get back from interviewing Wanda Johnson."

Milo paused before taking a bite of potato salad. "You're going to see her?"

"Yes. That's why I drove to Pie-in-the-Sky instead of walking."

"Don't."

"Don't . . . what?"

"God, Emma, use your head. For all we know, Moro may be hanging out there. I don't want you anywhere near that bastard."

"It's broad daylight," I asserted. "If I see a sign of him, I'll leave."

The hazel eyes bored into me. "Don't go near that trailer park. I mean it. What have I told you about taking chances? Christ, I feel as if I should have a full-time deputy to keep an eye on you."

Milo's expression daunted me. "Okay," I mumbled. "I'll phone her."

"You promise?"

I nodded.

He heaved a big sigh. "You scare me sometimes. After all the trouble I went through to snag you, I want to keep you around in one piece. Think about that."

I managed a small smile. "You worry about me too much."

"Bullshit. You've got lettuce on your front. I've always worried about you. I took a solemn vow to cherish you, which includes keeping you safe — and not just because I'm a sheriff. I'm your husband. Got it?"

"That works both ways. How can I keep you from getting injured or killed on the job?"

Milo sighed again. "You can't. I took an oath on that, too."

"I know." I couldn't stop looking at him. Maybe that was because I was terrified that someday I wouldn't be able to see him at all. "I love you," I finally said, in almost a whisper.

His face softened. "That's the best reason I can think of for not getting killed."

I called Wanda Everson Johnson as soon as I got back to the office. Surprisingly, she sounded glad to hear from me.

"I haven't seen you around town in ages," she said. "Deanna told me she'd gone to see you and the sheriff. Congratulations on your marriage, by the way. Dee's had the flu, which is why she hasn't returned your call. Is that why you phoned me?"

"Yes," I fibbed. "She was very upset when she visited us. Maybe she was coming down with it then. Of course, I know you both must be worried sick about Erin. Have you heard anything from her?"

"No," Wanda replied. "I'm convinced she's gone off with Rick Morris. I thought they'd broken up, but I suppose it was just a spat. Erin's very headstrong. I'm sure she'll be in touch soon."

"I take it you like Rick," I said.

"He seems like a decent young man. Not that I ever saw much of him." She dropped her voice. "It's not easy to entertain in a trailer."

Knowing Wanda only as a nodding acquaintance, I decided it wasn't up to me to offer advice. Vida would have drenched her in suggestions. Such as getting a job — which I didn't think she had done, given that she was at home during the noon hour.

"Did Rick live around here?" I asked. "I didn't recognize his name."

"No," Wanda replied. "He was originally from . . . oh, it begins with an *M*. I'm not sure I ever heard it before, but it'd been a logging town like Alpine. I think it's not far from Mount Rainier. He'd decided to drop out of college here, so maybe he was going back to his hometown. He mentioned there was a college nearby but he'd wanted to try going to school in another part of the state. I guess they didn't have some of the classes he was interested in here. I'm not sure what he intended to choose as a career. We never chatted much."

"So you think Erin and Rick may be in his old hometown?"

"That's my best guess," Wanda said. "It must be interesting, being close to Mount Rainier. I've never been there. If they stay in . . . whatever town it is, maybe I'll visit them and see the mountain."

"That'd be lovely." I winced. "Rainier is quite a sight. If you hear anything, would you let us know? We're concerned about Erin, too."

"Of course I will. You take care, Emma."

I rang off. Wanda's mind seemed to be wandering when it came to her younger daughter. Maybe she was incapable of facing up to serious problems. Like Vince Moro. I couldn't help but wonder if she'd seen him more recently than I had. Or if he was there in the trailer with her.

That was a very unpleasant thought.

SIXTEEN

Samuel Jonah Heppner was born on February 1, 1958, in Toppenish, Washington. His parents were Jacob and Sarah Heppner. He'd been christened in the Pentecostal church when he was six. One sister, Ruth, born in 1956; one brother, Amos, born in 1953, died in 1978. I paused over that statistic. Too late for Vietnam. Car accident? Illness? Maybe the Toppenish *Review-Independent,* the local weekly, had the answer. I tried to find a listing with the Washington Newspaper Publishers Association. No luck. I was a member, though the last big meeting I'd attended was twelve years ago. My reason for going to Lake Chelan had little to do with the *Advocate.* Tom Cavanaugh had been the featured speaker.

A little after two, Mitch interrupted my research. "Helena Craig's unreachable."

"Freeman has told her to keep quiet," I

said. "I'm not surprised. There's nothing we can do."

Mitch gazed at my Sky Dairy calendar. "The school board won't meet until early May — unless Freeman calls a special session, like he did with the porn issue at the high school. But it was held behind closed doors."

I nodded. "He'll do the same thing if he decides to fire Helena. She sounds feisty. I'll bet she'd sue the school district. Damn, I wish I knew her, but I can't keep up with everybody."

"Didn't Vida run something on her?"

"No. It was your predecessor once removed, Scott Chamoud, over a year ago. You might check it out before you talk to Helena."

Mitch was staring at my calendar again, but I got the impression he wasn't really seeing it. "I like a challenge. It keeps my mind off of other things. Maybe I'll give it a shot. Is that okay with you?"

"Sure." I smiled at him. "You see? I'm still not quite used to having a real veteran reporter."

He shrugged. "I'm not going anywhere — except back to my desk."

He did just that as my phone rang. "We finally got those blood tests back," Milo said. "Human blood in the wetlands, matching the human blood of the vic, and that matches the DNA that was found in the ATV. It's official, so now I'll give Fleetwood the news, too. And yes, we found out from Olympia that it's registered to Fernandez. Somebody didn't want that known. So far we haven't come up with any prints except his and the ones that belong to the kids who found it. We eating out tonight?"

"I forgot to call for a reservation," I admitted. "I'll try, but Le Gourmand may be booked. You know that people come from all over to eat there on weekends."

"Tell them I'm the sheriff and you're a food critic." He hung up.

I suddenly remembered that Bill Blatt planned on taking Tanya to dinner at the restaurant. I called Milo back.

"Oh, crap!" he exclaimed, followed by a brief silence. "Tanya's at my house. She mentioned having dinner with Bill but didn't say where. Maybe he's surprising her. The last thing they need is the old folks hanging out like chaperones. You want to drive over to Everett?"

"No," I said. "You've had a busy week. So have I. The Grocery Basket has halibut cheeks on sale. I'll pick some up on the way home."

"You're a hell of a good wife for not having had any practice."

"Maybe that's why." Once again, I hung up first.

I returned to my Heppner research. Toppenish was in Yakima County. Last December Vida had called the daily *Yakima Herald-Republic* to get background on an accident Mitch's son had been involved in while driving his Good Humor wagon. The child he'd struck had run out into traffic, but the investigating cops had found more than ice cream novelties in Troy's possession. He'd been arrested for dealing drugs. The Yakima source had been very helpful.

Before I could find the paper's editorial number, it occurred to me that maybe there was a closer source. Girding myself for more lewd comments from Janet, I dialed the funeral home. To my relief, Al answered, though his morbid manner was as unsettling as his wife's lewd remarks.

"Yes, Emma," he said as if he were confirming my demise, "I do have the mother of the deceased's contact number at the Guest House Inn & Suites in Monroe — suite B. It's a fine establishment, just off Highway 2 and conveniently located to Valley General hospital."

I hadn't asked for a testimonial, but I supposed it was better than having Al read my pre-death obituary. I jotted down the number and thanked him before ringing off.

When I called, a recording informed me that I could speak or press the room number or suite letter. No one answered. I'd have to try again later.

Vida returned shortly after I'd found the Yakima paper's listing. "Vinica Kramer is a Gypsy," she declared, sitting down and running a hand through her unruly gray curls. Apparently, she'd discarded the offending hat for good. I wondered if she felt naked without it.

"You mean she moves from place to place?" I asked.

"She may, but I mean she's a Rom, as she put it. I find that rather intriguing. I don't recall ever having met a Gypsy until now."

"I knew some in Portland," I said. "But a Gypsy named Kramer?"

"Her husband, Franz, is German-born. His parents came to this country when he was a child. Franz and Vinica have an older son attending Skagit Valley College."

"Is she a fortune-teller?" I asked — and felt guilty of an ethnic cliché.

"Yes," Vida replied, oblivious to my gaffe. "They moved here last fall, but she intends to set up shop — that may be the wrong term — when Kristina has recovered from mono. Franz is a carpenter and has gone to work for Nyquist Construction."

"That sounds like a story in itself," I said. "The fortune-telling, I mean. Another new business. Did you see Kristina?"

"No." Vida frowned. "Mrs. Kramer fears she may be contagious."

"Do you believe her?"

"I'm not sure, though I found her quite interesting. She asked me why I wasn't wearing a hat."

"Maybe she's seen you around town."

Vida was still frowning. "Before I could answer, she told me she was glad. The hat was tainted with evil. Maybe she knows my sister-in-law. There are some people who have unusual powers of perception and observation. I can see how she could cast a bit of a spell. I didn't recognize her, though she dresses in a rather ordinary manner. A bit more gold and silver chains, perhaps, but I'm not fond of wearing much jewelry. Pearls for formal occasions are sufficient."

I agreed, fingering the heirloom wedding ring Milo had slipped on my finger during our civil ceremony. I loved the simple gold band with its twin circlets of diamonds. It had once belonged to Grandma Olive Dodge. I changed the subject to my chat with Wanda Johnson.

Vida was disgusted. "She's living in a dream world. I recall Wanda as fairly sensible. If she wasn't, Meg wouldn't have been her friend."

"Maybe Wanda can't face a more dire fate for Erin than shacking up with her boyfriend in whatever small town Rick Morris is from."

"Perhaps. So foolish not to meet problems squarely, especially with children." Vida's frown returned. I wondered if she was thinking of Roger. But when she spoke again, it was of Vince Moro. "My nephew Billy related your confrontation with Wanda's ex-husband. Really, Emma, you should never have opened the door if you were alone."

"I've already heard the lecture," I said wearily. "Milo wouldn't let me go see Wanda, even in broad daylight. That's why I called her."

Vida's face tightened, but she nodded. "Prudent of him. Billy mentioned the address Vince Moro had on his driver's license." She stood up. "I must get back to work. Oh — do you want me to speak to the Fritzes? They live not far from the former Rasmussen house by the river."

Vida's intention to venture near the site of

a homicide victim's home didn't surprise me. She'd been shot by the killer while snooping around the premises during the murder investigation. My House & Home editor wouldn't let the memory of a near-death experience affect her curiosity.

"You don't mind going there?" I asked.

She shrugged. "The person who wounded me was killed by a cougar. A fitting end — though I'm not fond of cats in any form. Such proud, selfish creatures."

If I could never stay mad at Milo for very long, it was almost as hard to remain angry with Vida. I wished Leo were more inclined to leniency, but I really couldn't fault him. One of life's lessons is that you can't please all of the people all of the time. If you can please any one of them even part of the time, that's an achievement in itself.

On that philosophical note, I went back to researching Sam Heppner, a man who had never seemed to care about pleasing anybody. I wondered why.

I was able to track down a reporter on the Yakima newspaper who was kind enough to check out the death of Amos Heppner. He said it might take him a while, but he'd try to phone me back before five. It was now after three, so I hoped he wouldn't be called out on a hot story in the meantime.

I was considering other sources for Sam's background — the Pentecostal church came to mind if it was still around — when I saw a dark-haired woman heading purposefully for my cubbyhole.

"Mrs. Dodge?" she said, pausing on the threshold.

"Yes?" I replied, unused to being addressed by my married name in the workplace. "May I help you?"

"Maybe," she said, gesturing at one of my visitor chairs. I nodded. She sat down, carefully tucking her tan trench coat under her. "My name's Carmela Dobles. I've come from the sheriff's office. He wasn't in, but the receptionist told me you might help me sort through some confusion about my son, Joe Fernandez."

I was startled, and it probably showed. Folding my hands, I made an effort to regain my composure and noted that Carmela looked determined. Her dark eyes were intense; her piquant face was set. The brown slacks and beige turtleneck hadn't come off the rack. A car salesman in Portland had once told me that he always checked out a woman's shoes to judge how much she or her husband could spend on a car. I'd caught the telltale red inner heel on her pumps and recognized a Christian Louboutin signature sole even if I could never afford to own a pair. The Gucci handbag was another indication that Mrs. Dobles was definitely upscale. Maybe she came from money, but I didn't think so, though I wasn't sure why.

"I'm trying to claim my son's body from the local funeral home," Carmela said. "It appears someone else has also asked for his remains. Mrs. Driggers wouldn't tell me who it was. I've been informed that only Sheriff Dodge can give me that information, but he isn't in. Ms. Cobb — I think that's her name — suggested I talk to you, because you're the sheriff's wife as well as the local newspaper owner." She stared at me expectantly.

I grimaced. "I'm sorry. I don't understand what's going on, either. I spoke to the funeral home owner's wife this afternoon, and they also have to wait for the sheriff's response. Really, I wish I *could* help. I'm told your husband is recovering. I can't imagine how you must feel."

The dark eyes were shrewd. "I think you can."

For a split second I wondered if Carmela was part Gypsy. "Most of us don't get this far in life without tragedies. You strike me as a very strong person."

Carmela lowered her gaze. "I wasn't always that way."

"We have to acquire strength the hard way. How soon will your husband be released?"

She looked at me again. "Monday, probably. Nel will need rehab after we get home. He'll have to lie flat for the trip back to Visalia." She shook her head in apparent dismay. "He'll hate that. He's always in a hurry — which is how he ended up crashing his car in the first place."

"Was he here on business?" I asked.

"Here? You mean in . . . Alpine?" Carmela saw me nod. "No. He was going across the pass when the accident occurred. Apparently, your hospital is quite small. That's how he ended up in Monroe."

I nodded again. "Some of the other injured people were brought here. Given the severity of his condition, I was surprised he wasn't airlifted to Harborview Hospital in Seattle."

"I understand the medics weren't sure he could make it that far," Carmela said. "But Nel is nothing if not tough. The doctors at Valley General have been surprised at how quickly he's recovering."

"That's good. You're both lucky." I

winced, realizing that given the death of Carmela's son, that was a stupid thing to say.

She managed a wry smile. "You won't have to put up with Nel while he recovers at home."

I smiled back. "I've had experience with men who are horrible patients," I said, recalling Milo's gallbladder attacks. "But I do want to tell you how sorry I am about your son."

Carmela sighed. "I still can't take it in. He's my only child. Joe was . . . amazing." She shrugged and stood up. "Do you have children?"

"Yes, a son. He's a priest."

"You and the sheriff must be very proud of him."

"The sheriff and I don't have children together. Adam's father is dead." For a reason I didn't understand, unless it was some visceral bonding with this stranger, I went on: "I was never married to my son's father. They didn't meet until Adam was twenty."

Carmela's pert face sagged. "That's . . ." She shook her head as a glint of tears appeared in her eyes, but she swallowed and the small smile reappeared. "Life's a bitch, isn't it?"

"It can be. Then sometimes it's . . . not."

She nodded. "Ask your son to pray for me, for Nel, for Joe. I'm Catholic. Faith gets tested, and I've flunked a few times. But I can't walk away from it. In the end, what else have we got? Maybe it's all we need." She shrugged, turned around on her Christian Louboutin heels, and walked out through the empty newsroom.

For the next few minutes I sat at my desk wondering why Milo hadn't told me that the accident victim's wife was the mother of the murder victim. I wondered if she was the woman who'd come to see him during his off-hours. And why had son and stepfather happened to be in the same area at the same time? I should have asked Carmela more questions. I felt like kicking myself with my Nordstrom Rack sale flats. The only reason for the sheriff's discretion could be the familiar phrase he'd used on me over the years: "I can't talk about that because it's part of an ongoing investigation." But except for Erinel Dobles being Joe Fernandez's stepfather, what was the implied and possibly criminal connection? Maybe I should expand my research to Dobles.

One phrase stood out from what Carmela had told me about her husband being on

Highway 2. She'd said that Erinel — or Nel, as she called him — had been *going across* Stevens Pass. That indicated he was headed for Eastern Washington. Did that mean he had no idea his stepson was in the area? Was it by chance that they both were in SkyCo at the same time? It seemed unlikely. The Dobleses were from Visalia, in California's San Joaquin Valley. Joe Fernandez was supposedly from Wapato; Sam Heppner came from Toppenish. Both towns were in Yakima County. Maybe it *was* a coincidence. Ordinarily, I'd run all this by Vida. But unless she'd administered truth serum to Bill Blatt, she didn't know Sam was AWOL. I wondered if Milo or his deputies had checked again to see if there was any sign of Sam at his place on River Road. I'd do it myself, but I didn't want to miss the Yakima reporter's call. I was looking for a Pentecostal church listing in Toppenish when Vida returned.

"The Fritzes weren't home," she said in disgust. "I should've called first, but a surprise visit from the press catches people off guard. They often reveal more than they intended."

"What's to reveal if their daughter's pregnant?" I asked. "If Freeman expects her back before school's out in June, there's nothing mysterious about that."

Vida leaned on one of my visitor chairs. "All the more reason to find out if she knows anything about the other missing students. The Fritz girl was in some of the same classes as the Kramer and Ellison girls. Besides, it'd be interesting to find out who the father of her baby is. Not in a prurient way, of course."

"Of course," I murmured.

Vida looked at her watch, a gift from her late husband, Ernest, and the same one she'd worn all the years I'd known her. "It's going on four. I should have time to finish my advice letters. Three more today. What ever became of fidelity?"

"It didn't seem to mean much to Pastor Purebeck," I said.

"You hardly need to remind me," Vida retorted. "A poor example."

I smiled as I watched her stalk off in her splay-footed manner, dismayed but undaunted. And still hatless.

My phone rang before Vida reached her desk.

"Jay in Yakima," the reporter said. "I found a brief story from Toppenish dated February 8, 1978. Amos Heppner, twenty-four, died from a head injury during an altercation at a tavern. Three other men were treated at the hospital. Nothing noted about arrests or charges being filed. Sounds like an old-fashioned Saturday night drunken brawl. Is that any help?"

"Were the other combatants identified?"

"No, not even the dudes who ended up in the ER." Jay paused. "It's not that unusual. Toppenish prides itself on maintaining an Old West atmosphere. I take it your Alpine is a bit calmer."

"It *is* a former logging town," I said. "We haven't had anyone killed in a tavern fight since October."

He laughed. "Not bad. Dare I ask why you're interested in what goes on over here in this part of the state?"

"Family research," I replied. "Just getting the facts, Jay, in case it turns into a news story."

"We've got plenty of our own bad news," he said. "Yakima's one hell of a big county, second in geographical size to Okanogan. Feel free to ask if I can be of any more help. Not that I found much, I'm afraid."

I thanked him and rang off. I wondered what had caused the fight — and if it had driven Amos's brother out of town.

Halibut cheeks on sale cost me twenty-six dollars and eighty cents. Milo's appetite was wreaking havoc with my meager salary. Having lived mostly on frozen dinners that came in boxes before moving in with me, I realized he had no idea how much real groceries cost. I brought up the subject as he came through the front door, just after five-thirty.

"That's the welcome I get?" he asked, taking off his jacket and hat. "You're the one who always expects at least a kiss."

"I don't get paid for a week. You already blew my food budget."

"I didn't know you had one," he said, heading for the kitchen. "Hell, I offered to take you out to eat tonight."

"I know, but . . ." *Emma Dodge, nagging rival to the first Mrs. Dodge.* I came up behind Milo and put my arms around him as he was about to open the liquor cupboard. "I'm horrid," I wailed, pressing my cheek against his broad back. "Please kiss me."

He laughed as he turned to cradle my face in his hands. "Give me all the damned bills, not just half, you little twit. You're lousy with math anyway." He leaned down to kiss me — gently. "Still mad?"

I stared up into those mesmerizing hazel eyes. "No. I wasn't mad, exactly, just . . . upset. I hate being poor."

"You're not poor, you're just broke." He

let go of me, but not before kissing the top of my head. "Maybe one of these days Doc and I'll go halibut fishing up in Neah Bay. The season starts in the strait at the end of May. Two, three years ago when Doc and I were there we got one that weighed a hundred and thirty pounds."

My eyes narrowed as I watched Milo pour our drinks. "Isn't that a fairly good size for sportfishing?"

"It's not bad. Why?"

"That's *news*, you dolt. Two of you locals catching a big halibut? Jeez, Milo, that's three inches on page four."

My husband shrugged. "I suppose you'd have wanted pictures."

"Yes, pictures! I don't remember you telling me about that trip."

He handed me my Canadian Club. "I wasn't seeing much of you back then. You were too busy driving to hell and gone to be with Fisher."

"Doc didn't care if I was dating Rolf. He's as bad as you are."

"When Doc's here, he's got lives to save."

I just shook my head and led the way into the living room. "Forget it," I said, sitting on the sofa. "I mean, don't forget the next time . . . oh, hell, at least now I'll know you've gone somewhere when you're not here."

"That doesn't make much sense," Milo remarked, still unperturbed.

"Stop before I decide not to tell you about my research."

"Want to sit on my lap while you do that?"

"No. I've got to put the halibut you didn't catch under the broiler in five minutes. Anyway," I said, calming down, "I had a visitor today, Carmela Dobles. Why didn't you tell me she was Joe's mom?"

Milo's expression was stoic. "Because we're not sure who he is."

"Hasn't Mrs. Dobles seen the body?"

My husband shrugged. "Could be. That's up to Driggers. Did she say she had?"

"No." I grimaced, still beating myself up for not asking Carmela all sorts of pertinent questions. Maybe I felt a bond with her as the mother of an only son. Maybe somewhere along the way she'd lost the first love of her life, too. Or maybe I'd just responded to her as one woman to another. "Was she your visitor here?"

"No." Milo seemed to sense that I was upset. He changed the subject. "Get any research done?"

I nodded. "I didn't find out much background, except that Sam's brother, Amos, was killed in a Toppenish tavern brawl back in 1978. He was only twenty-four. No arrests, no names of the other participants."

My husband lighted a cigarette. "Cops involved?"

"Not mentioned in the article, according to my Yakima source."

"Damn," Milo swore softly. "Toppenish has its own police department. I'll check in with them. I wonder if they have records going back that far. If it was just a bunch of drunks, probably not. I'd need somebody with a long memory. Or a grudge."

"Should I call instead?"

Milo shook his head. "No. Maybe the Ol' Boy Cop Network won't be as tight-assed as the county sheriff's office. I shouldn't jump them too much. If they've got the Feds involved, they're in a bind. I remember how that goes from when I had to deal with them after . . ." His voice trailed off as he drank some Scotch.

"Go ahead. You know I don't burst into tears anymore at the mention of Tom's name." I smiled at my husband. "I got you instead."

"Even if I don't blab about an ongoing investigation or forget to tell you I caught some fish?"

"I understand the former, and the latter's

different." I stood up. "Speaking of fish, I have to put the expensive halibut under the broiler."

"Don't set it on fire," Milo called after me.

I ignored him. When I returned to the living room, I asked where he'd gone during the afternoon.

"I took a call about an abandoned car on River Road, so while I was out there, I checked Sam's place to see if there was any sign of him. There wasn't. In fact, his mailbox was stuffed, but it was the usual junk. I happened to see Marlowe Whipp on the way back from his route. He figured Sam hadn't checked his mail since Tuesday. He could've taken off later that day. His call to the funeral home may not have been from town. Did Mrs. Dobles ask you about the other request for the body?"

"Yes, but I didn't tell her who it was. I guard my sources."

"Good. Al tried to call Sam back but got no answer. He and Janet thought I'd had Sam make the call. I told him I hadn't."

I sipped my drink before I spoke again. "So why would Sam want Joe Fernandez's body? He'd have to give Al a valid reason, right?"

"Al doesn't make money on the side with

319

body snatchers." Milo frowned. "Are you thinking what I'm thinking?"

"I have to wonder. Carmela must've been married before she became Mrs. Dobles. What happened to Mr. Fernandez?"

The sheriff's expression was wry. "Maybe he never existed."

SEVENTEEN

"We could check that out on the computer," I suggested.

"Hell, how long would that take?" Milo responded. "It's like looking up somebody named Smith. Birth records would narrow it down. Damn, let me call Doe and ask her to give me the date on the vic's driver's license. She's working the desk tonight." He started to take his cell out of his shirt pocket. "Hey, guess who I saw at Gas 'N Go on my way back from River Road — Mickey Borg."

I was surprised. "Did you talk to him?"

"Are you kidding? He must have seen me in the Yukon first. He jumped in his car and took off. We aren't exactly pals. I wasn't stopping there anyway. You know I always go to Cal's Chevron."

"Me, too," I said and shut up while Milo called Doe. It took a little over a minute for him to get the information about Fernandez's date of birth. It was August 10, 1978.

"Six months after Sam's brother was killed," my husband murmured. "Maybe Amos was the kid's dad? Sam would be his uncle. It makes sense for him to claim the body if nobody else did."

"But Carmela showed up." I tried to sort through what little we knew so far. "Why would Dobles and Fernandez be in the same area at almost the same time? Come on, big guy, speculate a little for me."

"I am," Milo said. "Isn't that what we were just doing? Shouldn't you check the million-dollar halibut before it goes up in smoke?"

"Oh. Right." I hurried out to the kitchen. I flipped the fish over, grabbed my laptop off the bookcase, and resumed my place on the sofa. "Birth records in Toppenish, right?"

"Best place to start," Milo allowed.

I had some problems logging onto the site. "Damn! This is more complicated than it should be." I got up and handed the laptop to Milo. "You do this. I have to get the rest of dinner ready."

"I have to do all the work around here," he muttered as I headed back to the kitchen. "What's your password?"

"EMULARD95," I called back to him.

He muttered some more, but I couldn't hear him. Just as I was about to announce dinner, I heard him bellow, "Son of a bitch!"

"What?" I asked from the doorway.

Milo closed the laptop and hoisted himself from the easy chair. "Mother was Carmela Fernandez. Father was Carlos Fernandez. That doesn't tell us a damned thing."

"Then we know that Sam's brother wasn't the father, right?"

Milo sat down at the table and polished off his drink. "Not necessarily. They might've lied. The site does give the ages of Carmela and Carlos." He paused while I dished up the halibut. "She was seventeen. He was thirty-four."

"That's quite an age difference," I said, serving us each the scalloped potatoes and the asparagus before sitting down. "You look . . . dubious?"

"You're damned right I am," he growled. "I'm checking for a marriage license after dinner. I guess Carlos knocked her up?"

"Somebody did," I said.

"Good fish," Milo remarked. He paused before eating the asparagus he'd forked up and stared at me. "Why'd you say that?"

"Well . . . obviously, she had a baby. Oh! You mean maybe it wasn't Carlos's kid?"

"Could be. Family honor or some damned

thing. I'm glad nobody in your family made you marry some guy to make things look good."

"My parents were dead by then," I said.

"Right. Car accident after your brother became a priest. Is that why you got engaged to the guy you dumped when Cavanaugh came along?"

I nodded. "Don was older. He'd served in the army and was finishing his engineering degree. Ben was off on his home missions work. I guess I wanted to belong to somebody. Dumb idea."

Milo's cell rang. "Screw it. We're eating."

"What if there's a pileup in front of headquarters?"

"Doe can handle it."

The ringing stopped. "By the way," I said, "did Fuzzy call you?"

"You mean about the meeting Monday? Yeah. One o'clock. I'll have to be civil to Blackwell."

"You might have mentioned that to me earlier."

"And interrupt your tirade about running out of grocery money?" He shook his head. "Not a chance."

The cell rang again. Milo swallowed more halibut before looking at the caller's number. "Damn. It's Driggers." He clicked the cell on. "What now, Al? Did you lose the corpse?"

I watched my husband lean back in the chair as Al apparently droned on. "Okay, do what you have to, but if Mrs. Dobles isn't leaving until Monday, what's the rush? She's not buying a seat for the stiff, is she? You could send it on a separate flight. And no, I told you, I have no idea why Heppner . . . Right, but did he give you a reason? . . . Keep trying to reach him. If he doesn't tell you why he wants the body, it goes to the mother. . . . Sure, I can do that. Good luck." Milo stuffed the cell back in his pocket. "Nothing further from Sam, and Mrs. Dobles is getting impatient. They're discharging her husband first thing Monday morning."

"I hate to say this," I began slowly, "but do you think something's happened to Sam?"

"He wouldn't have called Al last night if he was lying in a pool of blood someplace. My guess is that he's wandering around the area, maybe doing a little fishing, maybe just . . . wandering. He likes to do that sometimes. It's people who drive him nuts."

I polished off the last of my scalloped potatoes. "Wouldn't some of the rangers have seen him?"

"They haven't been looking for him," Milo replied. "I didn't announce that he was missing."

"Maybe you should."

Milo shook his head. "No. That'd really piss him off. I have to take Heppner at his word. He wanted time off, he's entitled to it, and I'd be out of line. I can afford to lose Sam for a week or two, but not permanently. I don't give a shit if he's not a so-called people person. He's a hard and thorough worker. Loyal, too. That's all I ask."

"Like you, Sam goes by the book," I remarked. "By the way, why do you think Mickey Borg is back in town?"

"How should I know? I don't know where he went when he left town. He never sent me any postcards." Milo ate a last bite of halibut before speaking again. "I think I'll take Fred Engelman up on his offer to do some repairs, though. I can deal with his worrywart crap. Being shorthanded right now, I could use him to fill in at night in case whoever is on duty gets called away. As I recall, he can read and write."

"Good," I said. "Fred and Janie need the money. Mickey cleaned her out. Besides, Fred works for Blackwell. He can give you some dope on Jack if you ever need it."

"Blackwell's mill is just fine. Too bad he's

not. Got any pie left?"

"No. Yes. You had apple pie for lunch. You want blackberry pie for dinner? Jeez, you're hopeless!"

"Hey — do I look like I've gained weight?"

"Well . . . no, but you will if you . . . oh, never mind." I stood up to get the pie out of the fridge. "Do you want it warmed up?"

"Don't bother. Are you going to have some?"

"There's only one piece left. Did you eat some of it for breakfast?"

"Hunh. I don't think so."

Shaking my head, I handed over the last of the pie and sat down again. "I hope Vida doesn't find out Mickey Borg's in town. She might think he's snooping around here on Holly Gross's behalf."

"Why would . . . oh, I forgot. Mickey's the father of Holly's two other kids, right?" He saw me nod. "You think Borg's been hanging out with Holly since he left Alpine?"

"I've no idea," I admitted. "I don't remember when he took off."

"It's been two, three months since Darryl Gustavson took over the Gas 'N Go."

"I wonder why Mickey's here," I said, reaching over to brush some pie crust off Milo's chin. "Do you think he dealt drugs at the mini-mart?"

Milo chewed his pie, looking thoughtful. "If he did, Roger never mentioned him when he unloaded about who was doing what with the drug traffic. Neither did Holly, for that matter."

"Maybe she wouldn't if he was the father of her two older kids."

"Hell, with people like that, they'll rat each other out at the drop of a misdemeanor charge." He paused to eat the last bite of pie. "On the other hand, if Holly thought she could get some money out of Mickey for his two kids, she might've kept quiet. She sure isn't getting anything out of that jackass Roger. Hey, did you say he had a real job?"

"Incredibly, yes." As we cleared the table, I told Milo about Roger's new career with Party Animals.

"I saw that van go by when I was coming back from River Road," Milo said as we went back to the living room to resume our research. "Party Animals — sounds about right for Roger. Move over. We might as well sit together while we do this stuff. It might make it more interesting."

"Only if you keep your hands to yourself, Sheriff," I said in mock reproach. "Where were we?"

"Marriage licenses," Milo replied. "That'd be the Yakima County courthouse. If Carmela was only seventeen, she'd have to get parental consent. You do it. These keys are too small for my fingers."

"Then keep your fingers off my butt," I said, feeling his hand on my backside. "I have to concentrate."

"Okay, okay." He sighed and folded his arms across his chest. "I thought you'd have more fun doing research with me than with Vida."

"That's the problem," I said, squinting at the screen. "We'd both have so much fun we'd never be able to see the . . . damn, I think I need glasses. What does this say? It doesn't make any sense."

Milo took the laptop from me. "It's pet licenses, goofy. Let me do it. I can't screw it up any worse than you did." Cussing under his breath, my husband finally found the right screen — and after more cussing, he came up with the May 2 marriage license between Carmela Diaz and Carlos Fernandez. "Now let's see if we can find a marriage certificate," he said, switching to another site. Only minor cussing ensued, but Milo found it — May 6, 1978, St. Aloysius Catholic Church, Toppenish.

"That would've been the weekend of the

329

big Hispanic celebration of Cinco de Mayo," I said. "Nice timing for a wedding."

"Carmela had to get her parents' consent, being under eighteen," Milo noted. "I wonder what happened to Carlos."

"They divorced later." I tried to recall Carmela's exact words. "She obviously dumped Fernandez and later married Dobles. Or maybe Carlos died."

Milo closed the laptop. "Does any of this mean anything? It's Sam's hometown, his brother got killed there, Joe Fernandez was born there, and Carmela lived in Toppenish at the time of her first marriage. I don't know what the population was back then, but the town's about the size of SkyCo. You're good at these guessing games. What's your take on it?"

"The coincidence of them both being in the area really bothers me. Can I go *way* out into left field?"

"Why not? You usually do."

"Maybe this sounds weird, but it's all I can think of: they arranged to meet for some reason. What if they quarreled? And Dobles killed Joe."

Milo put a hand to his head. "Jesus. You're way up in the bleachers this time." He lowered his hand and looked at me. "So Dobles sticks around until late the next afternoon to make sure the guy's dead? The wreck didn't occur until around four-thirty. Fernandez died sometime during the middle of the night."

I grimaced. "But the body hadn't been found until just before the wreck." Milo looked at me without blinking — always a bad sign. "Okay," I went on, "it doesn't make much sense. But people do odd things. I don't suppose anyone spotted him in his fancy sports car? What kind was it?"

"A 2003 Boxster Porsche. It's damned near totaled. We've still got it in impound." Milo sighed. "I guess we'd better process it."

I was surprised. "You don't think I'm nuts?"

He chuckled. "Yeah, you're nuts, but sometimes you come up with something that's worth checking out, if only to prove you're wrong."

"I've been right about a lot of things over the years," I asserted.

"Like getting me to arrest the wrong guy ten years ago?"

"You thought he did it," I said. "He didn't deny doing it. You had evidence. It's not our fault he was covering for somebody else."

"It's still a pain in the ass." He put the

laptop on the coffee table. The hazel eyes sparked. "You want to roll around on the floor for a while? I need to work off that pie."

"That's work?" I said — and giggled.

Later that night as Milo was reading in bed and I was doing a crossword puzzle, he closed his book and turned to look at me. "I forget — where did Holly go after she collected her two kids from the foster parents in Sultan?"

"Centralia or Chehalis," I said. "I get them mixed up, because they're so close together off I-5. That's where Holly's sister lives."

"Right, Centralia." He chuckled. "I've stopped there a few times when I've been fishing the Cowlitz and the Toutle Rivers. They've got a hotel that used to be a brothel. The rooms are named after prominent citizens. One was for Floyd Duell, who was the mill superintendent here around 1920. I remember Grandpa Dodge talking about him."

"You went there because you thought it was still a brothel?"

Milo made a face at me. "I stayed overnight. It was a three-day trip. They've got a bar and a restaurant, too."

"We could go there on the honeymoon we've never had."

Milo set Tony Hillerman on the nightstand. "Too soon. The summer steelhead run won't be in for a while. You going to be all night figuring out what a three-letter word for a barking domestic animal is?"

I glared at him. "Are you timing me?"

"No, but I think I'll start."

I sighed in annoyance, put the crossword aside, and turned out the light. "Satisfied, you big jerk?"

"Yeah," he said, putting his arms around me. "How about you?"

I snuggled up closer. "I'm in my safe place. How could I not be?"

"Just doing my job, keeping you in protective custody. Good night, little Emma."

"Goodnight, Sheriff."

We both slept in the next morning. The Bourgettes didn't work on the weekends, and with any luck, neither Milo nor I would have to, either. Except, of course, that we probably couldn't stop thinking about the current homicide investigation.

Around ten o'clock, I was sufficiently awake to make coherent sounds. My husband had been up a half hour ahead of me and had just come inside from surveying

333

the area where the carport had once stood.

"You'd better start picking out appliances and whatever else we're going to need. You want to pay Lloyd Campbell a visit or go online?"

"I got dizzy looking at bathroom stuff online a while ago," I replied as I loaded the dishwasher. "It'd be easier to go to Lloyd's store. Do you want to come with me?"

Milo winced. "You have a hell of a time making up your mind. I don't think I could stand the aggravation. I'll do some fishing research. Trout season's coming up. I could use some new gear."

"Go for it. You have money to spend."

"Compared to what you're going to put out for new appliances?"

"Well . . . no. But . . . never mind. Maybe I'm not as awake as I thought I was." I offered Milo a feeble smile. "Should I actually order the stuff?"

Milo frowned. "Gosh, Emma, that's probably the only way it can get here to be installed." He reached into his back pocket. "Use this," he said, pulling out a credit card.

I was a bit tentative taking the plastic from him. "I feel like a kept woman."

"You are. I'm keeping you. You're kind of undersized, but I won't throw you back." He kissed the top of my head before heading to the front door. "I'm going to check out my fishing stuff at my place. If you need me, call. Lloyd might have a nervous breakdown while you're trying to make decisions. And don't go cheap. Quality lasts longer."

I made a growling noise in my throat, but I didn't think Milo heard me. Just as well. But it seemed strange not to be frugal. Unless, of course, it came to my wardrobe. I had an image to keep up, after all. Or so I told myself.

Half an hour later, I was ready to head for the appliance store. The phone rang just as I grabbed my purse.

"I'm at headquarters," Milo said. "Bill's car was parked in the driveway, so I didn't bother them. I figure they spent the night there. Anyway, I decided to come here and start processing Dobles's Porsche. Gould's helping me. Go for stainless steel in the kitchen."

"Why can't . . ." I realized my husband had already hung up. I headed along Fir to Alpine Appliance, which had expanded in the past couple of years to fill the block between Front Street and Railroad Avenue. Lloyd's son, Shane, was on duty.

"Hey," he said, greeting me as I came inside, "I hear you and the sheriff are remodeling. How's it coming?"

"Far enough that I have to order new appliances," I replied, not sounding very excited over the prospect. "I made a list."

Shane's fair skin seemed to glow as he studied the items, which also included the new plumbing fixtures. "This is quite a redo, huh? Are you going to Sky Blue Bath for this other stuff?"

"Eventually," I said. "Ever since Lee Amundson took it over, they've expanded quite a bit."

Shane nodded. "They've got more space, too, after moving to the old used-car lot on River Road. Okay," he went on, taking a ballpoint pen out of his pocket and clicking it a few times in what I hoped wasn't a mental calculation of the amount I was about to spend. "Let's start with refrigerators. They take up the most room. You want side-by-side or top or bottom freezing compartments?"

"I haven't thought much about it," I confessed. "Maybe side-by-side? It might be easier to get at things I bury behind each other."

Shane led me to a half dozen stainless steel models. "Speaking of burying, what happened to that guy who was in the wreck last Monday? That looked pretty bad. And a Porsche! That's really awful."

"He's improving," I said. "You drove by after it happened?"

"I sort of saw how it happened," Shane said, opening one of the fridge's doors. "Maybe I'm nuts, but I could have sworn that poor guy was forced off the road. Now, this is average size, so you might . . ."

"Forced?" I interrupted. "You mean . . . what?"

"I was coming back from making a delivery in Skykomish," Shane replied, petting the stainless steel as if it were the family dog. "The Porsche was ahead of me. You know just before that little curve on 2 after the ranger station?" He saw me nod. "A black sedan passed me going way too fast and cut in between my van and the Porsche. By the time I caught up, the sedan was gone and all three cars were still sort of going every which way. I was the one who called in the wreck."

"Did you stop?"

"Sure. But I was kind of shaken up, and a couple of other cars were already stopped coming from the other direction. Then one of the deputies pulled onto the highway — Sam Heppner — motioned for me to turn into town. I guess I was partially blocking the right-hand lane."

"Did Sam have you fill out a report?"

Shane shook his head. "I didn't actually see the collision, so all I could say was that the sedan was going really fast. Too many people who don't live around here do that all the time. I figured if Heppner wanted to find out if I did see anything, he'd have asked me later."

"Right," I murmured, wondering why Sam hadn't contacted Shane. "Is this on sale?"

"No, but the bigger one next to it is. Marked down two hundred bucks." He grinned at me. "Didn't you read our ad?"

"That's Leo's job," I replied. "Frankly, I didn't know I'd be buying appliances this weekend. I'll take it." After looking at only two models, I was already kind of dizzy. Or maybe it was Shane's account of the wreck that had set me off.

"Have you decided on a range or a cook-top and maybe built-in double ovens?" he asked, leading the way to another part of the store.

"I've always had a range," I said.

"Have you got the dimensions of your new kitchen?"

"No." I grimaced. "It's about twice the size of the one I have now." That was a guess, of course. "Maybe a bit bigger," I added lamely.

Shane ran a hand through his fair hair. "Well, cooktops are so easy to wipe up. Self-cleaning double ovens, of course. Stainless?"

"Yes," I said. "I'll take them."

"You'll . . . which ones?"

"Whatever you think is the best deal. I'm not very good at this sort of thing, as you've probably noticed."

"Gosh, it usually takes customers a long time to make up their minds." He grinned at me again. "I recommend the Whirlpool ones. They're on sale now, too."

"Fine. Now I need a built-in dishwasher. Are those Whirlpools on sale, too?"

"No, but the Maytags are."

"Okay. What about washers and dryers?"

"We're back to Whirlpool if you want the sale price."

"I do."

"Color?"

"Ah . . . do they come in stainless?"

"Sure."

"On sale, right?"

"You got it."

I sure do, I thought, and wondered if Shane had smelling salts on hand. "I don't know how soon they should be delivered," I said. "Probably not for another week or two."

"That's okay. I have to order the dishwasher and the washer and dryer. We sold out yesterday. The sale, you know."

I fumbled in my purse, trying to find Milo's credit card. I couldn't. Shane waited patiently, while I searched in the recesses of my big and overloaded handbag.

"No rush," he said kindly. "The Vardis just came in. Be right back."

I nodded vaguely at Professor and Mrs. Vardi before stepping out of sight to dump everything in my purse on top of whichever appliance I was standing by. It might've been an air conditioner. Or a trash compactor. Or one of Averill Fairbanks's spaceships. I was too rattled to know the difference. But the credit card finally surfaced, having been at the very bottom of my purse. I was putting everything back in place when Shane returned.

"The Vardis are looking at fridges, too," Shane said. "Let me run this through for you."

"Okay." I staggered over to the counter. Did I have the nerve to see how much I'd spent? I steeled myself — and waited, feeling as if Doc Dewey were about to tell me if whatever condition I had was terminal.

"There you go," Shane finally said, sliding the receipt across the counter. "You got some good deals."

"Unh," I uttered, my eyes widening at the total: just under five grand, tax included. My signature looked like a chicken had made it. I felt like a chicken — plucked. But it was Milo's money, though that didn't make me feel any better.

After getting into my car, I headed for the sheriff's headquarters, wondering if Milo had any idea of what appliances cost these days. I sure didn't. Or hadn't until buying what amounted to over a month of my salary as an impoverished editor and publisher.

To my surprise, Ron Bjornson was behind the curving counter. "I thought you quit," I blurted out.

"I did," Ron said with his off-center smile, "but the sheriff's short of people, so he asked me to keep an eye on things while he's working out back with some cars." He shrugged. "I guess Fred Engelman's taking on my chores."

"Yes. Now that Fred and Janie have remarried, they can use the money. Mickey Borg took everything, including the TV."

"That guy always was a prick," Ron said, then winced. "Sorry, Ms. Lord, for the rough language, but I saw him checking out a new Corvette the other day at Nordby Brothers. I sure hope Janie and Fred don't see him tooling around town in a hot new Vette."

"That'd be aggravating," I agreed. "I'd better find Milo."

"Awrrr . . ." Ron laughed in embarrassment. "I forgot — you're Mrs. Dodge now. That's nice. I mean, good for you guys."

"Thanks, Ron," I said, smiling as I went around the counter and toward the rear exit. "Say hello to Maylene for me."

If there was one thing I could say for Ron Bjornson, he didn't hold a grudge. His arrest as a murder suspect had occurred a few months after I'd broken up with the sheriff. To say Milo and I were not on good terms would be putting it mildly. In fact, we were both emotional disasters. The sheriff had some evidence against Ron, but he'd acted precipitously to show me up or just to show me. Neither of us had ever figured out that part. But when Ron threatened to sue the county for wrongful arrest, the sheriff offered a part-time job, which the Bjornsons desperately needed. Now that they both had full-time jobs at the college and their kids were grown, the family was in better financial shape.

I first noticed the ATV off to one side in the small impound area between the building and the railroad tracks. The Porsche wreckage briefly blocked my view of Milo and Dwight Gould. Moving closer, I saw that they were focused on a third vehicle, a midsized black Nissan sedan.

"Hi," I said diffidently. "I'm not here to pester you, but . . ."

Milo, who had been kneeling to study the car's right front tire, looked at me but didn't stand up. "If you've flipped out over picking a damned stove, save it, okay?"

I ignored Dwight's fierce glare. "I didn't," I declared, finding my spine. "I've got a witness to the Dobles accident."

The sheriff got to his feet. "We had two witnesses. A westbound couple from Spokane stated that the Porsche was going too fast and went out of control."

I felt smug. "How about a local?"

"Who?" Milo asked dubiously. "If it's Crazy Eights . . ."

"It's not," I interrupted. "It's Shane Campbell. You and your deputies apparently didn't ask for his statement." I glared back at Dwight just for the hell of it.

The sheriff turned away from me. "Finish up here, Gould. I'd better check this out. Ms. Lord isn't always a reliable source." He grabbed my rear as we went back inside. "Shane Campbell was on the scene? Goddamnit, nobody told me that. He wasn't

343

there when I showed up."

"That's because Sam Heppner told him to get out of the way. He was blocking traffic with his van."

Ron acknowledged us with a nod as we went into Milo's office. "Okay," my husband said, sitting in his chair while I parked myself across the desk. "I take it you were doing more than buying a fridge."

"I wasn't. I mean, I was buying a fridge, but Shane volunteered it. He happened to be right behind Dobles until another car cut him off. It appeared to be chasing down the Porsche."

Milo offered me a cigarette, which I accepted. He lighted both for us and handed me mine. "Go on," he urged — and scowled. "Why are you looking so sappy?"

"I'm not used to seeing you here in your civvies. It's kind of . . . um . . ."

He waved the hand that wasn't holding the cigarette. "Stick to business. What did Shane say he saw?"

I grew serious and related what Shane had said almost word for word, including the fact that Sam hadn't asked him to fill out a report. "Granted," I concluded, "he didn't actually see the other car force the Porsche off the road, but he was fairly certain that's what happened."

Milo's gaze was steady as he took a puff on his cigarette. "It probably did. That Nissan outside is the abandoned car I found on River Road yesterday. It's got some front-end damage with red paint that matches the Porsche. It looks as if we might be talking attempted vehicular homicide."

EIGHTEEN

I had a barrage of questions for the sheriff, but he silenced me by holding up his hand. "Before you ask, that's not the local car that was reportedly stolen from Ptarmigan Tract. We still haven't found that one. It belongs to Rocky and Sarah Swensen's older son, who's away at college."

"Do I know them?"

Milo made a face. "Rocky works for Blackwell. You'd know him and Sarah if you saw them, but skip the irrelevant questions. There's nothing in the Nissan to show who owned it or where it came from. It's got Washington plates, which we're running through the system, but my hunch is that it's stolen. The only thing besides finding the real owner is that whoever drove it filled up the gas tank. If we can track down where the gas was purchased, that'd help."

"Have you checked Cal's and Gas 'N Go?"

"Ron did that just before you got here. No luck." Milo leaned back in the chair. "Damn. This whole mess gets more screwed up as time goes on. It's supposed to be the other way around."

"Where was the abandoned car?" I asked.

"Almost to the end of River Road where it doubles back by the little bridge over Deception Creek. I wouldn't have noticed it if I hadn't wanted to check out a fishing hole there to see if what little snowpack we had changed the river's course." He took a last puff on his cigarette before putting it out in the Seahawks ashtray Tanya had given him to go with his coffee mug. "Why the hell didn't Heppner ask for Shane's statement? The jackass didn't even tell me that an Alpine Appliance van had been at the scene. Maybe he really was coming down sick."

"You thought he made that up?"

"Well . . ." Milo fingered his chin. "I wondered after he asked to go on leave the next day. I can't remember Heppner ever calling in sick."

"Maybe he was sick inside."

My husband stared at me for a moment. "Yeah . . . that sounds more like it, given whatever the hell's going on with him. Oh — did you actually buy any appliances, or did you just dither a lot?"

Grimacing, I took out the receipt and pushed it across the desk. "Here. Don't pass out. I almost did."

"Jesus! Five grand? What are they made of — solid gold?"

"Everything was on sale. I think."

Milo expelled a big breath. "Inflation, I guess. I haven't bought an appliance since . . . hell, I never bought an appliance. Mulehide did all that. She liked picking out stuff for the house."

"I thought I'd have an aneurysm. I must've done all this in fifteen minutes. It's a wonder I didn't run over somebody coming here."

The sheriff shrugged. "It's fine. Your stuff is pretty old."

"Some of it came with the cabin, and it was old then. The Bourgettes suggested that we could donate what we don't want to Father Den for the women's shelter."

Milo nodded. "That's a tax deduction. Go ahead." He stood up. "Now just go. I've got work to do."

"It's nice again today, so maybe I'll do some gardening," I said as he walked me out of his office. "Since my little log cabin is turning into a stately country home, I feel as if I should hire a landscaper."

"Do that. Mountain View Gardens is coming out next week to start on my place. I'll cut a deal with them."

"Milo . . ." I looked up at him in reproach.

"Hell, you just spent five grand on appliances. Do something fun."

I couldn't resist. "Maybe I'll pay Francine Wells a call instead," I said over my shoulder.

"There *are* limits," Milo warned me in a stern voice.

I kept going.

Instead of heading for Francine's Fine Apparel, I retraced my route to Nordby Brothers, at Sixth and Front. Only one of the siblings — Trout — was in the showroom extolling the marvels of a new Chevrolet Malibu to a young couple. I held back, waiting for the pair to fish or cut bait.

They did neither, the young man finally saying that they'd think about it before heading out the door.

"Emma." Trout greeted me with a big, almost sincere smile. "Are you looking to replace that Honda?"

"Not yet," I said. "I take it those two who just left were looky-loos."

"From Everett," Trout replied. "So many people come up here because they think we'll be a lot cheaper. Sure, we can give them a good deal, but Skunk and I aren't a charity."

I laughed. "You're also the only GM dealer for miles around. Would it kill you to take out a bigger ad?"

Trout grinned. "Hey, you doing Walsh's job? He's damned good at twisting arms."

"No," I said, growing serious. "I hear Mickey Borg's back in town. Did he make you richer by buying that Corvette?"

"Wow," Trout murmured, "news travels fast around here. Yeah, he drove it right off the lot. Can you believe he put down ten grand cash as the first payment?"

I tried to hide my surprise. "He did sell Gas 'N Go."

"Right, but still . . . where's he been since he left town? I asked him, but he shrugged and said, 'Here, there and everywhere.' Mickey couldn't wait to get on the highway to air it out, as he put it."

"So he left Alpine?"

"Who knows? I hadn't seen him around here for two, three months at least. I asked him what he'd been up to, but he didn't give me a straight answer. All the same, his money's good with me."

"As long as he's not printing it himself," I said.

Trout obliged me with a chuckle. "So what can I do for you, Emma? Isn't it time you drove an American car? First a Jag, then a Lexus, and now a Honda. Dodge is a good citizen driving that Yukon. Isn't it time you changed allegiance?"

"I'll have to eventually, but we're in the middle of a big remodel. I thought I'd stop in to make sure Leo was treating you and Skunk right."

"Walsh is good people," Trout assured me. "Now if I could just talk him out of that old Toyota. Jeez, that thing's got almost a hundred and fifty thousand miles on it."

"It still runs," I said, seeing a trio of young men who looked like college students enter the showroom. "I'll let you show these guys something they can't possibly afford," I murmured.

"At least they're dreaming the American dream," Trout said under his breath as he smoothed his tie and brushed back what was left of his graying brown hair. "Hey, there . . . looking for serious wheels or . . ."

I was getting into my trusty if aged Honda when I heard a horn honk. Not sure if it was meant for me, I looked across the street to see Mitch in his well-traveled Ford Taurus. As a longtime Detroit resident, he could hardly drive anything but an American car. Pulling a neat U-ie I wouldn't have dared in the middle of Front Street, Mitch parked behind my Honda. I walked to his passenger side as he rolled down the window.

"Guess what?" he said, leaning in my direction. "I ran into Mrs. Ellison when I went to pick up Brenda's meds at the hospital pharmacy. She's a nurse there. I remembered that her daughter was one of the runaways, so I asked if she'd heard anything more from her lately. She said she had, just this morning, when Samantha sent her a money order for fifty dollars as an early Mother's Day present. Apparently, the kid's got a job in Centralia."

"Centralia?" I echoed.

"Right." Mitch frowned. "I'm not sure where that is."

"About eighty, ninety miles south of Seattle," I replied. "Just off I-5. That's odd — Milo and I were talking about the town last night. Did Mrs. Ellison say where her daughter is working?"

"A hostess of some kind," Mitch replied. "Restaurant work, I suppose. She's too young to have a job in a bar. Anyway, her mom's thrilled. It sounds like the money must be pretty good. Tips, maybe."

"Maybe." I felt uneasy. "I hope Samantha

352

gets her GED."

"At least the Ellisons know where she is," Mitch said. "I'd better head home before Brenda starts to fuss."

"Say hello to her for me," I called, backing away from the Taurus.

Suddenly I wasn't in the mood to visit Francine's shop. Centralia seemed to be a theme for all sorts of things in the past few days. But I didn't know why. And that bothered me — a lot.

When I got home, I wasn't in the mood to pull weeds, either. Except for the front part of the yard and a stretch along the fence between my property and the Marsdens', there wasn't much garden left. The Bourgettes had dug up almost everything out back and along the sides of my little log cabin.

Instead, I decided to concentrate on my Heppner research. The only problem was that I didn't know where to look next. What I needed was someone in the Toppenish area with a long memory. Hating to be a pest, I called Dave Grogan, my venerable newspaper contact. He had been my adviser when I was buying the *Advocate.* Dave was retired now and living in Ocean Shores, near Grays Harbor.

After five rings, I figured Dave wasn't home, but he picked up on the sixth. The usual catching-up exchange ensued. I asked how he and his wife enjoyed their life of leisure; he queried me about the near-death experience Milo and I had undergone at the end of December. However, Dave didn't know about our marriage.

"Good for you, Emma," he said. "I always hoped you'd find somebody else after Tom Cavanaugh was killed."

I didn't tell Dave that I'd found Milo long before that happened, but cut to the chase. "Do you have anybody in your cerebral file who knows all of Toppenish's dirty little secrets?"

Being a veteran journalist, Dave wasn't surprised by the question. "Off the top of my head — which no longer has much hair — I can think of two. George Fairweather, who retired a few years ago as the *Yakima Herald-Republic* managing editor, and Charley Burke, who worked for the *Herald-Republic* and later for the *Spokesman-Review.* George is in Europe right now, but Charley should be around. I talked to him a week or two ago, lying a lot about our golf games. Let me get his number. He's living outside of Spokane, at Liberty Lake. Here it is . . ."

Our conversation wound down on the usual wistful yet bitter notes of why cable TV news was inferior to print media, if newspapers were all dinosaurs, and how glad he was to have gotten out of the business before reading in general and proofreading in particular had become lost arts. News, we agreed, was mainly dispensed by attractive talking heads who often didn't know rumor from fact. If there was one thing print journalists know how to do besides deliver the news, it's bitch. Dave and I were very good at it.

Charley Burke was outside doing something with his boat, according to Mrs. Burke. He'd be back only God knew when, but she'd have him call me and was the area code really 360? I assured her it was, thanked her, and hung up.

Realizing it was going on one o'clock and I was hungry, I was about to make a sandwich when Milo arrived with a Burger Barn bag. "I stopped to pick up lunch. I didn't know if you were home, but I figured I could eat two burgers if you weren't."

"Guess what? I can eat a burger. Did you get double fries?"

"Yeah." He set the bag down, hooked his arm around my neck, and kissed me. "I'll make the sacrifice. I had a late breakfast. So did you."

"I only had cornflakes," I said as he let go of me. "You always make yourself a big breakfast. I never have time to do that."

"You're never awake enough to find the stove. Speaking of stoves, what kind did you get?"

I blanked out for a moment. "Counter-top? With built-in double ovens? They're self-cleaning, by the way."

"No kidding. What'll we do around here for excitement without setting the kitchen on fire?"

I stared up at him. "We'll think of some-thing."

"Besides that, I mean." Milo ruffled my hair. "I don't see any sign of digging in the garden. Did you really go clothes shop-ping?"

"No."

"Good. Your closet's crammed with clothes. There's hardly room for mine. That'll change when the bedroom's bigger. Say, I was trying to find my shoes on the floor in there this morning and a pile of stuff fell over. Mostly pictures, including one of you and Cavanaugh in Leavenworth. But where'd that one of me come from? I look like an idiot."

I smiled. "I took that after you found the

gun that had been used to kill one of the California developers. I saved it because . . . I liked it."

"That was before we started dating."

"So?"

Milo shook his head. "I often wonder what was going on in your head all the years you didn't think you were in love with me. Let's eat."

"I was insane, okay? Get over it." I got out two plates from the cupboard. "I'll heat up the burgers and fries."

"Go ahead." He filled the plates. "I was right. That Nissan was stolen from a parking lot by the fairgrounds in Monroe. The owner reported it as missing to the cops Monday night."

I set the timer on the microwave. "So it was stolen just for the hell of it or to run Dobles off the road?"

"The latter," Milo said, sitting down at the table. "It makes more sense. *If* it was an accident, kids steal car, clip Porsche, dump Nissan in Alpine. That doesn't play for me. On that stretch, you're going too fast to turn off into town. You have to, especially with oncoming traffic, until you can turn off on the Martin Creek Road and double back."

The microwave buzzed. "Why?" I asked, setting the food on the table. "Nel Dobles is a Californian. You say this wasn't an accident. Thus, I deduce he had enemies. Please, Sheriff, enlighten me."

Milo made a face. "Don't be a smart-ass. That's what *I* want to know. It's spring break for most of the schools around here. It could be kids jealous of some guy in a hot car and wanting to do some damage. But there's one thing I haven't told you. Dobles is a fruit inspector."

I was puzzled. "Which means?"

"Fernandez was a fruit inspector."

"We grow fruit, California grows fruit. Are you saying Dobles and Fernandez planned to meet and talk about grapes?"

"I don't know what the hell I'm saying," Milo growled. "I can't get squat out of Yakima, but I don't think it's their fault. I doubt they know more than I do. It's the Feds who are screwing it up. For once, I'd like you to come up with one of your nutty ideas. I'd even listen to Vida yammering at me with some half-assed theory."

"Strangely enough," I said, "Vida isn't very interested in the case. Fernandez isn't a local, and nobody in SkyCo seems to be a suspect. She's too wrapped up in Roger's new job."

Milo downed three fries. "Great. The one time I might want to use what's under her crazy hats, she's a dud." His cell rang. Muttering under his breath, he barked, "Dodge," and listened to whoever was on the other end. "Shit," he said. "Okay, Dwight, I'll be there in ten minutes."

"What now?" I asked.

"Bob and Caroline Sigurdson reported their daughter as missing," Milo said. "I'm going out to their place on the Burl Creek Road. Bob is Blackwell's logging manager, so I don't want to piss him off just before I have to get together with his boss on Monday. I don't need any more guff from that asshole than I usually get."

"Which daughter?" I asked. "Don't they have two?"

"Amy or Antsy or whatever. They've got a son, Andy." Milo paused to take a last bite of burger. "The girl's not a teenager, so it can't be an end-of-spring-break fling."

"It's Ainsley, and she's Roger's girlfriend."

"Christ. No wonder she's missing. Maybe she's hiding from him." He grabbed four more fries and stood up.

"Can I come?" I gave the sheriff my most winsome look. "The woman's touch."

"Hell, no. Stay put!" He started out of the kitchen, then stopped just inside the living room. "Why not? Gould says Caroline's hysterical. Maybe you can calm her down.

If you stay here, you might invite Jack the Ripper in for a drink."

We didn't speak again until Milo turned off Alpine Way to the Burl Creek Road. "Okay," he said, "tell me what you know about this girl besides the fact that she's dumb enough to go out with Roger."

"She's an aide at RestHaven. That's why Roger volunteered. . . . Hey, I told you all this a long time ago."

"I try not to think about Roger if I can help it. As I recall from the dim, dark past, she started hanging out with him when they were still in high school. Have they been going together all this time?"

"I don't know," I replied. "Vida began mentioning them as a couple this past winter. Now that I think about it, she hasn't talked about Ainsley lately. She didn't say if she was at Dippy's birthday party. Vida usually doesn't miss a chance to gush about 'young love.' "

Milo made a disgusted face. "Let's hope Roger isn't mixed up in whatever stunt this Ainsley pulled." He slowed down by a white picket fence that enclosed a tidy Dutch Colonial two-story house. "You say they've got another daughter?" he asked, turning into a paved driveway.

"Yes, but I don't know anything about her.

I'm not even sure how I know that much. I'd forgotten they had a son."

Bob Sigurdson met us at the front door. He was a big man, not as tall as Milo but even broader. "Come in," he said quietly. "I told Caroline to lie down. She's a wreck. Women don't cope very well with a crisis."

For some reason, Bob didn't seem to notice that I was a woman; nor was he surprised that Milo was accompanied by someone who wasn't a deputy. The sheriff introduced me as Mrs. Dodge. I'd seen Bob around town, but I didn't really know him — or his wife. "I brought backup," my husband explained, "in case you needed some help with your wife."

"Very kind," Bob said, leading us into the well-appointed living room. "I made her take a couple of those Tylenol nighttime pills. I've got coffee on, if you'd like."

We both declined. Milo and I sat down on a peach-and-green striped sofa. Bob settled into a matching recliner. "I don't know where to start," he said, passing a hand across his high forehead.

"The last time you saw your daughter is fine," Milo responded. "We can back up later, of course."

Bob grimaced. "We saw Ainsley yesterday morning at breakfast. She left for Rest-

Haven — she's an aide there — a little before eight-thirty. Our other daughter, Alicia, drove her to work. Ainsley's car needs a brake job." Bob frowned, staring at his hands, which he'd carefully folded in his lap. "Alicia said Ainsley planned to get a ride home with one of the nurses who lives farther down the road, by the radio station. When she wasn't home by six — she gets off at five — we got worried. Caroline called the medical rehab unit, but they told her Ainsley had left at the regular time. We figured maybe she and the nurse had stopped somewhere. By going on seven, she still wasn't home, so we tried to get hold of Jennifer Hood, who's in charge of the unit. We couldn't reach her until almost ten. I wondered if the two of them had gone someplace, but . . ." Bob's face grew grim. "Jennifer thought Ainsley had a date. She told us Ainsley seemed sort of excited about it, but she didn't know who or what it was all about." He paused again, now gripping the chair's armrests.

Milo waited for Bob to continue. When he didn't, my husband posed a question: "Does Ainsley often stay out all night with friends?"

Bob shook his head. "Not as a rule. She has done overnights with girlfriends from time to time. We checked with everyone we could think of, but no luck. Either they hadn't seen her or they weren't home."

"You waited until this afternoon to call us," Milo said in a neutral tone. "Was that because you thought she'd still show up?"

Bob looked faintly pugnacious. "Well, yes. She's twenty-two — she's not a kid. I mean, she's entitled to have a life."

The sheriff nodded. "Does she have a current boyfriend?"

Bob's full face reddened. "She did, but they broke up a few weeks ago. Just as well, frankly."

Milo didn't speak, so I figured that was my cue. "I take it you didn't like him," I said. "Had they gone together long?"

Bob let out a big sigh. "About six months or so." He seemed to look at me for the first time. "Say — aren't you the newspaper lady?"

"Yes. Call me Emma." I smiled in what I hoped was a kindly manner.

Bob grimaced. "Ainsley had been seeing Mrs. Runkel's grandson. Roger Hibbert. He's not a bad kid, just kind of lazy and unmotivated. But Caroline and I . . . well, we felt she could do better, find somebody with a real future."

"Maybe," I suggested, "they got back to-gether."

"I doubt it," Bob said. "She never stayed out all night with him even when they were going together."

I kept my kindly look in place. "It might be different if they were reconciling. Long talks, sorting things out, considering a second chance."

Bob gestured at an oak mantel clock above the fireplace. "It's after two. How long does anybody need to talk?" He leaned forward, staring at me. "Do you think I should call Roger's folks or Mrs. Runkel?"

I didn't dare take my eyes off Bob. The question was for me, but I couldn't look at Milo. I knew damned well he'd love to have me say yes. So I did. "It wouldn't hurt," I said. "It's always smart to check with your children's friends and their families. You mentioned calling some of the other people who are close to Ainsley."

"Caroline did," Bob replied, sitting up straight again. "No luck."

Milo finally spoke again: "There's nothing I can do until Ainsley's been missing for forty-eight hours. As you said, she's an adult." He stood up. "Meanwhile, keep us in the loop."

Bob and I had both gotten to our feet.

"That's not very comforting," he grumbled. "You can't imagine what it's like to have a daughter and not know where she is or what's happening to her."

The sheriff's face tightened. "It's worse when you *do* know where she is and what's happening to her — and you can't do a damned thing about it."

Bob's skin flushed again. "Hell. I forgot what happened last winter with your family." He put out his hand. "Sorry. You, too, Mrs. Dodge."

After he saw us out and we'd gotten into the Yukon, Milo expelled a big breath. "That dumb shit thinks you're Mulehide. No wonder his daughter is dumb enough to hang out with Roger."

"Bob thinks Mulehide runs the newspaper?"

"Bob doesn't think, period." Milo reversed onto the Burl Creek Road. "Sure, he's got a good job with Blackwell, but Bob and his wife are all wrapped up in their own little world inside that nice house with their three nice kids. Dinks like that make me want to puke."

"Are you through?" I asked innocently.

"Yeah." He chuckled. "If you were Mulehide, you'd have told me I was being nasty because Bob probably makes more money than I do."

"Does he?"

"Hell, I don't know and I don't give a rat's ass."

"I don't, either. I didn't dare look at you. I knew what you were thinking."

Milo braked at Alpine Way and grinned at me. "It's a wonder he didn't refer to Caroline as the Little Woman. She's not. Built like a brick outhouse."

I laughed, then sobered as we headed up the hill. "I admit I wonder where Ainsley is."

"If she's smart — and she obviously isn't — she ran away from home."

"Oh," I said as we passed Pines Villa and Parc Pines, "I've got a call in to a former Yakima newspaper reporter who supposedly has a long memory. Maybe he knows what happened to Sam's brother. Other than that he died after getting beaten up in a tavern brawl."

"That may not tell us anything about Sam, though."

"Did Sam ever talk about religion?"

Milo turned left onto Fir. "Are you kidding? I doubt he ever believed in Santa Claus."

"His parents were religious. They went to the Pentecostal church."

"Maybe that explains why Heppner isn't religious. Those people are kind of far out, from what little I know about them."

We turned onto Fir. "I noticed that both his parents had biblical first names — as do the children — Amos, Samuel, and Ruth."

Milo glanced at me. "You're good. I'd never have picked up on that sort of thing. It might even mean something."

He turned into the driveway — and stopped. "We've got company. You recognize that Acura?"

"No. But it looks like a woman is sitting in the driver's seat."

"I'll have to park on the verge," Milo said, reversing and backing up. "What's going on around here? Have you put out a welcome mat I haven't noticed?"

"Don't ask me. You're the one with mysterious female callers. I only get drunken jerks."

We walked toward the house as an auburn-haired woman emerged from the car. "Ms. Lord?" she called.

"Yes," I responded, beginning to feel as if I were having an identity crisis. "Are you here to see me?"

Her gaze flickered in Milo's direction, but when she spoke, her words were for me. "Yes. I'm Helena Craig, from the high school. I have something I'd like to discuss with you, if I may impose."

My husband had already opened the front door. "After you, ladies," he said in a cheerful voice that didn't sound at all like him. "Don't mind me, Ms. Craig," he said, leaving the door open. "I'm just heading out to check my fishing gear. I'll leave you alone with the Little Woman." The big jerk closed the door behind us. I wanted to strangle him.

"You're sure this is a good time?" Helena asked, her attractive features a trifle strained.

"Yes! I mean, of course. Do sit. Can I get you something to drink?"

Helena had parked herself in the easy chair. "No, really. I hope I'm not interrupting your day with Mr. Lord."

"There is no Mr. Lord," I said, plopping down gracelessly on the sofa. "I use my maiden name for the newspaper. My husband is the sheriff." *And a world-class jackass,* I wanted to add but didn't.

"Oh! I thought he seemed familiar." Her fair skin grew rather pink. "I guess I'm used to seeing him in uniform. He's quite an imposing-looking man."

"He's tall," I said, trying to sound cordial but not quite making it. "What did you want to discuss with me?"

Helena seemed to have regained her aplomb. She crossed her long legs, which were covered in olive green wool slacks that matched her tailored jacket. "I understand that your reporter, Mr. Laskey, has been interviewing Principal Freeman. In fact, I believe he tried to reach me at home, but I was out. I called him earlier this afternoon, but there was no answer." She regarded me with a questioning look.

"He and his wife had plans to go out of town," I said.

"Ah. Well — that's why I'm here. I seem to be in the middle of a controversy. Apparently, I wasn't kept abreast of why some of our students appeared to have dropped out of sight, if not actually out of school. Mr. Freeman sometimes keeps information to himself."

"Typical of administrators," I allowed, finally feeling more congenial. "Especially educators."

"In any event, I'm sorry if I caused Mrs. Runkel any consternation when I was on her program. She's such a delightful woman. Very keen on education, of course, but I felt she might in some ways be . . . a bit old-fashioned when it comes to her ideas about contemporary teenagers."

I was tempted to be candid by saying that

despite an occasional burst of outrage for the sake of convention, Vida was virtually shockproof. But the admission might turn Helena into a clam. "Mrs. Runkel has some conservative views," I conceded. That much was true when it came to her staunch support of any Republican who could breathe without an oxygen tank.

Helena nodded. "That's why I didn't mention some of the tales I've heard going around among the students, especially the girls. Of course, much of this is due to those so-called Internet dating sites, which are — as you probably know — nothing but pimping."

Having gotten emails in my Junk file that obviously weren't confined to matching up prospective couples, I knew what Helena was talking about. For fear of getting a virus — or maybe even an STD if I opened any of them — I'd never actually read the contents. "Is this more than just salacious talk with the students?" I asked.

Helena made a face. "Frankly, it's hard to tell. They turn silent if I even appear to be prying. Or in some cases, they just laugh it off, dismissing it as some TV show they watched. I'm not saying that I believe any of our high school girls are involved. In fact, at least in one instance, I thought they mentioned the Skykomish and Sultan schools. Oh," she went on, leaning her head against the back of the easy chair, "it's a conundrum. Adolescents fantasize so much. But it's upsetting."

"Have you discussed this with Principal Freeman?"

Helena sat up straight again. "I broached the subject a week before spring break. He shrugged it off as silly chatter from too many movies and TV shows." She frowned. "I didn't realize you were married to the sheriff. I'm not sure I want him to learn what is basically hearsay."

"I'm a journalist," I said. "I know how to guard my sources. My husband and I walk a tight line to keep our jobs separate from our personal life."

"That can't be easy," Helena remarked in a bemused tone.

I smiled wryly. "We've had fifteen years of practice."

"I mustn't impose any longer," she said, getting up. "I feel better for airing my discomfort about our students. I don't suppose you have any advice on what I should do." She blushed again — and uttered a strangled little laugh. "I'm a counselor. I shouldn't have to ask anybody."

"Everyone needs to unload at some

point," I said, having risen from the sofa to join Helena by the door. "If I were you, I'd find the smartest and most trustworthy girl at the school and turn her into a spy."

Helena's gray eyes widened. "You're serious?"

"That's what journalists do when they want to get at the truth. In our case, we call such people 'leaks.' "

She put out her hand. "Thank you, Ms. . . . what should I call you?"

"Emma," I said, shaking her hand.

"Emma," she repeated. "I like that name. Maybe I can find an Emma at the high school."

With that parting sally, Helena left. I should have felt good for letting her unburden herself. But I didn't. I wished I hadn't suggested that she find a student spy. Maybe all the adolescent chitchat was just so many little bees buzzing around the halls of Alpine High. But bees' nests are dangerous. I didn't want Helena or an innocent teenager getting stung. Even bee stings can be fatal.

NINETEEN

Ten minutes after Helena left, Charley Burke called me back. If we'd ever crossed paths, neither of us remembered it. But, like everybody else in the newspaper business, he remembered that my name had been linked to Tom Cavanaugh's. That was no surprise, since Tom had owned his own West Coast weekly empire.

"Terrible thing when he got killed," Charley lamented. "Who took over his papers?"

I didn't want to divulge that Adam had inherited them, so I merely said that they were being run out of California by Tom's second-in-command, Phil Corrigan. In fairness to my son, he never used a nickel of his inheritance for himself but took some of the profit for his St. Mary's Igloo villagers and the other communities he served in his remote part of northern Alaska.

"So," Charley said after I'd apparently satisfied his curiosity, "you want to know something about a tavern fight in Toppenish back in '78? I was still working on the *Herald-Republic* then, though I moved on to Spokane the next year."

"Did you cover Toppenish on your beat?"

"Oh, sure, whenever a story landed on my desk. You got any names to toss at me?"

"Only one: Amos Heppner. It happened in February." I didn't mention that Sam's brother had died. Sometimes it was better not to give too much information but to let the source's brain roam unfettered.

"Heppner," Charley repeated. "Offhand, all that comes to mind is that big flood way back in northeastern Oregon. Before my time, but my old man grew up in Pendleton. Fairly close to Heppner, though Pa was born four, five years after the '03 flood."

Charley had paused. I hoped he wasn't going off on a tangent. "No connection that I know of to the Toppenish Heppner," I said.

"Probably not. There were quite a few bar brawls in Yakima County while I worked on the paper. More than one guy killed, usually with a gun or a knife. Do you know what happened to this Heppner?"

"He died as the result of a blow to the head," I responded. Time enough for Charley to get his memory up to speed.

"Oh, right. I got it: young guy, fight broke

out with some Mexicans. In fact, it was a Mexican tavern. A cantina, as they'd call it. Suppose I should say Latino or Hispanic, right? Anyway, he wasn't welcome. Well, it was a dumb stunt on his part. He called out one guy and they got into it, and then the whole place went nuts."

"Did you hear what started it?" I asked.

"Only later. It was over a Mexican gal who'd gotten knocked up by a white guy."

"Were the cops called in?"

"Probably not," Charley said after a pause. "Even back then, the Mexican folks were shy about doing that. Some of them might've been illegals, so they weren't keen on asking the law for help."

"Do you know if Heppner was the one who'd done the Latino girl wrong?" I asked.

"I do remember it wasn't him," Charley said. "White people have family honor, too. I figure it was probably a relative or a buddy of his. I think he had a brother, but I could be wrong. Is that any help?"

I was momentarily speechless, thinking of Sam. "Yes. Yes, Charley, I think it is. Do you remember anything else about the brother — or whoever it was?"

He chuckled. "Hell, I'm surprised I remember that much. But it was a cautionary tale for those of us with a nose for news and a risky habit of sticking it in the wrong places. And I'm not just talking about the minorities over on this side of the state. Some of those wheat farmers and orchard owners can be damned prickly, too. You'd be surprised at what goes on when the barn doors are closed."

"Dare I ask?" I inquired, having gotten over my temporary shock.

"Oh, hell." Charley let out a sigh that traveled all the way across the flat agricultural lands and over the towering Cascades. "Let's say some of these big spreads don't need a brothel in town and let it go at that. Okay? I may be retired, but I'm not stupid."

"I'm on the other side of the state," I said. "We have our own problems, as you well know."

"Sure. It all helps fill the front page. Too bad there aren't a lot of folks who read newspapers anymore. I got out just in time."

"I'm still in," I responded. "At least for now."

On that dark note, I thanked him and hung up.

Milo came home around three-thirty. He looked unhappy.

"What's wrong?" I asked, greeting him at the door with a kiss.

"Blatt's due to pull night duty," he replied, sinking into the easy chair. "I can't play favorites, especially when we're short-staffed and it's the weekend. I'll take over the desk tonight, and Tanya can stay here with you and then spend the night. That'll loosen up the schedule a bit."

I sat down on the sofa, Pepsi at hand. "Will you eat dinner here?"

Milo thought about it. "No. Why don't you and Tanya make something no man in his right mind would eat?"

"Maybe I will," I said, suddenly remembering that I'd been mad at my husband. "Creamed something-or-other. Don't you want to know what your Little Woman learned from Helena Craig?"

Milo laughed. "I couldn't resist. I figured it'd set you off so you might be ornery enough to get something out of her. What was it?"

I made short work of her visit. Before Milo could do more than shake his head, I launched into the conversation with Charley Burke.

"Holy crap!" he exclaimed when I finished with Charley's surmise about Amos's brother. "I don't know what to say. Heppner has a . . . kid? I mean, *had* a kid? No wonder he went off the rails. Jesus. That's damned rough. Now what do I do?"

"Keep trying to get in touch with him?"

"It's not working so far." Milo got out of the chair. "I need a drink. You want one? Hell, it's after four. Why not?"

"Yes, please. I'm kind of worn out from listening to people I don't even know."

Milo paused in the kitchen doorway. "Oh — in all this, I forgot to tell you Bob Sigurdson called to say that Ainsley showed up."

I grabbed my Pepsi can, took a last swig, and got off the sofa. "Where had she been?"

"Bob talked to Dwight. He didn't say. Dwight, being Dwight, didn't give a shit. I don't blame him. The Sigurdsons panicked." Milo started to head into the kitchen, then stopped. "Why?"

I'd come up beside him. "Because they're nice and didn't want something not nice happening to their nice daughter?"

He shrugged. "Screw it. I'm still reeling about Sam having a kid. Or *maybe* having a kid. This reporter guy might write fiction on the side."

"But it'd explain why Sam fell apart. Did he see the body when it was brought back from the river?"

Milo had opened the liquor cupboard but paused, leaning against the counter. "Yeah, he did. It was just before he was called to the wreck. He didn't say much when he came back, but that's typical of him. By that time, Sam was off duty for the day. Then he called in sick the next day." The sheriff looked at me. "It makes sense now. It even accounts for him not remembering to ask Shane Campbell to fill out an accident witness report. Shit. No wonder Sam wanted to claim the body. If only . . ." He slammed the cupboard door shut.

I put my hand on his arm. "You had no way of knowing. How could you? Sam isn't the kind to unload about anything, especially personal."

Milo sighed heavily. "Yeah, I know that. But just two months ago Gould goes off the job to bang his ex-wife. That's still a shocker. Now Heppner . . . just goes off. It makes me feel as if I don't know a freaking thing about my employees."

My hand fell away. "I know Vida, but she's driving me nuts lately. I understand Mitch's problems, but that's no help when he gets pissed off if I even look at him the wrong way. And Leo's threatening to quit. I *do* know these people, but I can't do much about how they feel or act. Don't beat yourself up. It's not your fault Sam's alleged son got himself killed."

Milo put his arms around me. "You're right, but it doesn't make me feel any better. Oh, hell, maybe it does." He moved back just enough to look down at me. "Walsh wants to quit? How come?"

"He'll be sixty-two next month. He misses California and he thinks Liza may finally take him back."

"Oh, crap!" Milo laughed. "Do I sense Ed lurking in the wings?"

"Please! Don't make it any worse!"

Letting go of me, he reopened the cupboard and took out the Scotch and the Canadian. "It's a good thing I had this Glenlivet that Bran gave me for Father's Day tucked in back, so you didn't hand it to Moro."

"I kept the good stuff. Where do you think Sam's gone?"

"Damned if I know," Milo replied, pouring my drink first. "He has to be touching base here or he wouldn't have called Driggers about the body."

Finishing his cocktail duties, he put a hand on my back and steered me into the living room. We resumed our usual places. Milo paused to take out his cigarettes, then stopped. "I'd better call Tanya and tell her she's got a dinner invitation."

I sipped my drink while Milo spoke briefly

to his daughter. "She sounds good," he said after disconnecting. "God, but I hope this thing with Blatt is real. Is it possible that Tanya could fall for a guy who's normal? That hasn't been her style in the past."

"I'd think that after the last one shot her and then killed himself, she might get the idea that maybe she was making some poor choices. You realize that if that happens, you and I will be related to Vida."

"That's crossed my mind. Maybe she'd start speaking to me again. I'm not sure that's good news."

"You've always liked her," I said. "I mean, when she isn't trying to take over your office along with the newspaper."

"She's . . . something." Milo took a drink of Scotch and finally lighted a cigarette. "You want one or are you quitting again this afternoon?"

"Oh, why not? Throw me one and the lighter, please."

My husband stood up. "To hell with that. I won't be home until after midnight. Let's get a little familiar." He parked himself beside me. "Not too familiar. I've got to get out of here in twenty minutes. You realize I don't get paid for overtime?"

"I did not know that. How come?"

"Because I make a decent salary and I

don't think it'd be right."

He lighted my cigarette and put his arm around me. I leaned my head against his shoulder. "Damn," I said. "I forgot I was mad at you this afternoon. I didn't come close to breaking my record of eleven minutes."

"You will someday." He kissed the top of my head. "Happy?"

"Yes. I'm getting used to it. I like it."

"Me, too."

We sat in comfortable silence for a few minutes, content to be together. The only sounds were an occasional car out on Fir, a crow cawing in one of the cedar trees, and Val Marsden's lawn mower. I could almost forget about the missing Sam Heppner, his murdered son, high school hookers, the annoying Nelsons, and office personnel problems.

"Are you asleep?" Milo asked after another minute had passed.

"No. Just cozy with you."

"What if we never left the house again?"

"We'd starve. Unless somebody would bring us food."

My husband sighed. "I don't think I could talk my deputies into doing that. Worse yet, Vida might show up with one of her gruesome casseroles." He finished his drink, kissed me lingeringly, and got up from the sofa. "I'll go change. Maybe I can get takeout from the Venison Inn. Don't they do that for MacDuff when he works late?"

"Yes. I'd better look through my ladies' luncheon recipes for something really dainty." The truth was, I was famished, never having had time to finish the burger and fries Milo had brought home for lunch. Maybe a hearty quiche with lots of ham would work. I ventured out into the kitchen to assume my role as kindly stepmother. Never having had a daughter, I rather liked that part of being married, too. At least when Tanya wasn't bunking with us on a regular basis.

I had the quiche in the oven before six. Tanya arrived about two minutes later, looking cheerful.

"Poor Dad," she said, pouring herself a glass of pinot gris. "He's been putting in some long hours. Does that make him crabby?"

"No, not really," I replied. "I mean, not any more than the job usually causes him to grumble. I'm used to it."

Tanya looked bemused. "It's odd to think how long you've known each other," she said as we went into the living room. Out of apparent deference to her absent father, she sat in the side chair on the other side of the hearth. "Except for coming here as a kid a couple of times for holiday dinners, I never got to know you. Bran and Michelle and I always hung out with your son and whichever other kids were here. We never thought of you as anything but a . . . hostess." She laughed, a bit embarrassed. "Then when Dad and you started dating, I just thought it was nice he had a girlfriend who knew how to cook. I never met the woman from Gold Bar."

"I got to know her fairly well," I said, though it turned out none of us — including Milo — really knew her. "Honoria was crippled, you know."

Tanya looked surprised. "You mean she couldn't walk?"

"She'd been pushed down the stairs in a domestic dispute," I explained, not wanting to offer details. "I always wondered if your dad started seeing her because he felt crippled inside after your mother left him and took you kids off to Bellevue."

"That's . . . strange." Tanya looked shaken. I almost wished I hadn't opened my big mouth. But she was an adult, and I saw no reason to shield her from the harm Tricia had caused Milo.

"I did my own damage," I confessed. "I should never have broken up with him the first time around. But the timing was wrong. I couldn't get over Adam's dad. I was emotionally crippled, too."

She smiled. "But you both got past it. Dr. Reed's been great treating my PTSD after what happened with my ex-fiancé. She's sensitive and yet sensible."

"I'm glad," I said. "She was widowed recently, you know."

"That's what I heard. Dad told me a little about that after Dr. Reed mentioned in passing that she'd recently lost her husband. I never saw anything about it in the newspaper. Did he live here?"

"Dr. Reed and her husband — he was a psychiatrist, too — came here from California in January. Their son's at UCLA. They wanted to hold the services down there, among longtime friends and colleagues. How was dinner at Le Gourmand last night?" I asked, anxious to change the subject for fear of revealing too much about Rosalie's private life.

"Amazing!" Tanya's face brightened, making her look almost pretty. "I knew that place was there, but I'd never thought much about it, except it seemed kind of weird for Alpine. Have you and Dad been there?"

"Oh, yes, several times over the years. It was our first real date, back in 1990, when it had a different name and different owners. I always have to translate the menu for him — and then he swears he still doesn't know what he's eating half the time."

Tanya registered more surprise. "You and Dad went on a date way back then?"

I'd taken another sip from my bourbon refill. "He didn't make a pass at me and I was disappointed. He told me only recently that he thought I was some religious nut because I was wearing a white blouse and a black skirt. He said I looked like a nun. And I felt there was zero chemistry between us because he was so . . . aloof."

Tanya was laughing. "That is . . . too . . . funny! No wonder it took you so long to finally get married. After you broke up the first time, he never really talked much about you until lately. I mean, while he was with me in the hospital. Even then, he didn't exactly go on and on."

"No," I said, "he wouldn't. It's not his style." Emboldened by the bourbon, I posed the question I'd vowed not to ask: "How are things with you and Bill?"

Tanya sobered. "Good. He's really a sweet guy. I hardly remember him from high school, though he was a year or so ahead of

386

me, and then we moved to Bellevue. You probably know he got burned by the woman he was engaged to."

"Yes, that happened around the holidays. Bill's very down-to-earth." I wouldn't mention Milo's endorsement of his deputy as a future son-in-law. That might make Tanya dump him on the spot. "Speaking of the high school, have you heard from Deanna since she was here? Her mother told me she'd had the flu."

"She called this afternoon," Tanya said, frowning. "She's still really worried. What's worse is that she thinks her mother has lost it. I wonder if that creep of an ex isn't bugging her. Didn't he come here the other night and try to get you to party with him and your neighbors? I saw something in the log about that, but Dad sort of blew me off."

"It was all kind of stupid," I said. "Vince Moro was drunk. Say, do you know any of your teachers who are still at the high school?"

"Oh . . ." Tanya leaned back in the chair. "I was only there for a year. Offhand, the only one I remember very well is the librarian, Miss Trews. I worked in the library during my free period. I heard she's retiring."

Having already given what might be bad advice to Helena Craig, I was more cautious with my stepdaughter. "Did you like Effie Trews?"

Tanya smiled. "She was kind of a fussy person, but dealing with kids who lost books, drew X-rated pictures all over them, and at one point set a copy of *A Tale of Two Cities* on fire in the library, she had her reasons. Why do you ask?" she inquired, looking justifiably suspicious.

"There are a lot of odd rumors going around the school these days," I replied. "You weren't in town, so you didn't hear Vida's radio program this week. She interviewed Helena Craig, the counselor. The main topic was dropouts, but I understand there may be some other problems. There are rumors about prostitutes being recruited from the local high schools. It may be just talk, but it's worth looking into."

"Shouldn't Dad be doing that?"

"Your father has his hands full right now. You might be able to help both of us."

Tanya was quiet for a couple of moments. "That's awful. Do you think Deanna's sister has gotten into anything that wild?"

"Not really. You've been gone from Alpine for so long that you've forgotten how rumors run like the Skykomish River on a winter rampage."

"Weird," Tanya said with a shake of her

head. "Oh, there's gossip in Bellevue, but it's not the same somehow. There's too much other stuff going on. I don't think I'll pass on that rumor to Deanna."

"Good. Your father's trying to ignore it, at least for the moment."

Tanya nodded. "Dad would insist I keep out of it. He's very protective of me."

"Of course." I didn't add that he was also protective of me. *Too* protective — it cramped my style. "It's a good thing Bill's got your back."

Tanya's hazel eyes sparked, reminding me of Milo. "I guess he does. I kind of like that idea."

I figured she should. He might have the rest of her, too. I hoped.

We spent the evening watching *When Harry Met Sally* and *Pretty Woman.* We both loved seeing them movies for what was probably the umpteenth time. Tanya had gone to bed and I was already tucked in when Milo returned, a little after midnight. He leaned down to kiss me, then frowned, pulling away.

"What's wrong? You look as if you've been crying."

"I have," I said, snuggling back down and smiling. "Tanya and I watched chick flicks.

We bawled like babies and had a wonderful time."

My husband just shook his head and ambled off to the bathroom.

I went to ten o'clock Mass, leaving father and daughter at the kitchen table. The priest subbing for Father Den was from Monroe. He spoke about his own flock, which, somewhat to my surprise, had a large Hispanic membership. Obviously, I wasn't keeping abreast of developments farther west on Highway 2. Maybe I was becoming a real Alpiner. "If," as Spence had once said, "it doesn't happen in Alpine, it doesn't happen."

As usual, I was skittering around taller fellow Catholics to avoid an Ed and Shirley Bronsky encounter. I'd managed to hide behind Brendan Shaw's broad back when Jack Mullins tapped my shoulder. I gave a start before turning around to greet the deputy and his wife, Nina.

Jack looked unusually serious. "Nina ran out of milk this morning," he said, keeping his voice down and putting an arm around his oft-maligned wife, "so I ran over to the 7-Eleven. I saw Sam coming out of the store, and I yelled to him. He took one look at me, jumped into his Jeep, and roared off toward the Icicle Creek Road."

"Poor Sam," Nina murmured before I could say anything. "I think he has a fatal illness and doesn't want to tell anyone."

"He's got something bothering him," I said, unsure of how much Milo's staff knew about Sam's defection. "Did he look as if he was sick?"

Jack ran a hand through his red hair, a futile gesture that never made it behave. "He moved fast enough. I didn't see him up close, but he looked as if he hadn't shaved in a few days."

"Depression," Nina said softly, her sweet face troubled. "It often accompanies a serious illness."

Jack was the flakiest of the deputies, but I've always felt he was also the smartest. He'd given his wife a swift, skeptical glance, but he didn't argue her diagnosis, misguided as it might be. Obviously, the sheriff's underlings were clueless about their fellow deputy's personal life.

"Did you want me to mention this to Milo for some reason?" I asked, feigning innocence.

Jack and Nina exchanged conflicted glances. "Oh," he began, "probably not. Sam's a peculiar guy. Maybe just the sight of me reminded him of work. He hasn't taken time off in . . . I don't even remember when. Maybe a three-day weekend to fish or hunt, but that's about it. Don't bother the boss. He's under the gun right now."

Nina, however, disagreed. "I think you should say something, Emma. If Sam's ill, he needs to see Doc Dewey. After all, he missed work last Tuesday because he wasn't feeling well. That's not like him."

"I'll think on it," I said, smiling, and not just because the Bronskys had driven off in their only remaining Mercedes. "Enjoy your Sunday." On that Pollyanna note, I headed for my Honda and went home.

"That didn't take long," my husband said from his easy chair. "Did your sub priest forget to show up?"

"Visiting priests are in a hurry," I replied, hanging my jacket on a peg. "This one is the regular at St. Mary of the Valley in Monroe."

Milo set the Northwest section of *The Seattle Times* aside. "Did you grill him about paying a call on Dobles at the hospital?"

"I thought about it," I said, sitting on the easy chair's arm. "Maybe the admission form didn't state that Dobles was Catholic. I talked to Jack and Nina Mullins. He saw Heppner this morning at the 7-Eleven."

"He did?" Milo paused in the act of caressing my back. "What happened?"

"Nothing. Sam was coming out of the store, saw Jack, and drove off in his Jeep. He's growing a beard, by the way." I hopped off the chair. "I need coffee. You want a refill?"

"I just got one."

"Where's Tanya?" I asked before I reached the kitchen.

"She went to my place to do some cleaning."

"Cleaning? As in housecleaning?"

"Right — I forgot to mention she's been doing some of that lately."

"Good. Then I won't have to." I poured my coffee and returned to the sofa. "She's showing a lot more spunk these days. I gather Dr. Reed's a big help."

"Reed's got all the right bullshit," Milo said with a wry expression. "Hell, whatever works. It's a good thing Tanya has coverage for this shrink stuff." He rubbed his chin. "So Heppner's still in civilization. I wonder where he's hanging out, if not at his own place."

"With his sister in Sultan? She might not tell you."

"True. They're tight. I get that now, after finding out the brother was killed. What do you figure? Amos Heppner went to the tavern to . . . what? Say his brother wanted to do right by the Hispanic girl?"

"That's possible," I allowed. "Or maybe he was trying to make peace with her family. Are we sure she's Carmela Dobles?"

"It fits. You know I don't like things that don't fit."

"So why do they get into a fight? They're anti-Anglo?"

Milo shrugged. "Could be. Prejudice comes in all forms and shades. Maybe it wasn't racial. How about religious? Catholic versus Protestant or, in the elder Heppner's case, Pentecostal?"

"Gee, big guy, you're speculating?"

"I can do that with you. You're the Little Woman."

"*Shut up.* If you don't stop it, I may become an abusive wife." I glared at Milo just for the hell of it. "You're right that religion might've been a big deal. But I've got a quibble. We know Carmela married another man, a Hispanic named Fernandez who put his name on the birth certificate. Is that legal if he wasn't the father?"

"Who'd know? I mean, that'd go through the courthouse in Yakima. Nobody there would pay any attention." Milo lighted a cigarette. "But how did Sam know what Joe

Fernandez looked like so that he recognized his corpse and went semi-nuts?"

"Good point. He wouldn't. Unless they'd met later in life."

Milo took a drink of coffee and sat back in the easy chair. "Damn. This is when I wished I pried into my staff's private lives."

"No, you don't."

Milo chuckled. "You're right. I'd have to listen to Mullins tell me how he and Nina have their discussions over every little damned thing that comes along. I might even have to hear how Blatt wishes his aunt didn't pin him to the wall and make him break every law enforcement rule on the books."

"Maybe," I said with a straight face, "Sam and Joe were Facebook friends."

"God. Now you're in Fantasyland. But you're right about technology. They could communicate in some form, and with pictures. It just doesn't sound like something Sam would do, though."

"You know what we're missing?" I said — and bit my lip.

Milo frowned. "What? You sitting on my lap?"

"No. Vida. I'm used to tossing ideas back and forth with her and . . . stop looking at me like that. She and I've come up with some loony stuff, but you know damned well we've also figured out a few things over the years. That happened because we colored outside the lines."

"Your office should look like a hallucinogenic nightmare by now."

"You know it's true," I said, just short of pouting.

Milo sighed. "Yeah, you've saved my butt a few times. But you have to admit, you always came at it sideways."

"It worked, didn't it?"

"Usually. Maybe. I guess." He sighed again. "So you want to bring her into the loop?"

"No. I don't think she cares about this one. The victim's not local."

"That didn't stop her before."

"But Vida's in a different place now. She's mad at you, so she doesn't want to help. More to the point, she really hasn't been interested in the murder investigation. I thought she was worrying about Roger, but he's got a job and she's glowing all over the place about that. She even wants to put him on a float in the Summer Solstice Parade."

"Oh, God!" Milo held his head. "That's worse than when Bronsky and his gang had the Mr. Pig farm float."

"Don't say that out loud," I cautioned.

396

"He might do the same thing with his latest venture into idiocy and self-aggrandizement."

"Is it too soon for us to retire and move to . . . Index?"

I took that as a rhetorical comment. "I guess I miss — excuse the word — speculating with her."

The phone rang. I picked it up. To my surprise, it was Vida. Maybe she really did have every house in Alpine wired for surveillance.

"I just returned from church," she said in an excited voice. "Amy and Ted told me that Roger and Ainsley have made up. Isn't that heartwarming news? I couldn't wait to tell you."

"Gosh, Vida, I didn't know Roger and Ainsley had broken up," I said, for Milo's benefit. "Was it just a spat?"

"Oh, certainly! Young love — so tender, so fragile, yet not easily discarded when it's deep and true. I won't keep you, but I knew you'd want to know. We'll talk more tomorrow."

"Yes, we'll do that," I said, hoping to convey at least a modicum of enthusiasm. "I'm happy that . . . you're happy." We rang off.

"Christ," Milo groaned. "So that's where

Ainsley was — with Roger. I feel like arresting Bob Sigurdson for ruining my Saturday afternoon."

"At least Bob and Caroline should be pleased that Roger has a job," I said. "I translated 'unmotivated' as 'lazy, worthless, feckless jerk.' "

"Let's see how long it lasts before Roger screws up. I hope he doesn't trash the van the company gave him."

"It doesn't belong to the company," I said. "Ted and Amy bought it for him second-hand."

"It's got a sign on it," Milo said. "I figured it belonged to Party Animals."

"Vida's been a little unclear about all of this. It seems to be sort of a freelance job."

"No kidding. Maybe I should check their business license to see if Roger hasn't made up the whole thing just to get some new wheels."

"Roger doesn't have that much imagination."

"You're right about that. You want to drive over to Leavenworth for dinner tonight?"

"Do you really want to do that? There'll be weekend traffic going both ways."

"I don't give a shit," Milo said, putting out his cigarette and standing up, coffee mug in hand. "All the time we went together, we talked about going there and we never did. Seeing that picture of you and Cavanaugh in Leavenworth made me jealous. Or maybe I just felt bad because I never followed through. Now let's do it."

"I went to dinner there once with Fleetwood."

"Great. That makes me feel even worse. We're going."

And Milo went — out to the kitchen. I remained on the sofa, smiling.

TWENTY

"Sausage?" Milo said in disgust as we started the descent from the summit of Stevens Pass. "Is that what *brat* means? I like sausage for breakfast, but I'll be damned if I'll have it for dinner."

"That's fine with me," I said, still perusing the AAA guidebook I'd brought along. "I'm not nuts about brats either. I'm trying to remember where I went with Tom. Or with Spence, for that matter. I *think* one of the places was the Café Mozart."

"*I'd* think you'd remember where you'd gone with Cavanaugh, at least," Milo pointed out.

"I was in kind of a daze. Don't you remember that after Tom and I got back some cranks had vandalized my poor Jaguar? You had to come over and, frankly, you seemed pleased to tell me it might be totaled."

"I was jealous, damn it. That happened the day after I walked in on you and Cavanaugh. I didn't even know he was in town. Find a place that you haven't been to with him or Fleetwood. I can't believe you came clear over here with that guy. Are you sure he didn't grab your ass?"

"Yes! We were discussing one of the murder investigations and didn't want to be overheard in Alpine. It was all business and we were home before dark, you big jerk."

"He must've been banging Rosalie even then," Milo said.

"Maybe. She'd been his shrink, you know."

"He probably invented being nuts to get her in the sack."

"Spence has had his own hard times," I said. "Long before he came to Alpine. The love of his life — back then, anyway — had drowned."

"He probably stuck her head in the bathtub," my husband said.

"Here — Andreas Keller. It sounds like hearty food."

"Good." Milo slowed down as we followed the Wenatchee River, its riffles touched by gold from the setting sun. "I've never had much luck over here in the past few years. Not enough fish planted," he said as we suddenly lost sight of the river at the edge of town. "Now, how do we find this place?"

"It's on their Front Street," I said. "Turn right when we get to the main part. The restaurant's in the eight hundred block."

As before, I was charmed by the Bavarian architecture. Like Alpine, Leavenworth had been a logging town and also a railroad hub but had lost both sources of income over the years. In order to keep the town alive, the residents had turned the place into a tourist attraction, with an almost year-long series of festivals, including Oktoberfest and a month-long Christmas celebration that ran special daily trains out of Seattle.

We found Andreas Keller easily, its typical Bavarian exterior decorated with a brightly colored spring garland on the ironwork by the entrance. After we got out of the Yukon, Milo sniffed the air.

"It smells different over here," he declared. "Even the dirt's a different color. Sometimes I forget just how foreign the other half of Washington is. People who don't live around here or never traveled through the state haven't a clue."

"Let's keep them that way," I said as we entered the restaurant. "Seattle and its suburbs are getting too big."

"Tell me about it," Milo said as we got in line behind a half dozen other people. "I hate that drive down to Bellevue. One of these days I have to take those annulment forms to Mulehide. She'll blow about six fuses."

"Maybe I should go with you. I've only met Tricia once."

He shook his head. "Not when I bring the stuff from the chancery office. But maybe you should get together with her first. Tanya's birthday is coming next month. Maybe we can all go down and have dinner. We'll eat out. Mulehide's not a great cook. It's been years since you've seen Michelle — damn, I mean Mike, since she changed her name after announcing that she's gay. You'll get to see her and Bran. Maybe you can meet his girlfriend Solange and Mike's partner, Carolyn." He winced only slightly, still not entirely comfortable that his younger daughter was a lesbian.

"I'd like that," I said as we were beckoned to a cozy corner table. "I should get acquainted with my other stepchildren."

"I've only met Carolyn once," he said after we'd been seated. "She seems nice. She's a nurse at a children's hospital in Portland."

"Yes, you mentioned that earlier." I stopped talking. An accordion player was blasting away only a few feet from us.

"Want to polka?" Milo said, leaning closer to be heard.

"I can't dance," I said. "The klutz factor."

"Same here."

We studied the menu until the accordionist had moved on. Milo went for the pork chops. I chose the rotisserie chicken, even though it was supposed to be a half. Any leftovers could turn into something Milo might not like for Monday night's dinner. We drank German beer and talked about our families in between intermittent serenades from what was now two accordionists. But the food was good, and just being together doing something out of our routine was a welcome change.

"That," I said as we walked back to the Yukon in the waning daylight, "is the first real date we've had in years."

"That sounds about right for you," Milo declared. "You tend to do things backward. You have a kid and wait thirty years to get a husband, then you get married, but two months later you finally go on a date with him. Let's walk a little. That German food's heavy."

We'd passed another restaurant and a series of small shops when I felt something bothering my left heel. "Hold up," I said. "I should never slip my shoes off in a public place. It's a bad habit." Sure enough, there was a pebble — or maybe a chickpea. I tossed it aside before putting my shoe back on. Milo was studying a bulletin board outside a camera shop that displayed pictures, apparently of Leavenworth's visitors.

"They have an ice race here every year," he remarked. "On foot. How many ambulances do they have standing by?"

"We could do that in Alpine," I said.

"No thanks. That'd mean extra duty for my . . . holy shit!" he exclaimed, peering more closely at one of the photos. "Unless I'm going blind, that's Nel Dobles."

I leaned against Milo to study the picture. "I'll take your word for it. I've never seen him." The man my husband was pointing to was with two other men, all of them smiling and holding up beer steins. He looked pleasant, probably even handsome, with dark hair and well-defined features. Milo scanned the other photos more closely.

"Here," he said, sounding as close to excited as the sheriff gets when he shifts into work mode. "There's Joe Fernandez. I'd bet on it, at least from his driver's license picture. He didn't look so good in person, being dead."

Joe was standing in front of München Haus Bavarian Grill, which we'd just passed. He was wearing a light blue shirt and jeans. His arm was around a pretty blonde who had her head on his shoulder.

"The camera shop's probably closed," Milo said. "I want to talk to somebody in charge at that restaurant. Let's go."

"Gee, I get to trot along on an investigation?" I panted, trying to keep up with my husband's long stride.

"I can't ditch you," he said over his shoulder. "You'd probably make friends with the town creep."

"Do they have one?"

"Every place does," Milo said as he led the way inside the restaurant. "We've got Crazy Eights Neffel for starters." He stopped, apparently looking for someone in charge. "Stay put," he murmured and approached the hostess. After a brief exchange, Milo gestured for me to follow him through the restaurant.

I trudged along behind him, past the restrooms and through an unmarked door that opened as if by magic. The man who greeted us looked a little like a cheerful wizard, short and stout, with a bald head, a gray goatee, and twinkling blue eyes.

"Hermann Obermeyer," he said with a faint German accent, offering his hand to my husband and then to me. "Come in, Sheriff. And Mrs. . . . Dodge, is it?"

The office was small and cluttered, not

unlike my own. There was only one extra chair. Milo didn't sit down, so I didn't, either. Obermeyer did, however. Maybe the sheriff's looming presence overwhelmed him.

After Milo had described the two photographs, Obermeyer looked puzzled. "We have so many visitors. Perhaps I should go outside with you to make sure I know which ones you're speaking of. Half of the people in them will be holding beer steins." The blue eyes twinkled some more as he led us out of his office, retracing our steps to the sidewalk bulletin board. It was almost dark by now, but the restaurant manager — I assumed that was his title — had brought along a flashlight.

"Oh, yes," he said at once when Milo pointed to Dobles. "He has been here a few times. Not so much to attend our special events, but passing through. This picture was taken with two visitors from Yakima. Mr. Dobles is from central California, I believe." Obermeyer frowned. "He is not, I hope, in some sort of trouble."

"No. He was in a serious car accident just outside of Alpine," Milo replied, "but he's recovering." He pointed to Joe Fernandez. "What about this young man?"

Obermeyer studied the picture for what

seemed like a long time. "Yes, I recall seeing him, maybe last summer. A rather . . . lively sort of fellow. Was he involved in the same accident?"

"No."

Typical Dodge, I thought, not going beyond the short answer that was bound to make the other person talk. I ought to know. He'd pulled that on me a couple of times, and I'd found it unsettling.

"I don't know his name," Obermeyer said, scratching his bald head, "but he was what I'd call a party boy. Always the beer, always the pretty girl, always just this far from making a fool of himself." He held up his thumb and index finger to demonstrate the narrow margin.

"Did he get into fights?" Milo asked in his most laconic manner.

"No. But once, at the beer garden, he came close. Somehow he made a joke, and everyone laughed. The hostility evaporated. He had a way with him. Is he in trouble over in Skykomish County?"

"No." Milo smiled and put out his hand. "This is routine. Thanks for your help."

"Of course, Sheriff," Obermeyer said, wincing slightly as my husband crushed his fingers. "Do come back to one of our celebrations. Your charming lady would enjoy herself." He sketched a bow for me.

"We might do that," Milo said, almost convincingly.

"Free brats for you both at München Haus," Obermeyer called as he headed back to the restaurant.

"Nice guy," Milo murmured as we walked in the other direction to the Yukon.

"But not a lot of help," I said.

The sheriff didn't say anything until we were buckling up inside the SUV. "I'm not so sure about that. We know that both Dobles and Joe have been in the area, though not necessarily at the same time. Dobles seems as if he likes to make an impression. Joe sounds like a goofball."

"Maybe he is. *Was,* I mean. You mentioned that Yakima isn't sure which side of the law he was on."

"Right." Milo paused, waiting to turn off Front Street to reach Highway 2. "But Obermeyer's description tells me something. Nobody takes a goofball seriously. It's a perfect cover. Now I'm damned sure he's a Fed. That means we may have a motive for murder."

"But in Alpine?" I said as we began to head west toward Stevens Pass and the summit. "That doesn't make sense."

"You're right. But I can't figure out what other motive there would be. Joe came to Alpine for a reason. For all I know, he intended to see Sam, if, in fact, they're related."

"You don't think that Sam . . ." The thought was so awful that I couldn't say it out loud.

Milo, however, knew what I was thinking. "No. Sam's reaction to recognizing Joe was what sent him off the rails. I doubt Sam knew Joe was in town. He'd probably arrived that night and met whoever killed him then. We've asked around. Nobody recalls seeing anybody who looked like Joe. If he had dinner — and the ME's report indicated he had, around eight that evening — it wasn't in SkyCo. We checked Skykomish and even Sultan. No luck. He probably ate in Monroe, which meant he didn't get to Alpine until later."

"You've got to talk to Sam," I said. "When's payday?"

"It was Friday. If you're thinking Sam needs money, forget it. He's as tightfisted as Gould."

I was silent again for a few moments. "I don't suppose you'll tell me who your mystery woman caller is," I finally said.

"If anything about her becomes official,

yes. Otherwise, it's unofficial."

"Nothing that could be remotely connected to Sam or Joe?"

"That's right."

I was looking at Milo, and he suddenly frowned. "At least I hope it's right," he said in an uneasy voice.

"Damnit, now you've made me curious. I think I'll drug you to make you talk."

The sheriff didn't speak until we were nearing the summit. "I've done some background on what my visitor told me. If I find out she's not running off at the mouth, I'll tell you because it'll become official. Like you, I don't deal in rumors."

"I didn't recognize her," I said. "Admittedly, I was spying on her through the Marsdens' fence."

"Of course you were. I really thought you'd try to crawl in through a window and listen from the hall."

"I wish I had. But I'd probably have fallen over something and given myself away."

He glanced at me and grinned. "That sounds about right."

"She seemed nervous."

"She was."

"Thirtyish?"

"About that."

"Pretty?"

"Kind of."

"Married?"

"Yes. That's it. You're done."

"Okay."

I did know when to give up — and shut up.

Monday morning Vida showed up wearing a pith helmet. "Where," I asked as Amanda stared, Leo gaped, and Mitch had to turn away to keep from laughing out loud, "did you get that thing?"

"It's not a 'thing,'" Vida replied indignantly. "It's authentic, made of pith, which comes from a swamp plant."

"You found it in a swamp?" Leo asked, trying to look innocent.

"Fie on you, Leo," Vida retorted. "My daughter Beth sent it to me. They had a safari night at the country club she and her husband belong to in Tacoma. Beth thought I'd enjoy wearing it. And I do. Have you no sense of adventure?"

"Not when it comes to hats," Leo replied. "I suppose that under the right circumstances, it could be quite . . . adventurous."

Vida caressed the band that went around the crown. "It's real. A lawyer friend actually wore it on safari last year. He donated it to the safari night auction for the Mary

Bridge Children's Hospital. Or is it a clinic? I don't recall, but it's in Tacoma."

"I've never been to Tacoma," Mitch said, having recovered from stifling his laughter. "What's it like?"

"It's quite large and very busy," Vida said, sitting down at her desk. "Too large and too busy, in my opinion, but not nearly as dreadful as Seattle. I often feel sorry for Beth because she has to live there instead of in Alpine, but her husband's law practice is very lucrative."

"And free hats," Leo noted.

Vida glared at Leo. "Not *free* hats! Beth paid a hundred and sixty dollars for this. The bidding was quite ferocious."

"I stand . . . or sit corrected," Leo said, running up the white flag and sinking his teeth into a raspberry Danish Kip had brought from the Upper Crust.

I chose a maple bar, being in a prosaic Monday morning mood. By the time the mail arrived shortly after nine-thirty, it dawned on me that the letters, emails, and phone calls about the mayor's plan were beginning to dwindle. That was typical of readers' attention span. I decided to follow up with another editorial to convince SkyCo residents that this was the wave of the future and they'd better get used to it. Of course, that wasn't necessarily true, but I'd say it anyway.

Leo came in a few minutes later to show me the mock-up he'd put together for all of our merchants who sold gardening and yard supplies.

"I know we ran something like this in our spring special edition last month," he said, "but everybody got off to an early start because of the warmer weather. I figured it wouldn't hurt to give it another shot. Harvey Adcock at the hardware store and the folks at Mountain View Gardens liked the idea, and then everybody else including Delphine Corson fell into line. I think I'll take her out to dinner just for the hell of it."

I was surprised, given that Leo had dated our local florist a few years earlier and found her too eager to take their romance to a higher level. "Isn't that a bit risky?" I asked.

Leo chuckled. "Just because my ex seems inclined to forgive if not forget doesn't mean I have to live like a monk. Say, I tried to track down that company Roger's working for, but I can't find a local or even an online listing. I asked the Duchess about it. She was kind of vague, though she did say their main offices were out of town. I wonder if she gave us the right name. I tried to Google them."

"Any luck?"

Leo shook his head. "I found several. One in Chicago, another in the Southwest, even one in Australia. But nothing local."

"It may be a subdivision of a bigger company. Call Amy, Vida's daughter. She ought to know."

"Good idea," Leo agreed. "I'd like to include them in this garden ad. They must do outdoor parties, including rentals like tents and canopies."

My ad manager went on his way. Vida and Mitch had left on their rounds. Maybe my House & Home editor was giving the Fritzes another try. I finished my editorial, though it wouldn't exactly rock readers out of their complacency. I was in a quandary about Helena Craig's confidences. If there was a story, it should go to Mitch. But for now, I'd hold off. High school hookers were as touchy a subject as I could think of. In fact, I preferred not thinking about them at all.

Mitch didn't return until after ten. He usually had covered the sheriff's office and the courthouse by nine-fifteen. I expected him to come into my office with major news but saw him pouring a coffee refill and picking up his second or third raised doughnut. I decided to get more coffee, too.

"Anything of interest?" I asked after he sat down at his desk.

"Yes, but I don't know what it is," he replied with a quirky expression. "It's the sheriff. Maybe you already know."

"I do not," I said, sitting in his visitor chair. "If I did, I wouldn't have to ask."

"Okay, I'll believe Dodge practices extreme discretion at home. It just seems strange when his wife is an inquisitive journalist."

"That's why," I said dryly. "I even tried feminine wiles early on, and he told me I didn't have any."

"But you married him anyway," Mitch said, sounding bemused.

"Yes. I couldn't resist his utter lack of charm. So what was or wasn't going on with the sheriff?" I asked after taking a sip of coffee.

"It was what wasn't. Everybody was very subdued. In fact, the only one who was around when I got there was Lori Cobb. Obviously, the sheriff had called a meeting. That's what took me so long. I had to go back to see if I could find out what was happening. I flunked. Even Mullins wasn't talking." Mitch bit into his doughnut.

"Keep checking," I said.

"Sure." He brushed crumbs off his brown

shirt. In March, he'd finally stopped wearing a tie to work. It was hard for him to shake his big-city ways. I'd had that problem early on in Alpine, too. "They've got three vehicles in impound," he went on. "I'd never looked out in back, but I decided to snoop a bit. One's the Porsche from the wreck that took out the milepost sign, the other's an abandoned sedan. Fong had told me that the ATV belonged to the murder victim. It was found by the landing strip near the Skykomish Ranger Station. Is the strip for public use?"

"I think so. It's mainly for emergencies, though. What are you thinking? Fernandez met someone who arrived by air?"

Mitch shrugged. "Why else would it be there?"

"I considered it a possible rendezvous point. Nobody goes there without a good reason. Maybe you should check with the ranger station."

"Wouldn't Dodge have done that?"

"Probably."

Mitch laughed and shook his head. "I'm sorry. I just can't quite figure out how you keep from trying to kill him."

"It's not always easy," I said, getting up as Vida returned, pith helmet at a slight angle.

"Well now," she said, marching over to

Mitch's desk, "I found a Fritz. The girl's very pregnant. Her parents both work for the state department of game. She was home alone. She calls herself Bambi."

I laughed. "That fits Miss Fritz if Mom and Dad work for the game department."

"True. She liked my helmet."

"I'm surprised," I said. "I'd think she'd be afraid you were hunting wild animals. Does she plan to return to school after the baby arrives?"

"Yes," Vida said, making her way to her desk. "Bambi seemed remarkably cheerful. She's giving the baby to relatives in Oregon. Medford, I believe. They're childless."

"Not pining for the father of the kid then?" I inquired.

"Not in the least. I don't think there is a father."

I followed Vida to her place as she sat down. "What do you mean?"

"People are very peculiar sometimes," Vida said, tugging at her left earlobe. "I gather she's carrying her uncle's child. That is, he was the sperm donor. I assume her aunt — who's actually her mother's cousin — is barren. If so, it would make rather a nice story, don't you think?"

"It would, if the family didn't object. It seems to me that Freeman is being a bit of a stick about this in keeping her out of school. Maybe the Fritzes didn't explain the situation. As a feel-good story, it's perfect for Mother's Day next month. I'm guessing that's when she'll deliver."

Vida nodded. "May sixth. I'll keep in touch. I think this is a first for Doc Dewey. Elvis Sung might have already done such a thing when he was still practicing in Hawaii. I'm always puzzled why people want to live on islands so far from anywhere else. They must feel disconnected."

"Adam loved the time he spent there in college," I said. "The people are very friendly."

"Yes, I suppose they would be." Vida turned thoughtful. "Isolated and all, cut off from the rest of the world. Rather like Alpine in the early days, when the only way into the town was by train. More sun and beaches, of course. I don't think I'd care for that."

It was pointless to comment on how much other people enjoyed the islands. I'd been there once, though it had been no pleasure trip. Just after purchasing the *Advocate,* I'd gone with Adam to get him settled in. The only sightseeing I had time for was of the campus and the dormitory. I felt cheated, but I was still adjusting to my new situation in Alpine. Adam had lived with me in my newly purchased little log cabin for only a month before starting his checkered college career. Once we arrived in Honolulu, he spent most of his time checking out girls. If I'd had a crystal ball, I would've figured it had to be badly cracked.

On the other hand, it was a good thing that I didn't have a crystal ball. If I did, I might have smashed it to bits.

TWENTY-ONE

Leo stopped in to ask if I'd like to have lunch with him at the ski lodge. I accepted the offer and ten minutes later we were seated in the restaurant section.

"If you tell me you're quitting, I'm leaving now," I said before looking at the menu, which I knew by heart anyway.

He chuckled. "No, it's not that. I just felt like a change of pace. I can only eat so much grease every day."

"I almost believe you." I told him about how Milo and I had gone over to have dinner in Leavenworth.

"I've driven over there a half dozen times," Leo said after we'd given our orders for the King Olav version of the Caesar salad. "Kind of a fun little town. Maybe I'll take Delphine there Wednesday night. If nothing else, the atmosphere will be interesting."

I smiled. "I recall you and Milo once talked about dating Delphine. Not at the same time, of course. Aren't you afraid she might rush you off to the nearest JP?"

"I made it clear a long time ago that marriage was a bad idea," Leo said. "Delphine's lonely. Her ex moved away after the divorce, right?"

"Yes. I never knew him. That happened before I arrived in Alpine."

Leo looked puzzled. "Vida never told you?"

"No. I gather she blabbed to you."

He shook his head. "Delphine told me. Her husband came out of the closet. He was the one who wanted out."

I laughed. "Poor Delphine. They had a couple of kids."

"Took the guy a long time to figure it out, I guess." Leo grew serious. "What's up with Vida? She took off like a rocket around eleven-thirty."

"I missed that. I must've been in the back shop with Kip. Was she upset or angry?"

"I couldn't tell. She'd been on the phone and so had I. The next thing I knew, she bolted out of her chair, grabbed her coat, and rushed off. By the way, I called Amy about the Party Animal outfit, but she wasn't home."

"Good grief, I hope it's not another Roger crisis."

"I don't think so," Leo said. "Just a few minutes earlier, when I told her I was trying to include Party Animals in our ad, she was all aglow. In fact, she mentioned that he had another assignment today. That's *good* news, for a change."

Our food arrived, and we moved on to other topics. Leo and I agreed that Mitch's spirits had seemed better the last few days, which meant Brenda must be improving. He asked about Tanya. I told him that she, too, was on the mend, thanks in part to Deputy Blatt's attentions. She had spent the night again with Bill at Milo's house.

"That's beginning to sound serious," Leo said. "Of course, it's a rebound romance for both of them. Those don't always work out too well. Mutual misery isn't a solid foundation for the future."

I agreed, but I felt that at least Tanya was seeing somebody who wasn't weird. We split the check and headed back to the office.

By one-thirty, Vida hadn't returned from lunch. I went out front to ask Amanda if she knew where Vida had gone.

"I wasn't here when she left," our receptionist replied. "I was in the restroom. I seem to spend half my time peeing these days." She caressed her bulging abdomen. "Pressure, according to Dr. Sung. It has to be a boy. A girl wouldn't make me so miserable."

"Don't count on it," I said. "Babies are tricky little creatures."

Despite her complaint, Amanda beamed. "I can't wait. July seems so far away."

"Trust me. It'll seem even further in June."

"Gee, thanks, Emma," she said. But she giggled.

By two o'clock, Vida still hadn't showed up. I was feeling antsy, so I left my cubbyhole and headed for the sheriff's office. If nothing else, I could listen to Milo growl at me about whatever was going on at his workplace. Mitch had considered checking in there again, but decided to hold off. Now that school was back in session, he'd headed up to see Principal Freeman and take some pictures of the not-so-happy students who'd been forced back into the classroom on a fine April day.

To my surprise — and maybe relief — everything seemed normal at headquarters. Lori was in place. Dwight was behind the counter, and Milo was in his office with the door open.

Dwight, of course, wasn't exactly delirious to see me. "You better not be bugging the boss about your remodeling project," he warned me.

"I'm not," I said, going inside the curving counter. "I have to ask his advice about what I should wear when we go out to dinner the next time. I think he'd like my green dress, but it's wool and the wrong season."

Dwight glowered at me and muttered something that was probably unprintable.

"Hi," I said, startling my husband, who was absorbed in some kind of reading material. "I have a query."

"About what?" he asked, not looking very pleased to see me.

"About the landing strip," I said, settling into one of his visitor chairs. "Why was the ATV there?"

"Because Fernandez was meeting with one of Averill Fairbanks's spaceships from Uranus. How the hell do I know?"

"Don't tell me you haven't thought about it," I said in mock dismay.

Milo leaned back in his chair. "I don't know that Fernandez was the one who left it there. His killer could have driven off in it and dumped it. No blood anywhere on the ATV, in case you were about to ask."

"Were there prints besides the vic's on it?"

"Several, but all of them smudged. Those things attract attention. The park rangers checked it out, too, after they heard about the kids finding it. And before you ask, they didn't see Averill's spaceship or anybody else's land there on Monday. I might've told you if they had."

" 'Might' isn't a very reassuring word," I said.

He shrugged. "So why are you really here?"

"Because Mitch told me something was going on this morning. A meeting, he thought."

"That's right." Milo sat up and leaned forward, lowering his voice. "I told everybody to be on the lookout for Heppner because he might be part of the investigation. I didn't go into details, just alluded to the fact that there was some Toppenish connection between him and the dead guy. And no, I did *not* suggest that he was a suspect. All I want is information, and that's part of his damned job, on leave or vacation or whatever the hell he's doing. Can you keep your mouth shut?"

I was annoyed. "Don't I always?"

He leaned back again. "That depends. Damnit, why do you look so cute? You're ruining my bad mood. Go away."

I stood up. "I will. Goodbye, Sheriff."

"Hold it." He got out of his chair and came around to where I was standing.

"Move away from the door. Don't look so pissed. All I want to do is hug you. Otherwise, I might go out and deck Gould just for the hell of it. Then I'd have to suspend myself."

I nestled against him. "I hate you."

"I know. Mmmm. Feeling you always makes me feel better." He let go of me and swatted my rear. "Now beat it."

I left, but I couldn't keep from smiling. Dwight glowered some more.

It was a good thing I'd stopped smiling by the time I crossed the street and got as far as the hobby shop. Vida's Buick was parked there, with one front tire up on the curb. Something was obviously amiss. She usually parked with such precision that the inches on each side to the diagonal white lines matched exactly. I picked up the pace, almost running by the time I reached the *Advocate.*

Amanda looked stricken, but I could already hear Vida's raised voice in the newsroom.

"I shall never give in!" she proclaimed to Leo and Kip, who seemed frozen in place. "Don't tell me about legal mumbo jumbo!" She stomped back and forth by Mitch's desk. "I won't have it! You hear me?" She yanked off the pith helmet and threw it in the vicinity of her desk.

"Vida!" I shouted. "What's wrong?"

She turned to stare at me with wild gray eyes. "Everything! That tart of a Holly Gross has gotten a court order to share custody and . . ." She burst into tears and would have slumped to the floor had Kip not rushed to steady her. Leo helped him guide Vida to her chair. Her glasses had fallen off. I picked them up and stood helplessly, wondering if I should call Doc Dewey.

Vida, however, seemed to be calming down. "I'm such a ninny!" she exclaimed, almost sounding like herself. But she was rubbing her eyes in that familiar gesture of distress. I winced, certain that I could hear her eyeballs squeak.

"Here, Vida," I said, standing between Leo and Kip. "Your glasses are fine. They bounced."

She stopped rubbing and took them from me. "Thank you. I shouldn't have come back to work. Now I've created a scene. That's intolerable. But there was nothing more I could do at Ted and Amy's. They're inconsolable, of course."

I steeled myself to ask if she'd talked to Rosemary Bourgette. "As the prosecuting attorney," I added, "she may have some advice for you."

Vida scowled at me. "You know I blame her, along with Milo and Judge Proxmire, for not putting together a tighter case to keep Holly in prison. If I want legal advice, I'll talk to my son-in-law. Or perhaps Marisa Foxx. She strikes me as a sensible sort."

"She is," I said as Kip and Leo edged away to their own workplaces. "Do you know if Holly intends to get Dippy in the near future?"

Vida sighed, her big bust heaving under the tan vest and purple blouse. "I've no idea. That is, the actual arrangement is for shared custody. What I wonder is if Holly will demand makeup time for being in prison, now that she's living with her sister after she was let out on bond. If so, that means almost five months. That seems very wrong for a felon."

I sat down in Vida's visitor chair. "How does Roger feel about this?"

Her eyes welled up with tears. "The poor darling doesn't know yet. He's on a Party Animals assignment out of town." She darted a look around the newsroom, which was now empty. Apparently Leo had followed Kip into the back shop. "What's worse — well, almost as bad — is that Roger and Ainsley's reconciliation didn't last. I gather they couldn't resolve their differences. I wonder if he'd enjoy an overnight with Grams when he comes back to town tonight."

I wondered the same thing, given that Roger was not a so-called adult. For all I knew, he still liked eating a gallon of ice cream and a vat of chocolate pudding. I couldn't comment on the idea. "For now, you should make an appointment with Marisa," I said.

"I shall. My niece Judi is her secretary, you know."

I did know. Another of Vida's sources, though to my knowledge, Judi hadn't been subjected to her aunt's inquisition as often as Bill and Marje Blatt. Judi was a Hinshaw and, thus, a relation only by marriage. Maybe Marisa had managed to insist upon her secretary's discretion.

I'd barely gotten back to my office when Mitch appeared. "Freeman's a brick wall," he said, standing in the doorway. "The two Pedersen girls have officially withdrawn from school. Their mother sent a note saying they were going to spend the next couple of months with their father in Maltby and go to whichever high school is around there."

"Ms. Pedersen told Vida they were with

their dad. Did you get some good pictures?"

"I think so. A couple of the track team practicing and the baseball team getting ready to play Arlington. A half dozen other shots inside the school, including an overhead view of the study hall. The custodian was replacing some lightbulbs, so I got up on the ladder. Lots of bowed heads, pretending to study. Or sleeping."

"Sounds good. We can use the track team on the front page and the baseball shot inside. Maybe the study hall one could go on page three opposite my editorial, which is also soporific."

Mitch chuckled obligingly and headed for the back shop. The issue was shaping up, though the real news couldn't yet be told. Not only was Sam Heppner a taboo subject, but all we had so far on Fernandez's murder was speculation. I was no more keen than Milo on going public with guesswork. Frustrating as it was for all of us, Mitch's article would be vague, the usual "ongoing homicide investigation," with a standard quote from the sheriff. Our readers wouldn't care. The victim was an outsider. They probably figured his killer was, too.

Shortly before five I called Tanya to ask if she'd be with us for dinner. She apologized for not letting me know sooner and said that an old girlfriend who lived in Sultan had asked her to spend the night. Shelley's husband was out of town on business, and she didn't like staying alone. Besides, she added, sounding a bit miffed, Bill was on night duty again. Better Bill than Milo, I thought and hung up.

I made a dutiful stop at the Grocery Basket, which took longer than usual. I hadn't done any big shopping in over a week. Betsy O'Toole, who was facing out the bottled juice section, noticed my almost full cart and grinned.

"Helping Jake and me feed our own hungry mouths," she said. "Thanks, Emma. How much has Milo added to your grocery budget?"

"In terms of money or items?" I shot back. "Try thrice."

Betsy laughed. "Thrice is nice — for us. Any way Leo could work that into our ad?"

"Dubious," I said, "unless you want a photo of me going to the store's ATM to get more cash."

Betsy laughed some more, her pretty face temporarily not showing the strain of the long hours she put in helping her husband run the store. "You didn't linger long after Mass yesterday. You missed the gossip about the high school."

I moved my cart closer. "Such as?"

"Some of the parents whose kids will be in high school this coming fall are thinking of sending them out of the area. To Sultan or one of the other schools in Snohomish County. Someone mentioned Eastside Catholic in Bellevue."

"Why?" I asked, figuring it was prudent to play dumb — and not too hard for me to do, since I wasn't sure what Betsy was talking about.

"Oh, you know the reasons some of the stricter Catholic parents give — birth control, abortion, blah blah. This time it's rumors about girls with loose morals who aren't being supervised properly at home or at school. It all sounds pretty outrageous to me. We sent our kids to Alpine High and didn't have any big complaints. One of the most outspoken is Shirley Bronsky. You know she subs at the high school sometimes, though she's usually in the lower grades. I thought I'd let you know what's current on the parish grapevine. Any chance of Milo converting?"

"He's already converting — our house into Hampton Court Palace. My husband's religion is fishing."

"That's true of a lot of guys around here. I'm glad Jake's not one of them or I'd be running the store by myself. Hurry back, Emma."

We parted ways. A few minutes later I was at the cash register, where the total came to a hundred and forty-six dollars and thirty-two cents on one of the sleek new registers the O'Tooles had recently installed. I figured I'd paid for at least two of them.

Milo was late getting home, arriving shortly before six. It was just as well. I was less than a half hour ahead of him and had just finished putting away the groceries. He entered the kitchen, setting a big brown paper bag on the counter before kissing me.

"I went to the liquor store," he said, shrugging out of his regulation jacket. "I replenished our supplies. Try not to lavish any of it on the Nelson gang and their hangers-on."

"I won't. Any luck tracking down Heppner?"

"Not yet. I'm going to change before I make our drinks. I don't see any sign of dinner."

"I grocery shopped," I called after him, since he was already out of the kitchen. I'd forgotten I had the leftover chicken from our Leavenworth dinner. It'd keep. If Milo had had a bad day — and who hadn't? — he might as well eat lamb chops. I already had the potatoes in the oven. I might have balked at the concept of two ovens, but that would be handy when I needed to bake and broil at the same time.

I was readying fresh broccoli when he reentered the kitchen. "Heppner doesn't want to be found," he said, taking Smirnoff vodka, Crown Royal whiskey, a highland Scotch with a label I didn't recognize, and a bottle of rum out of the paper bag. "It's not going to be easy looking for him. We have to play it low-key, with the deputies making so-called discreet inquiries instead of asking, 'Where the hell is that damned Heppner?' Even Gould will have to try to be tactful."

"At least you know he was at the 7-Eleven," I said cheerfully.

"Big help. Mullins already checked with them. He bought cigarettes. That's not exactly a lead."

"I don't recall seeing Sam smoke."

"He quit about eight years ago." Milo poured our drinks. "I guess his current crisis made him start again. Is Tanya coming?"

I told him she'd gone to stay with a friend in Sultan. "Shelley. Do you remember her?"

"Yeah. Nice girl. She married a civil engineer who works for SnoCo. They have a fairly big spread on the river. Hey — you've got lamb chops." He mussed my hair. "You look tired. Bad day at your place, too?"

"Yes. Vida had a meltdown. Go sit. I'll join you in two minutes."

Milo went out to the living room. I heard him sigh as he sank into the easy chair. By the time I flopped onto the sofa, he was smoking, sipping his drink, and looking as weary as I felt.

"Roger?" he said.

"In a way," I replied, kicking off my shoes. "Holly's got an order for joint custody of Dippy."

"Well . . . she *is* his mother."

"That cuts no ice with Vida. Also, Roger and Ainsley flunked reconciliation. Maybe she's smarter than we thought."

Milo snorted. "If she spent the night with Roger, she's still a dumb-ass. Where would they spend it? Not in that van, I hope."

"Don't ask me. It wouldn't have been at the Hibberts' house. I don't think Amy and Ted would approve." I paused to take a drink of Canadian Club. "Ainsley's old enough to have friends who might live on their own. Even if the Sigurdsons asked, they wouldn't rat her out."

"Not my problem," Milo said. "They're both adults. Legally, anyway. I figure Roger's still about twelve otherwise."

"That's generous. Say, what were you reading today when I came into your office? You hardly noticed I'd arrived."

"Oh — background on Visalia, where Dobles is from. I'd never heard of it, but it's good-sized, with a population of over a hundred thousand. I was trying to figure out how a food inspector who, I assumed, works for the state can afford a Porsche. I found zip on him. Maybe he inherited a bundle of money." He paused to sip from his drink.

"And?" I prodded.

"I learned a lot about the San Joaquin Valley. It's got a big Latino population, most of them getting screwed by their employers, especially agricultural workers. They raise several kinds of crops, but one of the biggest moneymakers is dairy cows. Reading all that makes me wonder how bad things are in this state on the other side of the mountains."

"Gee, don't tell me you're going on a social justice rampage."

"It wouldn't do any good around here," Milo replied. "Everybody is too damned complacent. Fuzzy's plan may fall flat for lack of interest. Hell, we can't even get a new bridge over the Sky."

"Blame that on the county commissioners," I said. "They've been debating the issue almost since I got here. It'll fall down before they do anything about it. All the more reason to get rid of them."

"Maybe you should write an editorial about it."

I glared at Milo. "I already did."

"Oh. Guess I should check it out. I've been kind of busy."

Never sure if my husband was kidding, I resisted the urge to dump the rest of my drink on his head and went out to start the lamb chops. They were good-sized, nice and thick. Milo would eat three.

The rest of the evening passed quietly. We both did our best to put aside the problems of the day. I was still getting used to the idea of having a husband to take care of me. All the independence I'd fought for so long and had come to cherish seemed to belong in a different world. I liked the new one much better. Whatever happened tomorrow wouldn't matter. We could cope with it together.

That, as it turned out, was an understatement.

TWENTY-TWO

Tuesday morning Vida was tight-lipped when she arrived only a couple of minutes after I did. The pith helmet had been replaced by a blue velvet beret that might have been jaunty if she wasn't so glum. But it was deadline day, which meant she plunged immediately into work.

It was only after I'd poured coffee and plucked a cinnamon twist from the pastry tray Mitch had just filled that I realized I'd completely forgotten to ask Milo about his meeting with Mayor Baugh and the county commissioners. I raced into my office to call the sheriff.

"What now?" he growled. "You can't miss me already."

"I missed asking you about the meeting with Fuzzy and the commissioners. What happened?"

"It didn't," Milo replied. "Hollenberg's sick. It's been put off until he either gets

439

better or croaks."

"You might — I repeat, *might* — have told me that."

"That nothing happened? Jeez, you must be hard up for news."

"I am, actually. There's a lot going on, but I can't go public. What's wrong with Hollenberg?"

"How do I know? The old geezer must be close to ninety. Call his wife. She's damned near as old as he is." The sheriff hung up.

Maybe Vida knew. She usually did. "What," I asked, going out to her desk, "is this about Leonard Hollenberg being sick?"

For once, Vida looked stumped, no doubt a measure of her concern over the custody battle. "I've no idea. I'll call my niece Marje." She picked up the phone. I went back to my office.

I spent the next half hour wondering how Mitch should write his story on the homicide investigation. He'd left on his rounds, so I hoped he could find out something that might be more interesting than "The Sheriff Is Baffled." I'd often threatened to use that in the paper when Milo was being particularly closemouthed. I supposed I couldn't do it now that we were married.

Vida tromped into my office a few minutes later. "I couldn't get through to Marje," she said. "The phones are always so busy first thing in the morning. I called Violet Hollenberg instead. Leonard has a bad chest cold. She's fussing that it could go into pneumonia. I suppose that's possible at his age, though Violet is a terrible fussbudget. For all I know, he merely has the sniffles. He was able to attend the commissioners' meeting last night, according to Mitch."

"Leonard *is* kind of old," I pointed out.

Vida pooh-poohed that idea. "Age is only a number. People who dwell on being old actually get that way. If Maud Dodd sends me one more compilation of everybody's aches and pains at the retirement home, I think I'll get the vapors. At least that suggests a rather pleasant and nostalgic ailment. Bunion removals, abscessed teeth, and all these replacement parts aren't news, they're a medical report. New knees, new hips, new whatevers. Most of those ninnies could use a new brain." She harrumphed and plodded off to her desk.

Mitch had already submitted his article clarifying the dropout situation at the high school. I was a bit skittish about running it, but Helena Craig had already gone public on KSKY, so I felt obligated to clear up any misconceptions. That five inches would go below the fold.

When Mitch returned, shortly after nine-thirty, he looked very pleased with himself. "I think we may have a lead story. Dodge is finally getting some word out of Yakima County about the dead guy. He'll let us know when everything's set."

"It's a miracle!" I exulted. "Make sure he does. He's probably forgotten — again — that it's our deadline."

Mitch's grin turned to puzzlement. "You mean he . . . ?"

"So he claims, though I recently explained why the paper doesn't come out ten minutes after it goes to the back shop. I suspect he's forgotten. Or doesn't remember which day is our deadline. I'd like to think he's putting me on, but I honestly don't know."

Shaking his head, Mitch went to the coffee urn.

Just to remind Milo, I called him.

"He's not here," Lori said. "I don't know when he'll be back."

"Did he leave town again?"

"I don't think so. Everybody's on high alert."

"Gosh, Lori," I said in mock amazement, "that smacks of news. Any way you could give me an idea of what it's about?"

"Not really," she replied, sounding as if she might not know. "It involves the state patrol, though. I only know that because two of their troopers were here a few minutes ago. The boss man left right after that."

"Okay. We'll stay on alert, too." I thanked her and hung up, then went to advise Mitch.

"The state, huh?" he said, licking some of a cinnamon roll's frosting off his lower lip. "That sounds like big time. Do you think it ties in with the murder vic?"

"I suspect Milo's been talking to Yakima," I said, deciding I might as well eat a cinnamon roll, too. I'd had only toast for breakfast, wanting to get out of the way before the Bourgette brothers resumed whatever they were doing that sounded very loud. "The only thing I know that you may not is a possible tie-in with the guy in the totaled Porsche. Shane Campbell was near the accident scene in his Alpine Appliance delivery truck. He's supposed to be giving a statement. He wasn't asked to do that at the time because he was blocking traffic."

Mitch made a face. "Is he thirtyish, fair-haired, kind of an all-American-boy type?"

"Yes. Why do you ask?"

"He was there this morning, talking to Dustin Fong. How come he didn't give his statement right after the wreck?"

"Heppner was the first deputy at the scene. He told Shane to move his van to keep the road open at least one way."

"That still seems strange," Mitch said. "Where *is* Heppner? I haven't seen him around for . . . a week now?"

"He took vacation," I replied.

"Kind of an odd time to do it," Mitch remarked. "A homicide investigation and spring break. As you've noticed from the log, there've been a lot more incidents of traffic violations, vandalism, and underage kids trying to buy beer. Shoplifting, too."

I shrugged. "Sam hadn't taken time off in ages. Milo figured he was entitled to it. He did report in sick Tuesday."

"That's what I was wondering about," Mitch said. "I thought maybe he had something really serious."

I didn't comment. Whatever Sam had seemed serious enough to keep him out of sight. But certainly not out of mind.

Fifteen minutes later, my archrival showed up. Spence paused to make his obeisance to Vida before entering my cubbyhole. "How is the enchanting Ms. Lord today?" he asked me, sitting in one of my visitor chairs. "Or have you arrived at the disenchanted stage yet?"

"Not even close," I said. "We're still in the honeymoon stage."

"I heard you two had been in that for at

least ten years," Spence retorted with a lascivious expression.

"That isn't exactly true," I said. "We went through phases of keeping our distance. So how is the lovely Rosalie?"

Spence stopped leering. "Lovely. Maybe I should exercise some restraint in teasing you these days. You've always had a knack for putting me in my place. I must confess I've found that rather intriguing."

"Not *that* intriguing," I shot back. "What's on your devious mind?"

"The sheriff, who, I am sure, is always on yours. Do you have any idea what's going on? Or should I have asked your reporter?"

"We're as deep in the dark as you are. Mitch and I were discussing that a few minutes ago."

"I suppose you know the state has been called in?"

"Lori told me that."

"Then we're both clueless." Spence leaned closer and lowered his mellifluous voice. "Is something bothering Vida? She's not herself."

"You're right. Holly Gross is going after joint custody."

"Damn." Spence glanced over his shoulder to make sure Vida wasn't trying to listen in. He saw that she was on the phone. "That's not good. For the kid, either. Oh, I know Holly is supposed to be living with her sister, who, like Caesar's wife, Calpurnia, is reportedly above reproach. However, I doubt Dippy remembers diddly-squat about his mother."

"Maybe," I conceded, "but she has her lawful rights. And let's face it — Roger strikes me as an indifferent sort of father."

"That is probably an understatement." Spence stood up, carefully making sure that the creases in his charcoal slacks were in order. "If you're free for lunch, we should talk. The ski lodge bar again? And don't say we've got to stop meeting like this. You have more wit than that."

"I'll bring my wit and see you around noon."

Spence made a little bow and took his leave.

As soon as he was gone, Vida came in to query me. "What, may I ask, did Spencer want? Is he upset about my chat with Helena Craig?"

"No," I replied, surprised that she would ask the question. "He asked if I knew more than he did about what's going on at the sheriff's office. I told him I didn't, which is true."

"Oh?" Vida seemed relieved. "Well, what

is going on?"

"All I know is that it involves cooperation with the state patrol. It could have to do with the murder investigation or even with the accident a week ago. Maybe they're consulting about replacing the milepost sign."

Vida wrinkled her nose. "I thought it might be something of interest locally. People who live in California have no idea about how to drive in the mountains. I wouldn't think it takes two law enforcement agencies to put up a new sign. Isn't that the highway department's job? I suppose it's bureaucracy — more wasting of taxpayers' money."

"I suspect it has more to do with the homicide," I said.

"I've never been to . . . where was the murdered man from?"

"Wapato, Yakima County."

"That part of the state is rather dreary. My late husband, Ernest, always felt that Washington and Oregon should be redivided by east and west of the Cascades, rather than north and south by the Columbia River. The eastern halves of both states have much more in common with each other than they do with the western halves. That makes more sense."

I'd heard the argument before and it wasn't without merit, but it came more than a century too late. "We're dependent on their agriculture, especially in Washington," I pointed out.

"Perhaps, though much of what we get in our local stores comes from California. Oh, well." She started to return to the newsroom, then stopped. "Goodness, my mind isn't in full gear today. I was suspicious about those Pedersen girls. I do not trust a person like their mother, who is so unfriendly and evasive. I checked with all of the local high schools in the Maltby area, and the girls are *not* enrolled in any of them. What do you make of that?"

"Poor record keeping?" I suggested.

"I don't think so." Vida ran a hand through her thick gray curls. "I didn't find a Maltby listing for Mr. Pedersen. Of course, I realize not everyone lists their numbers, especially these days with cellphones. But still . . . I wonder if the girls have a father. That is, one who lives in Maltby."

"It's grown a lot in recent years," I noted.

"Oh, yes. I believe it's somewhat larger than Alpine, though I can't think what's so attractive about it."

"It's rural, yet closer to Seattle and Bellevue."

Vida scowled. "That's an advantage? I think not."

Arguing was futile. "Face it, if their mother isn't concerned about them, then there's no reason we should be."

"I suppose," Vida said dubiously and shrugged. "I'd still like to get to the bottom of this." She stalked off to her desk.

I tried to put her worried state of mind out of my own to focus on the weekly guest op-ed piece. The current contributor was forest ranger Bunky Smythe, whose real first name was Baylor. Bunky wasn't a bad writer, but he was prone to peppering his article with statistics, mainly about the number of campers, hikers, and other interlopers who would visit our part of the world come summer. Taking his cue from the governor, who had already sounded the alarm about the possibility of drought and forest fires, he issued stern warnings, including to locals. Given that it had started to drizzle in the last half hour, his timing was unfortunate. However, if the recent weather pattern persisted, the light rain might be gone by afternoon. I corrected a couple of punctuation mistakes and zapped the column off to Kip in the back shop.

By eleven-thirty, there was no word from the sheriff's office, though Mitch had checked in only a few minutes earlier. The sheriff was still out. So, my reporter gathered, were most of the deputies. Maybe they were all looking for Heppner. I finished going over the letters to the editor and headed to the ski lodge to meet Spence.

I was pulling into the parking lot just before noon when my cell rang. "Breaking news," Mr. Radio said in an unusually excited voice. "Did you hear the sirens?"

"No," I replied. "Where were they? I'm already at the ski lodge."

"They were out on the highway. Some idiot in a sports car was trying to outrace the state patrol and went into the river. Sounds bad. I'm going to the scene. Care to join me?"

"Yes," I said. I'd try to get hold of Mitch, though, so he could bring a camera. I rarely bothered taking one with me, being utterly inept as a photographer. After Spence hung up, I dialed my reporter's cell, assuming he'd probably gone home to have lunch with Brenda. To my dismay, he didn't pick up. I'd try him at home after I got to the accident site. Maybe he'd left his cell in the Taurus.

As I headed down Tonga Road, the rain began falling harder. The wind had picked up and the dark clouds were moving south, obscuring Mount Sawyer just below the five-thousand-foot level. I kept my eyes on the road, knowing that even a little rain after a dry spell could make the asphalt dangerously slick. Maybe that's what had happened to the car that had gone into the river. I said a quick prayer for the driver and any passengers.

By the time I reached Alpine Way, traffic was already backed up to just beyond the railroad tracks. It appeared that nobody was moving across the bridge in either direction. I pulled over onto Railroad Avenue and parked in the Heartbreak Hotel Diner's lot. Apparently some gawkers already had done the same thing. There were at least two dozen people standing on the west side of the bridge. I spotted Spence's Beamer by the Alpine Falls Motel. As I drew closer to where the emergency vehicles were parked, I saw Milo among the official onlookers. He was easy to spot, being the tallest person in the group.

A state trooper stopped me as I tried to join the law officers, the emergency personnel — and Spence. "I'm sorry, ma'am," the solemn young trooper said, "but this is as far as you go." He pointed to a cordon that roped off riffraff like me from the scene of the accident.

Before I could plead my case, Milo strode over to where I was standing. "Let her through. She's mine."

The trooper looked embarrassed. "Sorry, sir. She's not in uniform."

"No problem," Milo said, grabbing my arm. "She's undercover."

"What cover?" I whispered as he led me off to join the rest of the official group.

"The one on our bed. Now shut the hell up."

Fleetwood was obviously trying not to smile. I waved at him discreetly before asking my husband what was going on, which seemed to be nothing, as far as I could tell.

"We're waiting for the divers." Milo gestured at the river, which, I realized, was running murky and faster than usual. "They got a lot more rain up at the summit, so there's runoff. The car, the driver, and the passenger are still down there."

I shuddered. "That's awful! How did it happen?"

"We'll talk about that later." The sheriff turned away from me to consult with one of the other state patrol officers.

I quickly called Kip on my cell. His wife usually made him lunch, so I assumed he'd be in the back shop. When he answered on the first ring, I gave him a quick rundown so he could post the news online and told him I'd get back to him via phone or in person, depending on how events played out.

"Darn," he said. "I'd kind of like to be there."

"You'd have to walk. Frankly, there isn't much to see right now."

"Just a thought. I know where I'm not wanted."

"You know where you're needed — and that's posting news online."

As soon as I rang off, Spence joined me. "Where's your camera?"

"You know I can't take pictures. I could use my phone, I suppose. It's the one I got for my birthday from my brother, Ben."

"I've got a camera. You now owe me lunch. Don't ask if I know what's going on other than what Dodge told you. The media is being kept in the dark. I can, however, conjecture."

"So do that," I said, as Spence nudged me a few feet away from the others. I couldn't take my eyes off the river, horrified by the fate of the two people inside the sunken car.

"It would appear — notice I use journalist-speak," Spence began, "that the sports car was possibly involved in a high-speed chase that probably started somewhere west of

SkyCo, so we'll assume it was the state patrol. I also presume that the driver turned off to Alpine but misjudged road conditions and was probably going at a high rate of speed. Ergo, he or she missed the bridge and went into the river."

I winced. "That's horrible. Who's in charge?"

"That burly guy your favorite bear is talking to. He's a captain, given that he has two bars on his uniform. I trust he'll show respect for the sheriff. I wouldn't want to see his nose get broken." Spence touched his own hawklike beak in a deferential gesture. Milo had done just that in retaliation for Mr. Radio's unsavory remark about our relationship.

"Milo usually plays well with other cop types," I said. "Where are the divers coming from?"

"Paine Field, via helicopter." Spence checked his Movado watch. "It's twelve-twenty. They should be here in ten, fifteen minutes."

"I'd better check in with Mitch," I said. Stepping away, I dialed his home number. This time he picked up. Explaining the situation, I told him he needn't rush, but to get to the river before one.

"Wouldn't you know news would break

during the lunch hour," he said in a glum voice. "Oh, well. That's the curse of a reporter."

I felt like telling Mitch I hadn't yet had lunch, but didn't. For all I knew, he was saying it for Brenda's benefit. I wouldn't trade places with him for the world. My better half wasn't an emotional basket case. He was, however, looking grim as he stayed by the state patrol captain.

Spence called my attention to some of the emergency vehicles trying to move off to clear traffic. "They won't need the firefighters or medics. Maybe they can open the road once the trucks are out of the way. The backup must be pretty bad by now. I'll do a quick remote broadcast." He moved away as far he could without falling into the river.

The sheriff finally loped over to join me. "The rain's starting to let up," he said, squinting skyward.

"Skip the forecast. Why was this car being chased?"

"Damn. I knew I should've ignored you," he said, adjusting the hood of my jacket. "But I have to pretend you're official."

"I am official," I said. "I'm the press. What's Spence supposed to be? An FBI agent?"

"I didn't see him arrive. Oh, hell, I don't

give a shit, but Godfrey over there is a stickler for keeping out anybody who doesn't belong."

"The press always belongs," I said in my most formal voice.

"Tell that to Godfrey. He thinks the press is a bunch of ghouls."

"Then I won't give him credit for this. Whatever this may be, which I sure as hell don't know because you're being a jerk."

"No, I'm not. I can't tell you anything because the ID on the accident victims hasn't been verified. You think I'd take the word of the state troopers just because they're law enforcement types?"

"Yes."

Milo sighed. "The real problem is that they don't know who the second victim is except that it's a woman."

"Oh. That does make a difference, I suppose. Are they local?"

Milo hesitated. "No. That . . . stop asking questions, okay? You're being a pain in the ass." He looked up at the sky again. "That copter should be here in a few minutes."

"I can't help being a pain. I'm hungry."

"So am I. What's for dinner?"

"Leftovers."

"Left over from what?"

"The chicken from Leavenworth."

"Shit. More chicken?"

The sound of copter rotors could be heard, though we couldn't see anything. The landing strip was out of sight. With all the trees along the highway, we probably wouldn't be able to watch it land. It'd take the divers a few minutes to cover the ground between there and the accident site. If the traffic didn't move faster, they might have to walk.

"As long as we have time to kill," I said, "so to speak, tell me what you learned from Yakima County."

Milo shot me an annoyed look. "Not here. Stop nagging. Go pester Fleetwood. I have to make sure Fong and Mullins are still awake." He headed for the cruiser parked on the verge not far from the bridge.

I couldn't hear the copter, so I assumed it had landed. The unneeded emergency vehicles had headed back into town. The young trooper I'd talked to first was directing traffic in one direction at a time. The vehicles, which included cars, trucks, and a couple of RVs, crept along, either because of the backup or the curiosity of their drivers, who had been caught up in the drama. I thought of the old saw about watching a train wreck: no matter how ghastly it was, onlookers couldn't stop staring. Human nature is fascinated by horror. Otherwise, there'd be no TV audience for gruesome celebrity murder trials.

Spence had rejoined me. "You're short," he said.

"I know that," I retorted. "So what?"

He grimaced. "May I finish? You probably can't see over the gathering, but a state patrol car has gone to fetch the divers."

"Oh." I offered him a faint smile. "Will they jump right in?"

"I assume so. Not that there's any rush," he added grimly. "How squeamish are you?"

"Unfortunately, I am."

He nodded once. "I recall that your beast-like husband let you off the hook at viewing a heart attack victim not long ago."

"And you stood in for Rosalie because she was on the point of collapse. Very gallant of you and the sheriff."

"May I remind you that the corpse was Rosalie's husband?"

"I didn't know that at the time," I said.

"Here come the divers." Spence took my arm as we retreated a few yards from the river. It had almost stopped raining. A glance at the road revealed that traffic was beginning to move — if slowly — in both directions. I saw Mitch's lanky figure crossing the bridge and waved at him.

"Your minion," Spence murmured. "Deal with him as you will while I do another quick remote about the divers' arrival."

I brought Mitch up to speed. "That's all Spence and I know. Law enforcement is being tight-lipped. As usual."

Mr. Radio had strolled back to join us. "Ever done this before?" he asked my reporter.

Mitch uttered a short laugh. "Often. Ever heard of the Detroit River or the Great Lakes?"

"By Jove, I have," Spence replied. "I spent some time in Chicago."

We were standing close to the north end of the bridge, having moved farther away from the official onlookers so that Spence could hear himself think while he did his brief update.

"There they go!" The cry came up from one of the cops. I guessed it might be the young trooper who had accosted me. I knew it wasn't Milo. Calling attention to himself was taboo under any circumstances.

Spence was back on the air; Mitch had snapped several photos in rapid succession; I stood like a dummy in the window of Francine's Fine Apparel. Except that I wasn't nearly as well dressed. I did, however, notify Kip that the divers were in the river.

Now we'd play the waiting game, except for the young trooper and Jack Mullins, who were hustling the gawkers off the bridge. Maybe they were afraid it'd fall down. To my dismay, I saw that one of them was Ed Bronsky. He could cause an overload all by himself. Naturally, he was protesting to Jack, but he lost the argument.

After dispersing the pedestrians, Jack stopped when he saw me. "Ed claimed he was part of the media. What's the deal with Sheriff Pig?"

"Don't ask," I said.

Jack laughed, shook his head, and moved on.

The divers suddenly resurfaced and came ashore. They were talking to Milo and the state patrol captain. All four of them turned around to look at what seemed to be some kind of crane on a flatbed truck. I hadn't seen it pull up.

"They're going to get the car out," Spence said in an unusually solemn tone. "I assume there's no rush, so no need to pry open the doors. I should've guessed as much."

"I wonder how long that will take?" I murmured.

"Maybe half an hour," Mitch said. "I'll stick around if you want to go back to the office."

I was undecided. "Let me see if I can talk to Milo."

Taking my time, I headed toward where the law enforcement group had gathered near the divers. After another minute or two had passed, the sheriff broke away and came over to where I was standing.

"What now?" he asked. "I'm not giving you any quotes."

"Guess what? I don't want one. All I want to know is how long it'll be before they raise the car."

"Depends." He glanced at the river. "Could be days."

I refrained from stamping my foot. "Come on, big guy. I'm up against a deadline."

"Today?"

"Milo . . ."

He started to reach out to me, then stopped and shoved his hands into his jacket pockets. "I'm not sure. They have to set up. When that drug dealer let his car roll into the river a couple of years ago, it took close to an hour, but we had a snowstorm back then. If you've got a deadline, you might as well go back to the office. Mitch, too. I'll call when they're ready to bring up the car, okay?"

I smiled up at him. "Thanks . . . Sheriff."

"No problem." He turned around and

walked away.

I relayed the message to Mitch. "I drove," I told him. "My car's at the diner." I suddenly realized I couldn't see Spence. "Where'd Mr. Radio go? Don't tell me he's interviewing the state patrol captain."

"No," Mitch said as we started walking across the bridge. "He decided to track down some of the locals who were watching the spectacle. Names make news, even on the radio."

"Not a bad idea. I just hope Ed doesn't offer himself."

"Ed," Mitch said under his breath. "He's a character."

"He is. Especially as Mr. Pig." On that more jocular note, I got into my Honda and returned to the *Advocate.*

Amanda was agog when we arrived, asking a barrage of questions before she suddenly rushed off to the restroom. Both Leo and Vida were out, but Kip came into the newsroom to ask how soon we could post an update. I told him we were waiting to hear from the sheriff.

Only twenty minutes passed before Milo called. "I'll make this quick. Two dead, driver and passenger, both from Centralia.

Mickey Borg and Holly Gross. Details to follow. I've got work to do." He hung up.

TWENTY-THREE

I was stunned. But I also had work to do. I called Mitch into my office and gave him the shocking news.

He was incredulous. "You mean the hooker from the trailer park standoff? And who's this Borg guy? The name sounds familiar."

I glanced into the newsroom. Vida was still gone, but Leo was back and on his phone. "Mickey was another of Holly's customers and also the father of her two older kids. She's been living in Centralia with her sister since she got out on bond. Mickey was in town recently and bought a Corvette from the Nordby Brothers."

Mitch was still looking slightly dazed. "Are you going to write the story, or should I?"

I hesitated. Mitch didn't know as much of the background as I did, but on the other hand, if there was more coming from the sheriff's office about whatever Milo had learned from Yakima, maybe I should do that one and let my reporter take on the river tragedy. The priority, of course, was for Mitch to get photos. He took off as soon as I told him the story was his.

Fifteen minutes later, Vida exploded into the newsroom, shrieking her head off. Leo was so startled that he dropped his cigarette and had to pick it up before it burned a hole in his pants. I rushed out of my office, trying to figure out if Vida was having a fit.

But she was jubilant. "Crime does not pay! Justice has been served! God's in his heaven and all's right with the world!"

I felt like saying that it depended upon your point of view. Or quoting Ben, who did not believe that God ran our lives from some heavenly computer. Life was, after all, about free will.

Vida took notice of my presence and rushed to hug me. "It's a miracle," she enthused while I wondered if she'd broken a couple of my ribs. "All our troubles are over," she went on, letting me go. "What do you wager that Holly had come here to take Dippy?"

I hadn't thought about it, but she was probably right. "I'm very happy for you, Vida," I said, and meant it. "I wonder if

465

Holly's sister will keep the other two children."

"That doesn't concern me," Vida responded, going over to her desk and sitting down. "I already called Amy. I happened to have KSKY on as I was driving back from interviewing Marcella and Dan Thorstensen about their Thailand trip. Spencer announced it just minutes ago. I almost drove off the road."

I remained standing by her desk. "Does Roger know?"

"Not yet. He's on another assignment. I think."

Leo got up to get a coffee refill. "Congratulations, Vida. Are you going to start speaking again to the sheriff, the judge, and the prosecutor?"

I wanted to kiss Leo for asking the question. But Vida frowned. "I'm not sure. We'd never have had to go through all of this had it not been for Holly getting out on bond."

"But," Leo said, "if she hadn't, she'd still be alive and in jail. God works in mysterious ways."

Vida gave him her most owlish expression. "That's so. I hadn't yet thought that through."

Mitch returned, looking pleased with himself. He paused halfway to his desk, aware that something momentous was going on. Vida repeated her news. I wondered if she'd somehow finagle a way of putting it into the *Advocate,* at least in "Scene." I flinched at the possibility: "Happy daddy Roger Hibbert has adorable Dippy all to himself," or some such saccharine drivel. I'd delete it on the grounds that it was too self-serving for the great-grandmother who worked for the *Advocate.*

I returned to my office while Vida regaled Mitch with her big news. After a few minutes, he joined me to say he'd gotten some good shots.

"I focused on the car itself — a Corvette," he said, showing me the pictures he'd taken. "The body removal was too grim."

"Not for Vida," I said quietly.

"Right." Mitch looked askance. "Anyway, here's a good one of Dodge watching the car being lowered onto the ground. Think he'll mind? I know he doesn't like having his picture taken for the paper, but the state patrol captain is next to him, so it speaks well for law enforcement in general. What do you think?"

Milo stood with his fists on his hips, the stance giving him an air of authority. The burly captain was a good four inches shorter and looked a bit like a bullfrog. "They both appear suitably somber," I said. "And official."

"I'll go with that one, then. Have we got room for the divers? They always make good pictures even if they're on dry land."

"Fine. Good work. I'll see when the sheriff's available. I still haven't heard the latest out of Yakima County. If you're on overload, I'll handle that one, okay?"

"Your call," Mitch said, not sounding miffed for a change.

Lori Cobb told me to hold off. The boss was still dealing with the state patrol. She didn't add that he was probably meaner than cat dirt, as Vida was sometimes prone to say when she was vexed.

I checked with Leo to see how our advertising was coming along. "Just a little over sixty-forty," he said. "Good news of a sort. Did Amanda tell you about that big classified ad Tiffany Rafferty is running?"

"No. I'll ask her."

Amanda had just gotten off the phone. "Tiffany came in person with it," she said. "She's a little weak in the writing skills department."

"No kidding. I heard she's working part-time at Parker's Pharmacy, courtesy of her grandparents' influence in being the original owners. She's clerking, not dispensing prescriptions. She took over from Jessica Wesley, the current owners' daughter, who's attending the University of Washington at the Bothell campus."

"Tiffany's selling the sports memorabilia her late husband, Tim, collected," Amanda explained. "Walt's a huge baseball fan, so I hope he doesn't read the ad. Leo told me that some of Tim's items are worth a lot of money. We can't afford stuff like that with a baby on the way and looking for a house. Tiffany got them appraised by a guy who was staying at the ski lodge a couple of months ago. You may recall he ran an ad in the paper. She sold a few items to him but saved the rest."

I remembered that Tiffany had been seen at the ski lodge back in February with a man who was dubbed a mysterious stranger, probably because nobody recognized him.

"I hope she does well by all that," I said. "Tiffany's had a rough life, especially recently."

Amanda nodded. "I hope she finds a man to take care of her. In some ways she reminds me of me when I was younger — and dumber."

"You were never dumb," I said. "How about 'flighty'?"

"That's good." She struggled out of her

chair. "It's time to make another flight to the restroom." And off she went.

By three o'clock, I was getting antsy. Not only was Mitch unable to finish his story about the river deaths without official confirmation of what had led to the tragedy, but I couldn't start on the information Milo had gotten from Yakima. I switched on KSKY for the hour-turn news. Spence was repeating what we already knew, so he was still in the dark as well.

As I turned off the radio, Leo stepped into my office. "I just got a picture of the Kiwanis Club at the Mariners game. Have we got room?"

I looked at the more than two dozen smiling faces, all of whom I recognized. "It'll have to go inside," I said. "See what Kip can do. We don't want to diss our advertisers."

"The M's lost. But according to Harvey Adcock, they had a great time. I watched part of the game — Cleveland's pitching did them in."

I nodded. "Milo and I missed it. We're not optimistic."

"Early days, as they say. It's only the third week of April." He looked at the picture. "Cal Vickers's hairline is moving faster than the M's infielders. I hadn't noticed that in

470

person."

"He usually wears a cap at the gas station," I said.

Leo chuckled and headed to the back shop. I reached for the phone — and stopped. It's a funny thing about words and how people say them. We hear what we expect to hear, but sometimes we miss what the speaker intended to convey. Maybe because I write to earn my living I'm more conscious of nuance, even after the fact. I thought back to over a week ago and my conversation with Janie Engelman. Suddenly I had an insight. I didn't feel enlightened as much as appalled.

It was going on four when Milo called me. I left immediately to go down to his office. The clouds had lifted, though the sun was skittish, as befit an April afternoon. Traffic on Front Street was back to normal. There were no state patrol cars outside of the sheriff's headquarters. It looked like an ordinary day in Alpine. Except, of course, that it wasn't.

Spence pulled up in his Beamer just as I got to the double doors. I waited for him, not in the mood to bother being annoyed by his presence.

"Allow me, madam," he said, opening one

of the double doors for me.

"Thanks," I murmured.

Dustin Fong and Lori Cobb were the only ones in the front office. They both looked tired but greeted us in their usual polite manner. "Go right in," Lori said. "He's waiting for you."

Spence's gallantry was still in place as he opened the swinging door in the counter to let me go first. I walked woodenly into the sheriff's office, where Milo sat with a lighted cigarette and a weary expression. None of us spoke until after Spence and I had parked ourselves in the two visitor chairs.

"Okay," my husband said. "Here's how this played out. The rumors about high school hookers turn out to be true. I got a tip the other night when a woman named Dawn Harrison came to see me after hours." He paused to look at me. "She asked for Heppner first because he was the only law enforcement person she knew by name. Sam was the one who cuffed her sister, Holly Gross, after the trailer park standoff."

Spence eyed me suspiciously. I knew what he was thinking. "I wasn't at the meeting," I said. "The sheriff made me leave the house."

"Sorry," Spence murmured before turning back to Milo. "You do go by the book, Sheriff."

"You bet your ass I do," Milo shot back. But he said it quietly. "The Lewis County sheriff contacted me to say they knew who was procuring if not actually running the girls. It was, as you've probably guessed, Mickey Borg and Holly Gross. It seems Holly not only couldn't go straight but had to get back in the game. The state was brought in yesterday. Before they could gather enough evidence, they got word from Mrs. Harrison that Holly and Mickey were coming up here to collect Holly's son by Roger Hibbert." Milo paused to put out his cigarette just as Spence lighted up one of his Balkan Sobranies.

I finally found my voice. "The state patrol chased them all the way from Centralia?"

Milo shook his head. "It started out on Highway 522 outside of Monroe when Borg picked up speed and a state trooper went after him. That Vette was doing over ninety most of the way. Outside of Sultan the trooper called in the plate number. That's when it turned into more than chasing down a speeder."

"Christ," Spence said softly. "That's some incredible driving on Highway 2."

"Why," I wondered out loud, "didn't they keep going and try to elude the cops?"

Milo regarded me with an ironic expression. "I'm guessing, which you both know damned well that I hate, but Holly was probably obsessed about getting the kid back. It was worth a speeding ticket to her. They had no way of knowing that the law was on to them for procurement. Frankly, I suspect — as does the state patrol — they've been running the girls, too. Mickey had plenty of money to throw around. He had his own place down there in Morton, a few miles out of Centralia."

A former logging town that began with an M. I recalled Wanda Johnson saying that was where her daughter was living with her boyfriend. If he was still around. Unless, I thought, the boyfriend was involved with prostitution.

"So," Milo said, leaning back in his chair, "that's about it. The state and Lewis County will take over from here. We just happened to get caught in the middle."

Spence checked his watch. "In that case, Sheriff, I'm off to do an expanded broadcast on the hour turn at four." He stood up. "Are you coming, Emma?"

"No. I'm waiting for Mitch." It was a lie, but I didn't care.

"Oh. Aren't you going to rush to put this online?"

"Go away, Spence. I'll have *all* the details

in the *Advocate.* I've got a date with a deadline."

"Of course." He nodded at Milo and departed.

"Well?" the sheriff said after Spence had left the premises.

"You were going to tell me what you heard from Yakima."

"So I was." He offered me a cigarette, and I took it after asking him to light it for me. "Mr. and Mrs. Dobles have gone south," Milo said, looking slightly more relaxed. "Not only was Dobles Joe's stepdad, but he helped get him his job — as a federal agent working vice."

"A fruit inspector has that much clout?"

"Like Fernandez, he works undercover for the Feds. Dobles owns his own company, inherited from his father. They make farm equipment. The guy's versatile. Why wouldn't he give his stepson a leg up?"

"Were they both here because of Borg's hooker ring?"

"Yakima says that's why Joe was here. Dobles had been at the federal courthouse in Seattle and thought he'd meet Joe while they were in the same area. They were supposed to have a late lunch Monday at the Cascadia in Skykomish. But Joe never showed because he was dead. Dobles didn't know that, so he headed for Wenatchee, figuring his stepson was working a case."

"But he got run off the road," I said. "What will happen to the girls who got lured into the hooking?"

Milo sighed. "We'll get names of locals tomorrow. I hope there's no more than Samantha Ellison and Erin Johnson."

"Both Pedersen girls are missing," I said and related what Vida had told me.

"Damn." Milo slapped his hand on the desk. "I've been checking some of those so-called dating sites on the Internet. What's with these kids who fall for that? When I think about Tanya or Mike doing anything like that, I . . . well, I can't even think about it."

"Then don't. They're both a little old for that sort of thing now."

"Right." He lighted a cigarette for himself. "You look kind of odd. Do you feel okay?"

"Yes, really. I just had a weird idea a while ago. Maybe I need to think about it. It's been a crazy day."

"That's an understatement. One good thing — other than busting the hooker ring — is that Mickey didn't kill anybody else on his wild ride."

I bit my lip. Maybe I should get the weird idea out of my system. "Maybe not today.

But he killed Joe Fernandez."

Milo stared at me as if my hair were on fire. "What the hell are you talking about?"

"Mickey was in town Sunday. I don't know how he got to Monroe unless he ditched his own car and stole the one you've got in impound. Did you check for prints?"

"Yeah, but we didn't find a match in the system. As far as I know, Mickey's never been busted, at least not in this state. He's been one slippery dude, though. You may be right about him selling drugs out of the mini-mart. How do you know he was here when Joe was killed?"

"Janie Engelman has an odd speech pattern that's hard to follow. She came in last Monday with a wedding picture of her and Fred. She griped a lot about Mickey. He'd made off with her TV, along with everything else he could get his hands on. She rattled on about complaining to Mickey that Fred had to listen to the Mariners play the White Sox that day on the radio. It was a Sunday, with a noon start, according to my Mariners schedule. Then I mentioned Mickey having left town. Janie said she hoped he had — *by now.* That indicated he was still in Alpine Monday morning or at least late Sunday night."

Milo puffed on his cigarette. "I don't

know if it's harder to listen to Janie or to you. That's the flimsiest piece of speculation I've ever heard."

"You've got a better suspect?"

He sighed again. "No. But I will check for prints. I'll get hold of the state to take them off Mickey's corpse. How would Mickey know who Joe was? Where's the point of contact?"

"A bar? A tavern? At the Big Toy in Old Mill . . ."

Milo held up a hand. "Okay, okay. I'll rely on forensics instead of Emma Does Disneyland. They should build a fantasy world in Anaheim just for you and your so-called theories."

"Hey — if Mickey was already suspected of being involved in prostitution, isn't it possible that Joe set up a meeting with him?"

"Yes, it's possible, maybe even reasonable. You might've said that first. But why the fish hatchery?" Before I could speak, Milo kept talking: "I suppose it makes sense because nobody would be around at night."

"Was Joe armed?"

Milo shook his head. "If he carried, his killer might've stolen his weapon. We don't know who left the ATV by the landing strip. My *guess* is Joe. It's still a guess that the abandoned car ran Dobles off the road. If

Borg's prints are on the Nissan, I'll consider it. But don't quote me."

"Gosh, Sheriff," I said, "I was memorizing your every word. You haven't yet gotten to 'dumbshit.' "

"Give me time. Give me a reason why Borg would know who Dobles is." He paused, fingering his chin. "Unless Joe told him the Feds were on Mickey's trail. I'll let the D.C. brain trust figure that out. Borg's dead. He's out of my jurisdiction. How about you getting out of my office? I've got so much damned paperwork to do that I won't be home until ten."

"You're kidding, I hope?"

"Only a little. I'll be lucky if I make it by seven."

As I stood up, Dustin Fong came into the doorway. "Mullins ticketed Roger Hibbert for no taillights. His grandma's going to be mad."

Milo groaned. "Shit. Blatt can run interference on that one."

"Yes, sir." Dustin returned to the front office.

I blew Milo a kiss. "See you later, Sheriff. I feel better now. But I'm sorry for Holly's kids. The two older ones have lost both parents. I don't care how rotten they were. It is still sad."

"Not your problem." He raised his hand in a farewell salute.

What was left of the afternoon flew by. I wouldn't get home on time, either. There was no story to write about Joe or his stepfather as undercover agents. But I did a brief article about Dobles's release from the hospital and apparent recovery. I considered mentioning that he was the stepfather of the murder victim, then realized that was a bad idea. If I didn't speculate in public, I didn't want readers speculating about why the two men happened to be in the area at the same time. Besides, they were outsiders. The locals wouldn't care.

Mitch had done a good job on the accident. He hadn't needed any prodding to contact the state patrol. In the process, he'd found out that not only was Mickey Borg speeding, but that he and his companion, former resident Holly Gross, had been wanted for questioning in regard to possible charges of procuring under-age prostitutes. If that didn't grab readers' attention, nothing would. The downside was that nobody would bother to read my editorial. Of course, most people didn't read it when the front page was dull as dishwater.

It was already after five when I realized that I hadn't seen Vida since I'd left to call on the sheriff. Mitch and Leo were still in the newsroom, so I asked if she'd left early to celebrate.

Leo spoke up first: "She got a phone call just before you got back and took off like a Boeing 747. No idea what that was about."

Mitch stood up and stretched. "I was on the phone with the state patrol. All I saw was a blur."

Amanda was equally ignorant. "I did see her drive away. I'd just come from taking the rest of the classifieds out to the back shop."

"Maybe," I said, "somebody staged a takeover at the retirement home. I'll make sure Kip has all her copy in."

My techno-wizard told me that as far as he could tell, the House & Home page was set to go. "This has been a really crazy day," he said. "When I was in high school, I didn't know much about hookers. I mean, I heard rumors about women in town who lived off of men, but teenaged girls? That's pathetic."

I agreed. "I'm going to check the wire service to see if there's anything local that may have come in this afternoon."

"Mitch already saw the first stories on Borg and Holly going into the river. No details, just that it was during a high-speed chase by the state patrol. Do you think we can beat the met dailies on this one?"

"Probably not," I replied. "Although nobody expects big stories to come out of SkyCo. The only way that will happen is if they do their homework between now and mid-evening. *The Seattle Times'* news deadline is ten, except for sports scores."

"You and Dodge made headlines last December."

"Don't remind me," I said.

Both Mitch and Leo had left by the time I went through the newsroom. As I expected, the AP had only the bare bones about the river deaths. I did find a story on a proposal to expand the Alpine Lakes Wilderness area. That was close enough to be of local interest.

I poked my head into the back shop at five-thirty to wish Kip good luck, adding, as I always did, that he should call me at home if there were any problems. Getting into my car, I noticed that the air smelled fresh after our spring shower. Instead of taking my usual route up Fourth, I drove along Front to see if Milo was still on the job. I spotted his Yukon in place. I also saw Bob Sigurdson coming out of the sheriff's office. That piqued my curiosity. Maybe he'd stopped in after work to apologize for bothering Milo on a Saturday. But judging from the grim expression as he got into his SUV, I thought not. I waited for him to pull out, ignoring whoever was honking at me from behind.

Bob reversed so fast that he almost ran into an oncoming forest service truck. I zipped into his parking place. When I went inside, Lori was gone, but Dustin, Jack, and Doe Jamison were congregated behind the counter. They all looked somber.

"What's happening?" I asked.

The trio seemed to have gone mute. Jack finally spoke: "Roger's in big trouble. Dodge and Dwight have him in the interrogation room."

I leaned against the counter. "What did Roger do now?"

Doe also found her voice. "We got an online anonymous tip this afternoon that he was involved in the prostitute procurement." She turned to Jack. "You take it from there."

"He had his taillights out, so I stopped him on Alpine Way," Jack said. "Just because he's such a jackass, I asked what was in the van. I expected some lip, but he cooperated. Sure enough, he had party stuff, but not much of it." He paused, brushing down his unruly red hair and making a face. "I noticed Roger didn't have a business license posted in the van, so I checked out the company through the state. They never heard of Party Animals. I was off duty by then and when I got here, I found out Bob Sigurdson had showed up to see Dodge." He paused again, looking at Dustin and Doe. "Should we go public?"

Doe shrugged. "Bob filed a complaint. It's official."

Dustin nodded agreement. "Bob's daughter Ainsley hadn't told her parents where she was the night she went missing. She'd been with Roger. He'd tried to talk her into turning tricks down in Morton. He made it sound like being a hostess at a club. I guess Ainsley isn't too swift. She told her sister about it. Alicia's younger, but a lot sharper. She thought it sounded beyond weird and said to dump Roger ASAP. Ainsley met him Sunday to tell him she was done. Then Alicia insisted Ainsley tell their parents. Bob was still here when Roger was brought in. We had to restrain him from decking the dumb kid."

I'd leaned an elbow on the counter so I could prop up my head. "Oh, my God! What's Vida going to do?"

"Bill's at the Hibberts' house now," Jack said. "I guess Amy called her about the ticket. She was probably there when Dwight busted Roger at home about ten minutes ago."

"How," I asked, still trying to deal with this latest blast of bad news, "did Roger get mixed up with this low-life crap in the first place?"

Jack held up his hands. "Holly, I suppose. For all we know, they've been in contact ever since she got out on bond."

That was plausible. I asked if Roger was upset about Holly's death.

"I don't think he knew about it," Jack said. "Roger seems to live in a world of his own. I had to go four blocks before I could pull him over. He had one of those Bluetooth things in his ear."

"Is he being charged with anything?"

"We don't know," Doe replied. "Dodge and Dwight haven't had enough time to get the dumb jerk to spill his guts. The boss man probably hopes he can throw the book at him, along with that mounted steelhead on the wall."

I realized I couldn't yet give the news to Kip. What was even worse, I didn't know how to handle it.

Dwight appeared from the interrogation room area. "The fat bastard asked for food. Who wants to go to the Burger Barn?"

"I'll go," Doe said. "I didn't get lunch, being on patrol while the river crisis was going on."

Dwight handed her a slip of paper. "Here's what the son of a bitch wants. That's two chocolate malts to go with the grub."

"There goes petty cash," Doe said, and made her exit.

Dwight went back to the interrogation room. "I guess," I said, "there's no point in me sticking around. I didn't get lunch, either, though I seem to have lost my appetite."

Jack chuckled. "Think how hungry your better half will be. He's probably about ready to eat one of Roger's fat arms."

"Guess I won't make leftovers," I mumbled as I headed to the door. "I'll be in touch."

After I got into the car, I wondered if I should go to the Hibberts' to see how they — and Vida — were coping. But I'd be intruding. Worse yet, I wasn't up to facing my House & Home editor. What I really wanted was a stiff drink and the comfort of my little log house. The rest of the world seemed to have gone insane. Maybe I was going nuts, too. The town, which had looked so normal a few hours earlier, seemed the same. But I knew that like a seismic fault lying dormant under the earth's surface, the impact of Roger's latest misdeeds had shattered Vida's world forever. And there was nothing I could do to help her.

TWENTY-FOUR

After I'd changed clothes and made a drink, I realized I had time to turn the leftover chicken into my white sauce lasagna. Milo liked that, and I always made more than even he could eat. Pasta seems to multiply when it's boiled. Shortly before seven, I was putting the baking dish in the oven when the doorbell rang.

Once again, I had trouble seeing through the peephole. I could tell it was a man, but not much else. In fact, in the dying light of day, he looked as if he had a beard or at least some heavy dark stubble.

"Who is it?" I asked, remembering Milo's warnings.

No response. I was about to ask again when my caller finally spoke: "It's me, Sam Heppner."

Aghast, I opened the door. I hardly recognized the errant deputy. He probably hadn't shaved for at least a couple of days. Sam also looked thinner, and his sharp, jutting nose seemed to dominate his angular face.

"Where's Dodge?" he asked.

"Still at work," I said.

"His Yukon isn't there."

"Maybe he's on his way home. Do you want to sit down?"

Sam looked around the living room as if he were searching for contraband. "Thanks," he said, sitting in the side chair by the hearth.

"Can I get you something to drink?"

"Got any beer?"

"Yes. Need a glass?"

Sam shook his head.

I grabbed a bottle of Henry Weinhard's dark ale out of the fridge and poured a short shot of Canadian into my almost empty glass. "Here," I said, handing him the ale. He'd already lighted a cigarette.

"Thanks." True to form, Sam remained a man of few words, but at least they weren't surly. In fact, he looked and sounded tired.

I sat on the sofa. "You haven't been here in a long time."

"I've been on leave."

"I meant here, at the house."

"Oh, right." He paused to drink some ale. "Did they pick up the Hibbert kid?"

"Yes. Milo and Dwight have been interrogating him. Maybe they're done by now. Otherwise the Yukon would still be there."

"He might've gone to see the prick's parents."

"He might." My jaw dropped. "You tipped them off, didn't you?"

"Yeah. I've been on to that kid ever since the trailer park mess."

"You knew he was up to something?"

"Hell, punks like him don't change. Dodge let him off too easy."

"He did that for Vida, not Roger. The kid was a help with the information he had on the local drug operation."

Sam inclined his head. "Yeah, the boss was in a bind. But this time he's nailed him."

"Yes." Now *I* was reduced to monosyllables, unable to stop fretting over Vida. But the booze had given me courage. "Sam, why did you fall out of sight? We were all worried about you."

He was looking at me, but I sensed he wasn't seeing me. "It was Joe," he finally said. "I never met him. Carmela sent pictures."

"He was your son." It wasn't a question.

Sam nodded once. "Her father wouldn't let me marry her. I wasn't Latino. Or Catholic. She was so young. She couldn't stand up to him."

I remembered Carmela's comment about not always having been a strong woman. "Did your brother try to intervene on your behalf?"

Sam sighed and passed a hand across his forehead. When he looked at me, his dark eyes were shadowy. "You know about Amos?"

"Don't get mad. I was trying to help Milo find out what had happened to you. As I mentioned, we were worried."

He sighed again. "My brother went to that tavern to try to reason with Carmela's dad and two of her brothers. You don't reason with drunks, especially when it gets personal. I didn't know he'd gone there until after it all came down." Sam shook his head. "What a waste. He was a hell of a guy."

There was nothing I could say that would comfort Sam. He'd probably heard it all and found it meaningless. Instead, I changed the subject. "What happened to Carmela's first husband?"

"Road accident outside of Wapato. He was drunk. I didn't find out about that for a long time."

"But she sent you Joe's pictures."

"That was later, after she married Dobles and moved to California. She didn't dare keep in touch with me before that. Carlos

Fernandez was a real creep. Dobles is a decent guy."

"What about your parents? I mean, would they have approved if you had married Carmela?"

"Hell, no." Sam stared at me. "They were rock-ribbed Pentecostals and anti-anything-but-white. Prejudice cuts every which way."

"Did you see Carmela while she was here?"

He looked away. "Yes. For about an hour in Monroe."

"That must've been hard."

"It was." He still didn't look at me.

"She's a strong woman."

"She's a good woman," he said, finally meeting my gaze. "A good wife to Nel. She was a good mother."

"I believe she never had any other children."

He drank more ale and shook his head. "She had problems when Joe was born. No more kids for her."

"I don't know what to say," I admitted.

"There's nothing to say. Carmela and I said it all to each other. Everything changes in life. But some things don't change."

I felt tears in my eyes. I wouldn't cry, though. It might make Sam crack. He seemed so brittle. No, I realized — he was fragile. Or were they the same thing? "So you were actually working while on leave?"

"Right. My brother-in-law's with the state highway department. They had some big road problems down in Lewis County last month and needed extra help. Phil went down there and heard about the cathouse at Morton. I got suspicious, with Holly on the scene."

"Did you mention it to Milo?"

"No. The boss doesn't like guesswork."

I was puzzled. "Did you suspect Roger had killed Joe?"

"Hell, no. Roger's too chickenshit to confront anybody. I knew Joe worked vice. Even Carmela never had any idea where or what he was doing undercover. But I suspected there was a tie-in between here and what was happening in Lewis County."

"You must've wanted to know who killed Joe," I said.

Sam grimaced. "That was up to Dodge and the Feds. Finding Joe's killer wouldn't bring him back. I wanted the trash who hired Roger. Hell, what's worse than ruining a young girl's life by selling her?" He looked away. His thins lips pressed together. I didn't know how to respond. Sam finished his ale and got to his feet. "I guess the boss man is still tied up. Thanks for the drink.

Sorry to bother you."

"It's no bother. I am so sorry for what happened to Joe. Really. He sounds like he was a great guy."

"I guess he was. That's Carmela's doing."

I put my hand on Sam's arm. I'd never touched him before and almost expected him to recoil. But he didn't. "That's not quite true," I said. "So much of what we are is genetic makeup. Why do you think Joe became a cop?"

A nerve twitched on Sam's temple. "I never thought about that."

I let my hand fall away. "You should."

Sam hesitated after opening the door. "Maybe I will. Thanks, Emma." He stepped outside, then turned to look at me. "Tell Dodge I'll be back at work tomorrow."

"I will," I called after him.

I waited until he got into his Jeep. It was almost dark. I grieved for Sam's loss. And for Carmela's, too.

There was still a small streak of light above the rugged mountain peaks that surrounded Alpine. Maybe in some corner of Sam's world there was a light, barely perceptible but never extinguished. After closing the front door, I realized Sam hadn't told his story to Emma Lord or Emma Dodge. I sensed he had confided in *me,* a woman.

Maybe he didn't hate the gender. In fact, maybe he had somehow idealized women in his younger years. Or he suffered from guilt. His disinterest in the female species wasn't because he had no love to give, but because he'd given it all to Carmela.

I opened my laptop and wrote the story about Sam's role in breaking up the hooker ring. I'd clear it with Milo, of course, though I knew it would come as a surprise to him. I called Kip to tell him we'd have late-breaking news. If there wasn't room on the front page, he could squeeze in a box directing readers to wherever he could place the article.

Dealing with Roger's arrest was heart-wrenching. For openers, I didn't know what charges were being brought against him. I reminded myself what journalists do: write up the facts, fill in the blanks, get confirmation, and ignore personal feelings. As I tapped away, I felt like I was on autopilot. Roger was a perp, Vida played no role in the story, and I was an instrument of communication.

When I phoned Kip to say I'd finished the story, he asked what it was about. I told him he'd find out when I zapped it to him. He sounded puzzled, but somehow I couldn't give voice to Roger's treachery. Kip had his hands full. He had no time for guessing games.

Half an hour later Milo finally arrived, just after eight-thirty.

"Just hand me the freaking bottle of Scotch and don't ask any questions," my beloved moaned as he came through the front door. "Jesus, but I'm beat!"

I didn't demand a kiss, just got out the Scotch and thrust it at him. He looked surprised. "You really aren't going to say anything?"

I shook my head.

Milo set the bottle on the counter and took me in his arms. "God, Emma, what would I do without you? Everybody else is nuts."

I merely looked up at him and smiled. His kiss was hard but brief. "Hey," he said after releasing me. "You can say *something.*"

"Dinner's ready when you are. Go change. I'll make your drink."

"Okay." He mussed my hair and left the kitchen. I turned the lasagna down to the oven's lowest setting. It was done and would stay hot until Milo was ready to eat.

When he came into the living room, where I was on the sofa, I asked where Tanya was.

"As crazy as it sounds," he replied after

taking a deep drink from the Scotch I'd put next to the easy chair, "she went to the Hibberts' house with Bill. I guess he needed backup handling his aunt Vida."

To heck with filling in the gaps on the news story. I asked the question that was my personal priority: "How is Vida?"

Milo grimaced. "Shell-shocked. That's the best way I can put it. By the time I showed up, she was just sitting and staring off into space."

"Did you try to talk to her?"

"Not really." Milo paused to drink some Scotch. "I went over to her when I first got there and put my hand on her shoulder. I told her I was sorry. She didn't say anything. Tanya had talked to her earlier. I guess she was in denial at first, saying somebody set Roger up."

"Yes, that'd be her first reaction." We both sat in silence for a few moments. Then I asked what charges had been brought against Roger. "I do have a deadline, you know," I added.

"That was a tough one," Milo replied, scowling. "Without more proof, I could only charge him with two counts of contributing to the delinquency of a minor — the Ellison and Johnson girls. I tossed in an attempted try with Ainsley. It's enough to keep him locked up until we get the rest of the information from the state tomorrow. Then we'll go for the vice and conspiracy charges. The dumb prick's in deep. Of course, the state will go after the Party Animals outfit, too."

"That's enough for me to give Kip," I said. "I just wish Vida had kept her eyes open after the trailer park disaster."

"Even if she had, there was probably no way she could've stopped Roger from getting involved in this lash-up. As his parents, Amy and Ted are more to blame than Vida. They're a couple of washouts."

I nodded vaguely. Vida had dominated all of her daughters. She was so strong in so many ways, yet she seemed to have produced weaklings among her own offspring. "Sam was here," I finally said.

Milo almost dropped the cigarette he'd been lighting. "No shit! What the hell was that all about?"

"He thought you were home. He had something to tell you." As Milo listened without interruption, I tried to recount Sam's story word for word. I concluded by saying he'd be back on the job tomorrow.

"Good God," my husband murmured. "So Sam wasn't having a breakdown, but was freelancing. I can hardly believe it. In fact, I can't believe a lot of what's happened in the last few days."

"I don't think it's all sunk in with me. I wonder if Vida will come to work tomorrow. Maybe she'll spend the night with Amy and Ted."

"Vida's tough," Milo asserted. "The only thing that means as much to her as Roger is her job. My money's on her to show up tomorrow. When do we eat? I'm about to pass out from hunger."

"Now," I said, getting off the sofa. "It's leftovers."

"What?" he exclaimed, following me out to the kitchen.

"It's lasagna. I, unlike Vida, have some talent around a stove."

"And other places," he said, grabbing my rear as I leaned over to remove the baking dish from the oven. "Food comes first. If I regain my strength, maybe we can have dessert later."

As we lay in bed that night while Milo read a Vince Flynn thriller and I worked a crossword puzzle, I realized I was stumped in the bottom right-hand corner. "The clue is 'sheriff's assistant,' " I said. "It's six letters, but it's not 'deputy,' because the clue going down is 'Bizet opera.' That has to be

Carmen, which ends in an *n.*"

"Work it out the other way," he advised, obviously caught up in whatever action-packed scene he was reading.

I put in "stay" for canine command, making the first letter of the unfinished word a *y,* followed by an *e* at the end of "ease." Picking up my crossword thesaurus, I figured it wouldn't take long to scan words that began with *y* followed by *e.* "Ha!" I exclaimed. "I'm done. It's *yeoman,* sheriff's underling, and, as an adjective, meaning staunch, sturdy, and loyal."

Milo looked up from his book. "Six letters? Too bad it's not seven. You could have put in 'Heppner.' "

ABOUT THE AUTHOR

Mary Richardson Daheim started spinning stories before she could spell. Daheim has been a journalist, an editor, a public relations consultant, and a freelance writer, but fiction was always her medium of choice. In 1982, she launched a career that is now distinguished by sixty novels. In 2000, she won the Literary Achievement Award from the Pacific Northwest Writers Association. In October 2008, she was inducted into the University of Washington Communication Hall of Fame. Daheim lives in her hometown of Seattle and is a direct descendant of former residents of the real Alpine, which existed as a logging town from 1910 to 1929, when it was abandoned after the mill was closed. The Alpine/Emma Lord series has created interest in the site, which was named a Washington State ghost town in July 2011. An organization called The Alpine Advocates has been formed to preserve what remains of the town as a historic site.

www.authormarydaheim.com